Praise for these other novels from *New York Times* bestselling author
CHEYENNE McCRAY

VAMPIRES NOT INVITED

"Something weird is going on, and it is up to half-human half-Drow Nyx to figure out what it all means. The versatile and talented McCray is slowly unveiling a supernatural society fraught with menace and plagued by prejudice and discord. Her Night Tracker series continues to be fast-paced and populated with intriguing characters. Hang on, for McCray is about to send things into overdrive."

—*RT Book Reviews*

"Set in an intriguing new world, romance, adventure, and non-stop action fill the pages." —*Romance Reviews Today*

"If you enjoy a kick-ass heroine, a sexy romance, and a compelling story that leaves you begging for more, this is the series for you." —*Nocturne Romance Reviews*

"An excellent continuation of the compelling Night Tracker series." —*Fresh Fiction*

NO WEREWOLVES ALLOWED

"Nyx is back and ready to kick more butt in the second installment of the Night Tracker series . . . McCray introduces some interesting secondary characters that add depth to this developing world. As always, there is a seductive sensuality mixed in with the hair-raising adventures."

—*Romantic Times BOOKreviews*

"McCray has written a wonderfully hot story that has characters we will love . . . beautifully fleshed-out, believable, and intelligent. The storyline is fascinating, intriguing, and fast-paced. This book is a fantastic page-turner that has great romance, lots of the paranormal, adventure, thrills, and chills."

—*Night Owl Romance*

"Interesting characters, [a] fast-paced plot, and fascinating world-building make this a must-read."

—*Fresh Fiction*

DEMONS NOT INCLUDED

"The hot new Night Tracker series promises plenty of thrills and chills. McCray does an excellent job establishing this world and its host of intriguing characters. The action is fast and furious, and the danger escalating. Add in some sexy sizzle and you have another patented McCray gem."

—*Romantic Times BOOKreviews*
(Top Pick, 4½ stars)

"McCray weaves a supernatural tale of mystery, murder, and blossoming romance. *Demons Not Included* has a well-rounded cast, a captivating storyline, and plenty of suspense to keep readers guessing."

—*Darque Reviews*

DARK MAGIC

Winner, *Romantic Times* Reviewer's Choice Award for Best Paranormal Action Adventure of the Year

"McCray does a stellar job layering the danger, passion and betrayal. Awesome!"

—*Romantic Times BOOKreviews*
(Top Pick, 4½ stars)

"Action, romance, suspense, love, betrayal, sacrifice, magic, and sex appeal to the nth degree! [McCray's] heroines kick butt and run the gamut from feminine to tomboy, and her heroes . . . well, they're all 200% grade-A male. YUM! Her love scenes left me breathless . . . and I'm surprised I have any nails left after the suspense in this last book."

—*Queue My Review*

"Vivid battles, deceit that digs deep into the coven, and a love that can't be denied." —*Night Owl Romance*

"A fabulous finish to a great urban fantasy . . . Master magician Cheyenne McCray brings it all together in a superb ending to her stupendous saga." —Harriet Klausner

SHADOW MAGIC

"Erotic paranormal romance liberally laced with adventure and thrills." —*Romantic Times BOOKreviews*
(Top Pick, 4½ stars)

"A sensual tale full of danger and magic, *Shadow Magic* should not be missed." —*Romance Reviews Today*

"Cheyenne McCray has created a fabulous new world. You won't be able to get enough!"

—Lori Handeland, *USA Today* bestselling author

WICKED MAGIC

"Blistering sex and riveting battles are plentiful as this series continues building toward its climax."

—*Romantic Times BOOKreviews*
(4 stars)

"Has an even blend of action and romance . . . An exciting paranormal tale, don't miss it." —*Romance Reviews Today*

"Sure to delight and captivate with each turn of the page."

—*Night Owl Romance*

St. Martin's Paperbacks Titles By
CHEYENNE McCRAY

NIGHT TRACKER NOVELS
Demons Not Included
No Werewolves Allowed
Vampires Not Invited
Zombies Sold Separately
Vampires Dead Ahead

LEXI STEELE NOVELS
The First Sin
The Second Betrayal

THE MAGIC NOVELS
Dark Magic
Shadow Magic
Wicked Magic
Seduced By Magic
Forbidden Magic

ROMANTIC SUSPENSE
Moving Target
Chosen Prey

ANTHOLOGIES
No Rest for the Witches

VAMPIRES DEAD AHEAD

CHEYENNE McCRAY

St. Martin's Paperbacks

This is a work of fiction. All of the characters, organizations, and events portrayed in this novel are either products of the author's imagination or are used fictitiously.

VAMPIRES DEAD AHEAD

For information address St. Martin's Press, 175 Fifth Avenue, New York, NY 10010.

EAN: 978-0-312-53269-7

Printed in the United States of America

St. Martin's Paperbacks edition / December 2011

St. Martin's Paperbacks are published by St. Martin's Press, 175 Fifth Avenue, New York, NY 10010.

10 9 8 7 6 5 4 3 2 1

To Mom, with love from your darling dotter.

'Tis now the very witching time of night,
When churchyards yawn, and hell itself breathes out
Contagion to this world: now could I drink hot blood,
And do such bitter business as the day
Would quake to look on.

—*Hamlet*, William Shakespeare (1564–1616)

WELCOME TO NEW YORK CITY'S UNDERWORLD

Present Day

Dark Elves / Drow: live belowground in Otherworld, never aboveground. Except for me. I'm unique—sometimes I wonder if that's a good thing.

Demons: not a problem. We plan to keep it that way.

Dopplers: these shifters can transform into *one* specific animal form—unlike Shifters, who can choose whatever animal form they want.

Dragons: you think fire is hot?

Fae: you asked for it. Don't blame me if you get a headache—*Abatwa, Brownies, Dryads, Dwarves, Faerie, Gnomes, Goblins, Nymphs, Pixies, Sânziene, Sidhe, Sirens, Sprites, Tuatha, and Undines.*

Gargoyles: there's a reason birds poop on statues.

Light Elves: can we say "Divas of the Otherworlds"?

Mages: powerful male wizards.

Magi: young, precious, omniscient female beings whom Trackers are sworn to protect and keep hidden safely away.

Metamorphs: can shift into human form, mirroring any human they choose before practicing criminal activities against humans. These jerks have no redeeming qualities. None.

Necromancers: did you have to ask? They talk to and raise the dead.

Ogres: Kermit isn't the only one who's green and eats flies.

Seraphim: not your average Angels.

Shadow Shifter: in my opinion their ability to shift into shadow form is pretty cool. But you *do not* want to tick one of them off. Do. Not. Make. Them. Mad.

Shifters: like I said, these guys can choose any animal form they want.

Sorcerers/Sorceresses: I never knew some Sorcerers could be so sexy.

Specters: haven't seen one and don't plan to.

Succubae and Incubi: avoid them. Just stay away. That's all I have to say.

Trolls: me, Troll. You, dinner.

Werewolves: some of the good guys. Until the full moon.

Witches: females born of norm parents but with strong magic.

Zombies: don't even go there.

Vampires: Stay tuned and see for yourself . . . because they are dead ahead.

PROLOGUE

It was a night made for danger. A night made for passion.

A night made just for her.

The sports coupe hugged the street as Monique took the steep San Francisco hill a little too fast. She loved to drive the silver Mercedes-Benz SLS AMG. It was impossible to beat human technology despite the norms' lack of magic.

Among the Light Elves, Monique was a being of great magic, but she still enjoyed human innovations. Why simply use the transference when she could enjoy the power of her vehicle, the sleek elegance of it.

Tonight she needed an outlet, and flying through nighttime traffic in this fashion was one of her favorite ways to relax. What she had planned next was an even more exciting way to let herself go.

It was a chilly January night, a trying night, and the Vampire tragedy she had come upon in the Haight-Ashbury district had topped it off quite unpleasantly. The Soothsayers still had the crime scene frozen until the Paranorm Task Force cleaned up any paranormal aspects of the crime and wiped out the memories of any human witnesses.

What a great asset to have when trying to keep the general population from freaking out at some of the bizarre sights they saw when paranorms were inhabiting the city with them. Humans would never understand. How could they?

Monique had barely made it back to her home in time to change into a short, strapless little red dress with a matching jacket that had a mandarin collar. She added decadently high red heels. At her throat and on her ears, wrists, and fingers were glittering diamonds and rubies mined, fashioned, and warded in the belowground realm of the Dark Elves, in Otherworld.

Males of every race of beings loved her exotic looks. She'd let her long dark curls float free around her face, hiding the delicate points of her ears.

Light Elves were generally apathetic when it came to norms and paranorms alike. She and Rodán, however, were among the rare few who believed that their people had a duty to protect those who could not protect themselves. And that included all paranorms as well as norms.

The majority of U.S. Proctors left most of the dirty work to the Night Trackers. Monique preferred hands-on leadership. That practice and the power of her magic were two reasons she made such a good Proctor and why she was chosen to lead all Peacekeepers in San Francisco. It is also why she had the respect of the Trackers who worked under her.

Her cell phone purred through the speakers in her car. She glanced at the navigation screen as the caller identification came up. She recognized the number as Rodriguez's.

"Answer," she said out loud, and when she heard the soft click she said to her lead Tracker, "Hi, Michael."

"The cleanup on Haight is finished." Rodriguez's voice was deep and smooth, like warm caramel, one of her favorite human treats. If she weren't Rodriguez's Proctor, she'd have had the Shifter male in her bed already.

Monique pushed a handful of curls over her shoulder. "Anything else to report?"

She heard the shrug in Rodriguez's voice. "The usual. Harley and Jonathan had to rein in a few rogue Werewolves." Monique glanced up at the full moon as he spoke. "Lee ended up with two of the beasts on her hands."

Monique swung the car around a corner and reached the St. Francis Hotel in Union Square. "Great job tonight, every one of you."

Rodriguez gave a low laugh. "That's what you always say, Mo."

"Because I have the best Trackers a Proctor could hope for." Monique smiled, but it faded as she narrowed her brows in concentration. "Let everyone know we're meeting tomorrow night before you head out to track."

"You've got it," he said. "Sweet dreams, Mo."

"I'd wish the same for you," she said, "but I have a feeling you have other things in mind." Like she did. "Have fun."

As Rodriguez ended the call, Monique turned the car into the parking garage of the St. Francis and pulled up to the curb just outside the rear entrance. She opened the sports car's doors and slipped out her long legs while allowing the attendant to assist her in stepping into the cold.

Being Elvin she was naturally protected from changes in temperature and from the generally cool environment of San Francisco. She barely noticed the chill night air as it brushed her skin.

She tipped the man before he valet-parked her car, then gave a slight inclination of her head to the doorman as he held the glass door open for her.

A brief feeling of guilt made her hesitate when she reached the opulent hotel lobby. How could she have such a fetish, to be with a Vampire?

Not a real Vampire, of course. She would never choose to be with an actual Vampire, with any being so inherently evil as those creatures.

But the feeling it gave her to role-play . . . the feeling of danger and the forbidden. Like a human with a drug addiction, she needed this. Wanted this.

Monique inhaled, raised her chin, and headed toward the bank of elevators. Nothing wrong with fantasies that didn't cross the line. She only enjoyed human men dressed up like Vampires.

The males the agency set her up with regularly were so realistic, down to their scent of dirt and age. It had to be a special cologne designed to make the whole experience that much more intense and satisfying. Whatever it was, it added to the incredible intoxication she felt from these connections.

Before she pressed the button for the elevator, she drew

a heavy cream-colored envelope out of her clutch. Inside the envelope was a keycard as well as a piece of stationery inscribed with a room number. She didn't really need to, but she checked the paper again.

Every one of these nights she indulged in something different. Sometimes the evening started at a hotel bar or maybe a coffee shop. At a seemingly chance meeting, she would be approached and engaged in conversation. She loved the natural, realistic cat-and-mouse game that ultimately ended in a luxurious hotel room with her satisfying her lust.

Tonight was different. She was to go directly to a room. Would there be instructions? Perhaps a "bellman" dropping by for assistance.

The last time she'd been in the St. Francis was some time ago, and she was pleased to find that tonight's room was in the original section of the hotel. She loved the decor reminiscent of the hotel's beginnings.

Who would it be? She gave a little shiver as she thought of the male who had played Vampire to her last night. It was never the same male who she was set up with, though. Too bad, because last night had been amazing, as she had told the agency. It was so realistic down to the moment when he'd bitten her. She'd felt like she'd been taken by a true Vampire.

Naughty Mo, she chided herself.

Elves were elegant, always moving with the fluid grace inherent to their race. Her heels didn't make a whisper of a sound as she stepped out of the elevator and walked toward the suite that had been arranged for her. When she reached the door, she smiled then slipped the keycard into its slot, heard the click, and pushed open the door.

The room was dark save for candle flames flickering from every surface. The suite had the heady, sweet smell of roses. Candlelight reflected off at least a dozen vases filled with roses of every color imaginable.

She wasn't Drow, of course—the Dark Elves who lived belowground—so her vision wasn't as acute in the darkness as theirs was. Still, she had little problem taking in everything in the room with a glance.

Including the man standing in the shadows to her right. A man dressed in a dark suit, his long black hair flowing over his shoulders but drawn away from his face so that she saw the hard angles and planes of his pale features.

Her breath caught when her gaze met his, and she was immediately lost in the depth of his glittering black eyes. It was the same man she'd been with last night. That never happened because she always insisted on variety. She didn't know this male's name and he didn't know hers. It was the way she preferred it.

"I cannot say that I am not pleased it's you," she said as she set her red satin clutch on the velvet cushion of a chair near the door. "I enjoyed last night very much."

The thrill of her first encounter with him caused a tingling low in her belly. The night had started out in an exclusive club, with him approaching her as a stranger might. It had ended beyond her expectations at the St. Regis Hotel.

The man smiled, and fangs flashed in the candlelight. So realistic.

"I am pleased as well." He moved toward her as he spoke then took her hands in his when he reached her. He dipped his head and kissed her cheek. "It is most welcome to be in your company once again."

He even sounded formal, as if he were as old as his scent. If he was a true Vampire, he might have been a Master.

The male held her at arm's length and studied her face, lingering at her brown eyes. A little shiver ran through her as he slowly looked down, pausing at her throat before continuing. He trailed his gaze over her firm breasts, the taper at her waist, and down the length of her bare legs to her feet, which were still clad in the high heels. Last night he had wanted her to leave on the stiletto shoes she'd worn.

What would he want tonight? She knew what she wanted.

When his eyes met hers again, she swallowed. His gaze immediately dropped to her throat again. She could almost feel his fangs sliding into the vein that pulsed there now, throbbing for his attention.

"I'm going to take you someplace you will love." His

voice was husky as he moved toward her, so close his chest brushed hers.

She tilted her head. "We're not staying here?"

"I have something special planned for you." He bent and scraped his fangs down the column of her throat before letting them rest at the vein that pulsed, begging for him. His voice was deep, mesmerizing. "Dare to go with me?"

Monique let out a soft moan. Her thoughts clouded with desire. "Yes." Her own voice sounded husky. "I'm ready."

Monique peered at the house through the window of the male's black BMW. He had pulled into the driveway of an incredible Queen Anne Victorian home in Pacific Heights, one of the oldest and most affluent parts of San Francisco.

It wasn't possible that an escort could afford such a fabulous place, even to rent. The male must have inherited it, or perhaps borrowed it for the night.

The darkened house had an almost eerie feel to it as he walked her to the front door. He unlocked it then put his hand beneath her jacket at the small of her back and guided her over the threshold.

It was as dark inside the house as out, and she had to blink a few times before her eyes fully adjusted. The door closed behind them with a *thunk* that caused her heart to jump.

"Come." He took her hand and she let him lead her within the dark house, through an elegant room of Queen Anne furnishings. They continued past a staircase, into a modern-looking kitchen, and up to a door beside a glass-fronted pantry.

Monique's heart beat a little faster as he opened the door and gestured for her to walk ahead of him. Through the door she saw a pair of wooden railings and steps leading down to an even deeper darkness. A basement or a cellar perhaps.

She hesitated. The combination of anxiety and anticipation thrilled her like nothing else. It was all part of the high that drew her in again and again.

Monique met the male's black eyes, which almost seemed to glow. No, *that* was her imagination. Yet they seemed amazingly bright in such dark surroundings.

She tried to step back but found he had a firm grip on her wrist, which startled her. "Release me." The last two words sounded deep, throaty as she put magic behind them. Magic meant to command, to be obeyed.

Instead of releasing her as he should have, though, his lips curved into a sensual smile that reminded her of last night and how good he'd made her feel. So incredibly fabulous. The power she'd put into her voice faded with her words as he brought her to him.

It was lust for this male. Lust that made all her defenses lie down like newborn pups that didn't have the strength to protect themselves.

The male's gaze was almost hypnotic as he moved closer to her and took her hands in his. He lowered his head and brushed his lips over hers. His mouth was cool, firm, masculine. Monique closed her eyes, and her lips parted to accept his kiss. She breathed in the scent of earth. It was stronger now, and she wondered if it came from the cellar or was entirely him.

"You will love this." His breath was cool on her cheek as he moved his mouth to her ear. "I promise you."

Monique felt a sense of fuzziness that she'd never experienced before as she walked through the doorway with the male. She didn't waver on her heels as they walked down the steep staircase together into the dark. Her steps were firm, deliberate, yet silent.

When they reached the bottom she blinked and narrowed her eyes, trying to make out shapes in what was an enormous basement. She frowned. It looked like rows and rows of coffins. A few steps away one of the coffins was open. It was white with pink satin lining.

"You have coffins." Amazing how the agency had taken this to another level, she thought. She played the game. "Why do you have coffins? What *is* this? It's beyond freaky."

The male's fangs gleamed white in her vision as he grasped a handful of her curls in his fist. She gasped as he brought her hard up against him and yanked her head back by her hair.

"What self-respecting Vampire wouldn't have coffins in his basement?" he said with a devious smile.

He moved so fast Monique never had a chance to think about what was happening. She gave a cry as he sank his fangs into the artery in her neck.

Her mind spun. She wanted to fight but she couldn't. She felt frozen, unable to move. Instead of the sensual, sexual feeling she'd experienced last night with this lover, she felt light-headed. As if she was truly being drained of her blood.

As if this was real.

Monique went limp in his arms. He continued to suck from her, drawing her lifeforce from her through the fluid that gave all beings life.

She tried to summon her magic to protect herself, but it was a vague attempt. As if she was poking at the male with a stick and hitting stone instead of a flesh-and-blood being.

The room seemed to spin as he raised his head and smiled. Blood coated his fangs. Real blood. Her blood.

"What . . ." The words came out as a forced whisper ". . . did you do to me?"

"My lovely Monique." The male spoke her name as if it were a beautiful treasure.

Confusion piled on top of confusion. "My name . . . how do you know?"

"I know much about you, Monique," he murmured as he nuzzled her hair and breathed in her scent.

Her skin felt cold and her mind numb, as if she were trapped in a fall of snow, her body heat evaporating with every minute that passed.

"I do what I must for the survival of my people." The male kissed the skin along her jaw. "You have now been bitten twice. With the second bite, you become one of us."

Realization came to her but it was far too late. "You are a real Vampire," she said slowly, her tongue feeling almost too thick to speak.

"And when you wake, so shall you be." He raised his head and smiled. He still supported her limp body with one arm. He ran his fingers down her neck with his free hand.

The place he'd bitten her tingled and burned. "A powerful Elvin Vampire, like no being ever known before."

"Elvin Vampire." The desire to giggle rose up inside her but she was too weak. "There is no such thing."

"In ten days there will be." The male scooped her up in his arms.

Her head lolled to the side as he cradled her to his chest. He carried her the short distance to the white coffin with the pale pink satin lining.

She thought she caught the scent of a human—but that was absurd. Why would a human be with her and her Vampire lover?

Dimly she was aware that he was setting her down inside the coffin. When she lay on the plumped satin, her head resting on a small pillow, she stared up at him. "Who are you?"

Triumph mixed with malice flashed across his striking features as he crouched beside her. He gripped the lid of the coffin. "My name is Volod," he said right before he slammed the lid shut.

Volod. The name was familiar to Monique's fuzzy mind. But then it didn't matter anymore as she passed into oblivion.

ONE

"Another Tracker is missing." Rodán set his wineglass on the white tablecloth of our table for two in the exclusive paranorm hot spot Some Other Place. "Kennedy appears to be gone."

The hum and buzz of the restaurant and bar filled the pause as I digested Rodán's statement. Another Tracker?

A busboy stopped by our table and cleared our dinner dishes after asking if we were finished. I waited until he was gone before I responded to Rodán.

"Kennedy, from Seattle?" I frowned as I spoke. "Any idea what happened to him?"

Rodán slowly shook his head. "The Proctor Directorate's investigation teams have found nothing."

"That makes how many?" I asked.

"One Proctor along with eight Trackers." Rodán's handsome Elvin features remained amazingly impassive, his crystal-green eyes betraying no emotion as he spoke.

"What does the GG have to say about it?" I asked.

Rodán looked thoughtful. "The Great Guardian has other matters that concern her at this time."

"More important than the disappearance of paranorms who are important to the safety of this world?" The GG drove me crazy in the ways she chose to "help."

"It is not for us to decide where her attention is best suited, Nyx." Rodán was gentle yet firm in his statement.

"I'm having a hard time believing what's happening." I shook my head, and my cobalt-blue hair tickled shoulders bared by my strapless Versace minidress. "There's something very wrong going on." A brilliant understatement.

Rodán gave a deep nod. "Exceptionally so," he said, making me wonder for a moment if he meant my understatement.

I shuddered at my next thought. "Unless Zombies are back."

"We are well and rid of Zombies, Nyx." Just hearing Rodán say "Zombies" made me shudder again. It had only been a few months since we'd faced the threat, but it seemed like it had been days ago.

"Desmond thinks we're rid of them permanently." The silk of my dress slid across my thighs in a soft caress as I crossed my legs at my knees. My light amethyst skin contrasted with the black material of my dress. "I do have faith in him."

"As do I." Rodán took another sip of his Chardonnay and I watched the play of muscles in his arm, beneath his golden skin. "Which is why I planned to speak of Desmond with you."

I cocked my head. "What about him did you want to discuss with me?"

"The Great Guardian and I have spoken." Rodán leaned forward, his forearms resting on the tablecloth. "I intend to offer the Sorcerer a position as a Night Tracker."

Surprise made me blink. First of all, Rodán never told me about his choices for Night Tracker candidates. Second . . . *Desmond?*

"Desmond has qualities that would benefit our team," I said. "He isn't the sword-and-dagger type, though."

A slight smile curved Rodán's lips. "Indeed he is not. He has other talents that would serve him well."

I smiled, too. "I am not being negative, Rodán. The thought just caught me off guard. I actually think Desmond would make a terrific addition. Providing you can convince him to join the Trackers."

"That may be a challenge." Rodán gave a nod of acknowledgment, his long white-blond hair shimmering beneath the low lights with the movement and revealing the points of his ears. "Desmond has been a loner, but after seeing what he and the Trackers did together to strike down his enemy, Amory, I know the difference he can make with us."

"Ah." I sipped my Chardonnay. "I wondered why you were telling me about a candidate. You never have before."

"That will potentially change, Nyx." Rodán's expression grew more serious. "I want you to take a larger leadership role."

I stilled and set my wineglass down. "More than being in charge of special teams?"

"Yes." Rodán studied me. "You have proven yourself to be an effective leader. You are respected by others, and you have a charisma about you which is not learned. You were born with it," he said. "You will still primarily track but you would be involved in more strategy development, training processes, and team assignments."

Surprise kept me from speaking as he continued.

"I am not considering you full-time in another position by any means," Rodán said as he continued to study me. "However, having more responsibility in the overoperations will make better use of your skills."

When I finally found my ability to speak, I said, "I had no idea you thought of me this way."

Rodán's gaze was focused, intent, as if he was evaluating even my response. "As a Night Tracker you have already provided balanced leadership, and your judgment is sound.

"I am thinking of one behavior, however, that must change," he added. "This has nothing to do with my feelings for you outside of being your Proctor."

"Okay." My words were slow and deliberate. After what had happened during the Zombie op, I was wary of what he might say. "What in your opinion do I need to work on in relation to the soundness of my judgment?"

"The only caution I have, you have heard before," Rodán said. "You are an exceptional Tracker. However, at times you have had no regard for your own personal safety. You need to think through what is best overall, before you jump into certain situations.

"For example," he continued, "too often you have charged forward without waiting for backup. It has almost cost you your life on more than one occasion. An effective leader needs to remain alive or he or she cannot be effective. Do you agree?"

I wanted in some way to fire back that I'd done what I'd had to. As a Drow princess, I was raised around warriors. I had trained as a warrior myself. Dark Elves don't sit back and watch, they act. But I knew Rodán was right.

With an inward sigh, I brought my fingers to the collar I'd worn to favor my father. When I considered the last operations, I had to admit Rodán was right. I'd put myself into some pretty bad situations, including getting injected by a deadly virus. Dark Elves are aggressive fighters, but they still lay battle plans and work as a team.

My restraint, to a point, during the last case may have had more to do with my team than me. They had been adamant that I not charge in on my own without them like I had during previous ops. They'd been right, and I'd known it.

"Yes," I said, "that's fair. It's not easy for me, though. It's my nature to give it everything I have, despite the dangers, but I understand what you're saying."

"Consider what I have to say." Rodán wore a serious expression. "I believe you above all those others you track with have the skills necessary to lead the entire team. Under my guidance, of course. I don't have all the details worked out, but I wanted you to know what I was thinking for your future."

Wow. I took a deep breath. "It means a lot that you have so much confidence in me and my abilities."

"You have earned it." Rodán steepled his hands on the tabletop. "Time and time again on operations you have been assigned to you have proven to be an exceptional leader. I only have the one concern."

"I think I understand." I clasped my hands in my lap. "But I'm not management material. You *know* me—I can't sit back and watch."

"I would never expect you to do so." Rodán smiled again.

"That is not the Nyx Ciar I know." I felt perplexed at his words, but he continued. "I am only asking for a little restraint on your behalf."

"Can I think about it?" I brushed my palm over my belly, absently smoothing the silk of my dress. "I need a chance to let this digest. Not only that, but I do have my PI agency to consider. I'm not sure adding extra responsibility as a Tracker will help me in my day job as a PI."

"Of course." Rodán raised his glass and sipped his wine. I watched the movement of his throat as he swallowed, observed his fluid grace as he set his wineglass on the table.

"It is my intention to groom Colin to take a leadership role," he said. "I would like him to start leading a special ops team."

Warmth spread through me at the sound of Colin's name. Yet that warmth was followed by the feeling of confusion that had plagued me ever since my and Adam's breakup and Colin's insistent pursuit of me.

Now was not the time to think of either of the two males. Detective Adam Boyd was no longer in my life, and Colin, a Dragon paranorm, wanted me to take things a step farther with him.

It was times like this—being comfortable with my Drow appearance in this paranorm restaurant, and not worrying about how I looked at night—that made me realize it could never have worked with Adam. I couldn't look like I did right this moment and be out with him. However, I didn't have those same reservations with Colin, as far as dating another paranorm went.

Still, at this moment there were more pressing things to consider than my love life.

"Is Desmond the only new Tracker whom you and the GG are considering?" I asked.

"I believe Tristan would make an excellent Night Tracker also," he said. "The Guardian agrees."

"My brother?" I thought about him as a Tracker candidate. Tristan had been locked in a stone for twenty-two years, but to him it had been as if no time had passed. He'd returned not recognizing me—I was no longer the five-year-old kid sister I'd been when he disappeared. He was now in Otherworld visiting with our parents.

"I hope he can be convinced," I finally said. "Though he was an artist before he was taken, never a warrior, I think he could be a tremendous Tracker."

"Tristan has always been a warrior," Rodán said. "A warrior with an artist's skills. It is time to use all of his abilities. As a Tracker he could add much to the team with some training.

"We'll let him out in the field with you for a couple of days to give him an idea of what a Tracker's night is like," Rodán said. "Then we'll send him to the training program in Chicago. Once he's fully trained, we'll team him up with an experienced Tracker in New York City."

"Rodán!" The pair of voices exclaiming his name came from a pair of blond Nymphs who stopped at our table. They looked like excited, giggly airheads as they bounced up and down on their toes. I recognized them—they were backup singers for Festival, a new paranorm rock band that I'd seen for the first time last weekend.

"Trixie." Rodán nodded to Nymph One. "Bubbles," he said to Nymph Two.

Trixie and Bubbles. I had to bite my tongue to keep from laughing. It may not have been the first time I'd heard their stage names but it still got me. By the looks of the pair of airheads, I wondered if those *were* stage names, or their real ones.

I settled back in my chair to watch. This should be good.

"We haven't seen you for a while." A small pout was on Trixie's lips. "Bubbles and I were just saying how much—" The Nymph glanced at me then back at Rodán. "—we have missed you."

I didn't think that was exactly the sentiment she'd wanted to express.

Then Bubbles said, "After we perform at the Pit next, are you going to invite us back to your chambers?"

Uh-huh. That statement confirmed what I'd been thinking.

I toyed with the stem of my crystal wineglass as Rodán gave them a smile that was entirely sensual. Rodán couldn't help it. He could simply have been trying to be polite, but no matter. His expression would still have the power to set a female on fire.

"I will talk with you beautiful ladies at another time." Rodán said it in a way that was appealing rather than off-putting. "At this moment I am enjoying Nyx's company."

"Can't wait," Trixie said with a giant exclamation point in her voice. "We'll see you soon."

Bubbles nodded with enthusiasm, her blond curls bouncing. "We'll be ready."

I bet they would.

Rodán gave a slight inclination of his head. "Have a good evening, ladies."

The bubbling airheads slipped into the crowd in the bar but I could still hear their giggles. I wanted to roll my eyes but I smiled at Rodán instead. "Your adoring public."

Rodán leaned back, holding his wineglass. He looked at me for a long time without saying anything.

I tilted my head. "Are you all right?"

"You know that for you I would give up everything," he said quietly.

My cheeks burned a little at the intimacy in his expression and in his words. "We both know you couldn't, Rodán." I continued even though he looked like he wanted to say something. "It's how you're wired. You're a sexual, sensual being and I get that," I said. "You would never be happy with one person."

"With you . . ." He looked thoughtful as he paused. "With you everything was different. You make me want to be with you alone."

I was surprised. I had never heard Rodán say this before in quite this way.

"Then why weren't you?" I said, more out of curiosity than anything else. "You continued to see others while you and I slept together. If I made you feel different then why didn't you stop inviting others to your bed?"

During the time I was with him, I'd never considered Rodán enjoying sexual pleasures with others as abnormal. He'd invited me to join in on the experiences, but I'd always refused. It wasn't my thing.

"One female would never satisfy you. Oh, maybe for a time, but I refer to a lifetime," I went on before he could respond. "I could never share the man I decide to be with. It just wouldn't happen."

His green eyes were dark with something I couldn't identify. "For you I would give it all up."

Warmth filled me as I studied the beautiful male sitting across the table. Rodán was truly like no other. Not a soul on this Earth Otherworld—or any Otherworld for that matter—could fully compare to my Proctor, former lover, and friend who was dear to me in more ways than I could count. What I felt for Rodán was different than my feelings for any other man.

"You know that I love you," I said quietly. "But I've always known that you have desires, you have lust for others. And I realized, in the end, I couldn't change that. I simply am thankful for our deep friendship now."

Rodán opened his mouth to speak but I pushed back my chair and got to my feet.

As he stood, his slight smile and a slow shake of his head indicated his understanding.

"I'm late getting to work and my boss is real hardcase," I said as I gave him a teasing look.

"Your employer told you to take the night off," Rodán said with an equally teasing expression. "Perhaps you should listen to him."

"I don't think listening is one of my strengths." I moved toward Rodán and tilted my head to kiss his cheek. "I'll consider your offer on the leadership position," I said as I drew away. "Not the girlfriend spot."

Rodán took my hands and kissed my cheek in return. "You would be the one, Nyx."

At the same moment, three females came toward us from the direction of the bar. They were dressed in next-to-nothing.

When they reached us, two of them took one of Rodán's arms and the third said to me, "You must learn to share."

Rodán met my gaze and I raised my hands, amusement rising in me. "See? Have fun."

He smiled at me then at the females who had swooped down to take him away. "One moment, please," he said to them. "I will join you shortly."

"You'd better," one of the females said with a coy look on her delicate features. "Or we'll hunt you down."

With another smile, Rodán gave a nod to the threesome, and they headed back to the bar.

He took my hands in his. His grip was firm, comfortable. "Good night, sweet one." He brushed his lips across my cheek, and I kissed him again before I stepped back.

I turned and headed out of the restaurant and into the night. My Corvette was parked in the underground lot, and the parking garage's dim lights shone off the sleek black car. Some Other Place wasn't far from my apartment which was at 104th and Central Park West. It was early yet, so I'd have enough time to change into my tracking gear and head on out.

The late-April night was clear and cool. As much as I enjoy the change in seasons, I'd been so ready for spring and was glad to see it.

When I reached my building, I parked, walked past my PI office on the ground level, and headed upstairs to my apartment.

Through Mrs. Taylor's apartment door I heard her television blaring the latest reality TV show and I smelled cigarette smoke. Terror, her Chihuahua, yipped three times as I walked by.

Kali, my blue Persian, hated Terror. I thought the rat-like dog had been lucky that Kali hadn't gotten hold of him.

I reached my floor and came to an abrupt stop.

Adam.

He'd been standing with his shoulder hitched up against the wall, but when he saw me he straightened.

So many feelings rushed over me as I met his warm brown eyes. Pain, desire, confusion, and love. Mostly love.

Adam's sable-brown hair was ruffled as if he had just combed his fingers through it, adorable and sexy. His hands were stuffed into his bomber jacket, the brown leather well worn. At six-two he had me beat by about six inches in height. He had a lean, muscular build.

"Hi, Nyx." He looked nervous. "Can we talk?"

"This is so unexpected, but sure." I swallowed. "Come on in."

My spine tingled as he stood behind me and I used a little bit of my air elemental magic to unlock my door. I opened the door and walked inside then held it open for him.

The love I felt for Adam and the pain over our breakup never ceased to make me feel weak, and not at all like the strong female and powerful warrior that I am.

I tossed my black clutch onto my white sofa and faced Adam. It was hard to keep my voice steady. "What do you need to talk with me about?"

Adam hesitated. "I met someone. I just thought you should know."

I felt light-headed, as if my head was separating from my body. I mentally drew it back and straightened my shoulders. Adam had met someone already?

"You were right when you broke up with me in December," I said. "It wouldn't have worked between us. You're a norm, I'm a paranorm, and our worlds would never meet."

Adam looked at the floor and then at me. He smelled so good. Of leather and his masculine scent that I had loved so much. "I never expected to meet someone else," he said. "Not after you, but I have.

"I know how you and I both feel about each other and always will. But we know why it ended." He lowered his voice "I just wanted you to hear it from me, Nyx."

"I'm happy for you," I said and then was surprised that I meant it as much as I did. "I want you to be happy."

"I am." He cleared his throat. "I think you would like Keri."

Hearing the female's name made my stomach twist. Maybe I wasn't as totally over Adam as I'd thought I was. Or maybe it was just hard imagining another female with him at all.

I studied his brown eyes, looking for signs of doubt. There were none. "You love her, so I'm sure I would like her."

Adam held my gaze then started out the door. He paused and kissed the top of my head. "A part of me will always love you," he said quietly.

"I feel the same way." I looked down at him again. "I'll miss you."

"I'll still be around." He gave me his adorable smile that showed off his dimple. "See you, Nyx."

I nodded then closed the door behind him.

For a moment I leaned with my back against the door and closed my eyes.

Adam had found someone else. It was truly over. It was final. This was real. Adam was gone from my life, no matter what he said about seeing me around. Something told me I wouldn't be seeing him at all.

Mentally setting aside everything that had happened tonight, I went to my closet. I pulled on black leather pants over red silky panties and a black leather top. The outfit was both durable and perfect for fighting when I tracked—and, well, beneath it all I just had to have something frilly even when I was tracking.

Maybe a battle was what I needed to get my head on straight. I strapped my weapons belt on and headed out, determined to find a good fight.

TWO

"Reese?"

Reese frowned into the darkness. The feminine voice that had just spoken his name when he answered the phone was familiar but he couldn't place it. He mentally blocked out the sound of traffic from the Santa Monica Freeway that edged his downtown LA territory as he concentrated on the phone call.

"You've got him right here." Reese squared his feet on the asphalt of the parking lot. He closed his eyes and sent his energy through the phone, his Shifter senses searching for whoever owned that voice. "Who's this?"

Before he could identify the female with his senses, she said in a hushed, frantic whisper. "It's Monique."

Reese opened his eyes and straightened. His skin tingled like it always did before something bad was going to go down.

He was beyond surprised. Monique, the San Francisco Proctor, had been missing for weeks. She was a friend, someone he liked, trusted, and admired. If he hadn't been so slammed with the volume of activity in his territory, and if they'd had enough Night Trackers to cover it, he would have gone to San Francisco to join the search for her. In a heartbeat. Unfortunately LA was short of Trackers, as were the neighboring cities.

"Mo? Are you okay?" Reese held the phone tight to his ear. "Where are you?"

"I need your help." Monique's voice trembled, something

he'd never have thought of from the Elvin Proctor. "Something horrible is happening and I need someone I can trust. I know I can trust you. Are you alone now?"

"No one else is around right now and of course you can trust me." Reese kept in the shadows as headlights flashed in his direction. "Where are you?" he asked again.

Her voice lowered, and he had to concentrate to hear her. "I'm near the entrance to Griffith Park on Crystal Springs Drive. Come now and signal me twice when you're there."

"You've got it." Reese began preparing himself for the shift, thinking of one of his favorite animal forms. "I can tell Curtis to meet—"

"No. Don't bring the Werewolf." Monique said the words so sharply that it made him pause. "I need you to come alone—you'll understand why when we meet. I can't have anyone know we have spoken. I'm in danger. I need someone I can completely trust to help and I know you can."

Alone. A bell rang in his mind. A warning bell.

"All right." Reese raised his left arm and glanced at his watch. Nearly midnight. "I'll be there in ten minutes."

"Thank you." Monique sounded genuinely relieved, and he wondered if he had just overreacted. "Hurry. Please."

"Be right there." He snapped his phone shut and started to slip it into the holster on his weapons belt.

Instead he opened the phone again and dialed the number for one of the Trackers who covered the more-than-four-thousand-acre park. Katy answered on the third ring.

"Are you at home right now?" Reese asked.

"Yep," Katy answered. "What's up?"

"I need you on backup right away, just around the corner from your place," Reese said to the Witch. He explained the call he'd just gotten from Monique and added, "Stick to the shadows and don't let her know you're there."

"Gotcha." The Witch's soft voice belied the power she wielded in the spoken word. "I'll leave right now. I'll be waiting and watching."

"Thanks, Katy." Reese flipped the phone closed and shoved it into the holster.

Reese visualized an eagle, picturing its beauty, its strength, everything about it down to the last feather on its body.

A rush of sensation washed over his skin, like ice water, followed by warmth that reached every nerve ending in his body. One moment he stood in the parking lot and the next he took to the sky, shooting up until he was high above the city. A sense of exhilaration filled him as he rode the wind until he was over the main entrance to Griffith Park.

Reese circled above but didn't see Monique, or any other being for that matter. He let out two piercing cries to let Mo—as well as Katy—know he was there. He doubted he'd see Katy, who likely would have cloaked herself in a Witch's glamour. Being Elvin, Monique would be virtually impossible to spot, too. But if anyone else was around, he should hopefully see them.

Monique stepped from the shadows and looked up. Reese soared downward, straight for her. He landed in human form at a jog about twenty feet from where she stopped. With a quick sweep of his gaze and an outreach of his senses, he slowed and walked to the Elvin Proctor.

Reese hadn't thought it possible for one of the Light Elves to look so concerned that she appeared almost frightened. The Elves were known for their stoic beauty, even during the worst of times.

Monique was lovely in jeans and a red blouse, her dark curls wild around her delicate, exotic face. Her completely feminine features belied the amazing skills she had as a Tracker and a Proctor. With her Elvin strength and intelligence, she was as tough mentally as she was physically.

She looked pale yet radiant in what little lighting there was at the park entrance. It was so good to see her, and he felt a flood of relief that she was alive.

"Where have you been, Monique?" he said, "The paranorm world is on its ass about all the missing Trackers—and you, a Proctor. It's all anyone's talking about."

"Reese," she said as she moved toward him. "Thank you for coming so quickly." She went on before he could say anything. "There's so much no one knows. I've been working undercover to find the other Trackers. It had to be kept secret."

Reese cocked his head as she neared him.

"It all had to look plausible to those who have taken the missing Trackers," she said.

"Rumors and speculation abound on who is responsible for this," Reese said.

Monique nodded. "I have something important to talk with you about. I need you to be a part of this operation."

Reese raised an eyebrow but let Monique continue.

"No one can know," Monique said. "You must turn up missing like all of the others."

"I'll consider it once I hear more from you," Reese said. "Who or what do you think is responsible?"

Monique lowered her voice, even though they were alone. "You're right in part. But this isn't the place to get into details."

Reese gave a nod as he studied Monique. Something stirred within him. Like the feeling of setting out on the hunt. He was going to be in on the action from the inside.

"I have a place where I'm staying near Anaheim." Monique gestured in the direction of the city. "I want you to come with me now and meet with our small undercover team," she added. "I want to make certain, though. You have told no one, correct?"

Reese hesitated.

"Reese, I have to know, have you told anyone?" Monique repeated.

"I'm sorry." Reese felt a tinge of embarrassment that sent heat creeping up his neck. "You turn up missing and I get a call from out of the blue with you asking to meet me alone. It didn't seem right with all of the Trackers missing to not ask for a backup. It's what you would have told me as a Proctor."

"Reese, who knows?" Monique sounded a little panicked. "Who have you told? Is there someone else here?"

"Katy, the Witch," Reese said. "She's watching right now."

Monique straightened, seeming to compose herself. "Call her in."

Reese said in a normal tone of voice, "Katy, it's all good. No danger."

No answer.

"Katy? Are you there?" Reese turned to look around him.

"Reese, Vampires are here!" Katy's voice resonated throughout the park. "I can smell and sense them."

The magic in the Witch's voice was powerful enough that Reese felt it to the soles of his feet.

"What's going on, Mo?" His voice came out in a growl.

Monique took a step forward. "Reese—"

He stepped back.

Something was wrong. Bad wrong.

"Reese!" Katy cried out as he stared at Monique. He took his gaze off the Proctor long enough to look over his shoulder.

He gave a cry of rage as he saw Katy lying on the ground, lifeless, blood trickling down her neck, a Vampire crouched over her.

His heart beat faster. Adrenaline pumped through his veins.

The shift came over him fast and sudden, and he roared as he became seven hundred pounds of tiger flesh—muscles, sinew, jagged teeth, and three-inch fangs.

Reese sprang onto the Vampire and slammed him onto the ground. He tore into the Vamp, ripping out his throat and shaking him like a rag before flinging him aside.

His roar reverberated through the park as he stood over Katy's body. He turned his head to look back at Monique and growled deep in his throat.

A redheaded female Vampire walked from the trees, glaring at Monique. "I don't know why he keeps you around. Look what you've done."

Monique scowled. "Shut up, Elizabeth." The redheaded Vamp stilled, anger burning in her eyes like green fire. "We prepared for this," Monique added.

Reese narrowed his eyes and growled again. What could they possibly do to him? Another growl rose up in him as he saw Vampires surrounding him, holding tranquilizer guns. He would have laughed if he were in human form. Norms' animal tranqs did not work on Shifters.

But he shouted out as the Vampires started shooting him

with darts, the needles stinging as they buried themselves in his huge body.

Before he could tear into the Vampires, the world started to spin around him. Darkness turned into light turned into darkness in his mind. Something different was in those tranquilizer darts.

Reese felt himself falling out of the shift . . . his body returning to his human form.

The moment he became human, Monique grabbed him in an embrace, startling him.

Fangs and a flash in her eyes told him all he needed to know. Monique was one of them.

It happened too fast.

"So happy you came," she said, right before she sank her fangs into the vein at the side of his neck.

Confusion followed by survival instinct sped through Reese. He struggled, but almost immediately felt like all of his strength was being drained from his body. He went slack and was shocked to realize that Monique was strong enough to hold his weight.

Monique was some kind of Elvin Vampire. No . . . No. The thought didn't truly compute in his mind.

She stilled. Reese's mind swam. He'd never felt so weak in his life. The Elvin Vampire slid her fangs out of his neck and licked the spot she had just pierced.

The strangeness of it all made everything feel surreal. Monique let go of him. He dropped to his knees and fell forward. He managed to land on his palms so that he was supporting himself on all fours.

Reese shook his head, trying to knock the fuzziness from his brain. Katy screamed. The sound cleared his mind. He was aware of more than one being around them. Several beings.

"We know what your weakness is, Shifter. You have no choice but to join us," came a smooth, deep male voice. "We had a special tranquilizer made that was formerly known only to Shifters."

Reese's mind swam.

"In twenty-four hours I shall be the one to bite you and

turn you. And then you shall be in my control. Yes, you will actually want to obey me. Hard to believe, isn't it? But true."

Reese barely was able to move away from Katy before he collapsed. Vaguely he heard voices. The voices turned into a murmur, and he faded away.

Two for the price of one.

Volod smiled as he looked down at the Shifter, who'd transformed from an enormous tiger to his significantly smaller human form. He was still a big male, probably two hundred pounds, all muscle.

The Witch was a bonus. Seth was the only paranorm from his super-team who hadn't succumbed to the Witch's voice. A Shadow Shifter, Seth had transformed into shadow before the voice could affect him. He shifted back into human form beside her, just in time to take her down without her having a chance to say another word. Thereby freeing everyone else from her thrall.

"Excellent." Volod gave a nod of approval to the recently made paranorm Vamps circling him. The Shifter Tracker, Reese, and the Witch Tracker, Katy, made up a total of eleven for his "dream team." One Proctor, ten Trackers.

As soon as Reese and Katy were fully turned, Volod would have them trained with the others.

And then the conclave. Volod would reveal his team and his plan when the group of head Master Vampires in the United States gathered for their quarterly meeting.

With the conclave's backing, Volod intended to take back his New York territory—

And exact revenge on those who had destroyed his world. Revenge against those who had murdered his brother, Danut.

The Drow bitch and the mightier-than-thou Elvin Proctor wouldn't be so smug when he was finished with them.

They would be his and serve his every command.

It was a far more satisfying thought than simply killing Nyx Ciar and Rodán. Far more satisfying.

THREE

SOME PEOPLE ARE LIKE SLINKIES:
NOT REALLY GOOD FOR ANYTHING, BUT THEY
STILL BRING A SMILE TO YOUR FACE WHEN
YOU PUSH THEM DOWN A FLIGHT OF STAIRS.

"What are Slinkies?" my brother, Tristan, asked as he looked from Olivia's T-shirt to me. The early-evening wind tossed his cobalt-blue hair around his face. With his equally blue skin he would be difficult for New Yorkers to see at night, as long as he stayed to the shadows.

I laughed. "I'll get you a Slinky of your own."

"And then I can demonstrate," Olivia, my PI partner of almost two years, said with a decidedly evil look in her dark eyes.

"Only with the Slinky." I elbowed her. "Not by pushing Tristan down the stairs."

"What's the fun in that?" Olivia looked at him then at me again, devious expression still intact. "If not Tristan, how about we push Colin—"

"Not." I lightly punched her shoulder.

Olivia was six inches shorter than my five-eight, but a dynamo of a petite package. A martial arts expert and former NYPD officer on the SWAT team—not to mention that she'd grown up with five sisters—Olivia DeSantos was a force to be reckoned with.

She gave a nod in Tristan's direction. He had tilted his

head back and was scenting something on the night breeze. Probably a lot of somethings, since this was New York City.

"He won't stop looking at my boobs." She put her hands on her hips. "I feel objectified," she added with total innocence in her voice.

I laughed and gestured to her melon-size breasts. "They don't grow them that big in Otherworld."

With her flawless dark silk skin and her exotic looks, that probably wasn't the only thing Tristan had been looking at. Olivia was half Kenyan and half Puerto Rican, a stunning combination. I'd noticed Tristan watching her when he didn't think she was paying attention.

Olivia's penchant for wearing T-shirts with amusing sayings, as well as jeans and Keds sneakers, didn't take anything away from her sensual looks. Once she started talking, though, everyone saw Olivia in a far different way—a tough streetwise cop turned private investigator who jumped into everything as if she were bulletproof.

"So . . ." Olivia gave me a sly look. "How's the fire-breathing hunk?"

My cheeks burned as if the fire-breathing hunk had scorched them with his flames. I turned away before forcing myself to look at her again.

"I'm not sure I want a relationship right now." I cleared my throat. "I have a lot to think about."

Olivia surprisingly didn't give any kind of smart-ass remark. "Fair enough."

"Adam found someone," I said. "He stopped by tonight to tell me."

"She's a ballerina." Olivia studied me. "I helped Boyd out with some information on his last case. She was his case."

"Why didn't you tell me?" I wasn't sure whether I should feel hurt or appreciative.

Olivia's gaze remained firm. "I thought about it and I really wanted to. But it just didn't seem right. It was so hard not to say anything. Still, I figured it was his job to tell you, not mine."

Slowly I nodded. "You're right. It was better coming from him. Thank you."

She tilted her head. "Are you okay with it?"

"Yes." I smiled. "I want the best for Adam. And if it's this ballerina, then that's great."

From the corner of my eye I saw my brother stepping off the curb—right in front of a taxi.

"Tristan!" I lunged toward him, grabbed his arm, and jerked him back onto the sidewalk.

The cab's horn blared and the whoosh of air as it passed blew my hair out of my face. I released Tristan's arm and held my hand to my pounding heart. "You can't step in front of moving vehicles. You'll get flattened." I added, "Not to mention a big blue guy might have freaked out the cab-driver."

Olivia gave an unladylike snort. "You're talking about New York City cabdrivers. Nothing freaks them out."

He gave me a sheepish look. "This place is most unlike Otherworld."

"No kidding." I grimaced. It was Tristan's first excursion in preparation for becoming a Night Tracker. He was leaving in the morning for his training in Chicago.

"You need to get used to Manhattan before we turn you loose on the city," I continued. "That means *be careful*. Besides, Father would kill me if anything happens to you after we finally got you back."

It'll be a while before he'll be an effective Tracker, I thought. *Almost gets hit by a car . . .*

My brother looped his arm around my shoulders, his blue flesh looking darker against my pale amethyst skin. Drow have skin tones ranging from blue to purple to dark gray—all shades that blend in with the night and shadows.

Tristan gave my shoulders a light squeeze. "I still cannot believe how much you have grown, little sister," he said in the language of the Dark Elves. His English was perfect thanks to my human mother teaching him when he was young, and he could read and write the language just as easily.

"I'm not so little anymore." I smiled. "Especially now that we're the same age."

"It doesn't matter that time did not pass for me when I was captured in the stone," he said. "You will always be my little sister."

We were both twenty-seven now, a fact that was strange to us since I had been five when he was taken from my family by Zombies. Fortunately all that was history now, and I had Tristan back.

"I know you want to look around," I said. "But stay close and don't get off the sidewalk."

Tristan grinned, squeezed me to him one more time, then released me and walked to the storefront window of a camera shop. It was close to midnight and the traffic wasn't too bad where we were on Amsterdam Avenue.

"So Rodán wants to give you more responsibilities than you already have," Olivia said when Tristan turned his attention toward a traffic signal that had just turned red.

As I nodded, Olivia shook her head. "I think you're the best they've got," she said. "But what do you think you are, Superwoman? Like you don't have enough to do with running a PI office and being a Tracker."

"I haven't decided anything yet." As we stood at a crosswalk, I frowned and met her gaze. "I just don't know if I want to take on that kind of leadership role. There would be a lot that goes along with it, maybe more than I realize."

"No kidding," Olivia said. "But if you want to do it, go for it. You'd be damn good."

I heard the faint vibration of Olivia's cell phone and she drew it out of the phone holster at her hip. Her features subtly changed when she checked the caller ID screen.

I cocked my head. The expression on her face had been one of genuine pleasure, in a way that I'd never seen from Olivia before.

She held the phone to her ear. "Hey, Scott."

My eyebrows rose. Olivia's tone had a sensual edge to it that surprised me.

With my Elvin hearing I could have eavesdropped and

listened to "Scott," but I never intentionally violated a friend's privacy.

"Perfect," she said after a moment. "Everything will be waiting." She lowered her voice, but I still couldn't help hearing her add, "Especially me."

Olivia tucked her cell phone back in its holster as she turned around to face me. "What?" The tone of her voice and her expression were now more like the Olivia I knew and loved.

"Am I being left out of everything now? Since when did you start seeing someone named Scott?" I put my hands on my hips. "And since when did you start to look and sound sappy over a guy?"

"I did not look or sound sappy." Olivia narrowed her eyes at me. "It's just a guy I met a couple of weeks ago at the dojo." She was a black belt in karate and worked out regularly in Midtown.

"You've been dating a guy for two weeks and haven't mentioned him?" I gave an incredulous look. "You've been holding out on me."

"It's nothing." She shrugged. "We've mostly been working out together."

"I caught that word," I folded my arms across my chest. "Mostly. So what else do you do?"

"We've been out a couple of times," Olivia said.

"What's he like?" I asked, letting my arms fall to my sides again. "Come on. Tell me."

"Fun. Outgoing." She smirked. "Kinky."

I laughed. "Only two weeks and that's a word you'd use to describe this guy you've been hiding away. Kinky?"

Olivia shrugged again. "You asked and you said I've been holding out on you."

I opened my mouth to attempt to get her to elaborate. A tingling sensation ran down my spine.

"Time to track," I said. "I sense some Metamorphs doing what they do best—getting into trouble."

FOUR

The following afternoon I signed for two small packages and set one of them beside the mail bin as the agency door closed behind the delivery person.

Afternoon light reflected through the glass door, illuminating the sign advertising our office to other paranorms.

NYX CIAR
Olivia DeSantos
PARANORMAL CRIMES
PRIVATE INVESTIGATORS
By appointment only

It was Friday and I'd spent the morning catching up on office work. Mostly paperwork—things that had to be done but were my least favorite things to do.

I turned my attention back to the boxes and mail that had just been delivered. I set aside the mail and used a box cutter on the first package. It contained some kind of electrical gadget that I figured Olivia must have purchased for the remodeling of our office. She'd spent the past two months taking us from my version of high tech to her version.

That meant we didn't just have a large-screen computer monitor each any longer. Now we had an entire wall that could be a single screen or several, depending on what we were researching or briefing each other on. We had headsets and any number of other gadgets.

I had no idea what the gadget was in the package I'd just opened. I shrugged and set it aside before moving on to the next box.

When it was open I dug out the paper—and pulled out a spiked leather dog collar and a leash. I frowned. The package must have come to the agency by mistake. I looked at the return address—simply a stamp with the initials PP and then an address. I glanced to see who the package should have gone to and saw that it was addressed to Olivia.

Weird. Unless she'd gotten herself a dog—a rather big one—then this had to be a gift for a friend. We had several Doppler friends whose animal forms were large dogs, but I didn't think she was close enough to any of them to buy them a collar and a leash. Not to mention the fact that even thinking about putting a collar on a Doppler was reason enough to get bitten.

I didn't like to call Olivia on her days off if it wasn't really important I put the items back in the box and set them on her desk.

Fae bells tinkled and I looked over my shoulder, away from the stack of mail, and at the office door.

"Colin," I said as the gorgeous blond male pushed the door open and stepped inside. A cool April breeze followed the Dragon into the office. The scent of spring was in the air.

He gave me a sexy smile that made me feel warm in a smooth sweep from my scalp to my toes.

"Hey," Colin said as he moved toward me. Fae bells tinkled again as he let the door close behind him.

I set the package down and turned to face him completely. "What's up, Hot Stuff?" I couldn't help a smile of my own as I called him by the nickname Olivia had pinned onto the sometimes fire-breathing male.

"I'm kidnapping you." Colin put his warm hands on my upper arms and bent to brush his lips over mine. It was just a whisper-soft kiss, but it was enough to singe me.

"Kidnapping me?" I said, thinking of all the possibilities that went with that idea.

Then beating those ideas back down again. I'd told Colin I wasn't ready for a relationship, and he'd understood. Adam had broken things off with me just a couple of months ago.

Adam might have been able to move on right away, but I was hesitant. More than anything, I think it was fear that held me back. Fear that any new relationship might end just like mine and Adam's had. I wasn't so sure I wanted to try my heart out so soon.

"I'm taking you out for an early dinner and a movie." Colin leaned back against Olivia's desk. His biceps and the muscles in his forearms flexed beneath his golden skin as he braced his hands on either side of the desktop. He wore a blue T-shirt and blue jeans that molded to his hips and thighs extremely well.

Soft burnished-gold eyes, long glittering gold hair, and well-cut masculine features made Colin the Dragon one of the sexiest males I'd ever met. Rodán was the only male I knew who was even more gorgeous than Colin, and that wasn't an easy accomplishment.

"How does Indian food sound?" Colin said as he watched me walk toward my desk.

"Delicious." I went behind my desk and brought my Dolce & Gabbana handbag out of the cubby beneath my desktop. "I'm starving."

"You do realize, of course," Colin said with a sensual expression, "that I intend to keep you the rest of the day. You need a break."

"Says who?" I moved back around my desk and reached him. He was six-four, and I had to tilt my head a little.

"Says me." Colin took me by my arm and guided me to the front door.

On the way I grabbed the packages that I'd left beside the mail basket. "This package came for Olivia. We have to go right by her apartment anyway, so I think I'll drop it off for her. She won't be back in until Monday."

Colin shrugged. "Sure. Just gives me more time to be with you."

I smiled at Colin again. It was easy and fun to be around

him. I didn't have to worry about what I did or said, and I could be out with him any time of the day or night.

Before we left I ran up to my apartment to change into jeans, a soft cream-colored cashmere sweater, and my black leather Elvin boots. I combed out my hair, the blue highlights shining in the inky black.

Colin's co-op was in Queens so he'd taken his black Dodge Viper to pick me up. From my office we drove to Olivia's apartment building on Gold Street in the Financial District. Colin parked and I grabbed Olivia's packages.

The doorman was away from his post—something that would have ticked off Olivia. She felt if she was paying for a doorman, "he'd damn well better be there."

Colin and I took the elevator up to the fifth floor then walked the few feet to her apartment door.

I started to knock when I heard a sound like a muffled scream. My heart started racing. Colin and I looked at each other.

"Did you hear that?" I said, keeping my voice low. "I think Olivia's in trouble."

Colin nodded, a grim expression on his face.

Another muffled scream. It was hard to tell if it was Olivia or not. A few more muffled sounds followed.

Colin tried the doorknob. Locked. I motioned for him to move away and used my air element to unlock the door. The mechanism clicked. The muffled sounds in the apartment stopped. I dropped the boxes I was carrying.

At the same time Colin flung open the door, I threw up a shield using my air element again, to protect us in case any weapons were fired our way.

No one was in the living room.

Another muffled scream. Coming from the bedroom.

I hurried across Olivia's small living room to her bedroom.

Heart pounding, I peeked around the door frame.

My eyes widened and I realized my mouth was hanging open. I snapped it shut as I took in the scene in a quick glance.

Olivia was strapped to her bed, spread-eagle. Her ankles

and wrists were secured with leather cuffs to chains, the chains attached to standard-issue handcuffs around each metal bar of her bedpost.

A collar was tethered by a chain running to the sides of the bed frame holding her head taut. The way she was restrained, she wasn't going anywhere.

Blindfolded, she screamed, the sound garbled because in her mouth was a red ball secured by two black straps around her head. She wore only a pair of black panties.

In a quick sweep of my gaze around the room I saw all that I needed to see. More leather cuffs, chains, locks, rope, various leather straps, a small leather paddle, a black leather hood, an eye mask, a riding crop, and other items I couldn't quite identify were all on the foot of the bed.

Colin made a choked sound from behind me and I clapped my hand over my mouth, trying to keep from laughing.

Where was the guy who'd restrained her like this? Maybe he was in the bathroom.

Given her futile flailing against the restraints and the garbled cries, it was obvious that Olivia was too pissed to be happy about her situation. I went to her, trying to keep my composure, when all I wanted to was burst out in laughter.

I moved forward to take off her blindfold and noticed the red writing on her black panties. I almost did start laughing but managed to control myself.

Flip Over to Spank

I tugged off her blindfold, and she stopped struggling. She looked shocked to see me and then her eyes quickly narrowed. She tried to say something but the ball gag was too big for her to talk around. I saw a clasp on one strap, near the ball, and I unfastened it. As pissed as she was, I was almost afraid to take it out of her mouth.

The moment I did, she shouted. "I'm going to kill him! He left me here. I can't believe he left me here."

Her face was flushed, perspiration on her skin, her dark hair sweaty at the roots.

"Who?" I said, trying to keep a straight face.

"Scott. That's who." Olivia glanced over my shoulder and saw Colin, who was grinning. "What are you laughing at, smoke for brains?"

Seeing Olivia like that and her total indignation was too much. It was also too Olivia. I started laughing so hard I didn't think I could stop.

"Let me out of here." Olivia narrowed her eyes at me. "Before I add you to my hurt-maim-or-kill list."

"If I can stop laughing," I said between gasps for air. "I think I know now what the collar and leash are for that just came in the mail."

After this I had a feeling Olivia would be strapping down and collaring Scott rather than the other way around. If he lived through today.

I heard the sound of the front door closing. Apparently Olivia did, too, because she screamed, "I'm going to kill you, Scott!"

Colin peered around the doorway from the bedroom. He stepped back, out of the way of the male who appeared in the doorway.

He was a fairly tall, good-looking human in a gray T-shirt, blue jeans, and athletic shoes. He had dark hair that curled a little at the ends, and his eyes were a brilliant blue.

His rugged looks belonged to an outdoorsy, athletic kind of guy. The T-shirt stretched taut over his chest and biceps showed just how fit he was. I had to say, Olivia had great taste—at least in the looks department. I didn't know about brains.

Right now the guy wore a sheepish expression. He was carrying a plastic bag with a drugstore logo and a paper bag of something that smelled like Chinese takeout. Knowing Olivia like I did, kung pao chicken, broccoli beef, and steamed dumplings was my guess.

"You must be friends of Olivia." He looked from me to Colin. "This must look a little strange."

"Kinda," I said with a grin.

"Kinda strange?" Olivia shouted. "A lot strange is you

leaving me alone. *Get. Me. Out. Of. Here.*" Olivia snarled each word. "And then I'm going to kill you, Scott."

"You said you liked the idea of being left alone and not knowing where I was . . . and you wanted to experience a little fear." Scott set the Chinese take-out bag on the nightstand closest to him while maintaining distance from Olivia. "Weren't you a little scared?"

"That doesn't include leaving me alone in my apartment cuffed to the damn bed so I can't move, blindfolded and gagged." She jerked against the cuffs, rattling the chains. "I can't believe you took off. And you actually stopped to get Chinese food? Are you serious?"

He raised the drugstore bag. "You're the one who forgot something at the drugstore and I had to run to get them—remember? And Chinese was right next door."

Olivia growled and the flush in her cheeks grew darker. "Isn't there a brain in your head? You don't leave someone alone restrained and gagged like this."

It was just too much. I held my arm to my stomach as I gasped for more breath, trying to stop laughing, but failing miserably. "I'll do it. I'll let her out."

It took only a little of my air magic to make the cuffs drop away from her wrists and ankles.

"Why didn't you do that to begin with?" Olivia scowled and sat up in the bed as she shook the cuffs the rest of the way off. "You could have let me out ages ago."

"What's the fun in that?" I repeated what she'd said last night and grinned. "Besides, I needed time to take this all in."

I thought Olivia was going to throw one of the cuffs at me. Instead she tossed it on the bed, stood, and glared at Scott. "I'm not finished with you," she said.

"I certainly hope not," he murmured, and in the smoldering, sensual look he gave her, I could see exactly what Olivia saw in him. The guy was totally hot.

Olivia just got off the bed, glared, then turned and marched toward her bathroom.

When I saw the back of her panties I started laughing all over again at what was written across her ass.

Spank Here

"You'll pay," she grumbled before she slammed the bathroom door behind her. "All three of you."

It was so Olivia. She didn't seem the least bit embarrassed.

I grinned at Colin and Scott. "This should be good."

FIVE

Colin and I had an early dinner at a restaurant on Cedar Street that served terrific Indian cuisine. Afterward he wanted to go to a movie at a downtown theater. He loved movies. Being from Otherworld, Colin had never known anything like them and had been hooked from the first time he saw one. It was still early enough that I could go to a movie and not shift until at least half an hour after it ended.

It was a comedy, and by the time it was over my stomach hurt from laughing so much. Between one of the funniest scenes I had ever witnessed—walking in on Olivia—and the movie, my stomach hadn't stood a chance.

As we walked back to his car, Colin looped his arm around my shoulders. "How about my place for a beer or two?"

Colin enjoyed a good Belgian, and I'd found I liked them as well. I nodded. "Sure."

He lived in a nice co-op on Sixty-sixth Road in Queens. I simply loved being around Colin. I didn't even mind shifting from human to Drow, or vice versa, during my time with him. As long as I had a place to shift in private, I was more than happy.

"Wonderful," I said after I took a long drink of the beer Colin had handed me. "Next to martinis this has to be my favorite." I winked at him. "Even better than an elderflower Tom Collins."

He gave me an embarrassed grin. I liked to find ways to tease him about the time we met after he'd been putting on the Dragon charm in a talent competition at the Pit. It had taken Hector three bottles of St. Germain elderflower liqueur to counteract the effects of his paranormal charm on all of the female patrons once his show was finished. I'd never let him live that one down.

"How about some popcorn and another movie?" Colin was really good at changing the subject.

"Sure," I said with a smile before I went into the guest bathroom to shift.

When I came out, Colin had an old-fashioned stovetop popper out. The corn kernels rattled in the bottom of the pan as he shook it over the gas heat. In minutes the kitchen smelled of popcorn. When it was finished, we took a big steaming bowl of it into his large living room to share. We set it and our bottles of beer on the coffee table.

While Colin picked out a movie, I parked my butt in our favorite place to sit: on the floor in front of the coffee table with our backs against the sofa. The popcorn was good and buttery as I ate a handful of it and waited for him to set up the movie.

He hit the controller, and a huge screen dropped down over the large flat-screen TV that was hanging on the wall. A few seconds later the screen lit up from the ceiling projector and the lights dimmed.

"Now, this is the way to watch all of the movies you collect, Colin," I said. "Love it."

"This is one I haven't watched yet," he said as he slid down beside me. "The reviews on the Rotten Tomatoes website look almost too good to be true."

"What movie is it?" I asked as his shoulder brushed mine.

Colin grabbed a handful of popcorn. *"The Terminator."*

"You haven't seen *The Terminator*?" I raised my eyebrows. "You will love it."

He looped his arm around my shoulders. I rested against him until the action scenes became so intense that I was leaning forward almost digging my nails into my palms. It was fun getting to see others doing all of the fighting for a change.

When it was finally over, I sagged against the couch. "That was great."

"Guess you could call us a pair of action junkies," he said. "You would think we'd get tired of it after what we do every night as Trackers."

"Never." I looked up at him and smiled.

"You know how much I care about you, don't you, Nyx?" Colin said as he lightly stroked my arm.

I tilted my head to look at him and saw the depth of emotion in his eyes that made me catch my breath.

"When I'm with you I feel complete." Colin brushed strands of hair away from my face. "I don't know how you feel and I won't ask you to tell me. I just want you to know how much you mean to me."

Colin lowered his head, and butterflies danced in my belly as his face moved closer. He brushed his lips over my mouth, so soft at first that it made me give a little moan. Then he pressed his lips more firmly to mine.

His kiss was amazing. Fire and passion mixed in with the depth of his caring.

When he drew away, my gaze met his. "You make me feel so good, Colin. Cherished, cared for, protected."

"That's because you are." Colin cupped the side of my face.

"You get me." I shifted so that my face was close to his. "You understand me in a way that no one ever has before. We're so alike in so many ways."

Colin smiled. "You're beautiful, funny, intelligent." He tugged on my hair, and I looked at the contrast of the blue strands against his golden skin. "You're adorable, too."

Then I tugged his long hair. "Talking about something adorable, let's talk about you."

"Me?" Colin laughed. "Stuffed dragons are adorable. Real Dragons aren't."

"Well, you're entitled to your opinion." I twirled the strand of hair around my finger. "We just disagree on this subject."

Over the past six months I'd come to know Colin fairly

well, but there was still a mystery about him to me. I wanted to know more about him. He seemed to be a bit uncomfortable talking about himself, but I wasn't going to give up.

"I was just thinking earlier today how little I really know you." I trailed my finger down his finely carved biceps. "There's a lot behind you in your past that I know nothing about. I want to know you."

"Uh-oh." Colin threw his head back and looked up at the ceiling. He had that crooked smile on his face that I loved. He slowly brought his head down and his eyes met mine. "Do we have to do this?"

I gave a single nod. "Yes."

"Okay. Ask away, Nyx Ciar," he said. "What would you like to know?"

There was something about the mixture of his confident expression with his smile. He had me. Forget the questions, I wanted to kiss him.

"Okay," I said. "Let's start with how someone who is as hot as you isn't taken already."

"What?" Colin shook his head and laughed. "That's your question? How about you just get to know me better and you come up with your own answer on that if you don't already have one. Next."

I rolled my eyes. "Well, so much for the 'ask away' comment."

He shook his head. "I said ask away, I didn't promise I would answer away."

So many strong males could not talk about their feelings. I hoped Colin was different. I needed that in a man, but this wasn't starting so good.

"Let's begin with how you ended up in this Earth Otherworld." I continued to stroke his arm as I spoke. "Why did you leave your part of Otherworld?"

Colin cocked his head and looked more serious all of a sudden. "Those are memories I don't like to think about. Let's try another."

I was beginning to understand why he didn't have anyone. I was an open book, but I couldn't even get out of him why he left his Otherworld and why he wasn't involved in a relationship.

"This isn't going so well, is it?" I said, adding a smile. I didn't want to frighten him off by pressing too hard. At least not just yet. "But I want to be with someone who's a little more transparent than a brick wall."

Leaning forward, I got right up in his face and poked him in the side with my index finger. "You don't want anyone to know you, do you, Colin? Is there a gate somewhere to this wall you have built around you?"

I gave him a quick kiss on the lips and sat back.

A bit of a pleading look came to his eyes. "Can't we just do more of that kissing stuff? I am better at that than talking about myself."

"Let's make a deal." I braced myself on my elbow and forearm. "More kissing after more telling."

Colin shook his head with a look of resignation on his strong features. "You have quite the persuasive way about you, don't you, Nyx?"

I leaned back into him and gave him another poke in his side and a kiss that lingered a bit longer this time. "I've been told that."

"You're right, I don't talk much about me. I'll admit I'm guarded." Colin was talking in a quiet tone. "I guess life has made me that way. I have a story, a journey, like all people do. Some of that story I'm proud of, other parts, well . . . not so much."

He looked down before he continued. "There are things in my past that I haven't talked about with anyone. But I will tell you. There's something about you, Nyx, that makes me feel I can trust you. Something about even the way you're asking now. You want to know me, and you are so accepting of me and what I am. I've seen that quality in you with so many paranorms whom others aren't accepting of."

I hadn't seen Colin so serious before. "Now you have me wondering about this dark past." I laughed. "What are you, a serial killer?"

Colin smiled. "I do have somewhat of a dark past, but nothing like that."

"Then tell me," I said.

With a sigh, Colin started talking. "My parents died when I was a child. I was sent from home to home—foster families, as norms would call it." He shrugged. "I was rebellious, angry, and I had a temper."

"You?" I raised my brows. "You're so even-tempered now."

At that, Colin laughed. "You have no idea how hard I have to work on that."

He grew a little more serious again. "That anger and temper manifested itself into me going into Dragon form and spewing fire to show how tough I was. Frequently I ended up in fights, always needing to prove myself. To show everyone that I was somebody."

I thought about that little boy he'd been and my heart hurt for him. A young Colin, desperate to fit in but not knowing how to do it without anger.

"And then one day I more than lost my temper, Nyx." Colin looked away from me for a moment before he met my gaze again. "It was over something that didn't even matter. But I burned down an entire village."

My eyes widened. "An entire village?"

"Yes, it was an accident, but I did it when I blew up. I was kicked out of my Otherworld." He sighed again. "You can imagine why."

"You were kicked out of your Otherworld? It must have been so hard for you to be alone." I squeezed his hand in mine.

"It was better than the alternative," he said. "They thought about putting me away in prison, but they decided the strongest punishment they could impose was banning me from the world I grew up in and the only world I knew. Turning me out into a place I knew nothing about."

He continued, "And to some extent they were right. It hasn't been easy. I've never truly felt at home anywhere."

"Wow," I said. "That must have been so very hard. What did you do next?"

"I traveled to different Otherworlds in my human form," he said. "I even petitioned a king I worked with and asked if he could do anything, saying I would continue to work for him as a Dragon, protecting his princess."

"The king you mentioned when you were talking with my father," I said.

"King Durkin." Colin nodded. "He was a good man and a good king. But in the end, he could do nothing for me, though he wanted to. He knew I'd made a mistake that I regretted."

"Then what?" I asked.

"I went to two Otherworlds and never felt accepted as a Dragon. Then I had the opportunity to come here, to the Earth Otherworld." Colin dragged his hand down his face. "A Sorceress owed me a favor, and she used the transference to get me here. I couldn't do it myself the first time."

I tilted my head to the side. "When was that?"

"Long enough ago for me to learn human ways and to become at ease with the human language," Colin said. "I did one form of metalwork or another over the decades."

"How old are you?" I asked.

Colin looked thoughtful. "On my birthday next, I'll be one hundred and two. Give or take a couple of years."

I stared at him. "Really?"

"Your father is over two thousand years old," he said. "I'm but a babe next to him."

"True." I gave him a teasing grin. "But in Earth years you're robbing the cradle." I shifted myself so that I could study him more easily. "What about relationships?"

"I was in a few relationships in the other Otherworlds that I lived in." Colin said. "Paranorm females loved the fact that I'm Dragon because it made me out as some sort of bad boy." He gave a little smile. "Females like to play with the bad boys. But I never got them to get serious."

He continued, "So I dated a few norm women. After the first couple, one of whom I was in love with, I knew it wouldn't work out. When it came down to it, as a Dragon I was too different," he said. "They knew they couldn't take me home to Mom and Dad and tell them I was a Dragon. So I avoided serious relationships to protect myself. I decided just to have fun."

"That's why Adam and I broke up—the fact that I'm so different." I still felt a little sad, but it didn't hurt as much now. "How could he explain having a wife whose skin changes at night? He wouldn't have been able to, and it wouldn't have been right for him to miss out on family and friends' events and sleepovers because his wife turned amethyst after dark."

Colin kissed me. "We're a lot alike, you and I."

"Yes," I said. "I like that." I paused. "You don't seem to have anger issues now."

"I've had to temper my anger," he said. "I've really had to work at it. I don't regret my past . . . it has made me the man I am today . . . a better man than I was. But I still fight aspects of my nature." He held my gaze. "I need someone who understands it."

"I get it. There are things I have to work at, too."

"I didn't want to be that person, the one who loses control like I used to." He rubbed his face with his hand again. "I learned to turn that on with the bad guys, and have avoided burning down villages ever since."

His gaze looked faraway for a moment. "Not a day goes by that I don't think of what I did to my own village. Not one day goes by I don't think I would like to go back and see the people I grew up with. And I think about the danger of that happening to the people I care about. I can never let that happen. I can never lose control like that."

He continued, "So when you bring this up, Nyx, it's hard to talk about because it forces me to dwell on a past that I'm not proud of, and I feel like I have left behind. But you want to know me, to understand me . . . Well, this is me. Do you want to leave now?"

"Leave?" I said. "Are you serious? None of us is perfect. I respect you for not being bitter. For being willing to change aspects you didn't like of yourself.

"So many say people can never change," I went on. "That is not true. Life has a way of changing people. You either become bitter and defiant and angrier. Or you recognize and take responsibility for areas where you've fallen short and change them. You changed, Colin. You are not that person."

"Thank you for saying that. I would like to think that I have changed. Being a Tracker helps. It allows me to direct the anger and flame those who deserve it."

"Thank you, Colin." I smiled at him. "You shared a lot."

"More than I thought I would," Colin said. "I haven't told anyone that since I left my Otherworld. It's all you, Nyx. That persuasive side of yours."

"Persuasive side?" I asked.

"Have you forgotten so soon? Time to pay up, Nyx Ciar. The kissing for telling."

Colin jumped on top and pinned me down and smothered me with his kiss. It wasn't too hard for him. He was met with little resistance.

He drew back and studied me with his burnished-gold eyes, the passion in them making me catch my breath.

Something twisted in my abdomen and my heart beat faster. I tried to swallow but my throat was too dry. All this time Colin had been so good about giving me my space. But now I saw desire there that was almost too much for him to hold back.

Then he kissed me harder, deeper, and I kissed him with the same fierceness. I brought my fingers up to the sides of his face and slid them into the soft strands of his long hair.

Thought really didn't come to me. It was all about caring and need and the deep affection I felt for him.

Colin clasped his hands around my waist and without breaking our kiss he rolled us so that I was straddling him.

He slid his hands into my hair and caressed my scalp. I felt myself slipping, wanting to be with Colin in every way possible.

To catch my breath, I drew away from Colin and immediately missed his lips, his taste. I met his eyes, which were now like liquid gold.

He moved me so that our foreheads touched and we still

held each other's gazes. "You know I would never push you into anything you're not ready for."

I twirled a long strand of his hair around my finger and gave a little smile. "Thank you, Colin."

He kissed me lightly before settling his hands on my hips. "I'll wait for you, Nyx." His voice was soft, sensual. "I'll be here when you are ready."

SIX

Volod's impatience with the conclave had him grinding his teeth. When would the idiots be finished with mind-numbing shit that wasn't of any true value to the Vampire race?

Smoke curled from torches bracketed along the walls of the New Orleans meeting chamber. The North American Vampire Conclave met biannually at this location deep beneath the city. Every April and October the leading Vampires from across United States and Canada gathered.

Human workers had been enslaved over 150 years ago to build the chamber along with a network of well-guarded tunnels. All had survived the years well, thanks to Vampire blood mixed into the mortar. It made for an impenetrable, indestructible place for New Orleans Vampires to use and for the conclave to meet.

Now Volod was here, ready to change the fate of Vampirekind.

And to avenge his brother's death . . . as well as seeking revenge for the destruction of all he had built in New York.

Volod glanced at Monique, who stood in the back of the room to await his signal. His beautiful Elvin Vampire looked stunning in a long black dress with diamonds glittering at her throat and ears. Her dark hair flowed over her shoulders and down her back in long soft waves. He pictured the last time he had bedded her and the way her dark eyes looked right before she sank her fangs into his own throat.

Her scent and race were masked by a spell the Witch had

used to keep those in the chamber from knowing that Monique was more than just a Vampire.

What a prize. Like Elizabeth, Monique was an incredible beauty. Her demeanor and mind set her apart, however. He had never thought of a paranorm as appealing, but this one was different. Her exotic looks and the powers she possessed were alluring.

Monique's lust for Vampires had led to her capture. He felt her energy and desire for him, but she was a professional and kept control.

Next to Monique stood Elizabeth in a long blood-red dress, her red hair swept up and rubies strung through the ringlets. The crimson shade on her long fingernails matched her lipstick. Her green eyes, so much like her dead brother, Drago's, were luminescent in the near darkness.

Elizabeth's jealousy and pettiness were already evident with this new addition, but she needed to know, as she had in the past, he would not tolerate her dictating what he did and with anyone. He had taken Monique for a purpose . . . the sexual connection he sensed between them was a bonus.

But now was not the time for such thoughts. He shook off his mental wanderings and looked to the conclave.

The current Vampire prolocutor, Nicholas, stared at Volod with his small, deep-set blue eyes and bushy brows that gave him a permanently gruff look. He had maintained a love of whiskey, long after his death and rebirth. If he hadn't been a Vampire, he likely would have had a red flush to his cheeks.

Nicholas gave Volod a nod, an indication that it was time for him to take the floor.

Volod strode from the back of the room into the center of the chamber. Seventeen regional conclave members—including five representatives from Canada—sat behind a blood-red curtained table that lined the back of the chamber. Each Vampire dignitary wore black robes along with an absurd headdress that looked like a human chef's hat.

Volod would have smirked if he weren't in attendance for such an important reason.

"My brothers and sisters," Volod began, addressing the conclave, "I am honored to be in your presence." With this conclave the rule was to "kiss ass," as humans would say. He nearly shuddered at the vulgarity of it.

"I have a most important purpose for being here," he continued. "Thank you for granting my request to speak to you."

The words tasted foul in his mouth. In truth he couldn't care less about the conclave. They were simply a means to an end and he needed what they could offer.

"Vampires have been kept in check by paranorms for far too long." He couldn't keep the venom out of his voice, nor did he care to. "We should have complete freedom to do as we were meant. To feed from and turn humans at will."

Marcus gave Volod a long-suffering look. "This is nothing new. Everyone here knows we have wanted to break out of the paranorms' control for years. It has proven futile and is not worth the risk of the destruction of our race. Have you something actually worthy of our time?"

A short but stout Vampire with a Napoleon complex, Marcus was second in line to be prolocutor if anything should happen to Nicholas. Volod thought that perhaps Nicholas should consider watching his neck around Marcus.

Volod ignored Marcus and slowly looked around the arc of the table, from one conclave member to the next. He held their gazes one by one as he spoke.

"I have an answer to this problem," he said, keeping the smile of triumph from his voice. "I have discovered a way to control paranorms rather than paranorms controlling us."

A murmur met his ears, a murmur of both curiosity and skepticism. He couldn't blame them for the skepticism. Too long had they tried to turn around the weight of control paranorms held over Vampires. Too long with no hope of obtaining their rightful position as rulers of the paranormal world.

"I have procured a list of all known paranorm weaknesses." Volod paused to let the words sink in to the now silent conclave, his announcement obviously surprising those in attendance.

Prolocutor Nicholas was the first to speak, his tone unreadable. "Please explain."

"The list I arranged to have secured gives us the information we need to defeat paranorms." Volod kept back a sound of impatience. He'd have to spell it out for the simpletons gathered at the conclave. "Every paranorm has a weakness, and this list allows us to exploit those weaknesses."

"You cannot expect us to believe such nonsense." Marcus made a scoffing noise. "If such a list existed we would have known about it long ago."

"Apparently not." Hair prickled at Volod's nape. He let some of his contempt for Marcus spill into his tone before he continued. "More important, the information includes a dossier of each of the Peacekeepers along with their respective skills, abilities, and weaknesses, both as a race and personally.

"Also listed are their quirks," Volod continued, "and, shall we say, the proclivities we can use against them. Among the listed weaknesses are little-known susceptibilities to toxins and other details that can be exploited. This list is a gold mine for us."

By their expressions it was obvious he had piqued the interest of the conclave.

"With this knowledge we can turn paranorms into Vampire-kind," he said. "Elite forces that will help us take control of the paranorm world."

Nicholas held up his hand in a motion meant to shut up Marcus, who had opened his mouth to speak again.

"Paranorm blood makes Vampires ill," Nicholas said. "If this was truly possible, what keeps a Vampire from becoming sick?"

"It does make us ill," Volod said. "For that reason there was never a reason to turn a paranorm. We of course had no taste for paranorm blood. If a paranorm is going to be turned, we must feed on a human just before or just after the taking of paranorm blood. When this is done the toxicity of the paranorm blood is completely neutralized.

"A paranorm is not a satisfying bite to a Vampire," Volod went on, "but this is not about quenching a thirst for blood here. It is about adding to our ranks for our purpose." Volod had learned this by trial and error on the subjects he'd turned prior to Monique. Even when he turned her, he'd had a human waiting in the shadows.

"Once a paranorm is turned, he can feed on others and turn them. Paranorm blood is not poison to others of their kind—in fact they love the blood of their own. Thus an army of these beings can be produced."

Nicholas fixed his gaze on Volod. "How do you know this will work?"

"Because I have done it myself." Volod gestured toward a door to one of the tunnels leading from the chamber.

At his signal, Elizabeth touched the massive door with her fingertips. Her power infused it with a soft orange glow. Stone scraped stone as the heavy door shuddered open.

When it was open wide, all ten Vampire paranorm Trackers, members of his "dream team," walked through the opening. The lovely Elvin Vampire, Monique, left Elizabeth's side to make her way toward Volod. She released the Witch's spell, and he caught her Elvin scent and the power she commanded.

Each Vampire paranorm made his or her way through the crowd to stand in a line just behind Volod.

Gasps of surprise traveled among the members of the conclave. Vampires could instinctively sense what race of beings a paranorm belonged to. His team of eleven included ten Trackers—Shadow and animal Shifters, Dopplers, Werewolves, and a Witch.

"That they are now Vampires is virtually undetectable—quite different than human conversions." Volod held back a smile at the fact that the bastard Marcus seemed at a loss for words despite his scowl. "Not only do they have Vampire strength, but they have retained the abilities and magic of their race."

"Very impressive." Nicholas gave a nod of admiration. "What exactly do you plan to do with them?"

"To create a paranorm army that has the power and skills

to eliminate the threat of reprise from paranorms," Volod said. "Thus we shall once again feed on humans and turn them at will."

Nicholas leaned forward, his arms resting on the tabletop, his hands clasped.

"What do you propose that the council do to assist you?"

"I want you to have knowledge of what I am doing," Volod said. "At times I will need resources that this council can provide. That might mean sending in more Vampire power from around the continent to various cities. We will work together and take back our world."

The power in Volod's conviction echoed in the chamber. "Now that we have assembled a team of skilled Vampire paranorms, we will next concentrate our efforts in New York City where the strongest Tracker foothold is, and we will destroy or turn all Peacekeepers.

"Once New York is taken," Volod continued, "we will move to Chicago, LA, San Francisco, Atlanta, Toronto, and other select major population areas. We will not stop until we have the control we need. We can expand this to our brothers across the world in Europe, South America, and Asia."

"Have you more Vampire paranorms in addition to these?" Nicholas asked.

"Only those I experimented on before taking Trackers." Volod glanced at his team before looking at Nicholas again. "I felt it important to do this slowly to ensure it was done correctly, one at a time. Thus it has taken us a while to experiment because every paranorm is different.

"I will continue to move forward deliberately and do this the right way," Volod said. "I turned one paranorm every ten days after ensuring the change had taken in the previous subject. Being a Master Vampire, I have total control over all those I turned myself once they rise.

"The Peacekeepers do not know who is behind the disappearances," he added. "We will continue to use that element of surprise to our advantage."

Volod didn't share that Monique had bitten the paranorm

Vampires the first time and he had turned them with his own bite the second time. Monique had control as well, but not like he did.

"Did you encounter any difficulties?" Nicholas asked.

"A few. During my experiments, before taking Trackers, I discovered that some Fae appear to be immune to being turned," Volod said. "Thus I eliminated those not susceptible. There are a few other species we are not certain about just yet, but most can be taken and turned it appears."

Nicholas gave a nod and looked as if he was contemplating all that Volod had told the conclave so far.

Alexander, the youngest member of the conclave at just over four hundred years of age, looked from Volod to Nicholas. "This is an extremely alarming proposition. Going after norms and paranorms seems far too dangerous.

"These paranorm Vampires are not proven," Alexander went on. "We on this council will see the reprisals. There are far too many paranorms compared with our number. What if these Vampire paranorms end up wanting to turn and then control us?"

Alexander continued with fervor. "Paranorms will wipe out Vampire-kind if we fail. At minimum, many of us will be destroyed, which was what we saw happen during the Rebellion. If it was not for surrender and the treaty, we would have been eliminated as a race." His voice rose. "We must maintain the current balance of power to avoid another paranorm slaughter of Vampires."

"Such coward's words." Cecilia faced Alexander in a sharp turn in her seat. The emerald pendant pinning her dark hair back glittered in the torchlight, and her elegant features were taut. "To expect us to be ruled by paranorms when there is the opportunity to rise up again is despicable. Allow the conclave to hear this out and consider it before we meekly reject the thought of such an idea."

Alexander tried to interrupt, but Cecilia continued. "If somehow the worst-case scenario comes to pass, and Vampire paranorms take over, how is that any different from what is going on today? What would cause them to want to stop us from feeding? From what Volod said, they want the paranorm blood."

Volod hadn't expected Cecilia to be so vocal on this subject, and to his benefit. With pleasure he listened to her go on.

"We desire human blood," she said. "The fact is, we are a weak race right now. A mere shadow of what we once were. There is not another race of beings as beaten down as Vampires. That has to change and if there is a way for it to be done, let it be done."

"Volod is worthless," Marcus said, and Volod clenched his teeth. "With his mini mission of rebellion, he could not even keep his small clan together in New York." Marcus glared at Volod. "His foothold there has been destroyed. He has proven to be a poor power-hungry leader, so do not waste anything on him, neither time nor resources."

Ignoring Marcus's comment, Volod interrupted. "These Vampire paranorms will be mine. You won't see a rebellion. I will be the one to bite these paranorms and turn them. They will be drawn to follow me. You are all aware of what happens when a Master Vampire takes his victim. They are his. It is no different here.

"Also," Volod continued, "my force will be only of the size I need to control our world. I think you need to see for yourselves."

Volod glanced at Seth, who gave a short nod before he faded into a shadow on the floor. A shadow that quickly moved and vanished among other shadows in the room.

A few members of the conclave made sounds of surprise and unease.

Seth reappeared, behind Marcus, with a dagger pressed against Marcus's throat.

"Call the bastard off!" Marcus tried to shout in anger but the blade was so close to his throat that his words came out in a strangled plea. A red mark appeared on his neck followed by a drop of blood rolling down his pale skin.

The conclave members to either side of Marcus moved as if to help the Vampire.

Katherine—formerly known by the unacceptable shortening of her name, Katy—the Los Angeles Witch stepped forward. Vampirism looked good on her. She radiated confidence and a quiet beauty that she didn't have before she was turned. She opened her mouth and started to speak.

Her beautiful Witch's voice echoed throughout the chamber as she spoke in a chant, weaving her spell. "Sit, all who dare to go against us, and do not move." When she heard protests coming from the immobile Vampires, she added a single word that came out far more powerful than any words she had spoken before. *"Silence."*

Immediately there was not a sound in the room, save for the crackle and hiss of the torches.

A feeling of satisfaction rose up within Volod. "Now that you've met Seth the Shadow Shifter and Katherine the Witch," Volod said, "I would like to introduce you to Daniel, a Shifter."

The conclave members remained silent, locked in the Witch's spell, as Daniel shifted into a lion. The Shifter's roar was so loud, it seemed as if the room trembled with it. He leapt forward toward Alexander. Papers scattered onto the chamber floor as he landed on the conclave table, his huge jaws within inches of Alexander's face.

Volod wanted to laugh at the fear he saw in every conclave member's expression. If he didn't need them and their resources, he could have had them all slaughtered by now.

"All of the Shifters and Dopplers maintain the fierce hunger and the basic instincts of their animal form," Volod said, "while keeping the intelligence and abilities of their race."

"Reese. Terrance." Volod gave them each a brief nod. "Both Shifters."

Terrance transformed into a snarling Doberman while Reese took the form of a tiger. Each joined Daniel on the table, the tiger in front of Cecilia, his nose nearly touching another member of the conclave, Wilhelm.

"I'm sure you have recognized these three as Dopplers." Volod gestured to the paranorms as he spoke. "Meet Kennedy, Jessica, and Rebecca."

Kennedy's body expanded, his height increasing as he shifted into a grizzly bear; Jessica became a ferret and Rebecca, a raven.

"You may wonder whether such small creatures as a ferret and a raven have enough strength to be a part of a Vampire paranorm army," Volod said. "Let me assure you, they can do things that no other paranorm or Vampire could. Attacking from the air like Rebecca or squeezing into small places like Jessica."

With a slight movement of his fingers, Volod indicated that Elliot and Jorge take their Werewolf forms. In seconds both were snarling, vicious wolves.

"You think they look fierce now?" Volod flashed his fangs as he smiled. "Wait until the full moon. A Werewolf Vampire is truly a sight to be seen . . . and avoided."

Volod held his hand out to Monique and she took it as he presented her. "Please meet the lovely Monique, a Proctor. As you can see she is Elvin, more powerful than you would likely believe.

"Paranorms have a desire to feed on their kind," Volod continued. "To a one they believe this is a better life for them . . . they believe their friends who have not been converted will have far richer lives as Vampires.

"Perhaps you have wondered if they would they go up against their own friends and do what it takes to turn them . . . or destroy them." Volod smiled at Monique and gave a slight inclination of his head.

Monique vanished.

Several conclave members gasped.

From beneath her glamour, Monique's voice rang clear in the room. "The answer is yes, we shall do whatever it takes. We believe the Vampire way of life is the only way of life."

"We are not capturing the unskillful or foolish," Volod said. "We have strong, committed paranorms."

"You have given us an effective demonstration." Nicholas made a confident gesture that meant the paranorms were to take their places behind Volod again.

If the conclave prolocutor was affected by the display, he

did not show it. However, other members wore expressions ranging from furious to impressed.

"Please return," Volod said to his dream team. The paranorms acknowledged him and went to stand behind him, changing back to their human forms.

When the paranorm Vamps had gathered around him again, Volod took a casual relaxed stance. He was in fact anything but relaxed. He wasn't sure his gamble would pay off.

"You see how fast my team works." Volod projected his words so that he could be heard clearly throughout the chamber. "All of these Vampire paranorms can do amazing things that include battling humans and other paranorms. Of course humans would be child's play and hardly worth their time or talents."

Marcus was nearly trembling with fury, so much so that he was obviously finding it difficult to speak.

"I want to do this in a manner that meets the conclave's approval." As he spoke, Volod let his gaze meet that of each Vampire seated at the long table. "I do not wish to go against you."

Nicholas folded his hands in front of him. "What are you proposing?"

"First, I need your approval and commitment to this mission. Second, I need resources and would like them quickly," Volod said. "I wish to have a sizable group of your best Vampires from around the country." He paused and put the menace he felt into his voice. "We need bodies to back up our Vampire paranorm army. The meaner and more ruthless, the better. However, I do need those who respect authority."

Nicholas looked to either side of him at the members of the conclave. "Does anyone have questions for Volod before we take a vote?"

No one spoke. Nicholas called in an aide, who then handed a piece of paper to each member. Each Vampire wrote a single word on his or her piece of paper before handing it to the aide.

When the aide had collected them all, he handed the sixteen pieces of paper to Nicholas, who put in his own. Volod did his best to keep his expression calm as the papers were split into two piles, one larger than the other.

Nicholas counted the papers in each stack then folded his hands again on the tabletop.

"The conclave has spoken." Nicholas met Volod's gaze. Nicholas's eyes were dark, intense. "You may have whatever you need to allow Vampire-kind to once again rule the paranorm world."

SEVEN

I STOPPED FIGHTING MY INNER DEMONS
WE ARE ON THE SAME SIDE NOW

"Do those inner demons like being spanked, too?" I said with a grin when I got a look at Olivia's T-shirt as she walked in the door of our PI office.

"Wouldn't you like to know?" Olivia smirked and tossed her Mets sweat jacket onto her desktop, causing a dozen sticky notes to flutter on the surface of the desk. A towering stack of thick folders teetered.

"Heh." I closed the file folder on a Metamorph case I'd been dealing with and set it beside my large-screen computer monitor. "Truth is, I'm not sure I *want* to know."

I should have known better. Olivia took that statement as a challenge.

"You can't tell me you haven't thought about a little tie-up play." She flopped into the chair behind her desk. "Considering where you're from and all."

"All the more reason to avoid it." I grimaced. "In my world it's not a choice. It's an expected way of life in the Drow culture. I only escaped it because of my human mother's influence over my father. I guess it might be different to give up control out of choice. In my world, it's taken. That is not alluring to me."

"That doesn't mean you haven't thought about it. Besides, you can be the one to take control, which might be what you need." Olivia put her elbows on her desk as she leaned forward. "Be honest. You've thought about it with Colin."

Unexpected warmth crept into my cheeks. "I take it you got over being mad at Scott after Colin and I left."

A sly grin crept over Olivia's face. "Let's just say he made it up to me. Although I told him he has more making up to do. I'm not letting him off that easy. We started again where we left off and then—"

"Okay, okay, that's enough details," I said.

"Hey, the rest was even more creative." Olivia had a mischievous gleam in her eyes. "If you don't want any new ideas for you and Colin, that's fine. Change your mind, just ask." She loaded an eraser, aimed, and missed badly.

"Colin and I . . . we're not that far into a relationship."

"Well," she said, "my ideas will help jump-start it."

I thumbed through one stack of files on my desk, looking for a case on a pair of Pixies gone bad, and changed the subject from me and Colin back to Olivia. "Colin thought it was funny that you weren't even a bit embarrassed."

Olivia snorted. "Hasn't he ever seen a nearly naked woman before?"

"Apparently not one tied to a bed, ball-gagged, and blindfolded. Either that or it had been a while." I shook my head at the memory of a very indignant, very pissed-off Olivia DeSantos. "I told him he didn't know you very well if he thought a little thing like that would embarrass you."

Olivia gave a rather wicked smile.

"Haven't seen you in a relationship in a while." I braced my elbow on my desk, my chin in my hand. "And definitely not one where you've moved as fast as this."

Olivia shrugged. "Scott gets me."

"He gets you?" I grinned. "The guy takes off to get Chinese food and leaves you practically naked, tied up, and gagged, and you're saying he *gets you*?"

"Not everyone's perfect. Just needs a few rough edges shaved off here and there," Olivia said. "Besides, after I got through with him I don't think that's going to happen again. New rules for the fun-and-game times."

"I have to agree with Colin," I said. "That was one of the most entertaining scenes I have ever witnessed."

She patted the side holster she was wearing. "Tell Colin he'd better not breathe a word of that story or I'll find a way to douse his flames."

I grinned. "I have no control over a Dragon."

Olivia loaded a rubber band with an eraser and aimed it at me. I caught the eraser along with the one that followed. "Find a way," she said before she shot at me with another.

My XPhone played "Runnin' with the Devil" by Van Halen, one of my favorite 1980s hair bands.

RODÁN came up on the caller ID screen.

I caught the last eraser lobbed at me at the same time I brought the phone to my ear.

"Hello," I said as I flung an eraser back at Olivia, who ducked behind her monitor. *Chicken* I mouthed to her as she reappeared.

Fighting words.

"Nyx." Rodán's tone was not normally so grim sounding.

I lost my focus on the eraser war and one pinged off my temple as I frowned and spoke to Rodán. "What's wrong?" My instincts told me something was wrong and my instincts were usually pretty good.

"The situation with the missing Trackers has gotten worse." Rodán's words sent a chill through me. "There is of course the one missing Proctor, Monique," he said. "An additional ten Trackers are now unaccounted for."

My lungs burned as I sucked in my breath. "Eleven total are missing?" I looked at Olivia who now wore an intent expression as she listened to my end of the conversation.

"Dopplers, Shifters, Werewolves, and a Witch are among those who cannot be located. They are not just any paranorm Trackers. They are some of the best at what they do," he told me.

"And one of the Light Elves," I said, more to myself than Rodán as I mulled over his statement. "The San Francisco Proctor."

"Yes."

"Is there any evidence?" I tapped my fingers on the desktop. "Anything at all?"

"No evidence," Rodán said. "However, in most cases, humans have disappeared in the general vicinity of where each Tracker went missing."

"How do trained, skilled beings like Trackers and a Proctor disappear like that?" I glanced at Olivia as I spoke. Her forehead was wrinkled, and she looked deep in thought. "I would have thought it impossible a couple of months ago, before this all started."

"We can't sit idly by. I want to assemble two special teams," Rodán said. "And I want you to lead one of them."

"Okay." I said the word slowly. "What is our purpose? To solve the mystery or to make sure this doesn't happen to any of our own Trackers?"

"Both," Rodán said. "You will lead the team investigating what you can of the disappearances from here, while setting up measures to safeguard our own New York team. We must be proactive in ensuring none of our own join the ranks of the missing."

I nodded to myself. "Got it."

"We will keep each of the fifteen territories guarded," he said. "I will set up a meeting with other Proctors, but before that, I need someone I trust to begin looking into this."

We'd only had twenty-four Trackers until Tristan joined us, replacing Meryl. She was dead thanks to Zombies and the same Sorcerer who had imprisoned Tristan in a stone for twenty-two years.

"Even though he's not a Tracker—yet—I think Desmond would be a tremendous asset," I said. "I'd also like Olivia, Joshua, and Colin." My reasons for wanting Colin and Olivia were purely professional. You couldn't beat having a Dragon and a former NYPD officer on your team. Olivia's skills in tracking down people and information were exceptional, which made her an incredible PI, too.

"Excellent," Rodán said. "I would only have expected you to choose those who will most benefit your team."

"Is drawing the team together after tonight's Tracker meeting soon enough?" I asked. "That's still a good eight hours off." The Trackers met almost every night at nine at the Pit, and right now it was only one in the afternoon.

"Yes." He added, "I would like to meet with you alone tomorrow around four o'clock to see what you and Olivia have come up with between now and then. I'd also like to talk with you about the duties of your new position, should you decide to take it."

I appreciated the fact that he hadn't assumed. "Sounds good."

"I need to speak with Desmond," Rodán said, "so I'll invite him to tonight's Tracker meeting."

"Great." It would save me time trying to locate the Sorcerer. Rodán had much better methods of getting ahold of anyone than most of us.

"In the meantime," he went on, "I'll send you a list of the Trackers, the locations they are missing from, and the name of their Proctor, whom you need to contact to begin your investigation. Gather all the facts you can. Since Monique is a Proctor, I would like you to talk with her special team's leader, Rodriguez."

"Got it," I said. "Olivia and I will be all over this."

"Check your e-mail," Rodán said. "And Nyx . . . watch for anything unusual. Be on guard. You're good, but so were the Trackers who are missing," he added before he signed off.

I gave Olivia the details of my conversation as I took a look at the e-mail Rodán had sent. I brought up the document on the huge wall of monitors. It had recently replaced my collection of Otherworld weapons, which included Drow-forged arrows with diamond arrowheads.

With my go-ahead, Olivia had removed the collection and brought us up to date with current technology. I had to admit that the monitors were pretty cool.

Olivia hadn't stopped there with her technological revolution. Wireless headsets and direct access to major government and law enforcement databases were also among our upgrades into the modern and out of the Middle Ages, as Olivia liked to say. I'd told her many times that I came from a world forever locked in that age; compared with what I'd grown up with, we'd been cutting edge in our PI office.

We reviewed the document that I'd brought up using two of the monitors to make one supersize copy for us both to read. In the document, the missing Proctor and all ten Trackers were listed, as well as what race of paranorm they each were.

The information for each Tracker included his or her last known address, contact phone number, Proctor's name and phone number, the territory the Tracker had covered, and the date that each of them had disappeared.

Olivia's gaze swept over the document as she read it. "This gives us some basic information but doesn't tell us a whole hell of a lot."

I studied it and instinct kicked in. "It tells us that no Fae are missing, which could be significant. Of course that could mean nothing, too."

Olivia used an electronic pointer to highlight the timetable. "In every single case, the disappearances happened ten days apart, from the beginning of January to mid-April."

"With the exception of the two Los Angeles Trackers who vanished the same night." I nodded as I spoke. "The territories of those two were close to each other. One was a Shifter, the other a Witch."

"Two disappearing the same night," Olivia said. "That doesn't really fit the MO of the other seven."

"What's the significance of a ten-day lapse between disappearances?"

"You've got me." Olivia slipped on her phone headset. "Ready when you are."

I picked up my own headset. "I'll take the Proctor and the first five Trackers on the list."

She nodded. "I'll get started on the others."

I came to a complete stop and Olivia did, too. "It's been exactly ten days since the last disappearance," she said, saying what I was thinking.

"We need to have Rodán send a warning to all Proctors." I reached for my phone. "If that is significant, someone could be in danger tonight."

EIGHT

The Pit was rocking.

Rodán's nightclub was easily the best club in New York City for paranorms. Thanks to Rodán's magic, the Pit's location was shielded. New Yorkers and tourists never even noticed the entrance, which was beside the Dakota building at Seventy-second Street and Central Park West.

The place was packed. As a Tracker, I didn't have to wait in the long line at the entrance.

After checking his ID, the bouncer, Fred, let the Shifter in front of me through the door. All paranorms had to get an ID showing that they were of age according to their race. Elves came of age at twenty-five, while most of the Fae were only fifteen by Earth Otherworld standards. Beings aged differently.

"Hey, Nyx." Fred gave me one of his adorable puppy-dog smiles as he greeted me. He was a Doppler whose animal form was a beautiful golden retriever.

"I've got something for you." I dug in my purse then handed him a giant Milk-Bone, his favorite.

With a grin he pocketed the treat, thanked me, then let the next patron through the door.

Tonight Festival had the stage. The paranorm band included two Shifters on guitar, a Werewolf on keyboard and drums, and a female Shadow Shifter who was the lead vocal.

Also on stage were Nymphs One and Two, who had extended such "gracious" invitations to Rodán when he and I were out to dinner. I had to admit that Trixie and Bubbles had great voices as they sang backup for the Shadow Shifter, Leslie.

I waved at Fred before the crowd sucked me in.

I didn't think I'd ever seen the Pit so crowded. Bodies were slick with sweat from dancing. The higher body temperature of the mass of paranorms made even me feel warm.

Thanks to my keen Drow sense of smell, I was almost overwhelmed by the odors of the many races of paranorms crowded together, mixed with the smells of bar food and alcohol. I made my way toward the back corner where Trackers hung out every night before we hit the streets.

One of my closest friends, Nadia, perched on the arm of an overstuffed couch as she looked over Lawan's shoulder. Nadia had long, thick, gorgeous red hair and was a Siren from the Bermuda Triangle.

Lawan was a petite Doppler from Thailand whose animal form was a Siamese cat. She was just as beautiful as Nadia but with long black hair, dark brown eyes, and dark lashes. We'd almost lost Lawan to Zombies in December. Just the thought of Zombies made me shudder.

Ice, a cocky Shifter with white-blond hair and ice-blue eyes, slouched in a chair in the corner while Joshua, an Australian Shadow Shifter, sat in the chair next to him. With my sensitive hearing, I overheard them making rather lewd comments about some of the females in the club.

Knowing the pair, I wasn't surprised. Despite the fact that Ice could be a real ass, and Joshua on the sexist side, I considered both of them to be good guys overall and outstanding Trackers.

Kelly, a Doppler bunny, was flopped down on the other couch. Nancy, a Pixie, sat next to her, both of them engaged in an animated conversation with Hades, a Shifter.

"How's my beautiful girl doing tonight?" Colin's deep voice sent a shiver down my spine as he came up behind me.

I started to face him but he put his hands on my shoulders and massaged me.

"Amazing." I sighed and leaned into him. "Considering everything, I'm doing just fine."

He brought his mouth close to my cheek. "Popcorn, beer, and a movie tonight?"

"Mmmmm." I tried not to let out a groan of pleasure at the feel of his hands and fingers."I will do anything if you just keep that up."

"Anything?" he murmured close to my ear.

My face heated. "Almost anything."

"Too late to change it." I heard him take a deep breath as he nuzzled my hair. "You smell so good."

"Colin." I became aware of my surroundings. I couldn't let my and Colin's relationship become obvious to the others. I was one of their leaders, and I needed to maintain professionalism in everything I did. "Save that for later." I stepped away and faced him.

"Consider it saved." His sexy grin sent tingles through me. "Right where we left off."

"Rodán's ready for us." Angel shoved her long blond corkscrew curls away from her face as she joined us. Her intelligent diamond-bright blue eyes held a hint of concern.

"Rodán called me," she said when we were several feet away from the others. Colin stayed close by my side. "Interesting what you and Olivia came up with."

"What's that?" Colin said.

"Rodán will probably tell everyone just as soon as we're seated," I said as we walked into the conference room.

Twenty-four of us made it into the room, including Olivia, who came in last. Olivia was the only norm Tracker, and every one of the other Trackers had come to respect her and her abilities during our past assignments. The twenty-fifth Tracker was Tristan, but he was in Chicago, training.

When we were seated, Rodán came into the room. He was as regal and impressive as always. Something about his presence was usually reassuring, and right now was no exception.

I thought about what he'd said about me being the one for him, and it made me smile to myself. We both knew that it would never be, but my love for him as my friend and mentor was deep, strong, and everlasting.

When Rodán spoke it was with concern in his voice. "We all know about the missing Trackers and Proctor. Though all are on the West Coast, I feel compelled to get involved. Nothing remotely like this has ever happened. All were talented Trackers, experienced Trackers who disappeared with virtually no trace."

The room remained silent, all expressions serious, as we listened. "I had Nyx and Olivia look at the cases. It's difficult to do a lot from this distance, of course. But one thing is peculiar—every disappearance has happened ten days after the last one, except for two in LA who disappeared on the same night."

He paused as he looked from one of us to the next. "We are not sure of the significance of this. However, today is the tenth day since the last Tracker vanished."

A low murmur rolled through the room.

"Also peculiar," Rodán said, "is that humans have disappeared near the locations where each Tracker went missing. We're not sure this is related, but we need to consider it.

"I have made sure that every Proctor across the country is aware of these facts," Rodán said. "All will be on guard."

Angel frowned and folded her arms across her chest. "What can we do to help them?"

"I have called you together for two reasons," he said. "The first is that our New York Trackers have been considered elite among Peacekeepers around the country. We have always shown leadership and have been considered examples of what it takes to be an exceptional team. We will involve ourselves heavily in solving these mysterious disappearances."

Rodán continued, "We have our own cases to solve in each of our territories, so we cannot bring our full resources to bear. I have suggested to the other Proctors that we organize an experienced team, pulling from the ranks of Peacekeepers across the country. Each member of the special task force will be chosen for complementary skills.

"I have been requested by the Proctor Directorate," he added, "to head this elite group. I have agreed."

After a pause, Rodán went on. "Therefore, my full attention will not be with you. You all know what needs to be done. You don't need me at every turn."

He was dividing us into three groups, he explained. Angel's team would be ready in the event they were needed to help with the US task force Rodán was establishing. Until they were called upon, Angel's team, along with the rest of our Trackers, would monitor the fifteen territories that New York City was divided into.

"Desmond will also be a part of our group," Rodán said as the Sorcerer entered the room. "He will be aiding Nyx in trying to solve the mysterious disappearances."

Before meeting Desmond, I never dreamed a Sorcerer could be so hot looking. He appeared to be in his mid-thirties, but was much older. He had a swimmer's build, shoulder-length, almost wild wavy brown hair, and a day's growth of stubble.

Rodán went over what Olivia and I had come up with. He mentioned that a summit was being organized in San Francisco for the newly assembled task force. In the interim, a video conference would be set up from my and Olivia's PI office using the new monitors.

"The second reason for bringing this group together tonight is to emphasize that we, as Trackers, could be at risk here on the East Coast. Just because the disappearances have occurred on the West Coast doesn't mean we are immune. Again, these where skilled, experienced paranorm Trackers who were taken down.

"Myself and the other US Proctors have discussed the need to develop new rules among Trackers," Rodán went on. "We will work in teams only. We stay together as best we can and trust no one.

"When a disappearance occurs, we often look to people the victim knew and trusted, but this case is baffling because there are so many missing Trackers from diverse locations.

"Be careful out there," he concluded. "Be safe. Be smart."

NINE

"No one has seen Rodán since last night." Unease stirred in my belly as I set my phone on my desk and looked at Olivia. "He had an appointment with Angel at seven this morning and then a lunch appointment with her team at noon but he wasn't there."

Olivia shrugged. "She's a blond. She probably got confused on the time."

I rolled my eyes. "Considering Angel has an IQ equal to a savant's, I don't think so."

"Blonds get confused all the time." Olivia waved my comment away. "For that matter, Rodán is blond. It was bound to happen sooner or later."

I shot her with an eraser before she even realized I had loaded the rubber band.

"Hey." Olivia rubbed her temple but was holding back a grin. "Just sayin'."

"Uh-huh." I glanced at her chocolate-brown T-shirt.

I'M NOT SHORT
I'M FUN SIZE

"Oh, is that what you're calling it now?" I said. "Fun size?"

"Scott thinks so," she said with a wicked grin. "Real fun."

"Whatever you say, short stuff."

That earned me a volley of erasers.

"Besides, it's barely two in the afternoon," she said.

"Isn't that a little soon to start worrying about a big boy like Rodán?"

"You're right." I frowned. "However, not only did he miss Angel's seven AM appointment, but he missed the lunch appointment, too. He also mentioned the lunch appointment to Nadia, so Rodán was aware of it. It's not like him." I rubbed my arms as I felt an odd chill. "And something just doesn't feel right."

I picked up my phone and dialed the Pit. "I'll check with Fred."

Fred answered on the third ring. When I asked him about Rodán, he sounded puzzled. "Haven't seen him. He's never been late and he's never missed showing up for anything here at the Pit."

Another twist in my belly. "Maybe he went to Otherworld to see the Great Guardian."

"I dunno." I had the image of Fred scratching his head. "This just doesn't happen with Rodán."

"He's supposed to meet with me in a couple of hours." I rubbed my forehead. "He'll probably be back by then."

"Probably." Fred still had concern in his voice. "See you in a bit, Nyx."

Olivia and I spent the two hours before I left working on the possible link between the missing humans and the missing Trackers.

When it was time, I grabbed my handbag and walked the short distance to the Pit to meet with Rodán. It was still early. There was plenty of time to talk with him before the place started to get busy.

After I said hello to Fred at the entrance, I made my way through the mostly empty nightclub. The entrance to Rodán's chambers—which I'd referred to as the dungeon on occasion—was well hidden behind a wall of gray fog. Very few were favored enough to get close enough even to see the doorway, much less enter through it.

The fog smelled of rain and moist earth as I passed through and made my way down a torchlit passageway. At the end was an arched black doorway that looked as if it came from a medieval dungeon.

Torches flared to life at either side of the door when I neared it. To the right was an oblong black pad, and I placed my hand on its spongy surface.

My palm itched as the colors swirled beneath my hand until they stopped at blue, the same shade as my eyes. A brief burst of white light flared in the hallway from within the blue, just like the dangerous flash in my eyes when I'm angry.

Cool air swept over me as I entered his large bedchamber. I frowned. Normally it was warm in here, enough to cause me to break out in a sweat. The room's usual firethorn and woodland scent had faded. A hard ball started to form in my belly.

I passed the wall that had a huge framed oil painting of a Faerie and past a display of artifacts from Otherworld and the Fae places in the Earth Otherworld. Instead of glowing, the Dragon scale looked dull in the torchlight. And the Faerie cone—normally lit like a city within a pinecone—was dark. The Pixie dust in its jar didn't sparkle, and the Sirens' rare golden seashell didn't gleam.

With every step I took my heart beat faster and my throat grew drier. Something *was* wrong. I knew it with everything I had. Something was really wrong.

Another fog-shrouded wall led toward his den. The normally chilly air was almost freezing as I stepped through the fog to the landing atop a staircase. I walked down the steps to his den, my shoes soundless on the stone.

Rodán's den wasn't exceptionally large, much smaller than the bedchamber above and smaller even than my bedroom. Rows of heavy books and rolls of parchment lined the earthen walls, and wisteria climbed across the otherwise bare places.

All the wood, including Rodán's desk, had been commissioned from the Dryads. They didn't give anything up without a price, but this time I didn't wonder what Rodán might have paid.

The desktop was spotless as usual. It didn't look like anything was out of place in the den.

I clung to my purse as I stood in the center of the still, lifeless room.

Hair prickled at my nape, as if someone was watching me. I spun around then placed my hand over my pounding heart when I saw nothing.

How could everything be so awfully quiet?

The feeling of being watched didn't pass. Dread built up in me like a living thing. Like black snakes sliding through my abdomen and pausing to squirm just enough to make me want to throw up. Why was I having such an extreme reaction? Rodán hadn't even been missing for a full day yet.

I hoped he was with the Great Guardian. I'd have to kill him for scaring me, but I could live with that. At least then I'd know what happened to him.

Okay. I had to calm down. Look at things logically and not jump to conclusions. I needed to treat this like any missing person case.

I made my way back upstairs, trying to shake the eerie feeling that his empty chambers gave me.

I had to find out who had last seen Rodán.

"Fred." I reached the Doppler bouncer as he was letting a trio of Pixies into the club. It was way early, but Pixies like to party long and hard.

"Did Rodán show for your appointment?" Fred asked, his puppy-dog eyes looking big and worried.

I shook my head. "When was the last time you saw him?"

Fred's forehead wrinkled and he looked deep in thought. "Just after the Tracker meeting, around ten. He was talking to Angel. Then he went toward his chambers and she went out the front."

"Thanks." I offered him a smile because he looked so worried. "It'll be okay. We'll find him."

Fred gave a nod and tried a smile himself. "I know you will," he said despite the concern in his big brown eyes.

I patted him on the arm then left to see who else I could question.

Two waitresses and a barman later, I had as much information as before. Nothing more than vague recollections of Rodán in the nightclub through one AM. At least I had that much to go on.

I needed to use the facilities, but when I went into the restroom designated for females, I ran into Kathy, one of the Shifter cleaners who helped keep the Pit in order. I asked her if she'd seen Rodán last night.

"Backstage," Kathy said with certainty in her voice. "He watched from there until the band quit for the night, around one thirty in the morning."

My heart began to race a little. "Did you see him leave with anyone?"

Kathy leaned on her mop. "Those trampy Nymphs who sing backup for that awful band."

The same two Rodán and I had seen at dinner not long ago. Maybe he'd decided to take them up on the invitation they'd extended.

"Trixie and Bubbles," I said.

"Tramps." Kathy rolled her eyes. "The three of them left together. Arm in arm."

I thanked Kathy, went back out into the club, and dug my phone out of my purse.

When I reached Olivia I said, "Can you track down two Nymph backup singers for Festival? I only know them by the names Trixie and Bubbles."

Olivia choked with laughter. "You have got to be kidding me. Stage names, right?"

I couldn't hold back a grin. "No kidding."

"You've got it." Olivia cleared her throat and I heard the click-clack of keys on a keyboard. "What's up?"

I explained everything, from my search of Rodán's office to talking with the Shifter cleaner.

"Got it," she said just as I finished filling her in. She gave me an address on Fortieth Street, where they apparently lived together. "I'll swing by and pick you up at the Pit."

"Bring my clothing and weapons belt, please," I said. I

would have to shift soon. "Take my 'Vette," I added. I preferred my car over her bucket-of-bolts GTO anytime.

Five minutes later Olivia swung my Corvette onto Seventy-second Street and I climbed into the passenger seat. I realized my mistake as Olivia cackled, the wheels screeched, and we took off.

I braced my hands on the dashboard. "Should have let me drive."

"Buckle up and shut up." Olivia maneuvered through New York City like one of the cabbies who took people's lives in their hands every day.

I had to remind myself that if I could defeat Demons, Vampires, Zombies, and mad scientists, I could certainly live through Olivia's driving.

At least I prayed I would every time she drove.

After we made it to our destination alive and managed to find a parking spot, we went up to the apartment building. It was fairly nice. Not exceptional, but nice. We took the elevator to the fourth floor.

When we got to the apartment, we heard squealing laughter and the fast beat of music coming from inside.

Olivia and I looked at each other. "You don't suppose Rodán is in there?" she said.

I shook my head. "No amount of 'playtime' would keep him away from his responsibilities."

She knocked. The laughter quieted. We heard rustling sounds from the other side of the door, then nothing. Olivia knocked again, and we heard giggles and voices. Even with my Elvin hearing, though, I couldn't make out what was being said.

This time Olivia knocked harder. "Open up," she said. "We need to speak with Trixie and Bubbles."

Finally I heard the bolt unlock and the rattle of a door chain.

The door opened just enough to reveal Trixie's pretty face. "What do you want?" she said, almost belligerently.

"We need to speak with you and your friend." I spoke before Olivia could say anything.

"We're busy," Trixie replied. "You'll have to come back later this afternoon."

"It will only take a few moments," I said. "It's urgent. We need to ask you a few questions that can't wait."

"I said we're busy." Trixie started to shut the door.

That was all it took to set off Olivia. She stuck her foot in the way then hit the door with such force that the chain snapped and Trixie fell on her butt on the floor.

I'd only seen the Nymph from her neck up as she peered around the door. Now I saw that all she had on was a pair of black panties.

Behind her were three males and Bubbles and a disaster of an apartment. Clothing was scattered from one end of the living room to the other. Food and drink containers were on all the surfaces, not to mention lots of dust. Apparently cleaning was not on the top of these Nymphs' list.

"What are you doing?" Bubbles also wore nothing but panties. She glared and put her hands on her hips as she stood in front of the males, who were in various stages of dress and undress.

The three Shifter males looked a bit shocked that Olivia had broken in the door, but didn't seem to care much that we'd caught them in the middle of play. Actually they looked amused, not to mention intrigued, by having two more females in the room.

"Throw on some clothes and bring your asses out here," Olivia said to Trixie and Bubbles. "We have some questions for you."

Trixie scrambled to her feet, her beautiful face set in a scowl. "We don't need to put clothes on for you. If you're not comfortable with us like this, it's your problem."

That is so Nymphish, I thought.

Trixie added, "I don't care what you want, we're not answering questions. We don't have to tell you anything."

"Either you can do this nicely," I said, "or we'll get the Paranorm Task Force down here. They'll haul your butts off to the detention center and we'll question you there . . . dressed or undressed."

Bubbles looked flustered. "You don't have the authority—"

"We're Trackers." I gave her a long glare. "That gives us all the authority we need."

Trixie and Bubbles looked at each other then back at me and Olivia. Fear had started to creep onto their faces.

"Okay," Bubbles said.

Trixie nodded. "That's fine. Whatever you want. We didn't know."

As soon as they heard that we were Trackers, the amusement left the males' expressions. Olivia directed the Shifters to get their clothes on and leave or they'd end up in the detention center, too.

They were gone within seconds, not bothering to get fully dressed. The males just scooped up their clothing and bolted.

We stepped into the apartment and shut the door behind us.

"You were seen leaving the Pit last night with Rodán, and now he's missing." I narrowed my eyes at the pair as their faces started to pale. "We need to know what happened after you went off with him."

"He's missing?" Trixie's throat worked as she swallowed. She hurried to add, "We don't know anything."

Bubbles's eyes widened. "All we did was get him to go there with us."

"Shut up, Bubbles." Trixie narrowed her gaze. "We just walked to the car, right?"

"Um . . ." Bubbles shifted her stance like she couldn't decide how she should stand or what she should do. "Yes."

Olivia's voice was deadly, like a cobra ready to strike. "Don't give us this 'just walked to the car' bullshit. Details now or I swear you will look like a couple of beat-up Trolls who no one will ever want to hook up with when I'm done with you."

The Nymphs looked at each other.

"What did you mean when you said 'all we did was get him to go there with us'? Where is 'there'?" I asked. My stomach started to feel queasy again. "Tell me everything. And you'd better start this second."

"An apartment in the Wall Street area." Trixie rushed to

get the words out. "Like Bubbles said, all we did was get him there."

"And give him a tiny drop of potion," Bubbles said right before Trixie elbowed her.

"Potion?" Chills ran down my spine. "What did you give Rodán?"

The Nymphs looked at each other again. "A male and female met with us the day before yesterday," Trixie said. "They didn't tell us their names. She said she was one of Rodán's 'personal play friends' and was putting together something fun for him."

"He has so many females," Bubbles added.

"Somehow they knew that we know Rodán and that we . . . well, that we enjoy each other's company," Trixie said.

"They told us we needed to get Rodán to that apartment and get him to drink a potion." Bubbles looked anxious to speak, and this time Trixie didn't try to stop her. "It was whiteberry potion—but I think they mixed it with something else."

"Do you know what whiteberry potion is?" Trixie said. "It's an aphrodisiac like no other in the world."

Bubbles had clasped her hands and was now wringing them, obviously agitated. "They said they added something to it that was supposed to make it better. It was supposed to relax him."

"It was all made to be fun for Rodán," Trixie added.

The two of them were now talking a mile a minute.

Bubbles sat on a couch in the messy living room. "It was part of a sexual fantasy of his of being drugged and kidnapped, and to lose all control and to be taken by a male and a female in charge, the female had told us."

"Yes," Trixie said. "We love Rodán and thought it would be fun to make it happen for him. He had even mentioned a similar idea to us at one time. We were told that we just couldn't tell him what was happening. It had to be a surprise. We got him to the apartment, gave him the potion, then got paid."

Dread had built up like a huge weight in my chest. "Was Rodán conscious when you left?"

"He was just a little groggy, but he was fine," Trixie said, and Bubbles nodded. "We would never want him hurt. Is he hurt? What's wrong? What's going on?"

"So you were paid and you left." Olivia put one hand on her hip and leaned forward a bit as she glared at the Nymphs. "Was it only this male and female who were there?"

Bubbles gave Trixie a quirky smirk. "Well, sort of," Bubbles replied. "Part of the deal, besides the potion and money, was that we were able to play with two Vampire look-alikes and we left with them."

Olivia looked as stunned as I felt at that moment. She shot me a look of concern.

"Two Vampire look-alikes," Olivia repeated. "What happened with them?

Bubbles stopped wringing her hands. "We left and went to a place they had a mile or two away."

Trixie nodded. "We played with them. They were so real looking and acting. We've done the Vampire thing before and Bubbles loves it. I've never been as big on it as she is. Well, not until last night. It was totally amazing."

"Yes, they were amazing." Bubbles added, sounding like a teenager describing her first kiss with a new crush. "They even pretended to bite us and it seemed so real."

"It was an incredible time," Trixie said, interrupting her Nymph partner. "We're supposed to meet up with them again tonight for a second round."

I suddenly felt jittery as I asked what I really didn't want to know. "Let me see where you were bit."

"Right here." Trixie pointed to the right side of her neck. "But there's no mark. It felt like he bit me on the neck, then licked the spot."

Bubbles gave an emphatic nod. "It felt so real and it looked so real. They even had blood on their mouths."

"I don't know how they did it," Trixie said. "It was amazing. We were sort of out of it for a while, like we heard a real Vampire bite would make you feel."

Bubbles was grinning now. "Then we started to go down on—"

"Okay, that's enough." Olivia glared at Bubbles. "Where and when are you meeting them next?"

"Right here this evening, around eleven. We're not on stage tonight." Trixie stared at Olivia's ample breasts. "You two should come tonight. You would love it." She gave us each a flirtatious look. "*We* would love it."

"Yes." Bubbles looked excited, too. "Six isn't a crowd, especially with you two a part of it. I'm sure the two Vampire players would enjoy it."

"We're not interested in the kinds of games you have in mind," Olivia said.

But we would be there to see the Vampires arrive. The Nymphs just wouldn't know it, because I would bring a team cloaked by glamours.

"What we're interested in is finding Rodán," Olivia said.

I studied the two dimwits. "When was the last time you saw him?"

Bubbles shrugged and looked at Trixie. "Around two thirty this morning, I think."

Trixie screwed up her face in concentration. "We ended the show at two as usual, then met with Rodán, then went to the apartment. So yes, that's about right."

I was amazed these two could tell time. I checked my phone. Close to five thirty in the afternoon. "Going on fifteen hours ago."

"Is Rodán okay?" Trixie looked suddenly concerned.

I ignored her. "Get them to detention now," I said to Olivia.

"Detention?" Bubbles said.

Trixie's expression changed to panic. "We haven't done anything illegal."

I felt an urgent need to rush over to the apartment they'd taken Rodán to. I didn't have time to mess with them.

"Give me the address." I got out my phone and input the location when Bubbles gave it to me. I pulled out a pair of cuffs warded to keep almost all paranorms from getting free.

"We talked." Bubbles backed away. "We told you all we could."

Olivia was on the phone requesting PTF backup as I advanced on them.

"Give me any problems now and I'll make sure they give you the worst cells in the darkest, dankest places in the detention center," I said.

The Nymphs looked like they were about to burst into tears as they held out their wrists and I cuffed them. Two afghans were lying on the couch, and Olivia threw one around each of them.

As soon at the PTF arrived, Olivia and I hurried to the Wall Street address.

We'd called Colin, Joshua, and Angel for backup, and they met us on the street level after we parked the 'Vette. I gave them the rundown as we headed into the apartment building.

We showed the doorman our fake human law enforcement credentials. Paranorm creds just didn't have the same effect. The five of us split up into two groups. Olivia, Joshua, and I took the elevator. Just in case whoever was in there got wind of us coming, Angel and Colin headed up the stairs to cover that exit.

It didn't take us long to locate the apartment. The hallway was quiet as we stayed out of view of the door. Colin and Angel showed up at virtually the same time. Colin could have beaten us if he wasn't on the lookout for anyone coming down the stairs. Angel had likely zipped upstairs in her squirrel form.

I nodded to Joshua, who faded. The Shadow Shifter flowed over the carpet and slid under the door. For a moment everything was quiet.

The door opened and Joshua held it aside for us to join him in the apartment. "I don't know what happened in here," he said in his thick Australian accent. "But it doesn't look good."

It felt like the black ball of snakes in my belly was unraveling and curling, twisting and turning.

When I walked into the apartment I caught my breath. The place was a wreck. Crystal chandeliers lay in heaps. Furniture was splintered. Cushions were ripped to shreds. Paintings hung askew or lay on the floor in broken messes. Burn marks were on the walls. Blood was splattered on the wooden floor.

Colin stepped over what had been a vase but was now only shards. "What the hell happened here?"

Angel put her hands on her hips. "Damn."

"If he was here, I'd say Rodán put up one hell of a fight." Olivia said.

To realize that Rodán had been in some kind of battle here, but was now missing, made me feel even sicker inside.

The whole world seemed to tilt.

Something horrible had happened to Rodán.

TEN

"Rodán is missing?"

Nadia's words echoed in the Trackers' conference room, where all twenty-four of us and Desmond had gathered for an emergency meeting. I'd called the group together and not an hour later everyone was there.

I had to tell myself to maintain a professional calm as I responded to Nadia. "He was last seen almost seventeen hours ago," I said. "He missed three appointments that I know of, and as you all are aware, Rodán never misses appointments without notice."

Several in the room nodded.

Without Rodán we didn't have a leader, and no one knew that he had offered me a leadership position. I'd put on the mantle anyway. If there was a problem with any of the Trackers I'd deal with it then.

Angel stood at my side, her staunch support giving me a measure of comfort. The two of us weren't enough to replace Rodán, but we'd do everything we could to find him and to keep things running in New York City.

After I explained to the Trackers all that we knew, I said, "Given all the disappearances on the West Coast, I believe we need to at least consider the possibility that he was taken."

Just saying that made my stomach queasy.

"Do you think he was?" Lawan had surprise and concern on her face, expressions mirrored across the room.

"I don't know." I braced my hands on the back of the chair at the head of the table, the chair that had been Rodán's. "But we need to be proactive, so I've contacted Krishna." She was the Proctor over Long Island, Staten Island, and Ellis Island.

"Krishna put me in touch with the chairman of the Proctor Directorate." I met the gazes of the other Trackers. "He told me he would notify all of the other Proctors of Rodán's disappearance."

I continued, "Chairman James will handpick a Proctor to temporarily replace Rodán." I emphasized *temporary,* because we *would* find him.

A low murmur rolled through the Trackers that strengthened when I added, "That new Proctor will be bringing a team of twelve handpicked Trackers to assist in finding Rodán."

Bringing in a new team and a new Proctor was bound to stir things up, so I wasn't surprised when I saw uneasy looks.

"Tonight the Nymphs I spoke of will be meeting with a pair of males who may have been involved in the situation," I said. "The Nymphs believe that the males are actors pretending to be Vamps. I'm not so sure they're just actors."

Lawan's dark eyes were intent as she spoke. "You seriously think that these males may be true Vampires?"

"Yes." My emphatic response caused another stir. "Which means that Vampires might be involved in Rodán's disappearance."

Tracey, who was Romanian Fae, a Sânziană, frowned. "But we defeated Volod and his people over six months ago."

"As you know, we've suspected that Volod escaped." I put my hands on the back of the chair at the head of the table. Rodán's chair. "We can't discount the possibility that he could be involved."

Robert leaned back in his chair, his expression one of deep contemplation. He was a cougar Doppler, intense, focused, and silent until he was backed into a corner, or went on the offensive. When he spoke his words always meant something. "Do you think this has anything to do with the missing San Francisco Proctor and all of the Trackers?"

"It seems likely." I gripped the back of the chair tightly.

"We just don't have the kind of information we'd need to make that determination."

"What next, Captain?" Ice said.

Heat flushed through me. Normally Ice would have said something like that in a sarcastic tone, but tonight he sounded almost serious.

"I'm putting together a team to go back to the Nymphs' apartment tonight for their meeting with the so-called make-believe Vamps." I straightened and settled my hand on my sheathed Dragon-clawed dagger. "They're supposed to arrive at their place around eleven tonight."

No one interrupted, which I took as a good sign.

"Of course we need to make sure all of the territories are covered, so I'm going to take members of the existing special teams only." My dagger's grip felt comfortable in my hand as I squeezed it.

"Because the apartment is small," I continued, "I'll have a limited team with those who can shield themselves in glamour or shift into smaller forms. The team will include Joshua, Colin, and Ice." I gestured to Desmond. "We can always use a Sorcerer's services as well."

Desmond gave a slight inclination of his head.

"Angel will handle organization of territories to make sure everything is covered on that end." I released the hilt of my dagger. I was clenching it far too tightly. "See her if you have any questions in that regard."

I expected some kind of comment on my taking over, but everyone seemed more intent on finding Rodán.

Maybe it had something to do with Rodán choosing me to lead most of our special teams over the past nine months or so. They were used to me taking a leadership position.

Whatever the case, I was grateful.

When it was time to track, everyone left but the team I'd picked out to crash the Nymph-Vamp party tonight.

I gave the address of the apartment building the Nymphs lived in. We arranged to meet just outside the apartment half an hour before the Vamps—or Vamp wannabes—were supposed to arrive. That way we could get in beforehand.

"We'll observe as long as we can to understand their approach," I said. "When I give the signal we'll take the Vamps into custody—if I determine that they are in fact Vampires."

After we separated with plans intact, Colin and I walked in comfortable silence the short distance to my place. We had almost three hours left before we were to meet the rest of the team.

When we entered the apartment, my normally aloof brat of a cat ran out of the kitchen and into the entryway, straight for Colin as usual. I rolled my eyes as the Dragon picked up Kali and she started purring and rubbing against his chest.

"I'm the one who feeds you," I said to her. "Why don't you purr for me?"

"I can tell Kali is yours, Nyx," Colin said as he stroked the blue Persian. "She likes to snuggle close and rub against my chest."

"There's a difference. I'm loyal to those who take care of me." Kali gave me a look of disdain before she went back to purring and reveling in Colin's gentle strokes. Well, I had to admit he was a pretty fantastic guy. "And unlike Miss Kali, I don't shred my pretty lingerie."

I shook my head and got out some Fancy Feast, putting it in Kali's Waterford crystal dish. Colin set her down and she walked like a regal queen to her meal.

Colin led me into my living room. When he brought me to a stop, he wrapped his arms around me. I put my head against his chest and let myself sink against him. Some of the tension of the day lessened for the moment.

My fear for Rodán wanted to come out in a rush, and I had a difficult time holding it back. I couldn't allow myself to think of anything bad happening to him.

"Rodán is too powerful for anyone to hurt him." Colin kissed the top of my head and his lips tickled my scalp as he spoke. "He's countless centuries old, Nyx. At least as old as your father."

I met Colin's gaze, surprise widening my eyes. "He's as old as Father? How do you know that?"

Colin gave me a gentle smile and caressed my cheek. "You forget I have resources."

I tilted my head to the side. "What else do you know about Rodán?"

Colin secured me tighter in his embrace as he placed his hand on the back of my head and held me close. "Things you already know, Nyx. It wouldn't be easy to take him down. He's powerful. One of the most powerful beings I have ever met. I can't imagine that anyone could truly hurt him."

I breathed in Colin's masculine scent and let out a shuddering sigh. I found comfort in the clean smell of his T-shirt and his faint Dragon scent that's a little smoky but more like a campfire in the woods. An evergreen breeze with a tinge of smoke.

"Unless they took him by surprise." I closed my eyes and tried not to think about the mess in the apartment—and the blood. Whose blood?

Colin just held me as we stood there and I felt his warmth through the leather of my fighting suit. He felt comfortable, reassuring, almost convincing me that everything was all right. That we'd find Rodán and he'd be fine.

After I'd taken off my weapons belt and my boots, Colin and I sat on my couch. He put his arm around my shoulders and I snuggled against him as he used the TV remote to find a movie for us to watch.

Something so real and warm rose up inside me that I could barely hold back from saying anything about it to him.

My heart had healed over Adam. Not fully, because in some way I would always love Adam.

But Colin . . . the intensity of what I felt for him filled my chest and seemed to travel through every limb. I knew it then. Colin meant more to me than I had even realized. Could it be love, so soon after Adam? Was that possible?

My heart said yes. But my head told me to wait a little longer before I voiced it. Because when I did, I wanted it to be special. Not now when Rodán was missing and I was so worried. Later, when the time was right.

Right now while I was with Colin he helped me put aside my fears for Rodán, if only for that short window of time.

When it was time to leave I secured my weapons belt and pulled my boots on. Colin gave me a deep, sensual kiss before we left my apartment and entered the night.

ELEVEN

Instead of racing me to our destination—a race Colin always won—he took my hand. It was like I had blinked once and then we were there.

I'd never experienced anything like it. No pain, no getting sick from the transference. We were standing at my front door and the next thing I knew we were in the darkness in front of the Nymphs' apartment building on Fortieth Street.

"No wonder you always beat me in a race," I said as he released my hand. "Dragons are handy to have around."

He kissed the top of my head. We moved to the side of the building, where we'd arranged to meet the others. Joshua and Ice were already there. Desmond showed up not a minute later.

I rested my hand on the hilt of my sheathed Dragon-clawed dagger. "We're going to take these guys in. They have something to do with Rodán's disappearance, and we're going to get it out of them," I said. "But first we'll go in and observe. We need to know if they're Vampires or just a couple of Goth Vamp players."

I made a sign with my fingers. "This means subdue and arrest if they're not Vampires." I made another sign. "No holds barred. Do whatever it takes to take down the Vamps, without killing them."

I made sure everyone had silver handcuffs blessed with holy water along with garlic disks. I'd brought a couple of garlic-and-holy-water "grenades" recently designed for Vampires. It would be like throwing a smoke bomb into a room full of humans. The rest of us would smell like an Italian restaurant but the Vampires should feel pretty crappy with lungs full of garlic and holy water.

Colin and I cloaked ourselves in glamours. Desmond had worked with me on mine after the Zombie incident so I could now hide from most paranorms, too.

Nymphs wouldn't be able to see me for sure. I figured it had something to do with their one-track minds and their nature. Nymphs are happy and horny, completely sanguine. They're not a suspicious race of beings. Quite the opposite.

The Vampires had once been human so they definitely wouldn't be able to see me, a huge plus.

Joshua shifted into a shadow, and Ice chose his white mouse form. Desmond would hide somewhere in the apartment. As long as I had a hold of him he would remain hidden behind my glamour, but I needed to have my hands free once we were inside.

I looked at the time on my phone then shoved it back into its holster on my weapons belt. "The Nymphs should be home in about twenty minutes."

In shadow form, Joshua slid through the crack beneath the door. A moment later the locks rattled and the door squeaked open.

The Nymphs' apartment was just as messy now as it had been earlier. Clothing was scattered on the floor. Two pizza boxes were on one end table, and several tubes of lipstick in various shades sat on the other. Six cans of soda were on the glass-topped coffee table, a straw sticking out of one of the cans, bright red lipstick on the end of the straw.

Colin glanced around. "Shouldn't be too hard to find a hiding spot."

I stepped over a hairbrush, a tube of toothpaste, a rolling pin, and a pair of stockings. I got why stockings would be on the floor in the living room, but I didn't get the hairbrush or the toothpaste, much less the rolling pin. Truthfully, I didn't want to know.

Colin faded behind his glamour—not even paranorms could see through it—while Joshua and Ice took their positions. Desmond climbed over stacks of clothing and shoes on the floor of the coat closet and hid in there. Old standbys like coat closets were always handy.

I chose a corner where I could get a good view of everything and leaned up against the wall.

It wasn't too long before the Nymphs' giggles sounded from the other side of the door. Then came the rattle of the doorknob and the squeak of the hinges as they pushed the door open.

"I can't wait until they get here." Trixie immediately shimmied out of a thigh-high dress and was left standing in lacy red panties, no bra, as she talked to Bubbles.

Bubbles unzipped her own dress. "I want the tall one again. Gary is *so* hot."

"So's the brunette," Trixie said. "I'm more than happy to take Kurt again."

Vampires named Kurt and Gary? Vampires had names like Michael, Franklyn, Alexander . . . not what sounded like nicknames.

Bubbles went through a door that I assumed was a bedroom. She came back out with an armload of red and black lingerie. The Nymphs were giggling and squealing in delight as they talked about the males who would be arriving soon. They talked and talked while they tried on lingerie, gazing at themselves in a mirror that covered an entire wall.

"Isn't it great we look so much alike?" Bubbles said as she tugged up her corset, pushing her boobs until they could have been used as a serving platter. She sounded like she could hardly breathe from the tightness of the corset. "Males just love the idea of twins. So we make the perfect pair."

"These black panties go perfectly with this red corset," Trixie said. "I love the color contrast. You get so much more color when you wear panties instead of a thong."

I rolled my eyes. Who cared?

"Tomorrow night let's wear leather." Bubbles adjusted her garter and started pulling on a pair of stockings. "Those Shifters love the dominatrix look."

Trixie nodded, her blond curls bouncing around her face.

"You know, the Catwoman outfit just might go over well with those three."

Bubbles finished with her stockings and rummaged around the room, looking for something. "Sam loves to watch the others tying us up."

"So does Rick. I'm not too sure about the leash thing, but if they like it, I'll end up liking it. Whatever gets them hot. It's all just foreplay to me." Trixie picked up a tube of bright red lipstick that matched her corset.

"My favorite red heels are here somewhere . . ." Bubbles's voice trailed off before she rose up with a triumphant look on her face. She waved what looked like a magazine. "The newest edition of *Fetishwear Today* is here. I was wondering where it went."

"Did you see the feature on the new latex outfits including hoods? I love the bizarre look of some of them," Trixie was saying.

I really, really wished they would stop their mind-numbing banter, bouncing from one subject to another. If they giggled for much longer I was going to shoot them both.

What a couple of idiots. Nymphs have one-track minds—sex, sex, and wait, more sex.

Did I mention Nymphs are focused on sex?

A friend of theirs was missing yet all they were concerned with were the males who should be arriving soon and the latest sex toys and fetish outfits.

The Nymphs finished dressing, then put on a heavier coating of makeup and found their heels. They each grabbed an armload of scattered leftover lingerie and returned to the bedroom just as someone knocked on the front door.

"Just a moment," Trixie yelled. She came in a half run, half shuffle in heels so high they might as well have been stilts. Watching her taking little bitty steps in the heels, trying to avoid tipping over as she headed for the door was just comical.

Trixie opened the door.

"Kurt!" she squealed, which was worse than giggling. She kissed him and let him in the door before greeting Gary with another shriek of obvious delight.

The moment the males entered the room, my senses went on full alert.

These males definitely weren't human . . . they were something *Other.*

But what? Their scents were a mixture. One had a Shifter's scent of amber, but I also thought I caught the faint whiff of dirt.

And the other—a Doberman. Like a Doppler might smell if his animal form was one of that breed. But again the hint of dirt mixed in with the animal scent.

We had suspected they could be real Vampires, and I had a strong feeling now that we'd been right.

"Hold on a sec, guys. Let me get Bubbles. We wanted to enter together." Trixie exited the room with the itty-bitty shuffle steps. The Vampires could not take their eyes off her red panty-covered round ass.

Brother, these two were just too much.

The Vampires started to talk quietly.

"Okay," whispered Gary. "Follow the plan. We need to keep them busy for a couple of hours till we hit the twenty-four-hour mark. I'll give you the signal then. In the meantime, we'll have our fun with them. Then ten days from now, we will have our own personal Vampire play toys."

Vampire play toys. There wasn't a shadow of a doubt.

"Excellent," Kurt said. "Everything has to go right tonight. He was so angry with us because we didn't take them back with us last night. We need to get them tonight, but first we have to find out if they told anyone anything about last night. Just follow my lead."

"You got it," said Gary.

"He" was so angry last night? Who's "he"?

The airheads came shuffling in side by side. "Hi, guys, do you like our outfits? We dressed for you," Bubbles said. She grabbed Gary by the arm and pulled him to the couch, snuggling up to him.

Trixie did the same with Kurt. "If you'd like us in something else," she said, "we can show you all the stuff we have. Whatever you want. Do you like Catwoman?"

"You're both perfect just like this, ladies. You look amazing. You're so hot," Kurt said to Trixie as he nuzzled her throat. "So beautiful."

"Did you enjoy last night?" Gary was saying to Bubbles. "I couldn't wait to see you again."

"Yes." Bubbles hissed the word as she pressed her breasts against Gary's chest. "I loved it so much. I kept thinking about the Vampire look all day." Her voice was husky, much different from the way she'd sounded earlier.

The Nymphs had suddenly transformed from birdbrains to sensual and seductive. It was like they had totally different personalities with these two males.

When I was about to lose my mind from boredom, the Vampires told the Nymphs they wanted to take them out. Trixie and Bubbles rushed off to their bedroom to change once again.

"Wish we could take them now," Kurt said when the Nymphs were gone.

Gary nodded. "Yeah, but we have to wait." He tilted his head. "Why did we get here so early?"

"So they don't leave to see someone else," Kurt said. "You know Nymphs. Their attention span is only as long as the length of time a male is with them."

"True," Gary said.

"We'll take them back to the apartment and do it there." Kurt grinned. "It'll be fun. They look hot. Nothing like taking a hot Nymph and turning her."

"These two take the cake for having fluff for brains," Gary said with a laugh. "Can you just imagine what he will say?"

Kurt frowned. "Maybe it's not such a good idea turning them."

The Nymphs burst back into the living room, now dressed in tiny red dresses.

I dropped my glamour and gestured with one hand in the sign to take these Vampires down.

At the same time, I used my teeth to pull the pin from the garlic-and-holy-water grenade and lobbed it in front of the two Vampires. It fell to the floor and rattled across the wood.

Colin, Joshua, and Ice appeared.

The Vampires startled. The Nymphs screamed.

Immediately the Vampires recovered from their shock. The Nymphs did not.

Before the grenade could go off, the Vampire Kurt shifted into a Bengal tiger.

The other Vampire, Gary, transformed into a Doberman.

Both vicious, frightening creatures.

It didn't matter. The grenade would do the trick.

Garlic and holy water exploded throughout the room.

My lungs burned from the strength of the garlic. My eyes would have watered if I'd had tear ducts.

The Doberman snarled and the tiger roared. They each shook it off as if the grenade had just been a nuisance.

A *nuisance.*

Ice in his white jaguar form gave a powerful cry, lunged, and took the tiger down. They landed in the middle of the coffee table. A tremendous crashing sound as soda cans and glass went flying.

"Get out," I shouted at the Nymphs, who were just standing on one side of the room screaming. I was going to arrest them just for the annoying sounds they were making tonight. I owed them.

As the Nymphs ran through the front door and slammed it behind them, I summoned my elements.

Colin transformed into a smaller version of his Dragon form. He bellowed, his tail sweeping table lamps, pizza boxes, and lipstick off the glass-topped end tables, and then sent the tables themselves flying. They crashed against the walls, shattering.

The tiger clawed at Ice, whose white pelt was streaked red with blood. I'd never seen Ice injured in a fight before. The tiger was strong, stronger than any Shifter or Vampire should be alone.

Ice shifted into an albino boa constrictor and started to wrap himself around the tiger. The Tiger transformed into an enormous alligator with huge jaws snapping at the constrictor's thick white body.

I wrapped ropes of my air element around the jaws of the alligator, snapping them shut and binding them tight.

The albino boa constrictor morphed into Ice. Man is the alligator's only real enemy. I tossed Ice one of my daggers. He brought it down so fast toward the alligator's white belly that I thought Ice was going to gut the Vampire-Shifter. Ice pulled just short of slicing him open.

Colin blasted fire at the unnaturally large Doberman that yelped and ducked out of the way, only to run into Joshua.

The Doberman leapt up, snarling, its jaws going for Joshua's throat. Joshua swung his fist at the dog, which went flying across the room.

It hit the wall and transformed back into its Vampire form before it landed on the floor.

The alligator shifted back into its Vampire form with Ice still holding my dagger at its throat.

Vampires looked at each other. Stark resolution was on their features.

Before I knew what was happing, the Vampire-Shifter grabbed Ice's blade. With unbelievable, inhuman strength, Kurt brought the blade down on his own neck.

I watched in horror as the blade sliced through the Vampire's neck in a smooth, effortless, and flawless motion, as if I had done it myself.

He'd severed his own head.

The Vampire *had severed his own head.*

I jerked my attention to the Vampire up against the wall. Gary had a wooden stake in his hand that he'd pulled from his pocket, and was raising it up as if to drive it down and into his own heart.

Colin and I dove for him at the same time. I grabbed the stake and Colin grabbed the Vampire. "No!" he shouted. "I will not be taken!"

I straightened, holding the stake in my hand. "Yes. You will."

Colin tossed me a pair of silver handcuffs and I snapped them on the Vampire's wrists.

TWELVE

"We need to interrogate this scum," Ice said in a low growl that reminded me of his jaguar form.

"Nyx." Desmond's eyes had a half-wild light to them when I turned to face him. Desmond had an accent from the world he was from, and the Scottish-like brogue was strong as he spoke. "I have to go to the apartment where Rodán disappeared. Now."

"Why?" I said, feeling off balance from the intensity of his expression and the depth of conviction in his tone.

Desmond took my hand and led me away from the Vampire I'd just cuffed. "A moment ago I had a vision. Just a flash of one, but a vision nonetheless," Desmond said. "We can't wait."

"What did you have a vision of?" Those black snakes were back wriggling in my belly.

"It was brief. A flash." Desmond pushed his hand through his already messy hair, making it look in even more of a disarray than usual.

"What did you vision about, Desmond?" I tried to breathe, but a feeling of panic rose within me.

"Rodán," he said. "I visioned about Rodán."

Air didn't want to come into my lungs.

"We have to go to the place he disappeared," Desmond repeated and took a couple of steps away from me. "Once we're there I should be able to tell you more. I might even be able to show you."

Breathe in. Breathe out.

"Okay." I clenched my hands as I tried to keep calm. "But the others need to see, too."

I explained to Joshua, Ice, and Colin that Desmond had something to show us. We had to wait for the PTF before we could leave. Fortunately that took only moments.

In our various forms we were able to get to the Wall Street apartment quickly. Colin took me and Desmond, and Ice transformed into a snow-white falcon. Every form Ice took was white.

Joshua traveled as a shadow. He'd saved my life once when I'd been blasted out a window by Volod and fallen twenty-four stories. Joshua had shot down from the shattered window as shadow, passed me, then transformed into a human and caught me on the ground. I never knew how he got to me so fast.

When we were all together, we headed up to the apartment we'd been in earlier that day and made our way inside.

A horrible, sick feeling came over me as I took in the wreckage. I faced Desmond, a dread so vast building up inside me that it was almost crippling in its intensity.

Desmond had his eyes closed and a pale green light seemed to roll up and down his arms and over his body, something I'd never seen before. The tendons in his neck stood out, his muscles tightening until they bulged.

His body trembled as he seemed to absorb energy from the room. Negative energy, I thought. It couldn't be good.

Joshua, Ice, Colin, and I circled Desmond, waiting. I didn't know if I wanted him to hurry or not, because I was afraid of what I would see.

Desmond opened his eyes and held out his palm. A small ball of light floated above his hand. It reminded me of the first time he'd shown me Zombies in a hologram.

He released the ball so that it drifted up until it hovered in the air between us. He made a motion with his fingers and the ball expanded . . . until there were three forms floating in front of us all.

Nymph One, Nymph Two, and Rodán.

The Nymphs' bodies were slender and petite, their faces stunning, their hair long and golden. Their perfect breasts threatened to spill from the bodices of the matching red dresses they wore, and their nipples were hard enough to show through the gauzy fabric.

"Come to our place this time," Bubbles was saying to Rodán as he put his arms around each of their shoulders and walked them toward his chambers. "We have something we want to share with you."

Rodán paused, bringing the three of them to a halt. "What would that be?"

Bubbles gave a wickedly sexual smile. "You're going to love what we have in store for you."

"Absolutely *love* it," Trixie said.

No, Nyx wanted to yell. *Don't go.*

But Rodán seemed to gain more sexual energy from the way the pair looked at him, the excitement they appeared to have for the night to come.

"And what would that be, ladies?" Rodán repeated, his voice low and sensual.

Bubbles leaned closer. "We have whiteberry potion."

Rodán raised an eyebrow. "How did you come upon something so rare? Are you certain it's authentic?"

With a devious grin, Trixie leaned in close. "We gave a private performance to a very wealthy individual. And yes, it is real. We tried a tiny bit."

"And we've been saving it for you." Bubbles rose up on her tiptoes and nipped his earlobe.

"Not a drop will go to waste." Rodán kissed Trixie, then Bubbles. "Shall we go?"

I shook my head, wanting to tell this memory of Rodán that he was heading into a trap.

The hologram swirled, everything blending together like oils in a painting. Then the apartment we were in appeared—only everything was intact. It was exceptional, even by human standards. Rich mahogany furnishings, crystal chandeliers, original oil paintings, and polished wood floors.

All of it lying shattered and broken in the present.

In the living area, Rodán settled onto the couch, the cushions of which were whole and beautiful, not shredded. Trixie scooted onto his lap and straddled him. She kissed him and slid her fingers through the length of his hair.

"No fair hogging Rodán." Bubbles knelt beside him on the couch, took his hand in hers, and placed it on one of her breasts. He tweaked her nipple.

"Why is this still on?" Rodán lightly pulled at the material.

She gave a blissful sigh of pleasure and nuzzled his ear before tracing the point with the tip of her tongue.

Rodán's love of females and sex might be his undoing.

"First things first," Bubbles murmured. "A drop of white-berry potion."

Trixie leaned back as Bubbles brought a tiny vial to Rodán's lips. A minuscule drop landed on his tongue.

No, no, no! I cried in my mind.

Rodán frowned. "It should not taste bitter," he said. "White-berry is as sweet as a cherry—"

His words cut off and he suddenly looked dizzy.

Trixie and Bubbles watched him as if expecting something to happen.

"Wrong potion," he whispered. "Something's wrong."

"Is it working?" Bubbles said as she looked at Trixie. "He's relaxing like they said he would."

Rodán's eyes looked bleary and when he tried to move he seemed tired, lethargic. As my heart pounded and my mouth grew dry, I could almost feel his muscles turn to limp blades of grass, his bones tired and old, as though every year he'd lived was now etched upon him.

Unwanted thoughts and images came to me . . . As if Rodán was a frail being with no past, no future—instead of the Elvin prince he was.

My jaws hurt from clenching them so tightly as Rodán struggled to talk, struggled to move. I'd never seen him like that. Never. Rodán, helpless?

"You'll have fun, Rodán." Trixie kissed him on the lips and slid off his lap. He watched her stand, and she looked away. "You can come by and thank us tomorrow. We can get a double payback on this one. We love you, Rodán. Enjoy the experience."

Bubbles joined Trixie. "Where's our potion?"

"It will be given to you," said a female voice I thought I recognized.

When I saw her, I stepped back from the hologram in shock. The San Francisco Proctor.

"Monique," Rodán managed to say to the Elvin female, her name coming out raspy and impotent from his lips.

"Move." The power in Monique's voice had the Nymphs scrambling to get away from Rodán.

Monique sat beside him. She was gorgeous with her hair long and shining, dark around her shoulders and her delicate features. Her fair—no, pale—skin was a lovely contrast with her dark hair, and her pointed ears peeked through the strands.

A single diamond pendant glittered at her throat. She wore a tight thigh-high black dress, her legs smooth and elegant, and her feet clad in expensive designer shoes. She looked exquisite, one of the most beautiful beings I'd ever seen.

"It's so wonderful to see you." She reached out and caressed the side of his face. "I've missed you."

I sensed Rodán's feelings—something wasn't right about the beautiful female beside him. But his senses were dulled from the potion.

"Leave." Monique waved away the Nymphs with one hand. "*He* is in the sitting room. He'll pay you there and give you your vial of potion. A couple of males, the look-alike Vampire friends that you were promised, are in there with him. I'm sure you two will enjoy them very much."

Vaguely I wondered who was in the sitting room. The males had to be the two we'd dealt with tonight.

"Thank you," Trixie said, bubbly enthusiasm coming from her as she turned away.

"Have fun, Rodán!" Bubbles waved before she and Trixie giggled and ran toward a door on the far end of the living area. In moments they were gone, closing the door behind them.

"What has been done to me?" Each word sounded difficult for Rodán to say, almost painfully so.

"The only known thing that can weaken the powers of Elves is a potion made from the center of the eye of a Basilisk," Monique said. "Many beings died to produce this potion for you."

Potion from the eye of a Basilisk. As far as I knew, no one had used such against the Elves in centuries. I only knew about it from my father's stories when I was a youngling. It had been so long that my father had thought the recipe for the potion had been lost.

"Why?" Rodán didn't try for long sentences. It seemed that any effort made him weaker.

"It had to be done." Monique caressed his arm. "This is so very important and we need you to listen."

Rodán managed to straighten a little in his seat. Perhaps the potion wore off sooner than expected?

"We?" he said.

Through the connection I had with the holographic vision of Rodán, I felt him struggle to keep Monique from realizing that the effects of the potion were beginning to fade.

She shifted on the couch so that she could look at him better. "Soon you will meet him. Or rather you will meet him again. I understand you've had encounters before."

Rodán frowned. "Who?" he mumbled.

Monique's smile was radiant. She looked more beautiful than I could have believed possible for anyone to look. "I cannot express how pleased I am to have you here," she said. "To have you become one of us, and to know that I shall be the one who makes you one of us."

The female was making no sense whatsoever. She leaned forward as she cupped his face in her palms. "You feel so warm, and you look so good to me, Rodán."

"Your hands are so cold," he said.

Monique brushed her lips over Rodán's and he recoiled.

"*Vampire.*" Rodán looked stunned. "You have been turned."

Shock compounded on shock made me weak.

The San Francisco Proctor was now a Vampire?

Suddenly it made sense that the two Vampires in the Nymphs' apartment were also paranorms.

"What happened to you?" A hard look came into Rodán's expression. "Who did this?"

"It is not what you think." She was standing now, talking with her hands. "It is wonderful. Amazing. There is nothing like it."

Rodán narrowed his gaze. "There is *nothing* wonderful or amazing about Vampirism," he said as he pushed himself to his feet.

Monique flinched as he spoke, and she looked shocked that he was able to stand. "You have no idea of the truth. But you will." Then as Rodán took a step toward her, she yelled, "Backups."

Rodán turned to face a new threat. Six Vampires rushed the room and were coming at him.

I felt him using every bit of mental focus he had to generate power to fight through the cloud of the potion that now controlled him.

He seemed to sense something else to his left and turned.

And came face-to-face with Volod.

I almost screamed.

But for Rodán, it was as if he'd been expecting to see Volod from the beginning.

"Rodán." Volod smiled. "Listen to Monique. It will be easier for you."

The other Vampires were coming after him, and he glanced at them. Monique came up from behind. The San Francisco Elvin Proctor was powerful, but she could not possibly be a match for Rodán.

I sensed a power surge within him. He sent a mental blast of magic at a wooden table six feet away. The table exploded in splinters. Each leg split in half, leaving eight shards of wood.

A second blast of power sent the splintered legs hurling in different directions at the eight Vampires.

Six of the splintered stakes buried themselves in the chests of six Vampires.

All six collapsed. Dead.

But Monique and Volod were not affected.

How could that be? Rodán seemed as surprised as I was.

I'd seen the stakes make it all the way to their chests. But now wood lay in splinters before them. Some form of a shield must have stopped the entry.

Volod and Monique advanced on Rodán.

My heart beat faster as I watched the holographic scene unfold. I cried out and ran forward to help Rodán without realizing what I was doing.

The hologram vanished like sparkling dust all around me.

"No!" I looked around me and saw the grim faces of my teammates, then met Desmond's gaze as panic sent razor-sharp arrows of fear throughout me. "Bring it back."

"Step away," he said. I realized I was in the center of the room.

When I was out of the way, Desmond released another ball of light. My heart wouldn't stop racing so fast that it felt like it was going to burst through my chest.

The ball spun before it dissolved into images again.

Volod and Monique were going after Rodán.

Monique fired her own blast of power.

Rodán stood his ground. Somehow, despite the remnants of the potion, he still had the strength to withstand her. He sent a surge of concentrated energy her way and then one at Volod.

Monique gasped as she flew back, over the couch, and landed on her knees. Volod was thrust against the wall and then fell to the floor looking slightly dazed.

"You don't know what you are doing, Rodán." Monique slowly rose to her feet. "It is better for you if I do this. Don't fight me."

He held his hand up. His strength had not fully returned, but I could feel power building within him. Centuries of magic was breaking through the hold the Basilisk potion had on him.

Monique cried out as the strength of his next burst slammed into her and flung her across the room.

Glass shattered. Wood snapped and splintered.

He did not look. I knew he didn't feel any remorse. She was a Vampire now. An enemy.

Volod had recovered and was coming at Rodán. He flung his magic at Volod, wrapping thick ropes of it around the Master Vampire.

Hope built up inside me. Centuries of power were within Rodán to command. He was far older, far more experienced than the Vampire, who was a child in comparison.

But the Basilisk potion still reined in some of his power. He should have been able to fling Volod across the room and drive one of the pieces of splintered wood into the Vampire's heart.

Instead he fought to keep Volod wrapped tight in his ropes of magic. A fight that was weakening him in ways I was certain he'd never experienced before.

Volod's eyes gleamed red as he fought back.

Rodán gave an Elvin warrior cry like I've never heard before.

He dropped Volod and raised his hands. In his grip was pure light—a sword made of light. He swung the magical sword at Volod's head.

The Master Vampire dodged the blade, barely saving himself.

Rodán's raised his sword again.

He put all of his focus into going after Volod.

Monique grabbed Rodán's shoulders from behind, catching him off guard. Something she would never have been able to do if his senses hadn't been dulled.

Volod drew a handgun with frightening speed.

He aimed it at Rodán. Before Rodán could use his magic to knock it away, Volod shot.

The bullet slammed into Rodán's chest.

I screamed.

Rodán gasped, shock on his features as he looked down. The hole steamed, but no blood rolled out.

"A bullet capsule filled with Basilisk potion," Volod said as he rose to his feet. "That's one you won't recover from for a long time."

Shock made my body numb as I reached out, only to have my hand slide through the holographic image.

Rodán turned his head, his eyes suddenly more glazed over, and met Volod's gaze.

At the same time, Monique sank her fangs into the vein on Rodán's neck.

I clapped my hand over my mouth, holding back a scream.

In the next instant the Master Vampire was gripping Rodán tight as Monique drank from him.

"No!" I heard myself screaming. But I couldn't stop watching.

The combination of the Vampire sucking his blood and the Basilisk bullet left Rodán too weak to fight back.

My mind spun as Monique made sounds of pleasure and Volod grasped Rodán too tight for him to move.

The world started to fade . . . sounds became muffled . . . his breathing slowed . . . and somehow I knew his heart all but stopped.

"One more bite tomorrow by Volod, and you will be one of us," Monique whispered in his ear.

Everything faded away.

THIRTEEN

Terror for Rodán ripped through me like a jagged blade. My mind raced. I had to pull myself together.

"We have to hurry!" I swung my gaze to Colin's. "There's still a chance we could get to Rodán before he's bitten again. Vampires must wait at least twenty-four hours before biting their victim a second time in order to turn them."

Colin studied me. "That gives us less than three hours. We know virtually nothing about effects of Vampires on paranorms, though. Maybe the wait is less, maybe it's more. We don't know. We just know now that they can turn paranorms."

Less than three hours? What if that wasn't enough? I raised my hands as I spoke, my words coming out almost frantic. "We need to let the other Trackers know what happened. And I have to interrogate that Vamp we caught tonight myself, unless Max got anything out of him."

The Werewolf Tracker was a good interrogator, but since we hadn't heard anything from him I knew he hadn't gotten the Vampire to talk yet. "We have to do whatever it takes to track down Volod now. That *bastard*."

"I'll let the others know." Joshua came up to stand on one side of me, Ice on the other. "I'll text everyone an alert that a conference call meeting will start in fifteen minutes."

"Send out the call-in number and the access code with the alert," I said. "I want to make certain there is no confusion. Everyone is to be on it." I looked from Joshua to Ice and Colin. "I'll make the call from my conference line at my office. Any Trackers who would prefer to join us at the office, that would be fine."

Joshua gave a nod.

"After our call I'll interview the Vamp we caught tonight," I said.

"I'll go with you to interrogate him." Desmond came up beside Colin. "I'll know immediately if there's anything I can read from him." The Sorcerer added, "I do know a few interrogation techniques."

"Can you tell us anything more about what happened or where he is now?" I asked Desmond. I wanted to run as fast as I could, but I didn't know where.

He shook his head. "Not yet."

The clock was ticking. We had to find Rodán before it was too late. We *would* find him.

I called Angel and we made quick plans for what we'd be asking of the Trackers. Colin transported Desmond and me to just outside the PI office's front door. Ice and Joshua should arrive at any time.

Olivia was sitting at her desk when we walked into the office. She frowned as soon as she saw my expression. "What's wrong?"

My breathing wasn't coming easy. I felt like I was winded as I said words I didn't want to say: "Volod has Rodán."

"No, no, *no*. No way." Olivia sat back in her chair looking stunned. "That's not possible."

"I wish it wasn't." I went to my own desk. "We're going to have a conference call in a few minutes with the other Trackers, and then I have to go interrogate a Vamp."

Olivia's frown deepened. "How did this happen? How could this happen?"

I gave her a brief rundown of everything that had occurred. She'd hear more during the call.

She tapped a pen on the sticky notes on her desk as she spoke to Desmond. "You're absolutely positive that you're right?"

"I hate to say it, but yes." Desmond folded his arms across his chest. "My visions are never wrong."

Just talking about it made me sick. My chest felt tight. My whole body tense. My gut ached.

Within a few minutes Ice, Joshua, Angel, Nadia, Lawan, and Tristan arrived at my office. Colin, Olivia, and I made up three more. The other fifteen Trackers called in.

All of it was happening too slow. Much too slow.

I went through everything in more detail than what I'd given Olivia.

"We're going to work primarily in teams of two," I concluded. "Olivia and Angel will man the PI office, which will be command central since Rodán's not here."

"Man the office?" Olivia said. "You mean woman the office."

A couple of Trackers laughed, Olivia's comment adding a bit of levity.

Though I felt it, I didn't want to let indecisiveness enter my voice as I continued. The Trackers needed a leader now and I was giving them one.

"Desmond and I will interrogate the Vamp who's in custody," I said. "Because we believe that those responsible for the disappearances of ten Trackers and now two Proctors are here, no one will work alone.

"That means twenty-two of you will work in teams of two. Since there are fifteen territories and only eleven teams, some of you are going to have to double up on territories." I glanced at Angel. "As soon as I finish briefing you and give you your instructions, Angel will coordinate territories."

Those on the other end of the call were mostly quiet, everyone listening intently.

"Tonight you're going to find every Vamp who was anybody," I said. "Go to all of the known Vamp hangouts in your respective territories. Olivia will e-mail you a list by the end of this call. Check out every resource we have. Shake them all down and get anything you can. Follow every lead. Someone knows something." I added, "Call in on this number and speak with Angel right away if you believe you do have a lead."

I clenched my teeth before I added, "I really don't care at

this point what you do to the Vampires to get the information. As far as I am concerned, tonight, the Vampires have no rights."

The grim faces of the Trackers in my office echoed how I felt. "Time is running out to find Rodán. We only have two and a half hours left before it's too late."

After I turned the phone meeting to Angel, Colin followed me and Desmond out the door into the chill night air.

"Be careful," Colin said, and he kissed me. When I drew away, he took my hands and brushed his lips over mine again. "You call me the moment you find out where Rodán is. You will not go after him alone. I can be there in a second."

"I won't." I stepped away. "Promise."

I looked over my shoulder once as Desmond and I rushed across Central Park West to Central Park. Colin was watching me, his burnished gold eyes seeming to almost glow in the darkness.

Desmond and I ran to the huge Alice in Wonderland unbirthday party sculpture north of Conservatory Water.

I walked counterclockwise around the sculpture while reciting the poem—that made absolutely no sense—inscribed around the base. " *'Twas brillig, and the slithy toves did gyre and gimble in the wabe.*" Fortunately I had it memorized or I would never have gotten it out, I was so frantic.

It was a line from "The Jabberwocky," a poem by Lewis Carroll. I'd heard Lewis was a paranorm—a Doppler in the form of a big yellow cat—still living in New York City. I'd never met him.

The Shadow Shifter and Dryad guards didn't want to allow Desmond to go into the Paranorm Center with me. I had to pull rank. I was ready to do a lot more than that, but they let us through.

We jogged down to the detention center, which was run by the Paranormal Task Force. A female Doppler PTF agent escorted us and we hurried down the stone steps into dank areas I'd rather not be in.

The only thing that mattered was finding out where Rodán was and saving him before it was too late.

Gary, the Vampire-Doppler we'd arrested, had been put in solitary confinement. When we arrived at his cell, we looked through the small barred window.

The Vampire-Doppler was in the special Vampire cuffs, strung up in a corner in his human form. His head hung so that his chin rested against his chest. His toes barely reached the stone floor, and red welts striped his naked body.

Max turned to face the door, a whip clenched in his fist. In his eyes was the look of the Werewolf he was during the full moon. It made me shiver.

After we handed over our weapons, the PTF agent unlocked the door and let Desmond and I into the cell.

"Didn't work," Max said as we walked up to him. "He will be tough. I didn't know how hard to get with him, but I got nothing."

The Vampire's head rose and my breath caught. His fangs had extended, and they flashed in the cell's dim lighting.

I glanced at Desmond. He looked confident . . . powerful.

Considering what he'd done in our last major case with the evil Sorcerer Amory, who'd turned Zombies loose on New York City, I wasn't surprised that Desmond showed such strength in the face of the mess we were in. What was one hybrid Vampire to someone who'd defeated the creator of thousands upon thousands of Zombies, as Desmond had?

Desmond didn't say anything, just looked at me, waiting for me to take control of the interrogation.

I walked within feet of the Vampire-Doppler. "Where did they take Rodán?"

Gary raised his head and stared at me and Desmond. He was fairly tall with a wiry, powerful build. I frowned for a moment as something hit me.

On the list of missing Trackers had been the name Gary.

"Are you one of the Trackers who disappeared over the last few months?" I asked.

The Vampire-Doppler continued to stare.

"We don't have time to spend trying to get him to talk." I glanced at Desmond. "We have to *make* him talk."

Desmond raised his hand. A glowing green fist of light

shot out and wrapped itself around Gary's throat. He gasped and clawed.

"Tell us where Rodán is." Desmond spoke with slow, deliberate intensity as he relaxed the magical fist just enough that Gary wasn't choking anymore. "Do it now or this will seem like nothing in comparison with what I will do to you."

When Gary didn't answer, Desmond squeezed his raised hand and the glowing fist clenched tighter around Gary's throat. He clawed more as he struggled to breathe.

Desmond let up on the pressure then asked again, and again the Vampire-Doppler said nothing.

As Desmond held Gary in his magic fist, I spoke to the PTF agent on the other side of the door. "Can we get a persuasion chair in here?"

Plenty of times I'd "persuaded" paranorms myself, but I'd never actually tortured anyone. I didn't have the stomach for it generally, but today, with Rodán's life in the balance, I would do anything. Desmond, I knew, would have no reservations today or any day.

Desmond held on to Gary with the fist as two PTF agents brought the persuasion chair in the room. Then they unhooked the Vampire-Doppler from the chains that had held him up, but kept the special cuffs on his wrists.

The Sorcerer used the fist to drag Gary across the cell and into the persuasion chair. Then the female agents stripped him and strapped him in.

A metal head frame attached to the chair, fit over the top of his head and around the forehead. The band around the forehead was tightened.

The chair had a V opening on the seat. A metal stainless-steel collar about three-quarters of an inch wide was affixed to a rod at the bottom of the chair frame, and attached around the base of his testicles. It had an extension that was a small vise. They called it a "ball crusher."

The rod had a turnbuckle that was adjusted to pull his balls down taut until the Vampire made a vocal response, like a scream. If he moved at all, they would be pulled off . . . Or so I hoped. For a male, I am sure it was an understatement to say there was something intimidating about someone literally having him by the balls.

Max moved up beside me. I'd been so intent on watching that I had forgotten he was there. "Man, this guy just won't talk. I must say he has balls."

Anger burned through me hot and fierce. "If he doesn't talk now the only way he'll have balls is when we pick them up off the floor and hand them to him."

Gary flinched.

Good.

Max looked from Gary to me. "What would you like me to do now?"

"Call Angel and she'll give you instructions." I pushed my hair over my shoulders to get it out of my face. "And find Volod."

He nodded. "You've got it."

"Thanks, Max," I said. He gave another nod before he left the cell. The agent locked the door behind him.

I turned my attention back to Gary.

The Vampire-Doppler's muscles were chiseled, showing power in every fiber of his body. No matter the strength of his paranorm powers, or as strong as he was physically, he was no match for the magic in the restraints or Desmond's power. Everyone had a breaking point, and we would find Gary's.

"Where is Rodán?" Desmond released his hold on Gary's neck, and the Vampire-Doppler slumped in the chair. Desmond got into his face. "Talk or you're really not going to like what I'm about to do next." He held his hand out, and green flame danced on his palm.

Gary stared at the Sorcerer, anger in his gaze. His blue eyes were still in the stages of turning dark as they would be for the rest of his unnatural life. Unless of course that unnatural life ended tonight.

"This little flame"—Desmond bounced the magic fire on his palm—"will make you feel like every nerve ending inside you is on fire. You'll feel like you're burning alive.

"The good news is you won't die," the Sorcerer added. "You'll just wish you would. You will struggle and move around. You won't be able to help yourself." Desmond looked at the place where Gary's balls were trapped before looking back at the Vampire-Doppler. "When you jump, you might lose a couple of things."

My fury over Rodán's abduction, and over what the Vampires had done to me just months ago, kept away any speck of pity that might have been in me. Fear for Rodán burned like the fire in Desmond's hand, only a thousand times worse. Joining the horrible fear were white-hot flames of anger.

No, I didn't care what Desmond did to this Vampire. We'd do whatever we had to do.

When Gary didn't say anything, Desmond blew on the flame in his hand.

The flame leapt from his palm and landed in an explosion of sparks, encompassing Gary.

He shrieked, his body jerking and straining against his restraints, his muscles bulging as the magic fire sizzled on his skin. How his balls stayed attached to his body I didn't know, but it had to hurt.

"What are you doing to him?" I asked Desmond in a lowered voice. My heart pounded. The green fire unnerved me. "Don't kill him."

"Like I told him, he's not going to die." Desmond's gaze grew more intense, and the green fire popped and crackled while Gary screamed. "It's like burning in the flames of the human version of hell. Only worse." Desmond closed his hand, and the flames vanished.

Amazingly, the Vampire-Doppler's skin wasn't even blistered. The only sign he'd just been through an ordeal was the sweat rolling down the side of his face and coating his skin wherever it was visible. His breathing was erratic, as if he'd just been running.

"Are you ready to talk?" Desmond asked Gary yet again.

The Vampire-Doppler still said nothing, just glared. The Sorcerer held out his hand and once again green flame erupted on his palm. "Last chance."

I was pretty sure Gary was a former Tracker, which meant he would be hard, if not impossible, to break.

No, everyone had a breaking point.

Everyone.

Some took longer than others.

After two more times with the flames, Desmond asked for a tub of water for Gary's feet. By the look in his eyes, he knew what was coming next.

Ice-cold water sloshed out of the tub and onto the stone floor when two agents brought it in. The agents unstrapped his legs just enough to put his feet in the tub.

When the agents finished and left the cell, Desmond steepled his fingers together. Currents sizzled, bouncing from one fingertip to the next. The air filled with static. My own magic felt the pull.

"Gary, we're not giving up," I said. "We won't stop until you give us the information we need."

"So be it," Gary said, his voice deep, guttural.

Desmond looked at me. I gave a short nod.

He directed his magic at Gary's temples. It reminded me of an old black-and-white horror movie.

Streaks of white lightning shot from Desmond's fingertips to Gary's temples.

Gary shouted so loud I flinched. His entire body jerked like he was being electrocuted—which he was. Only magically.

Desmond drew his magic back and asked Gary again if he was ready to talk.

Again Gary refused.

And again Desmond blasted him with his magical electrical charges.

And again.

And again.

I paced the cell as Desmond continued. I wasn't giving up. No way was I giving up. We'd make this bastard of a Vampire talk.

My phone rang and I drew it from its holster on my weapons belt. I looked to see that it was Angel. "Robert just called in," she said when I answered. "Vamp told him that something big is going on. That the future will be different.

Vampires aren't going to be subservient to paranorms any longer."

Gary screamed in the background. I rubbed my temples. "That's it?"

"A couple of other Vampires have said similar things. That there's been 'hush hush' talk, something quiet going on. No one knows details though," Angel said. "I didn't want to bother you with that because it means nothing."

The desire to scream with fury rose up in me in a swift rush. Nothing. We were getting *nowhere.*

"Thanks, Angel," I said. "I need to get back to work."

She clicked off and I reholstered my phone. I ground my teeth as I went up to Desmond. "This isn't doing any good." I took him aside and kept my voice low. "It's time to use water. I should have thought of this before. Not only does he have any sentient being's failings when it comes to water, but his animal form is a Doberman. His fear is going to be even more intense."

Desmond stood in front of Gary, held his hands up, and let a ball form in both palms. It was different from the energy he'd been using. This was malachite green, smooth, fluid—it was like looking at water rippling inside an enclosed lake.

The orb started out the size of a baseball, but gradually grew as big as a basketball and continued to float above his hands, turning, spinning.

We looked at Gary. His jaw tightened. Desmond released the ball.

It bounced in the air like something on top of the surface of a body of water. Buoyant. When it reached Gary it hovered in the air.

Gary stared at Desmond. The Vampire-Doppler looked haggard, worn down . . . but obviously not worn down enough.

With a flick of Desmond's fingers, the bubble bounced forward and encased Gary's head.

It looked as if his head were in a fishbowl with murky green water. I could see his eyes bulge with a wild look as Desmond kept the water bubble over his head. Gary thrashed in his seat, straining against his bonds.

I was torn between what seemed so horrible—torturing another being—and the desire to make Vampires hurt. Any Vampires. For what they were doing to Rodán. For what they did to me just months ago.

Vampires were nothing but parasites. Leeches. They had no purpose in this Otherworld than to feed on beings or to drain them of their blood and turn them into Vampires. They had no other purpose in life.

Just when I thought Gary was going to drown in Desmond's magic water bubble, Desmond flicked his fingers and the bubble drew away.

Gary was soaked and gasping for air. Harsh, deep breaths. He looked exhausted, as if he might snap. But he didn't say a word.

Desmond used his fingers to direct the bubble back to envelop Gary's head. Again the Vampire-Doppler's eyes bulged as he fought against his bonds. This time Desmond added flame and electricity. I thought the Vampire was going to pull loose from the leather restraints.

"We only have fifteen minutes!" I shouted when the bubble was removed. "Tell us *now*!"

I don't know if it was the dangerous white flash in my eyes or the water torture, but Gary finally let it all spill out.

Gary screamed. "No more. Please, no more."

"Then tell us where Volod is." I felt the first twinge of excitement tonight.

"At the Hotel Charone." He looked beyond Vampire-pale, his lips nearly white. He looked almost . . . dead. Not just undead, but dead.

"In the Financial District." My heart raced. "Where in the hotel?"

"The . . . Suite de Paris." Gary looked like each word was painful to push out. ". . . big ceremony. Volod invited important Vampires from around the country. It had to do with his most successful accomplishment."

I whirled and grabbed my phone from my weapons belt. "See what else you can get out of him, Desmond," I said as a PTF agent let me out of the cell.

First thing I did was call Colin as I ran up the stairs and out of the detention center into the Paranorm Center. "Meet me at the unbirthday party. I'll be there in less than a minute."

After Colin agreed, I dialed Angel and gave her the information.

When I burst out into the night above the Paranorm Center, Colin was waiting for me. "Hotel Charone," I told him.

He grabbed my hand and in the next second we were standing a short distance from the hotel. No other Trackers could possibly be here yet.

"We don't have time to wait for the others." I looked at my phone. "Seven minutes." Fear shot through me as I looked at Colin. "Can you transport us straight to the Suite de Paris?"

Colin shook his head, surprising me. "I can't transport someplace inside a location that I'm not familiar with."

"We would need you to find out which floor the suite is on and where the stairwell is," I said. "Better to just get us to the front door. *Now.*"

FOURTEEN

Colin used his Dragon charm spell to get by the doormen and to elicit information from the concierge. I had pulled a glamour and stood next to him. Jitters ran through me. I could hardly stand still.

Three minutes if they held to the twenty-four hours. We only had three minutes to get to Rodán, to save him from a fate that was truly worse than death.

As soon as the concierge gave the information to Colin, I went straight for the stairwell. Colin vanished behind a glamour and I knew he was following me even though I couldn't see him.

I ran up the stairs. Every flight felt like a lifetime. Fourth floor. Seventh floor. Ninth floor.

Tenth floor.

Instead of slamming the door open, I pushed it and slipped through it. Vampires have unreal hearing and I didn't want my element of surprise ruined.

Colin and I raced for the doors to the suite.

They were closed.

And two Vampires stood guard outside.

Paranorm Vampires. A Vampire-Shifter and a Vampire-Werewolf. I was afraid they would be able to see through my glamour—a lot of paranorms could in the past. Good thing my father and Desmond had worked with me on perfecting my glamour. The Vampire paranorms didn't move from their posts.

I checked my phone. Two minutes.

Sure that Colin would follow my lead—or had the same idea I did—I went up to the Vampire-Werewolf. I saw his nose wrinkle and he looked around right before I grabbed his head.

I jerked his head down and my knee up at the same time so that my knee broke his nose. He started to make a sound but I was already using the momentum to flip him to the side, his head firmly in my palms.

As he went to the right, I twisted his head to the left and snapped his neck.

It would have killed a normal Werewolf. Not a Vampire-Werewolf.

He growled and stumbled to his feet as he grabbed his own head and twisted it back the way it should be.

My hand went for a wooden stake on my weapons belt.

To the side I saw Colin grappling with the Vampire-Shifter, who was morphing from one animal shape to another. Colin couldn't be seen, still behind his glamour, and the Vampire-Shifter looked like he was losing the fight.

I raised the stake and drove it toward the Vampire-Werewolf's heart. He couldn't see me but he must have sensed me there because he knocked my hand away.

The stake flew out of my hand and landed several feet away.

I dropped and rolled on the carpet, away from the Vampire-Werewolf. He was stumbling, trying to keep his balance. Blood no longer flowed from his broken nose. It had already healed.

Less than a minute. I didn't know the exact time but we had been fighting for at least ninety seconds.

I drew the mini crossbow with a stake made of silver and aimed it for the Vampire-Werewolf's heart.

The moment the stake pierced his chest, the Vampire-Werewolf collapsed.

I turned toward Colin and saw him finishing off the Vampire-Shifter with a swing of his sword. The Vampire-Shifter's head rolled across the carpet.

No time to wait for Colin. I jerked open the door to the suite.

Rodán was at the front of the room bound, and by the look in his eyes, he was drugged.

Volod was beside him. I had just enough time to see Volod slide his fangs into the vein at Rodán's throat.

"Rodán!" I screamed from behind a group of fifty or so Vampires who were all watching Volod.

My glamour dropped.

Volod jerked his head up. His eyes met mine. Blood coated his lips and fangs.

Rodán's blood.

Nausea gripped me, the desire to throw up taking me off guard.

"Get the Drow bitch," Volod snarled as he pressed Rodán's listless body to him. "But bring her to me—alive."

Heat roared through my body. I'd just declared myself in a room full of Vampires. Who now had their gazes fixed on me.

Not only did I sense the Vampires, but I sensed more paranorms who had been turned.

I didn't have time to look at Colin. The Vampires closest were almost on me before I could draw my daggers.

Two Vampires lunged for me.

Fire blasted them as an elephant-size Dragon appeared beside me. Orange-yellow scales glittered gold on its huge body, on the ridges along its back, and down its long, spiked tail.

The Vampires burst into flames as Colin fried them. Smoke filled the room, making it hard to breathe.

Fire wouldn't kill the Vampires, but it would slow them down before they regenerated.

In the time Colin had given me, I drew both of my Dragon-clawed daggers. I had to get to Rodán. Somehow I had to stop the process before Volod turned him.

So many Vampires were coming at us and so much smoke filled the room that I couldn't see Volod and Rodán anymore. Couldn't see a way toward them.

Colin roared and the whole room shook with his bellow. He stomped on furniture and swung his great spiked tail within the confines of the suite.

A half-charred Vampire burst out of Colin's flames and reached for me. I rammed one of my daggers through his chest and twisted, grinding out his heart.

I gave a Drow warrior cry as I raised my other dagger and sliced through a Vampire's neck. Her head tumbled to the floor as her body dropped.

"Can you see Rodán?" I shouted to Colin.

The big Dragon reared up to look over the crowd of Vampires and through the smoke. Then the Dragon dropped back down and shook its huge head.

My heart thudded as I raised my daggers to fight off three more Vampires.

The scream of a leopard twisted in my head right before it bounded out of the crowd. The huge cat knocked aside the Vampires closest to me.

A Shifter-Vampire.

I took a step back as the leopard crouched, ready to pounce.

Then more Vampire paranorms crept through the crowd and circled us. Dopplers, Shifters, Werewolves. All paranorms, but all Vampires, too.

Blood rushed in my head. Adrenaline spiked inside me.

Vampire paranorms stood around us and filled the distance between Colin and me and the door.

Surrounded.

Shouts came from behind me and throughout the room. I swung my gaze in a quick sweep. Some relief shot through me as I saw that several New York City Night Trackers had arrived.

Ice crept forward as a white jaguar, Robert beside him in cougar form. Max in Werewolf form gave a low growl as he came up from the opposite side. Joshua and Angel approached in human form.

A huge tiger Shifter rushed me. The white jaguar slammed into him. Both rolled to the side, snarling and fighting.

Angel snapped her whip, a cracking sound echoing throughout the room. A rottweiler roared and leapt toward her. She wrapped her whip around the big dog's body and jerked. With incredible strength, she yanked the rottweiler hard enough that it flipped end over end and came to a thud at her feet, entangled in her whip. She drew a wooden stake from her weapons belt and drove it home through the Vampire-Shifter's heart.

Joshua raised his flail and swung it at the lion Vampire-Shifter. The lion roared and batted the spiked ball away.

Max in Werewolf form went for the throat of a Vampire-Werewolf. The Vampire-Werewolf twisted out of the way and snapped at Max's neck. Max yelped as the Vampire-Werewolf ripped away a chunk of flesh.

A Vampire-Doppler, a raven, flew at my head. Before it reached me, Desmond shot a burst of his magic at the bird. Feathers floated down as the bird shrieked and tried to get out of the ball of light.

What was Volod doing? Where were he and Rodán?

Another Werewolf leapt toward me and I raised my dagger. Colin, in human form, swung his fist and hit the Werewolf in the muzzle. Bone snapped, the crack loud, and the Werewolf flew across the room.

A shadow rose up in front of me and formed into human shape. A Shadow Shifter. I'd never seen him coming. He grabbed me around the neck with one hand, holding me so close to him that I couldn't use my daggers.

I head-butted him.

Lights sparked behind my eyes but I caught the Vampire-Shadow Shifter enough off guard that I was able to throw him off me.

I whirled to see that my team was being circled by Vampire paranorms.

They were everywhere. Too many of them.

I clenched my Dragon-clawed daggers as Max, Angel, Joshua, Ice, Colin, and I stood against one another in the circle of Vampire paranorms.

My heart thudded, my mind spinning, as I looked for a way out.

A thud from the direction of the suite's doors. From the corner of my eye I saw Desmond walk in. "Get out," I shouted. "Desmond, get away."

He ignored me. Extended his hand. Green light flowed from his hand to the center of the circle. The light enveloped me and my team. Tingles skittered along my skin.

Colin put his hands on my shoulders.

Everything went dark.

A blink and then we were all in the center of my living room in my apartment.

"What?" I spun to face Colin. Desmond was just behind him. "What are we doing here?" I looked from one of them to the other. "Where are Volod and Rodán?" My whole body trembled as I spoke, frantic with fear.

Desmond shook his head. "It's too late, Nyx."

I went totally still. It felt like ice was slowly creeping over my body, making its way from the top of my head all the way down to my feet.

"No." I shook my head. "*No.* Take us back, *now.*"

"I'm sorry," Desmond said.

The world dimmed as it hit me.

My body started shaking violently.

Control of my elements slipped through my grasp.

Lightning cracked outside my apartment window. Wind shrieked. The windows shattered. Rain stormed through the window and into the room.

Furniture snapped. More glass shattered.

Splintered wood and glass shards began to spin within the room around us, as if we were in the middle of a hurricane. A piece of glass scratched my arm, but I hardly felt the pain.

Shouts over the storm, yet I barely registered them.

The room shook and trembled as my earth element rocked the apartment building. A cushion burst into flame and I was vaguely aware of Desmond putting it out with his magic.

Water soaked everything. My wet hair was pasted to my face and rain rolled down my face and body. The wind blasted me so hard it almost knocked me to the floor.

The whole room shook and shook and shook and flames burst throughout, so fast Desmond could barely keep up.

"Nyx!"

My name being called.

"Stop! You're going to kill us!"

Words that made no sense to me.

The next thing I knew I was in Colin's arms. We were on the floor and he held me, rocking me.

I trembled and shook and the room trembled along with me. Wind and rain whipped my and Colin's long hair around our faces, the water chillingly cold.

"Nyx." He spoke close to my ear, and somehow I heard his even tone. "Calm down, honey. Calm down. You need to get control over your magic and you need to do that now."

"Rodán." I said his name in a moan. The rain wetting my face made up for the tears I would never be able to cry.

Colin continued to rock me. "You can control it. You can do it."

Realization finally cracked through my pain. My magic was so strong, so powerful, that I struggled to reel the elements back in.

"There you go," Colin said. "You're doing it."

I tried to concentrate not on Rodán but instead on my elements. It was like hiccuping. I'd reel in my magic then lose a little when I saw Rodán's face in my mind. Reel it in, then another hiccup as I saw him again.

"Good job." I felt Colin's lips against my wet head.

It was over. The storm of my emotions was over—outside me. Inside they still raged.

"Bloody hell," Joshua said.

"Shit. What was that about, Nyx?" Ice stood above me and glared down, his arms folded across his chest.

Yet I thought I saw compassion in his ice-blue gaze.

Desmond just watched me.

I didn't care what any of the Trackers thought.

I pushed my wet hair from my face as I looked up at Desmond. There had to be a way to get to Rodán. It couldn't be too late. It just couldn't. "Help me find him," I said in a hoarse whisper.

The Sorcerer shook his head. "I'm sorry, but it's been done. Rodán is one of them now."

"No!" I scrambled to my feet and Colin followed me. I felt the room shudder a little as I almost lost control of my elements again. "I won't give up on him. *I won't.*"

Colin wrapped his arms around me from behind. I didn't know if he was trying to comfort me or subdue me.

"Rodán was probably pretending to go along with it," I said as I looked up at him. "He's not one of them. He'll *never* be one of them."

"You've gone too long without sleep." Colin drew me in close. "We'll sort things out after you get some rest."

I shook my head. "No. Are you serious. I don't need sleep. How can I sleep now?"

Colin rubbed his hands up and down my wet arms, but his warm palms did nothing to chase away the chill that iced my body.

I felt so helpless. So hopeless.

Nothing would ever be right again.

FIFTEEN

The spring night was cold but Volod didn't feel the chill as he, Monique, Elizabeth, and six of his Vampire paranorms stood in the Trinity Churchyard Cemetery.

Anger burned beneath his skin at the thought that somehow the Drow bitch had found him.

A sense of satisfaction cooled him again. Whatever the case, she'd been too late.

The waxing moon peeked in and out of thick clouds moving slowly across the dark sky. A breeze tugged at his long hair and at the black coat he wore over his black suit. As far as he was concerned, this was a special occasion.

Volod pushed away thoughts of his plans almost being wrecked—for now. He would deal with that problem soon enough.

In the three-century-old cemetery, many nearby headstones were badly eroded, some too worn to see the names. The remains of the humans would be no more than dust. Humans had not been buried here for over a century.

But Vampires were actively buried here. Only no human or paranorm was aware of that fact.

Volod glanced at Monique and Elizabeth, who stood beside him. Despite the fact they were on either side of him, he could feel the tension between the two, so much so that he found it amusing, even arousing.

Elizabeth had not taken well to Volod bringing Monique into his clan, much less the fact that she had shared his bed from the time he had turned her. That Elizabeth was not pleased was certainly an understatement.

Volod focused on the grave and allowed himself to feel some measure of grim satisfaction that this part of his plan had come to fulfillment.

However, capturing Rodán had been harder than he had anticipated. Even with all his precautions and preparation, he had underestimated the Elvin Proctor.

Volod stared at Rodán's catafalque as two of the Vampire paranorms shoveled freshly dug dirt on top of the modest coffin.

"Will it be any different for him as to when he shall rise?" Monique asked as she glanced from the coffin to Volod. "He is unlike others of our kind."

Monique had warned him that Rodán was ancient and powerful. Volod just hadn't grasped how ancient and how powerful she'd meant. Monique had neglected to mention that to her *ancient* was over a thousand years. To Vampires, it meant three centuries or so.

Volod was ancient. Yet a child compared to Rodán.

That thought had him grinding his teeth. But he had proven who was smarter, who had control. And now he was Rodán's Master.

"No, it will not make a difference," Volod said as he studied her. "Now he is like everyone else."

Monique said nothing and returned her gaze to the coffin that had almost disappeared beneath the dirt being shoveled onto it.

A feeling of jealousy bit at his consciousness, an emotion that surprised him. The level of respect Monique clearly had for Rodán, and the fact that Monique and Rodán had been lovers at one time, made Volod almost furious enough to eliminate Rodán when he rose and be done with him.

Almost.

He had let Monique bite and take Rodán's blood last night, but Volod had bitten him tonight. It would allow him to have a mental bond and the control he needed over the soon-to-be Vampire.

Much to his surprise, Volod still felt a bit queasy from ingesting Rodán's blood. Taking the blood of the human he'd had waiting had barely helped him recover. He had since directed one of his Vampires to discard her drained, lifeless body.

With every shovelful of dirt that landed on the simple coffin, satisfaction replaced his unrest. He wanted to watch until the coffin was fully buried—as if to reassure himself that, indeed, Rodán was dead.

And that he would become one of the undead.

When the coffin was completely covered with dirt, Volod raised his hand. A burst of his power spread over the grave in a hot red shimmer, sealing it and eliminating any traces of freshly dug dirt. It would look like it had been here for a century rather than having been dug that very night.

"This will hurt the Drow bitch more than anything you could have done." Satisfaction edged Elizabeth's tone before her voice turned bitter again. "It does not make up for Nyx having murdered my family, but it will do for now." She glanced at Volod. "You promised I could kill her."

Volod said nothing. It was true, at one time he had promised to give the Drow female to Elizabeth, but he had bigger plans for Nyx now. One day he would be ready to dispose of her, but not until he turned her, used her as he was using the other paranorms, then made her wish she was dead.

"Hers shall be a painful, excruciating death." Malice filled every word as Elizabeth continued. "I may cut off each of her body parts one by one and toss them into a vat of boiling oil."

"You sound like one of the Dark Witches." Monique gave a shudder from the other side of Volod. "So barbaric."

"Wait to see what I will do to you." Elizabeth's green eyes flashed an ominous red in the darkness. Monique ignored it and gave Elizabeth a look of bored tolerance.

He could almost hear Monique saying, *Whatever.* The equivalent of "fuck you."

Volod imagined a fight between these two. What male, Vampire, paranorm, or human, didn't savor that image? No special powers, just a good catfight. Maybe when things settled down he would arrange such a playtime. The winner got vengeance over the loser . . . and then got him for the night.

Elizabeth flashed her fangs and hissed. Monique ignored her, which infuriated Elizabeth even more.

Volod turned away. His gaze met Reese's, then Daniel's. "Guard this site until I return on the tenth day."

"Yes, Volod," they each said as they moved toward the grave to stand vigil.

The paranorms he'd turned had taken so well to being Vampires. He was beyond pleased.

Volod walked from behind the church and out of the graveyard to the street, where his limo waited.

A headlight cut through the darkness. The light illuminated the faces of the female Vampire and the Vampire-Elf, their beauty almost breathtaking.

Once the chauffeur opened the back door and they entered, Elizabeth and Monique sat on opposite sides of the bench seat in front of him.

Elizabeth reached into the limousine's small refrigerator then poured him a blood cocktail. She handed it to him, a seductive look on her beautiful features. She likely wanted to entice him to her bed, but he had no interest as he had in the past. As a Vampire paranorm, Monique could do the most tantalizing things to him.

However, he thought as he looked from one beautiful Vampire to the next, both of them in his bed at the same time would be entertaining. If they didn't kill each other first. Maybe he could get this and the catfight in the same night. There would be a time for all of this.

"I must feed." Monique looked out the window and back to Volod and pressed her palm to her chest. Like the other Vampire paranorms, she required paranorm blood. Human blood and synthetic blood just weren't the same. That much he knew. It was what this rebellion was about. "We are ready to go after our next targets."

Monique had expressed to him that she no longer thought

of herself as a paranorm. She lived for blood and turning paranorms to join what would eventually be a part of his Vampire paranorm army. An army that was slowly growing.

Volod studied Monique. "Are you prepared to deal with all five of the Paranorm Council members?"

"Yes, Volod." Monique gave a deep nod, lowering her eyes. It pleased him when she showed her subservience to him. "All targets have been identified and our team is ready to go after them within the next hour."

Volod reclined in his seat, vaguely noticing the flash of lights as the limo drove them to their destination. "Remember, I do not want any left alive but Council Chief Leticia."

Maybe three in bed he thought. Two paranorms and Elizabeth. Bedtime with paranorms could become rather addictive.

Monique nodded again, but killing the council was not sitting well with her. It was a lesson she had to learn. Lives must be taken when necessary. Eliminating the Paranorm Council was necessary.

"I wish to see their bodies." Volod let ice slide into his tone as Monique flinched. "I want to make sure none but Leticia survive tonight."

"Yes, Volod," she said.

Elizabeth smirked. "If she does not have what it takes to eliminate them, I shall."

Monique cut her gaze to Elizabeth. "They would be certain to destroy you. You are no match for any member of the Paranorm Council."

Fire flashed in Elizabeth's eyes. "If you are not careful you will not survive this night."

"Should I fear you?" Monique raised an eyebrow. "I think not."

Elizabeth snarled and raised her hands to claw at Monique, and Volod felt Monique's magic building within her. In no way could Elizabeth save herself if Monique attacked.

It seemed that Monique's power grew by the day, a thought that could have been concerning if he did not have such a perfect hold on her.

"Enough." Volod snarled the word. "You will respect each other. I will not have you fighting."

Both Monique and Elizabeth lowered their heads.

"I am sorry," Monique said.

Elizabeth avoided looking at Monique and said nothing.

Volod studied them a moment more. He focused on Monique. "Kurt and Gary—do you have further news of them?"

Monique nodded. "Just before tonight's celebration, Katy—I mean Katherine—visioned that Kurt is dead. Gary was taken by Nyx and her team of Trackers."

Fury flowed through him, hot and liquid. He reminded himself that the bitch would pay. She was paying the price already, and the cost had been something more than dear to her.

"Gary must have talked," Volod said in a growl. "Fools. They should have killed those two tramps the first night. I should have killed them for disobeying me. Now they were captured and they obviously talked." Volod worked to keep his composure. "But neither of them should have known about tonight."

"Someone must have told him." Elizabeth looked from Volod to Monique before looking back at Volod. "Then the imbecile talked." Elizabeth raised her chin. "If he hasn't already, he will ruin the advantage you have over the Trackers not knowing you are back and what you have planned."

"I am aware of that, Elizabeth." Volod gave the female Vamp a chilling stare that caused her to shrink back in her seat. "I do not require you spelling out what has likely happened."

Monique ignored Elizabeth. "Only two others knew in addition to the three of us. If not Elizabeth," Monique said without looking at the female Vampire who gave a low growl in her throat, "then it would be either Elliot or Reese. I cannot see Reese sharing that information. Elliot was friends with Kurt and Gary. He is probably the one who let them have the information."

"He will be dealt with immediately," Volod said as he thought of the exact way he would handle that.

Monique's tone was even, respectful. "I do not think we need be overly concerned with him."

"I will decide whether or not I need be concerned." The reprimand in his voice seemed to startle Monique, but he could not let her get away with making determinations for him any more than he could allow Elizabeth to.

Monique snapped her mouth shut, and he saw a flash of something in her eyes before she lowered her head. "Yes, Volod."

Volod shifted on his seat and crossed his legs. "Does the Witch think she can learn more?"

Monique nodded. "Katherine will scry again tonight and let me know the results."

Volod turned his gaze to the window again and watched the limo pull up to the brownstone he had declared as a meeting point should anything go wrong at the hotel.

Satisfaction rolled through him as he thought of Rodán lying in his coffin and of the pain that the bitch would be going through at this very moment.

Elizabeth and Monique followed Volod into the brownstone, which he'd purchased years ago. He'd had it gutted and remodeled so that the first level was one huge meeting room. The bedroom, kitchen, and bathroom that had previously been on that level were unnecessary for Vampires.

The basement level had also been remodeled. It served as their sleeping quarters with simple guest coffins lined side by side. Only Volod's coffin was apart from the others, as befit his position as their Master Vampire. The two floors upstairs served to keep prisoners as well as their human snacks.

Volod walked into the entryway and heard the buzz of conversation coming from the great room. Elizabeth helped him take off his coat and hung it on the coatrack. He didn't need the coat for warmth, but its style fit the occasion.

When he entered the great room silence fell. His shoes sank into the carpet as he walked the length of it to the fireplace. He'd kept it more to serve as a focal point for the room than for any warmth it provided.

Monique and Elizabeth followed him through the crowd of thirty-plus Vampires who had been waiting for him. When he reached the fireplace, Monique and Elizabeth stood off to one side. As close to him as he would allow yet as far away from each other as possible.

Volod ground his teeth as he looked through the crowd. When he spotted Elliot, he spoke to the Vampire-Werewolf. "Come here."

Elliot looked surprised but strode forward. The Vampire paranorm was large, what humans called brawny.

"You told Kurt and Gary about our plans for tonight's meeting." Volod managed to keep his tone even.

Elliot's expression changed from casual interest to fear. "Why do you say that, sir?"

"Why? Why do I ask you?" Volod kept his gaze fixed on the pathetic Vampire paranorm. "Do not lie to me and do not respond with questions. I need the truth. Now. You told them, did you not?"

Elliot cleared his throat. The beat of his undead heart increased. "I did. I'm sorry. I just wanted to make sure they were back in time to make it to the celebration. It won't happen again. I'm truly sorry."

"I will not tolerate this. Were you told you were not to say a word?

Elliot's throat worked as he spoke. "Yes, I was."

Volod heard his own words come out in a deadly chill. "Yet you talked."

"It will not happen again." Elliot's eyes had a pleading look.

Volod put power into his voice as he said, "No, it will not happen again."

The Vampire-Werewolf trembled.

Volod took a step toward Reese who was standing next to Elliot. In one quick move he drew Reese's sword and swiped it at Elliot.

The blade met Elliot's neck then sliced cleanly through. The head thumped as it dropped, followed by another thump when the body fell. Blood barely showed in the deep burgundy shade of the carpet.

"No, Elliot, it certainly will not happen again." Volod raised his gaze to meet everyone's in the room. "Leave and find your supper. The time is ours."

SIXTEEN

"Bethany, be at my home office within thirty minutes for an emergency meeting."

With his keen hearing, Volod heard the Siren answer on the other end of the connection.

The Fae representative, a Siren from the Bermuda Triangle, said, "Why? What's happened, Leticia? Why can't we meet in council chambers?"

"They have been compromised."

"Why do we need to meet so early in the morning?" Bethany asked in a sleepy voice. "It's only two AM."

"Something has happened. I cannot talk about it over the phone. It is urgent that all of you arrive as soon as possible. There are decisions we have to make now. Lives are at stake."

"What's the code word, Leticia?" Bethany sounded a little more awake.

"Solstice. I'll be on a conference call with the other council chiefs until you arrive. Now hurry."

"Good to know it's really you." Before she hung up, Bethany added, "I'll be there within thirty."

Volod watched as Janet, the female Vampire-Metamorph, hung up the phone and turned toward him, shifting out of Chief Counsel Leticia's form. "It is done, sir."

"Very good." Volod glanced at the real council chief, who sat on a nearby chair. "I thought Trackers and the Paranorm Council would be more challenging. Obviously I was wrong."

Although she was cuffed and gagged, in her gray eyes

Leticia amazingly had the look of someone who believed herself to be far superior to him. Special handcuffs, designed to impede paranorm powers and magic, would soon be on each of the council members, not just Leticia.

Volod studied the chief, keeping emotion from his features. He would wipe that haughty look off Leticia's face and replace it with one of fear. It was something he loved to see in his victim's eyes.

She would serve him. Earlier he had chosen to bite her himself to ensure total control over her once she was turned.

Leticia, a Doppler lioness, tilted her chin at a regal angle, arrogance in her demeanor. Her silver hair was drawn back in a knot at the base of her neck, but disarrayed, and her once elegant clothing was torn.

Volod had determined that the council members were more valuable to him as Vampire paranorms rather than dead. Turn and use them as he pleased. He motioned to a pair of his Vampire paranorms. "Take the council chief into her office."

Leticia looked at Volod with contempt before one of the members of his dream team lifted her from the chair and carried her through the doorway of the large Manhattan condo.

The Metamorph shifted once again into a perfect double of Leticia. Volod's team of Vampire paranorms moved through the doorway Leticia had been taken through. The next council member escorted through that doorway would be taken.

Volod stepped back into the shadows.

First to arrive was Eric, five minutes earlier than expected. "Leticia" met him at the door. "Come to my office," she said by way of greeting.

"What is this meeting about?" Eric was saying as she guided him through the doorway.

The moment the Werewolf was on the other side of the doorway, two Vampire paranorms grabbed him.

Shock followed by anger shot across the Werewolf's features, and he snarled and fought against the Vampires' holds.

With strength that Volod found impressive, Eric threw one of the Vampire paranorms across the room.

The Vamp hit the wall with a loud thud. The crash of glass followed as he dropped onto a small table that had held several glass objects.

Volod frowned. If they weren't careful, the next council members to arrive would hear the noise.

Eric snarled and fought but was taken down to the carpeting and restrained with silver-lined cuffs along with rope that had silver woven through it. He was gagged and dragged into the room where Leticia was being kept.

Volod gave a smile of satisfaction. Then he ordered his dream team and the Metamorph to take their places again.

Reginald opened the door and walked into the condo without knocking. Fortunately, the Metamorph was ready to greet him as Leticia.

When the elderly Shifter walked through the doorway that led to her office, he glanced at the mess across the room. Before he had a chance to digest what he saw, Volod's team attacked.

The Shifter fought surprisingly well, and Volod wondered at how much he had underestimated Reginald. He growled as he transformed into a tiger followed by a wolf, then a bear, each time slipping the grasp of the Vampire paranorms who were trying to restrain him.

Finally another Vamp was able to inject a serum made with silver into the Shifter's arm. Immediately Reginald dropped. He transformed back into his human form before he hit the floor.

The Shifter was removed from the room and taken to the office where the Werewolf and Leticia waited.

Moments later Volod watched as Bethany and Caolan entered the condo together. The Siren and the Light Elf paused when they crossed the threshold.

The Metamorph greeted them urgently. "We have little time," she said. "Come."

"Something is not right." Caolan reached for his sword,

ready to draw it. "I scent . . ." He looked puzzled. "I do not know."

"Yes, something is off." Bethany put her hand on a silver dagger at her side. "We need to leave."

"Everything is fine, do not be absurd." Janet glanced at where Volod was hidden and he scowled even though none of them could see him. Stupid bitch shouldn't have looked in his direction. She could give him away. "Hurry now," the Metamorph was saying.

"No, something is wrong," Bethany repeated. "I can smell Vam . . ."

A side door burst open. The Vampire paranorms who had been waiting outside rushed in to take care of the last of the council members.

Volod thought about ending the fight as Caolan unsheathed his sword and swung it at one of the charging Vampires. The lifeless head hit the floor and rolled. Bethany drove her sword through the chest of a second, who fell immediately.

Volod decided to simply watch. The two council members were no match for the six other Vampire paranorms who surrounded them. Katherine, the powerful witch from Los Angeles, held out her hand, and light sparked from her fingertips.

Energy suddenly seemed to leave Caolan and Bethany. They moved, but in slow motion. Jorge, the Vampire-Werewolf from San Diego, aimed a gun at Caolan that looked like a toy and pulled the trigger. A dart filled with potion made from a Basilisk eye pierced his shoulder.

Janet pointed the end of a fire extinguisher at Bethany and fired a stream of freshwater at her, drenching the Siren. Bethany cried out as if in pain. Sirens came from the saltwater sea—freshwater created a severe burning sensation on Siren skin and slowed them down.

Seth, a Vampire-Shifter, burst out laughing. "That was easy. Classic council members. They can tell Trackers how to fight, but they can't fight their way out of a wet paper bag."

Volod smiled to himself. This went exceptionally well.

Jorge nodded. "Cuff them and follow me. You council members might like to see your leader—the one you thought called this little meeting."

As the council members were led into Leticia's office, Volod strode in behind them. "Excellent," he said, letting his pleasure emerge in his tone. "The Paranorm Council is now mine."

Volod narrowed his eyes as he continued. "The very council responsible for the deaths of so many of my own. Death would be too good for each one of you." Satisfaction filled him as if he were feeding on a sweet young female. "You hate the thought of becoming one of us, don't you? But you will like it when it happens."

Bethany looked panicked and shook her head.

"Monique, choose four Vampire paranorms, and you may all have a bite to eat on me. The four remaining council members are yours for your dining pleasure." Volod rested his gaze on the council members. "I do not need the upset stomach their blood would give me. Especially when I have all of you here to do it for me."

Volod thought about the rush he'd had earlier when he'd bitten Leticia. How deliciously satisfying it had been feeding on a human afterward to clear the queasiness in his stomach.

Now he would sit back and enjoy the scene. He loved watching the fear on subjects' faces just before their necks were ravaged and their blood drained. That this was the Paranorm Council made tonight extra special.

The council . . . the powerful group that, along with the Trackers, had virtually destroyed him. And now he would see them added to the ranks serving him.

Not to mention, this would be just one more bit of anguish for the Drow bitch. He wanted Nyx to suffer, and that day would come.

Her leader, Rodán, taken, and now the council. He smiled, thinking of how Nyx must feel with the net slowly surrounding her and tightening. The thought gave him almost as much of a high as watching events here.

"I want you to remove the gags. Especially the gray-haired hag." Volod pointed to Leticia. "I want to hear the pleading cries before the meal is devoured."

Seth and Janet began removing the gags.

Volod gestured to Bethany and Caolan. "What is wrong with these two? They look drugged."

Katherine looked from the council members to him. "I shot a tranquilizer spell at them. It slows every aspect of the mind, including motor skills."

Volod scowled. "I prefer them conscious. I like to see the shocked look on their faces when they are bitten." He walked up to Bethany and sniffed the air. "I want to smell their fear, watch their futile struggle."

As he paced in front of the council members, looking them over one by one, he added, "I want the spell removed so that the two are bitten with clear heads."

"Yes, Volod," the Witch said.

Volod smiled at Leticia, his tongue taking a quick swipe of his lips as her gag was removed. "Just one more bite and you are mine."

"We shall never serve you," Leticia said as she glanced at her captured council members.

Volod smiled, his words cold, calculating. "I will break you soon enough."

He saw a hint of fear flicker in Leticia's gray eyes. *Finally,* he thought. He clenched his teeth and slowly paced the width of the office as his gaze moved over the other four council members. "Yes," he said more to himself than them. "It will be very useful keeping you alive.

"However"—Volod turned to Reginald—"perhaps I should consider eliminating you." The sour-faced elderly Shifter was angry and disagreeable. "You have lived far beyond the time you should have."

Reginald's face screwed up into a mass of tight wrinkles. "You may as well. I will not serve you."

Volod brushed aside the Shifter's words with a wave. "I will not waste my time with any further conversation."

His gaze moved to the Werewolf, Eric. "You were far easier to take down than I expected." Amusement flickered through Volod at the look of fury that met him. Eric's strength and agility had made him difficult to catch at first, but he had been subdued in a relatively short amount of time.

Volod looked over at Caolan, one of the Light Elves. "You are quite a prize, are you not?"

Life was back in Caolan's eyes. Volod wondered if it was fear he saw, too. If not for the bit of the Basilisk serum, the Light Elf would have persevered, but in the end, he too was Volod's.

It was not easy to put fear into these council members, yet now he felt the emotion in the room.

"One thing puzzles me." Volod went up to the extraordinarily beautiful blond Siren. "What do they call you again? What kind of a paranorm?"

"She is a water Fae, Volod." Monique answered for the silent Siren.

Water Fae. Volod stopped pacing as he sensed something different about her that reminded him of two other Fae creatures. They had been Undines, not susceptible to a Vampire's bite. Both had been bitten twice, and drained the second night. Neither had risen when it was time to, leaving them dead, not undead.

Could that have been why they had not turned? Because they were water Fae? If it was so, he would simply eliminate the water Fae rather than take the time for them to be bitten a second time then buried.

"Ah yes, a water Fae. Two others who looked much like you were bitten recently, and they seemed to be immune to a Vampire's bite. I have no use for a paranorm who can't be turned.

"You shall be a test." Volod gave a decisive nod. "If you do not rise, then I will know your kind are not worth dealing with."

Bethany scowled but lost none of her beauty. "To die would be a far better fate than to serve you."

Volod smiled again, letting the chill of his thoughts come out in his words. "You would go well with the decor in my bedroom. Even if you do not turn, it is very tempting to chain you to my bed for my pleasure. I just may do that."

The Siren's cheeks turned slightly green.

She began to sing.

For a moment Volod was too surprised to react. Her song was magical, magnificent.

He felt dazed as he watched Monique stride across the room. Monique slapped Bethany hard enough that the sound echoed throughout the room. Abruptly she stopped singing.

As he came back to his senses, Volod shook his head. Bethany had attempted to use her Siren's song against him.

Monique reached for a stack of papers on Leticia's desk and removed the large clamp. "Jorge, hold this Siren for me," she said calmly.

Jorge grabbed the Siren from behind, wrapping his arm around Bethany's throat.

Monique raised the clamp. "Let's see her tongue."

The Siren clenched her lips tight.

Jorge's forearm dug into the Siren's throat and her mouth came open, her tongue out.

Monique pressed the large clamp open, fit it over Bethany's tongue, then released it. The Siren groaned.

"That will shut you up," Monique said.

The pale green that had blossomed beneath her skin faded.

"Enough of all of this talk," Volod said. "Take them down, Monique."

Monique's eyes sparkled with excitement. Volod knew she had loved the faux-Vampire experience even before she was turned. She had shared with him that the real thing took it to ecstasy beyond her dreams.

For her it was all still something sexual, just as it had been before she was turned. She had told Volod that there was nothing better than to bite, then finish the night off with him.

Volod watched as Monique caught Elizabeth's eye. A

look of hatred from Elizabeth told Volod that she was boiling from the fact he had not chosen her to assist him tonight.

Monique looked away to the other Vampires. "Janet," she said, "take the big, and now not so bad, Werewolf."

Monique smiled as she stroked Bethany's arm. "I will take Miss Pretty here. The Siren."

Volod felt almost intoxicated as he watched Monique take complete charge. He especially loved it when she took control over Elizabeth.

"Elizabeth, take the shriveled one there." Monique pointed to Reginald, not even looking Elizabeth's way.

Elizabeth looked disgusted. "I don't need to be sick for days from biting a paranorm. There is no human to take after sucking on this wrinkled-up prune. Pick someone else, I won't do it."

"Katherine, the old guy is yours," Monique instructed without hesitation. It was as if she had purposefully ordered Elizabeth to bite Reginald, knowing that the Vampire would refuse.

Volod saw some fear in the council but was amazed at how they accepted their fate. They were unlike most humans, who screamed like frightened little six-year-olds when they realized what was happening. And observing the council, which had almost destroyed him, was more satisfying to him than biting ten humans. "Dinner is served," Volod said.

The paranorm Vampires stepped forward. Katherine walked up to Reginald. With her amazing strength, she gripped the old Shifter's upper arms with her hands. She showed her fangs a second before she buried them into his neck.

His only response was to close his eyes. His body twitched.

Janet would not have been much of a match for Eric, Volod thought, had it not been for the restraint system. The belts went around his waist and through his crotch to hold his wrists taut behind his back. They even held his ankles and elbows in place.

Janet grabbed a chair in front of the desk and pulled it up

to the tall Werewolf. Eric seemed to know that struggle was futile and only would make it all the more enjoyable for Volod. He obviously had resolved to not show emotion.

The Metamorph stood on the chair, looked into Eric's eyes, and then slid her fangs deep into his neck. There was no movement from Eric. He stood there as if nothing was happening.

Impressive, thought Volod. The strength of such a Paranorm would serve the cause well once he was turned.

Just as Eric was taken, Katherine was all over Caolan's neck, moving him back and forth like a lion trying to shake the life out of its next meal. Like Reginald, Caolan closed his eyes as he accepted his fate. Katherine continued ravaging him.

Monique tapped Katherine on the shoulder. "I'm glad you are enjoying the feast, but I think that's enough, Katherine. Leave a little flesh on him."

Katherine swiped her tongue over the bite marks, stopping the flow of blood, before she stepped back.

Volod smiled as he studied the Siren, who was watching in horror as her fellow council members were bitten. By the way her whole body trembled, he could tell that the blood dripping from the slumping paranorms and from the Vampires' mouths was obviously too much for her.

Monique turned toward the Siren and moved forward. Volod knew that given a choice, Monique preferred to bite males, but she would still relish this little pretty. Volod loved watching her take another, especially a female, and Monique knew that.

Bethany was cuffed from behind. She worked her tongue out of the clamp and spit it out. "You will regret this, you bitch," she screamed. "You were one of us. How can you do this? You were a leader."

Bethany backed up. Her cuffs dropped to the carpet with a soft thump. With terror on her face, the Siren bolted through the unguarded door.

"Stop her," Janet screamed.

Monique held out her hand. A half-inch-thick, twisted vinelike rope flew from her fingertips, extending through the door and around the corner.

A shriek came from Bethany, and Monique's face lit up. She looked like a little kid who'd just hooked the big one. She pulled quickly on the vine. Bethany stumbled backward into the room, the vine wrapped around her neck.

Staying in place, Monique jerked hard on the vine, spinning Bethany around. She continued to reel Bethany in until she was inches from her face.

"Thank you for doing that, Bethany," Monique said in a low, sensual voice. "I love, as Volod does, the futile struggle as he calls it, of such a prize. You made my night and his."

The eyes of the red-faced Siren looked like they were going to bulge out as the vine strangled her. There was no more struggle left within her. Suddenly the vine disappeared and the Siren was left gasping for breath.

Monique grabbed Bethany in what could have been mistaken for a lover's embrace. White fangs flashed before they were lost in the side of the Siren's neck. Bethany began to struggle hard, but she was no match for Monique, who continued to bite, her breathing as loud as if she were being pleasured in Volod's bed.

Monique finally pulled away from the Siren, who did not slump and quiet down like the others. The bite seemed to have little or no effect on her.

Monique looked to Janet. "Cuff her again. Use the full restraint system this time so there is no chance of escape. We will take her with us."

She turned to Volod. "I don't see much effect from the bite. You just might have a new adornment for your bedroom."

Volod nodded. "You know me well already." How he loved to watch the enthusiasm of Monique's attacks—no one he had ever known was a match for her.

"Have your team get them out of here, Monique," Volod said as he looked at her. "Then we will return to the brownstone. I want to see you in my suite."

She gave a slight bow of her head. "Of course."

"Elizabeth." He turned his gaze to the redheaded Vampire who stood just to his side. "Come with me."

He didn't wait for her, allowing her to walk in his wake. She would realize soon enough what her position with Volod had been reduced to. In the limo he chose not to talk with her. She did not break the silence.

While in the limo, Volod thought about how talented the Trackers were—yet stupid enough that he was able to take control of so many so easily. They hadn't seen any of this coming.

If he had their powers for his own, he could rule all.

His plan would gain him the same result, though. He *would* rule all—through the paranorms.

Unfortunately, the Trackers knew what he was up to now. The element of surprise was gone.

SEVENTEEN

As soon as they entered the brownstone, Elizabeth followed him upstairs. What an amazing twenty-six hours it had been, Volod thought. To capture and turn Rodán, and now to have taken control of the Paranorm Council.

It was time for a reward.

After he strode through a door into the bedroom of his suite and Elizabeth had closed the door behind them, he said to her, "Take off your clothing."

She paused and just looked at him. "Why?"

Volod narrowed his gaze and spoke with deadly calm. "You know better than to ask. Simply do as I have instructed."

Elizabeth seemed to make up her mind. Her demeanor changed and she slowly undressed as if teasing him with every movement. She let her hands slide over her body as she slipped out of her long emerald-green gown, which matched the color of her eyes.

By the way she met his gaze and touched her breasts ever so lightly, it was clear she was attempting to seduce him. When she finished undressing she started to walk toward where he stood near the door to the suite.

"Stand on the rug." He gestured toward the large oval rug at the foot of the massive bed. "And let down your hair."

Elizabeth obeyed, reaching up and pulling out the pin that held the curls in place. Her long red hair tumbled over her shoulders down to the small of her back. He felt an ache of need as he studied the stunning, naked female.

When a knock sounded at the door, Elizabeth looked casually in that direction, a smirk on her face. Likely she thought he had chosen her alone to join him in his bed tonight.

Volod sensed Monique on the other side of the door. "Enter."

Monique looked vaguely surprised to see Elizabeth, naked.

Volod gestured toward the rug. "Take off your clothing, put on the items laid out for you on the bed, and join Elizabeth."

Elizabeth's eyes widened. Monique's lips parted as if she was going to say something.

"Now."

Monique glanced at Elizabeth before she started to take off her own clothes. She had become accustomed to his insistence that in the brownstone she should wear elegant dresses that showed off her slim figure. She was to always appear as a lady.

Where Elizabeth wore gowns that reflected her station as a lady in a royal court centuries ago, Monique wore more modern dresses. Usually short enough to show off her legs from the middle of her thighs down.

Monique walked over to the bed. She removed the short black dress, as well as her stockings, panties, and bra. She looked at the items on the bed. Monique took a few moments to slide on the leather panties along with a skimpy bra made of thin leather strips encircling each breast. Small chains were attached and held the silver rings snugly in place around her nipples, emphasizing them.

She slipped on the high heels that would make her four inches taller than Elizabeth. There was a leather hood with a hole near the top. The face was completely open. At Volod's instruction, Monique put the hood on and pulled her hair though the hole, making it appear there was a single ponytail coming out the top. The edges tightened around her face as she tied the laces behind.

Monique returned and stood on the rug beside the naked Elizabeth. Desire stirred inside Volod as he looked from one beautiful female to the other.

"Elizabeth." Volod gave a nod in the direction of the bureau. "Take the two items in the top drawer out. You have used them before and know what they represent. Bring them back here and hand them to Monique."

Elizabeth's pale skin seemed to grow paler yet. From her expression he could tell that she realized what was going to happen—she had been there herself, decades ago. Only she had been in Monique's position.

Shock then a sort of rebelliousness was in Elizabeth's gaze. He liked that. The fact that she would hate what happened next stirred him only more.

Elizabeth returned to the rug holding a stainless-steel collar with rings fastened around it. A tiny padlock was attached to a hinged fastener.

"Elizabeth, on your knees." Volod pointed to the floor. "Monique, put the collar on her."

Only Monique looked surprised. Elizabeth knew all too well what was going to happen next. Anger radiated from her although she was clearly working to keep it hidden.

She shook her head. "No." She almost shouted the word as she shoved Monique away from her.

"Subdue her, Monique." Amusement flickered inside him—and lust. "Do whatever you need to do to get her on her knees."

Monique approached Elizabeth, who stepped away, hatred on her features.

The Elvin Vampire's power stirred within her, a palpable thing. For the first time Elizabeth looked concerned.

Monique raised her hands. Elizabeth gasped as invisible power wrapped around her. She struggled against a force they could not see.

"Bitch!" Elizabeth screamed. "You paranorm slut. Let me go!"

Elizabeth's mouth slammed shut, Monique's power taking away her ability to speak, effectively gagging her.

With her magic, Monique forced Elizabeth down onto her knees. She tried to get back up but Monique kept her in place. She held her hand under Elizabeth's chin and forced it up to look at her.

Unable to move, Elizabeth steeled her features as she knelt, but her whole body shook as she waited for Monique to put the collar on her.

"Monique, I want you to release the power you hold over Elizabeth." His eyes focused on the green-eyed redhead. "Elizabeth, do not struggle or you will feel my wrath. You know how this works."

Monique let go of Elizabeth. Her head dropped.

"Head up," Volod commanded.

Elizabeth's head raised and she stared at Monique with a look of both fury and sadness.

Monique seemed to recognize the symbolism, that she was being elevated to Elizabeth's former position. She was now Volod's. She kept her features calm, but he felt a sense of excitement and satisfaction radiating from her.

"Give her the collar and leash, Elizabeth," said Volod.

Elizabeth handed Monique the items.

"Now put the collar and leash on her, Monique. Lead her to the doorway and back over here." Volod crossed his arms over his chest as he looked at Elizabeth.

Monique took the collar from Elizabeth. She opened it and placed it around Elizabeth's neck. She secured it in place, closed the small padlock, and removed the key left in the lock. She then clipped on the leash. Elizabeth started to stand.

"I want you on all fours," Volod commanded. "Walk her around the room now."

Monique gripped the leash and started to walk but Elizabeth resisted. She pulled harder on the collar and began crawling slowly next to Monique.

Volod thought about the excitement of the vision before him. He loved the contrast of the power in Monique's dress and the submissiveness in Elizabeth's nakedness on the end of a leash.

The humiliation Elizabeth now felt gave him deep satisfaction. Another female Vampire had power over her. She avoided looking at Monique as she did what she'd been ordered to.

Monique led Elizabeth to Volod. When she was at his feet, she rose up onto her haunches. "Please, Volod." She tilted her head. "Please don't do this."

Volod grabbed her by the collar and dragged her up high enough that he could put his face into hers. "I'll always take care of you. That, you know."

She licked her lips. "Yes."

Volod kissed her, then he handed Monique the leash. "Now tether her collar to the ring on the frame at the foot of the bed. I want her facing me. Then join me in bed," he added. "She will watch, first."

EIGHTEEN

My eyes stung and I rubbed the bridge of my nose. Silence reigned as I stood in the PI office surrounded by all the New York City Trackers who could be out in the daylight.

The exception was Nakano, who was with the Vampire-Doppler prisoner. Those who could only come out after dark were on a conference call with us.

"The Pit is compromised now, so that's why we chose my office as an alternate location to meet," I said. "But I do believe we need to find a new, safer place to meet in the future."

Several of those around me nodded.

"What, are we reduced to hiding in holes?" Ice said. "That's not how Trackers operate."

"We operate smart," I said. "We have to stay alive to defeat this threat. If Volod and his Vampire paranorms find out where we meet, they could ambush us. We need to find the right place to do it."

I continued, "I contacted the chairman of the Proctor Directorate first thing and let him know what has happened."

"It doesn't seem real." Lawan stood next to Max and had her head resting against the arm of the big Werewolf. Her eyes looked red. "None of it seems real."

No, it didn't seem real. It was like a death.

It *was* a death, only worse.

Nadia had tears in her voice, tears I wished I could cry. "I can't believe Rodán is going to be one of them."

"Rodán will never be one of them." My words came out

in an angry rush. "This is Rodán we're talking about. He's too powerful and he would never completely turn."

"Monique was powerful, too." Robert spoke calmly, almost too calmly for me at that moment.

"That's true, Nyx." Nadia wiped tears from her eyes with her hands. "From what you and Desmond told us yesterday, Monique has completely succumbed."

The truth in their words stung, but it didn't make anything that had happened seem more real.

"We need to find Rodán's body." Ice's jaw was set, his normally snow-bright blue eyes dark with anger. "Before he rises."

Surprise made me unsteady on my feet. My mind spun at the thought of digging up Rodán's body and disposing of it before the transformation was complete. The very thought was admitting the hopelessness that I felt deep down.

"Find his body?" Lawan said, saving me from voicing the same thing.

Angel glanced at me, making it clear she was waiting on me to either speak or tell her it was okay to do so herself.

If I was going to assume leadership—and it seemed that was now expected of me—then that's what I had to do.

I squared my shoulders as my mind ran through all that needed to be done. "I'll appoint a team of three Trackers to try to locate Rodán's body." I swallowed. "And I'll take it back to Otherworld."

I looked over the Trackers. "Robert, Phyllis, and Nancy, you'll take on that responsibility. I'll discuss it with you further when the meeting is over." The Doppler, Werewolf, and Pixie nodded in response, their expressions grim.

Part of me was so shattered I didn't want to continue. I wanted to run upstairs to my apartment, curl up in bed, and pretend that none of this had happened.

But this was the real world and I had to get a grip.

I took a deep breath. "We need to figure out what is happening. What Volod is up to. What exactly he wants. And then we need to find a way to stop it. We just don't have any information. There are Vampires out there who know something, and we need to find out answers. Volod is no match for us."

"Volod is responsible for the missing Trackers." Dave leaned back against the desk, his arms crossing his chest. "He's back and he's hell-bent on revenge."

"So far," Robert said, "whether we want to admit it or not, the reality is that he has taken on very powerful Trackers and he is winning."

"It is obvious that he wants control of his Vampire world." Angel's long blond corkscrew curls fell down her back and she brushed them aside as if they were an irritant today. "He tried it before and failed. He wasn't going to just stop. We can safely assume he's after the same control he sought before."

"We know he is turning paranorms," Nadia said. "But how? What does he plan on doing with them?"

I nodded as I looked to the other Trackers. "We all know Vampires want the freedom to live their lives at the expense of others. Vampires never had a chance at keeping that freedom when paranorms came after them. Not a chance."

"They are simply no match," Angel said. "We all know they hate our suppression of their feeding on humans. The only thing that stops them has been our ability to control them. Now they are turning paranorms on paranorms. It's obvious this is all about a plan to gain the control they've never had."

I shook my head as I thought about what we were facing. "It's amazing that for all these years, there have been no Vampire paranorms. There was no such thing in the Otherworld. So how is it possible now?"

"Good question." Dave rubbed the stubble on his jaws. Werewolves tend to grow facial hair faster when it's getting close to the full moon. "Years ago, before the Paranorm Rebellion, a few paranorms were turned but immediately killed."

Robert looked thoughtful as he spoke. "Vampires have no taste for paranorms. Our blood makes them ill."

"Obviously he's figured out how to overcome that." Lawan raised her head from where she'd been leaning against Max.

It hit me then that Max was looking at her protectively, lovingly.

"He's probably willing to live with the distaste for paranorms if they serve his purpose," I said. "He likely figures making a few Vampires ill is worth it."

"Nyx is right. If not for the Trackers, Vampires would run rampant." Fere, a Tuatha D'Danann—a great winged Fae warrior from Otherworld—had his hand on the hilt of his sword. His wings would not be visible until he needed them. "The game has changed, however. He is coming directly after paranorms now, and Trackers no less, and making his very enemies his powerful allies."

"He has us in his sights." I tapped my chin with my finger. "He is coming after each one of us. We are now fighting our own kind who are magically strong and know our ways. These Vampire paranorms are powerful, much more powerful than the Vampires we're used to fighting."

Angel nodded. "Plus these aren't just any paranorms who have been turned. They were some of the best Trackers around. Volod did his homework."

"And they know our weaknesses. Remember, they have the list the Sprites took," Nadia added.

"They accomplished this with the element of surprise so far. They no longer have that." Joshua looked like he was working a problem out in his head. "Next time we'll be prepared for them."

"Yes." I nodded. "We're in a fight for our lives and those of our paranorm families. The humans also." I rubbed my forehead as I thought about the situation. "Our fellow paranorm Trackers had no idea of the threat, and as far as we know they were taken by surprise. Things have changed now. Next time we'll be prepared."

Fae bells chimed at the front door. An early-morning spring breeze followed Desmond into the office.

My heart rate picked up and I straightened where I was standing. "Hi, Desmond." A few of the other Trackers greeted him, too.

Desmond gave a slight nod in response as he worked his way through the crowd to my side.

"Do you have news about Rodán?" I hoped beyond hope for any news he could give me that would tell me there was a way to save Rodán. A childish wish . . . wanting to know that nothing bad could happen to a friend and mentor I loved.

Desmond shook his head. "I scried this morning, searching for answers. What I saw will give you little solace, but perhaps some."

"What is it?" Colin asked from where he stood behind me.

Desmond's long, wild hair seemed even wilder than normal, like he had a bad case of bed head. "I can tell you what paranorms are not affected by a Vampire's bite."

"Okay," I said. "Let's hear it."

Desmond looked at Colin first. "Dragons are safe from being turned by a Vampire bite." He moved his gaze to Nadia. "Water and amphibian paranorms are not affected. Sirens as well as Undines are safe."

The Sorcerer's gaze went from one Tracker to another. "Dopplers with sea animal or amphibian forms, and Shifters who can take those forms, are also not at risk like the rest of us."

He turned to me again. "And Drow. Drow are not affected by a Vampire's bite." Before I could express my surprise, he continued. "But since you are half human, Nyx, I do not know how you would react."

I nodded, relieved that at least Colin and Nadia were safe. As for me, I wasn't going to worry about that. I didn't intend to get caught.

But Volod had bitten me once, during our Vampire case months ago . . . all it would take was one more time.

I shook the thoughts from my head. "At least water paranorms aren't affected."

"Doesn't do us much good unless we're fighting the Vamps in the Hudson River," Ice said with his characteristic smirk.

Right then Ice's expression didn't bother me. The look on his face gave me a feeling of normalcy that I hadn't had for a while.

Nadia braced her hands on the desk she was sitting on. "Your brother, Tristan, should be safe. What about others?"

"No other Drow that I know of live in this Otherworld." I touched the collar around my throat as I thought about my father. He had fought hard to make me stay there, but I had finally won. "It's a close-knit society, and they keep to themselves belowground in Otherworld."

Fae bells rang again on the door. This time Nakano, a Japanese Shifter, walked in. Behind him was Gary, the Vampire-Doppler prisoner, followed by two PTF agents. Gary was locked into a compression suit.

"Glad to see you," I said to Nakano. I looked over at Gary. His suit's garlic-and-holy-water lining was obviously making him ill. The suit was like a human's straitjacket, but lethal to Vampires. The lining made them so ill they could hardly think straight, much less try to escape. Gary looked almost green instead of pale. Perhaps more than just a regular Vampire.

If making the Vampire sick didn't work, a cross was sewn to the front of the suit. If the Vampire made any sudden movements, the cross would burn into his skin, causing him excruciating pain.

Another important enhancement was a disk made from Dryad wood and infused with Dryad magic, which was affixed over the Vampire's heart. If the Vampire tried to escape, or if anyone but his Doppler PTF agent guards tried to take the suit off, the disk expanded into an eight-inch stake, piercing the Vampire's heart in a flash.

As if that weren't enough, a slim wire wrapped the neck, made from an alloy mined by the Dark Elves. In an escape attempt, the band would slice through the Vampire's neck, beheading him.

Considering Gary had tried to kill himself when we captured him, I wasn't so sure the suit was a good thing. The

Vampire-Doppler was still alive, so I certainly wasn't going to say anything that might give him any ideas.

As the other Trackers made room to allow the small procession through, I felt almost guilty for how bad he looked. After all, not that long ago he'd been one of us. The good guys. As for the suit, something about holy water and garlic made healing a lot slower for Vampires—and apparently Vampire paranorms.

When the sick-looking Vampire-Doppler was brought to me, I looked into his bleary eyes. "Hi, Gary."

He stared at me with a dazed expression and mumbled something I couldn't hear.

"All of this will be over if you just tell me what I need to know," I said as I looked up at him.

"How were you taken?" I asked. "How is Volod doing this?"

"A group of Vampire paranorms came at me in my territory. I never saw it coming," he said.

"How many paranorm Vamps are there?" I asked. "And how many Vampires?"

Gary looked away from me like he was trying to think of the number before he looked back at me. "Right now, over twenty-five Vampire paranorms, and he's brought in more Vampires from nearby states. Around another ninety Vampires."

I sucked in my breath. *Close to 115?* That was odds of nearly five to one against our city's Trackers.

I took a deep breath before I continued. "Where do the Vampires bury the dead before they rise on the tenth day?" I asked.

Gary seemed unsteady on his feet. I motioned for the Doppler agents to put him into one of the chairs in front of my desk.

I repeated the question. The Vampire-Doppler looked at me, his eyes unfocused. "I never buried anyone."

"I don't care what you've done." I frowned. "Where does Volod bury them?"

"It is different in every city." Gary sounded like he needed a glass of water. His words had a dry scratchiness to them. "We just came to New York. I don't know where he buries his dead here."

"We need to check all cemeteries in Manhattan as well as the surrounding areas," I said to the team I'd assigned to the task.

"Won't matter." Gary slurred his words. "I heard that Volod does some kind of magic thing. Makes it look like the grave was there forever. You will never be able to find any of them on your own."

"Then you need to help us." My patience was dissolving along with any sympathy I may have had. "You know what we can do to you."

I think he would have shrugged if he weren't in the compression suit. "Doesn't matter, because I don't know any more than that."

"We'll come back to that in a moment." I didn't want him to think I was giving up that easy. "What is Volod up to?" I got in Gary's face, close enough that I could smell the lining of his suit.

"I don't know." The Vampire-Doppler looked away from me, refusing to meet my eyes.

"Tell me now or I'll let Max and Nakano both have at you." The snarl in my voice was enough to make him flinch. "Or better yet, Desmond."

Fear swept across Gary's face, but he didn't say anything. I wondered if he was too scared to talk.

Desmond stood in front of him and extended his hand. From it the green fist extended and wrapped around the Vampire-Doppler's neck, just below his chin.

Gary made a gurgling sound, and then resignation was clear in the droop of his shoulders and his expression. He looked like a being who didn't care anymore. No matter what Volod might do to him. He just didn't want to experience more pain.

He swallowed. The wire pressed against his throat. Desmond kept the magic fist around Gary's neck. "Volod wants to create far more paranorm Vampires than he has. He wants an entire army."

Chills rolled over me. "An army," I repeated.

He licked his lips. "Volod plans to—"

A pinging sound. A red stripe across his throat. A stunned look on Gary's face.

Gary's head tipped forward. And fell from his shoulders and landed by my feet.

Shocked silence followed the head as it rolled across the office floor.

I looked at Desmond, who had a surprised expression. "Oops," he said.

Somehow his magic fist had set off the wire.

"What the—" Ice started when the Fae bells jingled yet again at the front door.

A male being entered through the doorway. He paused as he swept his gaze over us and looked at Gary's lifeless head on the floor. The male was a Dragon, and a powerful one if his scent and my senses were right, and they usually were.

He was a tall male, confidence and arrogance in his clear, dark eyes. His head was shaved, gleaming in the morning light streaming through the window. His well-muscled body hummed with strength and power.

"Private meeting." No amount of friendliness was in Ice's tone as he spoke to the stranger.

I walked through the crowd of Trackers until I stood in front of the male, who was about a foot taller than me. "Is there something I can help you with?" I wasn't in the mood to be polite yet I did a credible job of it.

The male looked from me to the headless body then back to me. He sniffed the air then scowled before looking back at me. "I believe it's a matter of what I can do for you."

His gaze was piercing as he glanced at the other Trackers—it was the kind of look that could instill fear in lesser beings. But we were Trackers. The intimidation factor wouldn't work with us.

"We're busy." I kept my arms loose at my sides, but I was

feeling anything but casual at that moment. I was limber, filled with anger, and ready for anything.

"Such attitude." The Dragon spoke with a smooth Cajun accent. "That will change."

Every Tracker in the place bristled. Ice pushed away from where he'd been leaning up against the desk.

"I am Armand Despre." The tall, powerfully built male spoke in a commanding voice. "Your new Proctor."

NINETEEN

The room was thick with tension as we all digested what the Dragon, who called himself Armand Despre, had said.

I had heard of this powerful Tracker before but had never met him. He had a reputation as the top Vampire fighter in all of our ranks. Still, I didn't need the pretentious entry and grandstanding attitude.

"Pardon us if we don't simply take your word for it." I held my ground beneath his arrogant gaze. "Who assigned you?"

An amused expression crossed the Dragon's features. "James, chairman of the Proctor Directorate, asked me to fill in for Rodán until he is found."

"We located Rodán early this morning." I swallowed back the bile that was rushing into my throat. "He has been . . . taken by Vampires."

Armand Despre stilled. "Vampires." He said the word slowly, each syllable deep with thought. "Are you certain?"

"Several of us were there when he was bitten." I couldn't show any sign of weakness by revealing the depth of the pain I felt. "It was the second bite."

The Proctor's gaze narrowed. "Rodán was turned?"

"He'll never be one of them." The defensive tone of my voice and my posture likely made it clear to the Proctor how much I cared for Rodán. I'd wanted to do the opposite.

Armand Despre brushed aside my words with a dismissive gesture. "If that is the case, he is gone. Now he is the enemy."

I had to bite my tongue as anger started rolling through me in waves.

"We have a team set to search for his body." Angel stepped up beside me. I was grateful for her support. "We'll find it before he rises."

"No." The Proctor's statement caught me off guard. "That is a waste of Tracker time and effort. We will take Rodán out when the time comes."

"Kill him?" I clenched and unclenched my hands. "You want to murder him?"

Armand Despre looked at me as if I were a Vampire who needed to be taken out. "It is not murder to kill a Vampire."

"We're talking about Rodán, not just any future Vampire." Angel touched my arm, but I shook her off as I spoke. "We owe him help before he becomes what he would never have chosen. Not just wait and murder him."

"You are the Drow female." The Dragon studied me. "You have served the New York City Trackers according to your reputation."

I hadn't known I had a reputation outside our local team, and his comment caught me off guard.

"I am not impressed with reputation," he replied, "but with action and results."

I ground my teeth. I'd action him.

Armand Despre put his hands behind his back and began walking back and forth among us. He looked to be forty at most, but likely he was far older than that. There was power in the way he moved, decisiveness in his gaze, arrogance in his posture and on his handsome face.

He addressed us like a military commander might address his troops. "We will arrange a meeting place. You will be introduced to my handpicked team of Trackers, and you will work with them in solving the disappearances that started on the West Coast and have now spread to New York City."

"How did you know this was related?" Ice said with a hard edge to his voice. "We only discovered for ourselves this morning."

"Clues have arisen." Armand Despre looked like he didn't appreciate having to give any explanations but was doing so to avoid further questioning. "And they have been tracked to this city.

"I have additional news for you." Armand's black T-shirt and jeans were snug around his biceps and powerful thighs. "Your Paranorm Council has been taken."

Angel sucked in her breath audibly. Other Trackers made sounds of shock and disbelief.

"When?" I said.

"From what information has been gathered," the Proctor said, "just hours ago."

It felt like a sweeping wave was coming toward us. If we didn't do something about it and soon, that wave could wipe out all of us.

Armand turned from me and faced the front door of the office. "I have brought a few of my Trackers here to join us."

Irritation made my skin itch. That's all we needed was to introduce a new team, led by an arrogant Proctor, when we were trying to coordinate our efforts.

Rather than just tinkling, the Fae bells at the office door started jingling in a fierce melody. I frowned as a female walked through the door with a pit bull on a leash and a falcon on one shoulder.

"This isn't an animal shelter," Olivia said from where she sat behind her desk. I glanced at her T-shirt.

I DON'T NEED A WEAPON. I AM ONE.

Yeah, and you'd better watch out, I thought. It was easy to underestimate Olivia—until you got to know her.

"This is Megan, a Witch." Armand extended his hand. "Along with Bruce, a Doppler." He gestured to the pit bull, then the falcon. "And the bird is Tate. Bruce just prefers to be in animal form on Megan's leash."

The Witch continued to hold the leash as the pit bull morphed into a male with the body of a middle linebacker.

The falcon flew down from the female's shoulder and seemed to hover in the air for a moment. Then Tate shifted into a tall, muscled, and heavily scarred male.

A short male with a runner's physique came through the doorway—but he didn't walk. He *floated.*

"Since when did Peter Pan become a Tracker?" Olivia said. A couple of those on my team laughed.

"Air is a Cloud Shifter." Armand sounded clearly annoyed, but Air didn't seem affected by Olivia's crack.

I'd heard of Cloud Shifters but never met one. They could float in human form or shift into a cloud, both useful skills for moving around and reconnaissance.

Armand gestured to the door again. "And meet Cindy." We all looked . . . and saw nothing. Then I noticed Ice staring at a black mouse scurrying in his direction.

Ice vanished and in his place, on the floor, was a white mouse, one of Ice's preferred forms.

The mice scampered toward each other and rubbed noses.

I blinked. Then glanced at Armand, who was frowning.

Dave rolled his eyes. "Get a room."

"I've got a shoe box." Olivia leaned over her desk. "Better yet, I can get one of those cages with two hamster wheels."

I shook my head. Olivia was in fine form today.

When Ice shifted, he rose up to his full intimidating height, his blue eyes glinting like sunlight on new-fallen snow.

Beside him, the black mouse shifted into a pretty, dark-haired female who was a couple of inches shorter than me.

I'd never, ever seen Ice look at anyone the way he looked at Cindy. His eyes had softened and his smile was almost gentle. But when he turned back at the other Trackers his characteristic smart-ass expression was fully in place.

"We grew up together." Cindy had a soft, pleasant voice. She looked like the girl next door. She smiled up at him. "It's good to see you, Ice."

The look he gave her was enough to tell me that he loved her—and somewhere along the way she'd broken his ice-covered heart.

"Can we talk without a head rolling around?" Olivia said as she pointed to the floor. I'd forgotten all about poor Gary.

Desmond approached me and I nodded. Too late to worry about triggering Vampire straitjackets now.

He raised both hands this time and emitted more green light. This time his light formed a cube around Gary's head and body. Desmond moved his hands in the direction of a corner of the office and we all watched the cube float there.

Then the cube shuddered—and began to shrink. We were mesmerized as the cube and the body inside it became smaller and smaller until it was the size of a golf ball. A loud *pop* and it vanished. All disappeared except for a small pool of blood the cube missed.

"That's a handy skill." Olivia jerked her head in Angel's direction. "Can you make blondie over there disappear?"

I smiled. Olivia actually liked Angel and enjoyed teasing her.

"You left a mess." The Witch looked at the pool of blood left on the floor and raised her hand. "I like to keep things tidy." She snapped her fingers and the mess disappeared.

"Why don't we get rid of our Shifter maids and hire Samantha here to snap her fingers?" Olivia said.

The Witch looked a little irritated and I thought perhaps it might not be a good idea to tease someone who could make things disappear. "Not Samantha. It's Megan."

Olivia shrugged. "Whatever."

"How did you find us?" Angel asked Armand, drawing attention away from Olivia.

"It wasn't difficult." The Proctor's arrogant demeanor had me grinding my teeth. "We are great Trackers, and great Trackers know how to find things. After all, the Vampires found you easily, so why not us?"

"Who do you think you are, penis head?" So much for drawing attention away from Olivia.

I mentally shook my head.

"What have you discussed in terms of a plan?" The Proctor turned to me. "Where are you and what has happened until this point? I'm aware of all that you have done until your last report yesterday."

This took me off guard. He actually cared what we had been discussing before he arrived? I'd expected him to just toss it all out the window and do everything from scratch. Perhaps that's what he was going to do anyway.

"We're dividing up in teams." I crossed my arms over my chest as I faced him. "There are twenty-five of us and fifteen territories to cover.

"Our priority," I continued, "is to shake down Vampires and get what information we can gather in order to find Volod and stop him. We're going to check every house, hole, bar, and haunt where Vampires are known to hang out."

Armand looked at me expectantly, and I went on. "Vampire attacks have been increasing. Rumors are rampant that Trackers have lost control and Vampires can feed now. We believe that someone knows something. We're going to shake as much as can be shaken and learn what we can."

When I finished talking, he slowly nodded. "A good plan. However, I will be taking charge from this point on."

I hadn't expected anything different.

"We aren't just fighting Vampires." Armand met each of our gazes. "We're fighting our own kind. And remember . . . the person next to you could become your enemy."

TWENTY

If the Vampires didn't kill Armand Despre, I might.

Only the light from the waxing moon illuminated the alleyway. My back brushed the brick wall behind me as I shifted my position behind the Dumpster.

I glanced at Armand. Complete arrogance was in the Proctor's gaze, his posture, his very presence. No doubt he had chosen me to serve as his teammate to keep an eye on me.

A sword was sheathed at one side and a dagger to the other as he knelt beside me. It seemed as though his complete attention was on the mouth of the alley, but I felt that he was as keenly aware of my presence as I was of his.

I leaned forward, and moonlight peeked through the cloud cover and brushed my skin. The moon's glow highlighted my cobalt hair and the light amethyst of my skin. I wrinkled my nose at the rotten scent of garbage coming from the Dumpster.

"I hope our intel is good," I murmured. "According to the Vamp whom Lawan and Max shook down earlier, we should see some action soon. At least if the Vamp was telling the truth and Vampires do meet up here."

"They do."

Those two simple words and the tone of his voice made hair prickle at my nape. His self-confidence and complete and utter arrogance were clear.

"How are you so sure?" I asked and then wished I hadn't.

"I sense they have been coming here a long time." Armand glanced at me. "And I smell them. I am never wrong on this."

He looked back at the alleyway. "There is no better Vampire hunter." It came out as fact.

The urge to slap him upside the head was strong. Someone needed to take Mr. Ego down a rung or two.

Colin's humbleness was the opposite of this guy's demeanor. Both had amazing powers, and from what I heard about Armand and knew of Colin, each was every bit as talented a Dragon. They just had different skill sets. Armand had chosen to be a Vampire specialist, and Colin had so many versatile abilities.

"How long have you been a Vampire hunter?" I asked to fill the silence.

"Many years now." Armand continued to stare into the night. "There is no one as good as I am." He glanced at me. "It is my specialty. I've been doing this for over twenty-five years, not to mention the fact that I am a Dragon."

More and more points in the I'm-not-too-sure-of-this-guy column.

"What made you decide to specialize in Vampires?" I was genuinely curious.

"Two of my closest friends were turned." He moved his attention away from me. "I had to kill one of them."

My stomach cramped at the thought of being faced with that dilemma. I couldn't imagine it.

"It is dangerous for a once-bitten Tracker to actually be going after Vampires," Armand said. "I have thought about taking you off this case."

"Who do you think you are?" I scowled. "I have been laying my life on the line for a long time as a Tracker. If you think I'd back off this case now, you don't know me well.

"I either go after Volod with your team," I continued, "or I do it alone. I'll worry about my personal risk. You don't need to. I've gotten on just fine for years with my approach."

"I worry what you could add to the other team if you are turned. If I become a Vamp," he said, "I expect you to kill me. If you are turned, I *will* kill you."

"I am clear what your position is."

"I'm on a mission. If I had it my way I would not stop

until every Vampire is dead. Because of the truce, of course, I can't kill one until he crosses the line or I'd kill them all."

"Where does that leave Volod's bunch today?" I asked.

"Everyone on Volod's team has crossed the line by my rules, so as far as I'm concerned they are dead."

I looked at the shadows lying across the alleyway. "Is the Proctor Directorate going to have anyone talk with the Great Guardian?"

Armand was quiet for a moment. "There is no one," he finally said.

I cut my gaze to him. "What do you mean?"

"Rodán and Monique were the only Light Elves with a connection to the Great Guardian," Armand said. "The directorate never expected to lose either of them, much less both."

That made my head spin. No liaisons to the GG? Someone would need to be.

My own senses kicked into gear at the same time Armand's body tensed. Vampires—I caught their odor of old dirt and must.

"Six." Armand stood, remaining behind the Dumpster, still close to me. He drew his sword, and the sharp edge glinted in the moonlight. "Vampires, not Vampire paranorms."

The rush of blood in my ears intensified as I placed my hand on my buckler. I didn't have that many sets of Vampire cuffs, and I didn't think they were going to volunteer to come with us.

And then I sensed them, too. They made no sound as they approached but I could hear them, smell them, feel them. They said nothing as they pressed back farther into the alleyway, almost upon Armand and me.

Armand shimmered and vanished as he pulled a glamour. I drew my own, grateful that at least the Vamps wouldn't be able to see me. It had taken a Master previously to sense me, and I could tell that none of these Vampires was a Master. And now not even a Master Vampire would detect my glamour.

The buckler at the front of my weapons belt felt cool beneath my fingers. The edges were sharp, easily able to slice a Vampire's head from his shoulders if necessary.

But these Vampires might have information. What Volod was up to. And maybe even what he'd done with Rodán's body.

Bastards. My hatred for Vampires grew with every day that passed. When Volod had bitten me and nearly killed me with a paranorm virus serum, I'd thought I couldn't hate anyone more than I did right then. Well, he had surpassed that.

And he would be mine.

Small stones and gravel crunched beneath shoes. A pair of the Vampires were laughing and joking around, which seemed bizarre for Vampires. I sensed the two were newly turned, which would account for the lack of dourness.

"Where's the bite party tonight?" One of the pair grinned. He looked cocky and sure of himself. He and Armand would have gotten along fine. "I'm thirsty. I could use a little fun and some real blood," Cocky added.

An older Vampire looked at the younger one with haughty amusement. "Beneath an old church in New Jersey."

"Just over the state line," said another of the older Vamps, this one more serious.

"Thanks for including me tonight. I was wondering, though. Before, you guys always said we had to be careful," Cocky said. "Now there are parties happening all over the place. What's the story on the Trackers backing off? Everyone I talk with has a different story."

"Supposedly Trackers are going down," Amused said, not looking so amused anymore. "And all will be changing in the Vampire way of life, to what it should be."

"That's cool with me," Cocky said.

One of the three Vampires who hadn't spoken interrupted. He was tall and lean and looked very hungry. "I don't know if they are going down. No one really knows. Rumors are that the Trackers aren't focused on us rank-and-file Vampires. They have other distractions."

Amused gave a slow nod. "I have heard the same."

"Groups of our people have started feeding freely on humans even though Volod has not instructed them to," Serious added. "I am not so certain that is wise."

"Volod? Volod is back?" Cocky asked.

"The story is that he is behind all of this," Amused said. "However, I don't know anyone who has actually seen him back."

Cocky changed the subject. "So what's happening at that party in Jersey?"

Amused looked at the other three older Vampires before returning his gaze to Cocky. "From what I understand, those who organized the party have a bunch of once-bitten humans in coffin storage beneath the old church. Supposedly at least two dozen. Hopefully that is true."

A fourth Vampire nodded. "Once everyone has arrived, the hosts will turn the humans loose. Then there will be a chase, with the winners getting to keep the prey they catch."

"I love, love, love it. Let's go then." Cocky jerked his head in the direction he had come from.

"I thought we were going after humans in the city," the other young Vampire said. He had an odd, nasally voice.

"Are you kidding—when there is a chance there are twenty-four once-bitten humans rounded up for a Vampire rodeo? Let's go see this for ourselves," Cocky said.

He went on, "I love seeing the look of horror on humans' faces. As the coffin is opened they experience one last thread of hope . . . only to be recaptured and bitten. I just love that game."

I really wished I could see Armand. At the same moment I saw a shimmer appear beside me where Armand had been standing earlier. He was still in glamour, but visible enough that I could see him.

"Let's follow them." Even though the Vamps shouldn't be able to hear us through our glamours, I kept my voice down.

With the readiness of his stance, the calculating look in his dark eyes, Armand looked like he wanted to wipe out every Vampire there, but he gave a nod. "Of course. They will lead us to something far more rewarding."

He was clearly relishing the opportunity to take on multiple Vampires.

Well, bring it on.

We followed the six Vamps back out to the street, where a Tahoe SUV and a Lincoln Town Car waited.

"Follow us." Amused walked toward the SUV with Serious.

"I will go with the first car," Armand said to me. "Can you make it into the second?

"Yes." At least I hoped I could.

I waited until Armand vanished then reappeared in the backseat of the Town Car. Cocky and Hungry had loaded up with Amused and Serious in the Tahoe. The other two Vampires went to the Lincoln.

Now I had to make it to the back of the Tahoe. I just hoped I could do it without throwing up.

I knelt on one knee, bracing myself with my fingers on the ground. I closed my eyes, picturing myself in the backseat.

Prickles ran up and down my skin. I clenched my teeth. And leapt forward in my mind. Before I opened my eyes I smelled the strong odor of dirt, heard the sound of the engine running and talk among the Vampires. Apparently Cocky thought everything was all about him because he was talking over the others.

I opened my eyes, still in a crouch, and found that I'd just done the transference behind the backseat rather than into it. My stomach pitched a little, but it was nothing compared with how sick I got when I did a transference across a long distance or through stone walls.

The two young Vamps, along with Hungry and another older Vampire, talked about the most boring subjects. I'd never realized what gossips Vampires were. Who was sleeping with who, what Vampire was feeding when he shouldn't be, just the disgusting ways of Vampires.

Sheesh. Get a life already.

Oh, yeah. Vampires have no life.

I was really hoping Armand was learning something useful on his joyride, because I certainly wasn't with Hungry, Amused, Serious, and Cocky. Give them pointy hats, white beards, and shrink them, and you'd have Snow White's seven Dwarves—Vampire style.

They obviously had no new information. At least we

could save humans, though, and these lowlifes would soon find out that Trackers hadn't disappeared.

When the Tahoe finally stopped, I was ready for a drink. Preferably a vodka martini with three olives on a cute little sword. More than that, I was really wishing I could just wipe these bastards out and move on to the next bunch.

The doors opened and the Vampires got out. I heard multiple voices and peeked through the window to see dozens of Vamps milling around an old church lit by the bright moon.

They looked like people out for a Saturday-night church potluck. Only sloppy joes, casseroles, potato salad, and watermelon were not on the buffet table.

I didn't sense any paranorms or Vampire paranorms. All of these Vamps had once been human before the bite had twisted their minds like a virus.

The church itself was dark, but the beings outside obviously didn't need the light. Vampires couldn't go inside a church, but I think they enjoyed the ability to be around one without bursting into flames. The small graveyard in the back likely made them feel at home.

I waited for the Vamps to get far enough away from the SUV that they might not notice me appear if for some reason I couldn't hold a glamour while I did the transference. I closed my eyes and imaged myself outside the Tahoe.

A quick rush of blackness then I felt ground beneath where I crouched. My heart pounded a little. I refrained from patting myself on the back for making two short transferences in a row. My father would be proud.

My glamour held. I straightened and looked around me and caught sight of Armand standing by the Town Car. I eased over to him.

"I'll call for backup." I started to reach for my phone but he put up his hand in a *stop* motion.

"Twenty to twenty-five Vampires is child's play." His gaze roved over the crowd. "I have heard of your skills. They will do. This is what it is all about. Let's have some fun."

My skills will do? I gritted my teeth. I forced myself to remain calm. And professional.

I gestured to the church. "The Vamps said something about the humans being kept beneath."

A Vampire moved to the walkway just outside the doors. In the background a cross on each door started to glow, warding against Vampires.

The tall, slender Vamp raised his voice to be heard over the crowd. "We are ready to begin."

Loud applause broke out, and hoots and whoops were heard as if kickoff before a big game was imminent.

"We will give the humans a two-minute head start," the Vampire said. "To make it more sporting."

Right. More sporting.

Anger burned beneath my skin, a hot flush creeping over me at the thought of what these Vampires were about to do, not to mention all that they had done up to this point. At the same time, I knew the annihilation these Vampires were about to experience.

"You can smell their fear from here." The speaker smiled as Vamps around him nodded and bared their fangs. "Prepare for an entertaining evening." He turned away and headed around the church to the east side. The creak of hinges of a gate opening was followed by the soft thump of the wood as it fell back in place.

Armand didn't even glance at me. "I will torch the Vampires to slow them down. You take the group of ten to the east. I will take the remaining sixteen."

I nodded. Sure. No problem. I was amazed at his self-confidence in taking sixteen Vampires on his own. More power to him.

"I will wait until the humans have been set free and are clear of the church." Armand still didn't look at me, just continued to study and evaluate the situation. "Wait until I have set fire to them all."

"You've got it." I placed my hand on my buckler.

Both of us, still in glamour, moved closer to the Vampires. We separated and I skirted the crowd toward the east side. The closer I got to them, the stronger their smell became. I sensed their hunger, their desire for sport.

A sort of excited hush fell over the Vampires. With my keen Drow sight I could see every bit as well as a Vampire, and I focused my gaze on where the tall, slender Vampire had disappeared.

Moments later came human cries of fear and terror. My stomach twisted. What they were doing was so sick, so vile. Vampires earned whatever fate they were dealt.

The hinges creaked again and I focused on the Vampire now holding the gate open.

Screams and cries and sobs became louder right before the first one ran out of the gate. It was a naked human male.

A second naked human followed the first, then another. They were being let out one by one.

The anticipation in the air thickened, the energy of the crowd like a pack of wolves surrounding their prey. Only these inhuman bastards were planning on playing with their meals first.

Ten humans came through the gate, wild-eyed with terror. A female stumbled and fell. The male behind her grabbed her by the arm to get her back to her feet before they both started running again.

When the gate closed I looked across the crowd for Armand. What was he waiting for?

A roar tore through the night followed by billowing plumes of fire from the west side of the churchyard. Shrieks and screams ripped the air. The mass of Vampires began charging in my direction.

Damn! They were all closing in on me, toasted and not.

A Dragon's bellow rang in my ears. More fire torched the Vampires, and heat brushed my cheeks as the flames neared me.

The first charred Vampire was almost in my lap when I flung the buckler. It sliced through the head of one Vampire then took out the next Vamp as well.

Two down, eight to go, plus whatever I might need to help Armand with.

In a two-fisted grip I raised one of my seventeen-inch-long, two-inch-wide Dragon-clawed daggers and gave a Drow warrior cry as I swung the blade. I beheaded the third Vampire.

I whirled to take on the fourth and blood bathed me as the regenerating Vampire's head flew off.

The next Vamp was too close to swing at. I ducked and rolled to the side into tall grass before getting to my feet. I leapt and forward-flipped through the air to land on the other side of the group I was taking on.

Armand was tearing off the heads of Vampires with his teeth. He was a massive Dragon, larger even than Colin, with ebony scales that gleamed in the fire he had produced.

No time to watch. A brief glimpse of Armand the Dragon and I was already drawing my second dagger.

Holding both weapons, I shouted another battle cry before I ran one dagger through the fifth Vampire's heart and twisted the blade. She dropped.

I swung at a sixth Vamp, but my blade glanced off his shoulder when he ducked.

I twisted and caught sight of Armand as he took human form again. His movements were smooth, unconcerned, confident. He used the sword that had been sheathed at his side in simple, effortless strokes.

The remaining five Vampires snarled and shouted as they came after me. I somersaulted forward with my twin daggers extended and cut the sixth and seventh Vampires at the knees. I jumped up, brought the daggers down on the backs of their necks. They were beheaded before their bodies hit the ground.

I backflipped away from the remaining three Vampires and landed about six feet away.

Not three anymore, it was now four. Another one had joined in.

My mouth tasted foul and my breathing came fast as adrenaline rushed through my body. Anger heated me as I thought about those poor humans running blindly through the forest.

As soon as we eliminated these Vampires we needed to get a search-and-rescue team out here. Also a Soothsayer or two to erase the humans' memories tonight.

Out of the corner of my eye I spotted one Vampire running away. Armand didn't see him. *Let him go,* I thought. He could report back to the others. Maybe word would spread that Trackers were alive and enforcing laws.

The last four Vampires approached me with caution in their gazes, but hate, fear, and bloodlust, too.

I gathered my elements and harnessed my air power. With my elemental magic, I bound the four Vampires together so that they couldn't move.

Armand's arms had turned into something like giant taut rubber bands extending out fifteen feet. As he stretched them, a wooden stake in each hand, he drove into the hearts of two of the Vampires he had left to fight.

Eliminating the four I had captured with my air element would be like shooting ducks in a barrel. Out of nowhere a fifth Vampire came charging at me. I'd thought there were just those four left. I lost my concentration as the Vampire grabbed me and drove me down to the tall grass we were in. I dropped my daggers.

The huge male slammed me onto my back, knocking the breath from me. He grabbed me by my shoulders and widened his mouth. His fangs extended, his head came down in a rush of motion.

I brought my knees up and planted my boots against his chest. I shoved as hard as I could, and the Vampire flew off me.

When I started to roll to the side, two of the other Vampires dove for me.

Fear made my heart thump faster but it added to my strength and cleared my mind, too.

I brought my elbow up into the throat of one Vampire and flipped him over into the one who'd descended on me.

A tangle of bodies landed on top of me and I struggled to free myself, using my upper-body strength to get away.

My legs were still trapped but I reached out and grasped the hilt of one of my daggers. The grip felt comfortable in my hand as I brought it up and swung at the Vampire closest to me.

She cried out as my blade found its way to her throat. Her head flew from her shoulders, and her body slumped backward. Four Vamps left.

I planted my boot on the face of the other Vampire on top of me and braced him long enough to sever his head. He fell over my legs but I managed to shove him off. Another down.

I scooted backward, away from the remaining three Vampires who were advancing on me from just a few feet away. As I was about to get to my feet, one of them lunged.

A burst of energy came over me and I shot forward from a sprinter's position. I put just enough space between myself and the Vamps.

I reached for one of the grenades at my belt, pulled out the pin, and lobbed it in front of them. It exploded in a rush of water and garlic. The Vampires flailed and cried out, temporarily blinded.

I picked up my sword and swung it at one of the Vampires. Another nice, clean swipe and he was headless. The other two were starting to gather themselves, but I didn't give them a chance.

My blade flashed in the dying flames left over from Armand frying the place. I neatly cut off one of the Vampire's heads.

The last Vampire reached me before I had time to think. He grabbed my hair and my shoulder and jerked my head to the side as his fangs came down on me.

A rush of fear of another bite, of becoming a Vampire myself, sent strength I didn't know I had soaring through me.

I twisted and grabbed the Vampire's head and brought it down as I rammed my knee into his face. At the same time I dropped my dagger and grabbed a wooden stake from my weapons belt.

With all my strength I jerked his head back by his hair, hard enough to expose his chest to me. Then I rammed the stake up and into his heart.

The Vampire crumpled. I let him drop.

I felt a presence behind me and whirled to face the next attack.

Instead I saw Armand casually leaning up against a tree, watching me. I was breathing hard, my heart pounding like crazy, and he could've been a patron watching a Broadway show.

I kicked the Vampire out of my way. I needed something to kick given the amused smile on Armand's face.

"Very impressive," he said.

I pushed my hair out of my face. "Just another day at the office. Now that you're so well rested, we have more tracking to do."

TWENTY-ONE

Lack of sleep was eventually going to get to me.

I rested my forehead in my hands, the desktop hard beneath my elbows, and sighed.

Fae bells jangled at the front door and I sensed Olivia walking in. I raised my head and met her gaze.

"You look like crap." Olivia pulled off her Mets jacket and tossed it on her desktop, right in the middle of the neon orange and green sticky notes.

"I bet Scott would like to see you try," I said as I looked at her T-shirt.

SOME DAYS IT'S NOT EVEN WORTH
CHEWING THROUGH THE RESTRAINTS

A sly grin crept over Olivia's face. "Wouldn't you like to know."

I leaned back in the chair. "Too much information."

"Well, we both enjoy the struggle but you don't want to hear about that." She paused as if considering. "Or do you?"

I rolled my eyes.

"You need to get some rest, Nyx." She walked around her desk and plopped into her own chair. "You've been putting in time all night and most of the days, too, ever since Rodán was turned."

"Five days." I let out a harsh breath. "And bad news in the city is getting worse by the hour."

Olivia faced her monitor and started typing on the keypad. "What happened last night?"

"More of the same." All of the blood and death was getting to me, too. "The Vampires in this city are getting out of control. They know our attention is divided and we can't focus all our efforts on taking them down. It seems to get worse every day."

She looked thoughtful. "What about Proctor whatshisname and that bunch he brought along?"

"Armand Despre probably thought he'd be able to take them all down on his own." I rubbed my eyes again. "And the Vampires are proving him wrong."

"You two make a hell of a team." Olivia stared at her monitor and moved her hands over the keyboard as she spoke. "Ever since you wiped out that bunch at the church in New Jersey, you've taken down more Vampires than the rest of the Trackers put together."

"I almost hate to admit it," I said. "But he's good, really good."

Olivia looked at me and smirked. "I have a hard time believing you aren't pulling your weight every night."

I shrugged. Armand made sure I got my share of the "fun." It irked me that he just watched while I cleaned up the last of whatever mess I was dealing with. At least he didn't try to take over everything just to show how good he was.

And I had to admit, he was probably the best Tracker I'd ever seen—and a Proctor on top of it. Talk about hands-on management.

Olivia pulled up an online newspaper's headlines. "This is sick," she said.

I nodded. I didn't want to believe what was happening. The city was in the grips of a panic with bodies turning up every day.

"Just like last fall." Olivia scrolled through other newspapers as I looked at the monitors. "Wannabe Vamps are being blamed." She glanced at me. "No one wants to hear the truth."

I turned away from the headlines. "Would you believe it if you weren't involved in the paranorm world?"

"Not a chance." Olivia shook her head. "Speaking of unbelievers, I talked with Wysocki last night."

I frowned. "She doesn't get it? After the last time we dealt with Volod, you'd think a New York police captain would be a believer."

"Oh, she gets it all right." Olivia took out her XPhone and read through some notes she'd made. "She just can't get anyone higher up to believe her."

"We've got to find Volod." I wished caffeine worked for me. I sure could've used a jolt. "Once again we didn't get any info last night worth anything. Whatever his next step is, he is keeping it quiet. Too quiet."

Olivia stopped flipping her pencil in the air and pointed it at me. "You know he's coming after you, Nyx. He's taken Rodán, he's taken the council. He's taking revenge on all of those who destroyed him.

"I think he plans to save you for last," she added. "You need to be careful. You aren't invincible and you have been bitten once. You probably shouldn't even be here."

"I can't hide." I sighed. "I'm being cautious and watchful. Volod won't win, Olivia. He will not win. But thank you for your warning and for being such a good friend."

Olivia resumed her pencil toss. "Oh, don't go getting sappy on me, purple butt."

The Fae bells at the front door did a gentle dance and tinkle, something that only happened when Megan, the new Witch Tracker, stopped by.

This time the pit bull Doppler, Bruce, and the falcon, Tate, weren't with her.

"Hi, Megan." It wasn't hard to smile at the Witch. If I hadn't seen her in action, I would have thought she was too sweet to be an effective Tracker. "What's up?"

"If it isn't Samantha Stevens," Olivia said. "Do you sneeze when you wiggle your nose?"

"I need to talk with you, Nyx." Megan parked herself in one of the two chairs in front of my desk, ignoring Olivia. Her shoulder-length blond hair swung forward. "I had a vision when I scried in my crystal this morning that involves you."

"Okay." I hated visions about me. I leaned forward, my forearms braced on my desktop. "What's it about?"

She bit her lower lip as she folded her hands in her lap. "It was about a gift I thought of giving you the other day."

"A gift?" I tilted my head to the side. "That's what you scried about?"

She gave a single nod.

"What is it?" I replied.

"I'm going to give you the ability to read minds."

"What?" As what she said hit me I shook my head. "No way. I don't need or want that ability, and I don't want any spells cast on me."

She leaned forward, a look of utter seriousness on her face. "You are meant to have this gift, Nyx Ciar of the Drow. It might last twenty-four hours, a week, a month. But whatever the case, it will last as long as it is needed, and it may come and go."

I raised my hands to ward her off. "No spells. Uh-uh."

"You need to trust me, Nyx." She spoke calmly, like a mother to her child. "As I told you, when I scry, I am never wrong."

"Well, maybe this time you *are* wrong." I stood up from behind my desk, afraid she was going to zap me with a spell before I could make my escape.

She got to her feet, too. Rather than a flowing dress like I was used to Witches wearing, she had on jeans, boat shoes, and a white-and-blue-striped blouse with a boat neckline. She was as fresh-faced and pretty as always.

"I can't leave until you say yes." There was a stubborn tilt to her chin that I hadn't noticed before. "It's important."

When I glanced at Olivia she shrugged. "Go for it."

"You're not much help." I turned to Megan again. "You're *sure* I need this ability?"

She nodded. "Very."

I let out a sigh, both nervous and resigned. "You promise this is temporary?

"Absolutely." She gave a *come closer* gesture with her hand.

"I really don't want to know what other people are thinking," I said.

"You'll appreciate it when the time comes." She raised her hands as I reached her.

"I suppose it could be useful in learning what the enemy is thinking." I furrowed my brow as I concentrated on what she wanted of me. "How difficult will it be to keep everyone else's thoughts out of my head?"

"I don't know," she said. "I've never had this ability."

I took a deep breath as I stood directly in front of her. "Have you ever done a spell to give it to anyone else?"

She took one of my hands. "No."

If she hadn't grabbed my hand at that moment I might have backed away. An electrical charge burst through my body.

I would have won any kind of tug-of-war match pulling my hand from hers, but I was afraid to mess up the spell she'd obviously started already.

"Close your eyes." Her voice had lowered to a tenor; rather than the airiness that it usually had.

I took a deep breath and shut my eyes. My body filled with warmth, like a heated river of honey slowly traveling through my veins.

My ears began to burn and my head tingled. It was like something was waking up in my head.

Be still, Nyx. I heard Megan talking in my mind. *I'm not finished yet.*

The tingling in my head increased and I bit the inside of my cheek to calm down. I felt a change start to take hold of me.

When the warmth began to fade, I expected voices to bombard me.

"You're crazy," Olivia said. "Completely crazy to let a Witch do something like that."

I looked at her. "Not crazy enough to let my boyfriend tie me up and stuff a gag in my mouth and leave me helplessly restrained while he goes out for Chinese food."

Olivia raised her brows. "It worked."

"What worked?" I said. "I can't hear your thoughts."

Sure you can. Olivia's lips weren't moving. *You just did.*

"Oh." I blinked. "So you didn't say the part about me being crazy out loud."

"Nope." Olivia shook her head. "But you really didn't need to read my thoughts to know that."

Was that Olivia's evil cackle in my head?

I turned my attention to Megan. "I don't hear anything coming from you."

"That's because I'm a Witch." Megan released my hand and stepped back. "If I know what to look for, I can block it with another spell."

"Lucky you." I jerked my thumb in Olivia's direction. "I keep hearing *ball gags, restraints,* and *Scott* from over there."

Olivia loaded a rubber band. I caught the eraser before it could hit my forehead. She was a great shot, but fortunately I was faster.

"Armand needs me, so I've got to go." Megan headed back to the door where the Fae chimes started dancing softly again. She grasped the door handle and looked over her shoulder at me. "Good luck to you," she said right before she walked out the door.

The door didn't shut, though. My Dragon came through. Colin looked at me and smiled.

So beautiful, came the thought as he walked toward me. My cheeks warmed. I felt more than heard a depth of affection for me that I hadn't realized existed. It was amazing what he was thinking. He loved being with me. I felt like I was invading his privacy, but it was all so good from him.

I held up my hands. "Fair warning. The Witch just cast a spell on me so that I can hear everyone's thoughts. At least I think everyone."

"Doesn't matter to me. I tell you that you're beautiful all the time and how much I care for you." Colin smiled as he reached me. "I have nothing to hide from you, Nyx. You don't need to worry about me."

"Are you sure it's okay?" I tilted my head to look up at him.

He leaned down and brushed his lips over mine. "Yes."

"I'll try not to," I said. "I just don't know if I can stop it.

Megan said I'll pick something up with certain individuals but not all."

"No worries," he said, and then I realized his lips weren't moving. *Maybe you'll start believing just how much I care for you.*

Heat flushed through me again. Instead of answering I gave him a quick kiss.

"If you could only read my mind right now, Hot Stuff," I said, "you would know the feeling's mutual."

"Come on." He took my hand. "Let's have lunch at my place. You know I make a great club sandwich."

Olivia hit Colin right on the nose with a rubber band. "Enough mushy crap. You need to stop before I gag."

"Do you have chips and Belgian beer?" I asked, ignoring my partner.

He grinned. "Barbecue and of course."

I felt renewed energy.

"Let's go." He took my hand and we headed toward the door.

I looked over my shoulder at Olivia. "I'm betting he will remember the handcuffs tonight, and he'll love it if you wear the leather panties."

An eraser pinged off the open door as I ducked.

"You'd better stop reading my mind or I'll kick your ass, Nyx Ciar," she shouted after me as I laughed and fled with Colin.

TWENTY-TWO

Still holding my hand, Colin took us through the transference to his apartment door in Queens.

He let us both in then closed the door. Colin's place was warm, comfortable, and welcoming and I loved it there.

In the kitchen he took out all of the ingredients for club sandwiches then handed me a beer. Normally my drink of choice was a vodka martini with three green olives, but not with Colin.

I tried not to hear his thoughts, but it was hard. Most of the time he thought about me, how much he loved being with me, having me with him. There were flashes about Volod and the battles he'd fought against Vampires since Rodán was taken.

"It's getting worse." I set my bottle down on the countertop as I watched him slice a tomato. "I don't think we can do this on our own. We need help."

"What did you have in mind?" Colin asked as he laid down strips of fried bacon over tomato.

I leaned back with my hands braced on the countertop behind me. "More Trackers, of course." I tilted my head as I voiced thoughts I'd been having. "And I'm wondering about Drow. If my father would allow any of my people to come and fight."

Colin raised his eyebrows as he finished a sandwich and put it on a plate. "What do you think he'll say?"

"Honestly?" I sighed and tapped one toe on the kitchen tile. "I don't know. Father will do just about anything for me, but I don't know which side of 'just about anything' this falls on."

"That's a lot to ask of your people, who have nothing to do with the Earth Otherworld." Colin stacked potato chips next to the sandwich then handed me the plate. "Fighting here would put not only his warriors at risk, but his people back at home as well. It would leave them with fewer reserves."

With a frown I stopped tapping my toe. "I hadn't thought about that."

"On the other hand," Colin said as he picked up his own sandwich, "if he has plenty of warriors to take on both tasks, then it can't hurt to ask."

I nodded. "He does and then some."

We took our plates and bottles of beer to the kitchen nook table and settled into two of the wooden chairs parked around it.

I said, "Each day that goes by . . . I just can't believe Rodán is gone. It seems more and more surreal. Like I'll run into him at any moment and that everything will be like it used to be."

Colin studied me with a thoughtful expression. "Obviously I didn't know him as long or as well as you, but I find it pretty hard to believe, too. I liked him and respected him as our Proctor."

I picked up my sandwich, looked at it, then back at Colin as I thought about what I was going to say. "I think someone needs to talk with the Great Guardian."

He paused, then his words echoed what I heard him saying in his mind. "What about the Proctors?"

"Armand said that Rodán and Monique were the liaisons to the GG." I squeezed my sandwich so hard a slice of tomato shot out onto my plate. "The Proctor Directorate never expected to lose them both before they could find a replacement for Monique. I don't think there's anyone else who can travel to Otherworld to the home of the Elves."

Colin took a drink of his beer then set his bottle down. "Does your father speak with the Great Guardian?"

I gave him a rueful look. "I don't think they're necessarily on the best of terms. Father has never returned home in a good mood after a meeting with the GG."

"And you've never been crazy about her." Colin smiled back before taking a bite of his club sandwich.

"She drives me nuts." I pushed my hand through my hair in a frustrated motion. "All of her riddles and the fact that she hasn't gotten us the help we needed when we needed it . . ." I shook my head. "I've never met her, but as irreverent as I've been, I'm not sure what kind of welcome I would get. I might do more harm than good."

Colin swallowed. Thanks to the Witch's gift, I knew what he was going to say before he said it out loud. "If Armand is right, you might be the only one who can get an audience with her. With your father's help."

I looked up at the ceiling and groaned. "There has got to be someone else. Like someone with skills in diplomacy."

He pointed a finger at me. "You have excellent diplomatic skills. Look how you handle Ice and Joshua. Not to mention Fere and Kelly. You treat everyone with respect and you smooth the waters when they need it. You keep everyone on track and professional. You have more than what it takes, Nyx."

I didn't need to read his thoughts to know that he meant what he said. I smiled. "Thanks."

"Why don't you finish that sandwich you've been playing with for the last five minutes," he said.

I knew when to shut up and listen to an order, so I did just that.

It wasn't easy, though. No matter how I tried not to, I could hear Colin's thoughts. How much he enjoyed club sandwiches and beer. A brief memory of tracking with the new Witch Tracker last night along with the pit bull Shifter and the falcon. But mostly me.

His thoughts were warm, genuine, real. He wasn't intentionally thinking them for me to hear. He meant them. How beautiful he thought I was and how much he cared for me . . . what he wanted to do with me.

Those thoughts kept my face warm.

As soon as we had cleaned the plates and put them away, Colin brought me into the circle of his arms. The kitchen light was bright and highlighted his long blond hair. His features were strong, masculine, but next to Rodán he was the most beautiful male specimen I had ever seen.

With my fingertip I traced the scaled serpent tattoo along his arm. It looked almost alive. Flames curled over Colin's shoulder from the serpent's mouth as it wound up and around his arm from his wrist to his shoulder. The tattoo almost looked like a living, breathing creature as it moved with the flex of his muscular arm.

I love you, Nyx, came the strong thought in my mind. I caught my breath.

Heat flushed through my body again and I swallowed as I met his gaze. So much feeling and emotion rose within me. Fear, hope, caring, and love. My heart filled with it, filled with the love that had grown over the months since I'd first met Colin of Campton.

My throat was so dry I thought that I wouldn't be able to get the words out without them sounding pale and insignificant compared with the strength of what he was telling me.

"I love you, Colin." It came out clear, and I hope filled with the meaning behind it.

He smiled. "I know."

I slugged his arm with a teasing punch, the arm without the tattoo. "Cocky, aren't you?"

With a knee-melting grin, Colin said, "When it comes to you."

I wrapped my arms around his neck and drew him down to kiss me. His lips were firm and warm, his taste masculine and seductive. His kiss was as steady and constant as he was. A male who was confident in who he was and who he loved. I sensed it all.

When he raised his head, I rested my forehead against his chest. My breathing wasn't steady—it was almost as rough as if I had just fought off a dozen Vamps again. His heart had an even thump to it. His presence warmed me as if his Dragon's fire was reaching out and enveloping me.

"Look at me." His voice was husky, his tone low and throbbing. "I want to see your eyes."

I brought my gaze up to meet his. The blazing warmth there melted me.

Then I realized I couldn't hear his thoughts anymore . . . I was feeling them.

He kissed me again and this time I felt both lost and found. Lost in the kiss, like I was traveling to some Otherworld I'd never seen before. And found because Colin was with me the entire way.

When he stepped back I ran my tongue along my lips, tasting him. For all the time I'd been seeing Colin, we had never taken our relationship beyond kissing and cuddling.

I knew a part of me had held back because it had been too soon after my breakup with Adam. But now that chapter had had a chance to close and I could move on.

I'd fallen for Colin long ago, but I'd wanted to make sure it wasn't just a rebound relationship. I found it was possible to love two men even as I let one of them go. Ever since Colin had shared with me who he was, his struggles, his vulnerabilities, it had taken my feelings for him to a different level.

This time I took Colin by the hand and led him into the bedroom, something I'd never done before.

He didn't seem surprised. He let me draw him close to his enormous, almost Dragon-sized bed.

I don't know if he kept me out, or if I was able to turn away his thoughts, but I wasn't hearing them, and for that I was glad. I wanted to know how he felt by him showing me.

His chest was hard, his muscles firm as I slipped my hands under his T-shirt and ran my palms over him. He felt warm and good to my touch. I pushed his shirt up and he helped me pull it over his head before he tossed it over his shoulder.

We kicked off our shoes and then I reached for the button of his jeans. I unfastened it and then slid the denim to the floor. He kicked them aside. I never knew boxer briefs could look so good on a man. I also never thought of a Dragon in them, and that made me smile.

Colin kissed my smile as he rubbed my shoulders through

my blouse. His palms felt wonderfully warm, the heat easily transferring through the material. He brought his fingers to the top button of my blouse and hesitated. His gaze seemed to ask me if I wanted him to go on.

I brought my fingers up to his and unfastened the first button myself. When my blouse parted he traced the curves of my body, up and around my breasts and the lacy bra covering them. His callused hands brushed my softer skin, and the pleasant feel of them made me shiver.

He pushed my blouse over my shoulders and I let it drop to the floor. His hands caressed my belly then along the waistband of my slacks before his fingers unfastened them.

With slow, deliberate movements, he pushed my slacks over my hips and panties, running his palms along the curves of my backside until the slacks slid down my thighs.

When I had stepped out of the material, he brought me close to him, pressing himself against my belly. The feel of him next to my skin was so inviting.

I tugged his boxer briefs over his hips to the floor and shivered at his naked male beauty. All that golden skin, firm muscles. His trim waist and powerful thighs.

Everything about him was beautiful.

"A Dragon," I said softly. "In the flesh."

"A princess." Colin let his palms slide up and down my bare arms. "Almost in the flesh."

I grinned up at him. "Dragons have a thing for princesses, don't they."

He gave a solemn nod and spoke as though he was totally serious. "Especially Drow princesses. Beautiful Dark Elves are our favorite."

I wrapped my arms around his neck and pressed my body to his. He felt so good and warm against me. "Oh, really."

"Yes, really."

"Are you using your mesmerizing power?" I teased. "Because you've sure mesmerized me."

"Have I?" He reached behind me and unfastened my bra. "Mesmerizing is a useful skill, yes?" he said as he pulled my bra straps over my shoulders and bared my breasts.

Happiness rose up inside me as he touched me. A feeling different from anything I'd felt before.

The look in his eyes took my breath away. "You are so beautiful, Nyx." His gaze met mine. "In every way imaginable. Your heart, your soul, your nature. Everything about you."

I bit my lower lip. The strength of his belief was obvious in each word.

"Funny," I said, my voice a little throaty. "I think the same thing about you."

"That I'm beautiful?" His expression was teasing.

"As a matter of fact, yes," I said. "You are gorgeous. So much so that I might need some of the elderflower antidote."

Colin laughed then kissed me again, rocking me from side to side as he kept our bodies flush together.

When he drew away he slid his hands up over my hips and hooked his fingers in the waistband of my panties. Then he slipped the panties down over my hips so they fell to my feet.

He took me by the hand and led me to the bed. I lay back on the soft pillow and looked up at him. He let his gaze drift over my body as if drinking me in from head to toe.

Colin braced his hands to either side of me so that he was above me. The heat of his body intensified, as if Dragon flames were brushing my body. He kissed me deeply and I knew I wanted him.

His words were soft and husky when he spoke. "Let me show you how much I love you, Nyx." I could see the love in his eyes, feel it in his presence.

As he held himself above me, his muscles bulged and his arms shook, as if he was holding himself back—barely.

I wrapped my legs around his waist and pulled him closer. I started kissing him with every bit of passion that was wound inside me.

His lips were firm, his taste so masculine. I clenched my fists in his hair and squirmed beneath him.

"I love how wild you can be." Colin's long blond hair brushed my face as he rocked against me, showing me just how turned on he was.

With a harsh groan, Colin dipped his head and licked each nipple with his warm tongue, then gently nipped at them with his teeth. I cried out as wild sensations traveled straight from my breasts to my abdomen.

Colin drew back, his eyes focused on mine. I felt as if I was held in a Dragon spell even though I knew he wasn't using his magic. No, this was a magic all our own.

He spread my thighs and settled his body between them. I moved beneath him, not wanting to wait, barely controlling my impatience.

And then I felt him against my skin before he slid inside of me.

Colin rocked against me, riding me. I couldn't help the sounds that came from me. Soft moans and whimpers that grew louder the more he drew it out.

Stars started to spin in my mind as an oncoming orgasm grew and grew inside me. It was so intense that I didn't know if I'd survive it.

And then I could no longer think, only feel as everything exploded inside me.

I cried out and then realized Colin was shouting his own release.

My body did not want to come down from such heights. Finally it eased and I gave a sigh of exhaustion.

Amazing.

Colin kissed me then snuggled at my side. I drifted off to sleep feeling safer than I'd felt in a long time.

TWENTY-THREE

Colin looked a little green after I took us through the transference from the Earth Otherworld to the belowground Otherworld realm of the Dark Elves. I did a credible job of not throwing up.

"Sorry." I took Colin's hand, and we stepped down from the transference stone. "It was my first time taking anyone with me." Not to mention my first time using the transference to get home. Usually my father did it.

"I didn't need to know that, Nyx." Colin squeezed my hand and smiled. "Next time, I drive."

I matched his smile. "Now that you know the way here, I guess that'll be just fine."

He kissed me and I gave a soft little moan. A thrill went through my belly as I thought of our afternoon together.

I had shifted into Drow before we left for Otherworld and wore black leather and my Elvin boots, as I did when I tracked. Colin simply wore jeans, a Breaking Benjamin T-shirt, and New Balance shoes. We both carried packs containing enough for an overnight trip to Otherworld.

"Nyx?" My father's voice boomed out as he stepped into his transference room.

"Hi, Father." I gave him a bright smile. "I'm home. And I brought company."

Father narrowed his gray eyes at Colin, assessing him. "Dragon," he said.

Colin nodded. "Yes, Your Majesty."

"Colin, this is my father, King Ciar," I said. "Father, this is Colin of Campton."

Father looked at him a moment more before he strode across the chamber and reached out his arm. They did the warrior hand-and-elbow grip.

Over two thousand years old, broad-shouldered, muscular, and powerful, my father was a male who few could contend with. If any.

His sapphire-blue hair flowed past his shoulders and light blue skin. As usual he wore leather breeches and boots, a sword sheathed at his side. The metal breastplate he had on was studded with precious gemstones mined by the Dark Elves.

Father gave a single nod to Colin, and they released their grip. In that nod I saw approval, and it made my chest warm. Father believed in his senses, and obviously they had told him that Colin was a great guy.

My father turned to me and held out his arms. He was so tall I had to stand on my tiptoes. He felt good and familiar as I caught his earthy scent.

"Ciar?" My mother's voice came from the entrance. "Did you send for—" She caught sight of me. "Nyx!"

My beautiful mother picked up her skirts as she hurried across the transference chamber toward me. Her sapphire-blue eyes had a glint of tears as she hugged me. "I've missed you," she said as she drew away and smiled her brilliant smile.

In Otherworld, after about thirty human years, beings don't age, or they age very slowly. My mother had been in her twenties when Father brought her to the belowground realm. She had been here almost thirty years, yet didn't look much older than she had when I was a youngling.

"I've missed you, too." I hugged her again, noticing her pale skin next to my amethyst flesh. Her skin was fairer than mine—when I was human—from living underground for so many years. She was about two inches shorter than me and I'd inherited her sapphire-blue eyes.

"Colin, this is my mother, Kathryn Ciar." I drew her toward him. "Mother, this is Colin."

"Dragon," Father said.

She looked interested. "I've never met a Dragon before," she said as Colin took her fingers and kissed the back of her hand.

"It is my pleasure." Colin gave her a smile.

Father took him by the shoulder and started walking toward the entrance to the transference chamber. "How do you know my daughter?"

"Why didn't you say you were coming?" Mother and I walked with arms around each other as we followed the two males.

"Wanted to surprise you," I said.

"Your father usually brings you through the transference." She looked at me. "Did your Dragon bring you?"

I glanced at "my Dragon" before I turned back to Mother. "I did it myself. I brought us both through the transference."

"What?" My father nearly bellowed the word as he came up short and turned to face me. "You are far too young to even have the ability, much less use it to bring someone through the transference."

"I, uh, never had a chance to tell you." I sort of hadn't wanted to tell him—yet. "I learned how to do it during that Werewolf op."

Father scowled. "You are too young," he repeated.

"Apparently not." I glanced at Colin, who had one brow raised. "I got us here just fine."

"Humph." Father turned away again. "We will discuss this later."

"There's nothing to discuss," I mumbled under my breath, then realized I was falling into the role I'd always played with my father.

When we reached the entrance, two guards stood outside. I looked at the guard on my right. Instead of the usual disdain for me that the warriors held, I saw interest. And was that respect?

I had trained with Father's warriors from the time I was a youngling. I'd grown up with a sword in my hand.

The problem was that Drow females are subservient to males. That was one thing Mother hadn't believed in for herself or for me. Father loved her so much that he didn't argue when she raised me to be the independent female I am. And I had Father twisted around my little finger. He would do anything for me.

So I grew up around warriors who did not believe I should be there. And I'd humiliated those I'd bested over the years.

I cut my gaze to the other guard on the opposite side of the door. His gaze was just as interested, and not hostile or cold in the least.

What in the Otherworld was going on?

Father laughed at something Colin said and clapped him on the shoulder. "We will have an ale at the tavern."

Who could argue with the king?

My parents' first meeting with Colin was going exceptionally well if my father was already inviting him for a drink.

Mother and I talked as we walked behind the two males. I was glad she didn't ask me about Colin even when we were a bit of a distance behind them. Dragons have exceptional hearing.

As we walked through the great hall to the passageway that led to the underground village, I leaned close to my mother and kept my voice low.

"Why are all of the males looking like that?" I said. "Like they're interested in me and even a little curious."

Mother tilted her head. Being the queen she was, she didn't look directly at the males to see what I was talking about, but I was sure she was glancing at them from the corner of her eye. "Honey, I have no idea. But your father might."

"No." I shook my head. "Let's not get Father involved."

"I don't blame you for that," Mother said with a conspiratorial note to her voice. "Your father would make their lives miserable for even looking at you."

Father and Colin dropped back so that they were with us as we entered the village.

"I have something I must attend to," Father said. "I will meet you at the tavern."

Colin smiled at me and walked beside me, my mother on my opposite side. "So tell me about this place," he said.

"The belowground world of the Dark Elves is a lot like aboveground, with a few exceptions," I said. "We don't have horses for transportation or oxen for work. But we do have pigs, sheep, and cows for food.

"In the Drow world," I said, "if males are not warriors, they work in the mines, own shops, barter aboveground, and fill other 'male' roles. Females take care of the younglings, cook, clean, and other 'female' jobs."

We walked into a tavern filled with laughter, talking, and the sounds of ale mugs thumping on the tables and the barmaid serving up orders.

The room grew quiet when Colin and I walked in with Mother. I didn't know if it was because we were with the queen, or because Colin was a stranger, or because everyone seemed to have taken some kind of fascination with me. Maybe it was all of the above.

We settled on bench seats at one of the picnic-like tables and the barmaid practically ran to my mother's side. I was certain it wasn't every day that the queen stopped by.

"An ale for each of us," Mother said with a pleasant smile. "Plus a fourth for the king."

When the barmaid rushed away, Mother turned to me. "Excuse me for a moment."

When Mother left, Colin squeezed my hand beneath the table. "See any friends around?"

I shook my head. "Because I wasn't raised in the same lifestyle as other Dark Elves, I never made many friends. I had servants who made polite conversation, but I think everyone was always a little frightened of me."

"Frightened?" Colin said. "How?"

"I don't think it's just because I'm both a princess and a

Drow warrior, but rather that I am *different*. No one else in my world shifts into human form. I am unique."

Colin studied me. "I can't imagine you not having friends here."

The thought hit me of how the Witch said the mind reading would come and go. I hadn't heard anything since my time with Colin. But that was fine.

I shrugged. "I was used to it. I didn't know anything different until I became a Tracker and I learned what friends really are."

The barmaid returned with four mugs of ale, setting the others at the empty seats for Mother and Father. She scuttled away.

"You sure stir up a lot of interest." Colin held his mug of ale and looked around. Just about every warrior in the place was looking at me.

"Do I have something in my teeth?" I said. "Because I've never stirred up interest like this before. Ever."

"No on the teeth." He grinned. "Let's find out about the other."

I opened my mouth to ask him how we'd do that when he turned to a warrior at a table next to us. "Did you have something you would like to ask Princess Nyx?"

"Yes." The young warrior looked pleased that he'd been asked, which was strangeness beyond strangeness to me. He was one of the younger warriors who'd started training just as I was leaving for the Earth Otherworld. I suppose that's why he didn't have any reservations answering Colin.

"What's your name?" Colin asked. "And your question."

"Alfric, sir." He nodded to Colin. "My lady," he said to me.

"We have heard tales," he continued, "that you are a great warrior in a different Otherworld. That you bested the same beings who stole and murdered our people."

My eyes widened. In Drow I said, "Zombies?" That was what this was about?

The male nodded with enthusiasm. "And other heroics. You are known well to us now as a warrior princess."

A warrior princess? I blinked at him. "I am?"

The young warrior gave an enthusiastic nod. "Yes, the stories say—"

He suddenly sat bolt upright, his gaze no longer curious but now steadfast, like any Drow warrior. The rest of the warriors in the tavern seemed to take the same cue as heads suddenly turned toward the entrance.

TWENTY-FOUR

A larger-than-life presence filled the room, and I turned to see my father walk through the tavern door. He lifted his hands, telling everyone to remain seated, then worked his way over to us.

My mother came in behind him. She must have gone out into the village for something.

As soon as Father seated himself and picked up his mug of ale, the warriors relaxed and went back to their meals and their own mugs of ale. Noise filled the tavern again.

"It is good you have come, Daughter." Father always sounded gruff, even when we were having a family conversation.

"How long will you be here?" Mother smiled, obviously pleased I was there. She made such a pretty queen. Despite the fact that she was human, the Dark Elves had grown to love her.

"Not long, Mother." I wondered how much time it would take to get an audience with the Great Guardian. "It depends on a few things."

"Such as?" Father asked.

I frowned as I thought about what I needed to tell them, and what I needed to ask my father. I glanced at the warriors around me and lowered my voice. "It's best we talk somewhere private."

Father studied me for a long moment then nodded. "First we will eat. Then we will talk."

The barmaid returned and Father told her to prepare a

meal for us. The tavern's cook and owner were bound to make sure it was a kingly feast.

While we waited, Father drilled Colin with questions. "Where are you from?"

"Campton, sir." Colin looked far from intimidated, unlike many others when they met the king for the first time. Colin had a comfortable presence that I loved.

"Ah." Father gave a nod. "How is old Durkin?"

"Last I saw King Durkin," Colin said with a smile, "he was still chasing off knights who want his daughter's hand in marriage."

"He must have more of a problem if you are no longer in his realm," Father said. "Dragons aren't easy to come by."

"It is true that my race is becoming much rarer," Colin said.

Fascinating. I'd had no idea Father would know the king of Colin's home.

Mother looked from Father to Colin with genuine interest on her face. "How many princesses have you guarded?"

"Over the ages there have been several." His gaze met mine. "None so beautiful or special as your daughter."

My cheeks grew warm and my belly flip-flopped because of the way he was looking at me. Colin had a way of making me feel cherished and beautiful, and loved.

Father cleared his throat. Colin turned his attention back to him, answering more of Father's questions and telling stories that had my gruff king of a father belly laughing.

Sheesh. I'd never expected this. But I loved it. My father genuinely liked Colin, that much was obvious.

The barmaid and servers brought out two hams, three beef roasts, two chickens, and a shank of lamb. Then came the vegetables, bartered from the Light Elves. Carrots, potatoes, cabbage, and corn pudding. The freshly baked bread and rolls smelled like heaven.

Father told the warriors in the tavern to share in our dinner. Not one of them declined. I don't know if it was because he was the king, or because they were hungry.

After such a delicious feast, it was hard to pack in dessert, too, but I managed. Fruit tarts and puddings were served and devoured.

When we were finished with dinner, the four of us walked back through the village and across the great hall to Mother and Father's chambers. In the sitting room, Mother sat in her rocker while Father reclined in an oversized chair. Colin and I sat together on a settee across from both of them.

The room was done in rich purples and blues. Mother had decorated it once she moved in, with elegant Queen Anne furniture bought in from the Earth Otherworld.

I sat up straight on the settee as I spoke to my father. "Rodán is . . ." I swallowed as I forced the words out. "Vampires got to him, Father."

Shock registered on Father's and Mother's faces.

"Rodán?" Mother held her palm to her chest. "He's . . . dead?"

"What happened?" Father said almost in a growl. He had never liked Rodán, but I knew he had respected him.

I wasn't sure how to say it, so I did the best I could. "He isn't exactly dead, he's undead. Or soon to be. Volod bit him and buried him and soon he will rise as one of them. He will become a paranorm Vampire."

Mother seemed to be holding her breath. Father's features took on a tight, angry expression.

I raised my hand. "Father, do *not* tell me I must move back to Otherworld, away from danger, because that's not going to happen."

For the first time, he didn't launch into a tirade about me coming back to Otherworld permanently. I was his princess—it was hard for him to stop being overprotective.

Mother moved to the settee, and Colin got up so that she could sit down beside me. She hugged me and for the hundredth time I wished that I'd inherited from her the ability to cry.

"I know he was special to you, honey." She stroked my hair, her motions soothing. "I'm so sorry."

"I am, too." I straightened and looked at my hands before meeting my mother's gaze. "I miss him," I said, my voice hoarse with pain. "I miss him so much. Even worse is that I might have to deal with him as an enemy. I just can't think of him that way, but I know that deep down, that is reality."

"Tell me what it is that you have come to talk with me about." My father's words brought my attention back to him. "I know you didn't come from the Earth Otherworld just to inform me of this." I wasn't surprised my father knew I had something to ask of him. He wasn't being callous, just matter-of-fact.

I leaned forward as I explained what had happened so far, all that we knew. Then I discussed what we believed would be happening soon, going into as much detail as possible. Colin interjected whenever I needed him to.

"We need help," I said after I'd filled Father in. "We don't have the resources in New York City to battle this threat."

"What do you want of me, Daughter?" My father probably knew, but was asking anyway.

"I want to know if you can send Drow warriors." I clasped my hands in my lap. "To help us fight this Vampire threat before they amass an army of paranorm Vampires. We must do this as soon as possible.

"We need skilled warriors," I continued. "Humans are no match for the paranorm Vampires. We lack numbers. A force of Drow warriors I could lead would give us what we need to go after them.

"The warriors cannot handle daylight, but then Vampires also come out only at night." I leaned forward. "The threat to the entire Earth Otherworld is so strong. I know it is asking a lot, Father, but I don't know what else to do."

Father was quiet for a long moment. Because he didn't immediately say no, I had some hope.

But finally he said, "I am unable to do this for the people of the Earth Otherworld."

Even though I had expected this, I felt deflated and hurt. "Why not?"

"I will not risk the lives of my warriors in a battle for beings from another Otherworld." He didn't raise his voice; he sounded genuinely concerned.

"It is against my policy to have my warriors risk their lives in a fight that is not theirs," he continued. "I would do it for you, Nyx. You are aware of that. However, I would be doing it for others, not you. It is not our affair."

"I understand." I sighed and looked at my hands. "But I thought I'd try."

Mother stroked my hair, her touch light and welcome. "What will you do now?"

I glanced up at her. "I need to talk with the Great Guardian."

"What?" Father looked surprised and not very happy.

"There's no one left who can speak with her." I forced myself to relax against the back of the settee. "Monique and Rodán are gone forever, and I'm told there are no other liaisons to the GG. I'm the only one with any sort of connection to her. We need help, and maybe the GG can give it."

Father still didn't appear to be pleased, but he slowly nodded. "I will inform the Great Guardian that you wish an audience with her."

"Thank you, Father." I took a deep breath and let it out. At least he would help me with this hurdle. "How soon do you think that will be?"

The springs on my father's chair creaked as he got to his feet. The rest of us stood, too. "I will contact her now," he said. "As far as when she will give you an audience, I do not know."

"I hope it's not long." I was so restless, I felt I needed to talk with her this very minute. "I don't think the beings in the Earth Otherworld have much more time."

"It will be when it will be." Father strode out of the chamber and closed the door behind him.

TWENTY-FIVE

"Wonder how things are going at home," I said as I walked the last few steps out of the belowground realm of the Dark Elves and into the late-afternoon sunshine of Otherworld. I ran my fingers along my Drow collar as I spoke.

"We'll be heading back soon." As the enormous stone covering the entrance shuddered to a close, Colin came up behind me and rested his hands on my bare shoulders. I leaned back against him and felt myself relax just a little. "And we will deal with Volod," he said.

I nodded and felt the slide of my hair against Colin's chest before I turned to face him. "The Great Guardian better have some answers."

Colin's lips were soft as he brushed them over mine. I wrapped my arms around him and hugged him back.

"Are you stalling?" He smiled as he drew away.

I started to protest then realized he was right. "I guess I am a little intimidated at meeting her in person."

"It'll all be fine." Colin took my hand and squeezed it. "Which way, O beautiful one?"

I raised our joined hands and indicated a path in the forest a little to our left.

"I don't know how Father arranged this meeting so soon." I started walking at Colin's side. "But I'm glad he was able to. We need to be getting back."

"Your father is a man of amazing stature," Colin said. "Rodán is the only other person I've known to have been in the Great Guardian's presence."

"Yes, he is a man of great stature." I sighed. "I just wish he could join us with some of his men. Just think what an advantage that would be. If Vampires can't turn Dark Elves, and Elves have superior strength and magic, it could make a real difference."

"Vampires are one thing." Colin squeezed my hand. "A Vampire paranorm force of former Trackers is as formidable a force as he would face." He continued, "Taking nothing away from Dark Elves, who can hold their own against any fighters, but this is a dangerous fight and your father knows it."

I frowned as I thought about this. "My father is not one to shrink back from a fight."

"I could see in your father's eyes that he wants to help." Twigs and dried leaves crunched beneath Colin's shoes. "It is not that he is afraid. He just has to think about his own people first."

"Of course." I heard the sound of a nightbird as it started to wake. "I have to get past the idea that my father said no to me. It's something he doesn't do. But I know it's unfair for me to put that on him and I understand his position."

"We'll find other ways to defeat Volod." Colin ducked beneath a low-hanging branch. "How far to the meadow your father told us about?"

"Not far." I stepped over a fallen log, making no sound whatsoever, unlike Colin who stepped on a branch. The large cracking sound echoed through the forest. Birds quieted.

I looked up at him. "I didn't realize Dragons were so noisy."

"You should see me when I shift."

"I have." I shook my head. "Let's just say it's a good thing we don't have to rely on you for stealth right now."

He bumped my shoulder with his intentionally, and I did a little sidestep but didn't stumble. I laughed and bumped him back and he did stumble a bit.

The forest grew quieter as we neared a meadow. From

ahead came the burbling sound of a small stream. The forest smelled so clean, of fresh air, pine, and rich loam.

My heart beat faster as we got closer to the meadow and my belly did a flip. What would it be like to talk with the Great Guardian?

We paused at the edge of the tree line. I caught my breath and wished Father could see the beauty here in daylight. Soft yellow sunshine, patches of purple and pink flowers dipping in the light breeze, and grass as green as a carpet of Drow-mined emeralds.

My boots skimmed over the tops of pale mushrooms at the edge of the darkened forest. Colin came up beside me. "Your world is amazingly beautiful, Nyx. This looks like a place I'd expect to meet the Great Guardian."

A small footbridge spanned the width of the stream, the water sparkling in the ebbing sunlight. The opposite end seemed to fade away into the forest. It was like looking into the distance, yet it wasn't that far.

I tipped my head back and looked at lacy clouds strewn across sky growing deeper blue with every passing moment. My skin wasn't tingling yet, but the night was on its way.

"Nyx." The sound of a sweet voice had me whirling and facing the bridge again.

A glow filled the meadow. I raised my hand in front of my eyes to block the strength of it.

When the glow faded enough to see, an ethereal being, beyond anything I could imagine, stood a few feet away.

Slender and fine-boned, she was almost as tall as Colin. She had long, delicate fingers that were folded in front of her, against the soft white material of her gown.

I'd never seen such perfect skin, or eyes as crystal blue. Long, glossy hair, pale like jasmine, tumbled over her shoulders to the soft grass at her bare feet.

Colin had a hold on my hand still, and he gently tugged as he bent to one knee. I found myself kneeling before her.

"Rise." She spoke like a queen, yet sounded young and sweet.

But when I was standing, through the crystal blue of her eyes I saw ancient wisdom that I knew I could never grasp. I could feel the Guardian's power, vibrant, tangible. Warmth and a tingling sensation traveled throughout my body like I'd never experienced before. As if I were being embraced by someone who I truly loved.

I felt no fear. The warmth and goodness of her filled me.

"Nyx, welcome." She smiled at me then inclined her head to Colin. "It is a pleasure to see you, Colin of Campton."

Colin bowed his head before looking at the Great Guardian again. "I never expected to be permitted to see you. Who am I to see the Guardian? I will forever remember this day."

She smiled. "Who are you? You are a brave Dragon who cares about others. You have righted your way and you are worthy of such time with me. I see great things for you. So yes, you shall remember this day."

When she returned her gaze to me, I wondered how I'd ever called her GG instead of the Great Guardian. My face burned at my lack of respect.

"I am pleased with you." The strength of her statement surprised me, and my cheeks grew even hotter. "You are a brave warrior. Most important, you are a brave warrior who cares for others before herself."

"Thank you." I could almost picture how small my words were in her presence. They seemed insignificant.

"What can I do for you?" she said.

"I'm here because neither Rodán nor Monique can be." I swallowed. "I am told there is no one but me who can speak with you."

"It saddens me." The Guardian's voice grew softer. "That two such as them should be lost to something so evil."

"How did you know about Rodán?" I asked. "I guess I have heard that you know all, but I wasn't certain."

She gave a sad smile that seemed to say, *Of course I knew.* Instead, she said, "Rodán is a good man. Now he will be tested."

Hope made me straighten. "Does that mean he'll be okay? That he'll come back to us?"

"That is not for you to know." The Guardian's face told me nothing as she spoke. "I will only guide you along what I believe is the right path for you."

"I'm sorry I doubted you." I don't even know where the words came from. "I am sorry I didn't believe in you."

"Now is when it is important to believe. You have seen me and heard me. Now is the test for you." She didn't look at me any differently than she had before. "You are young, and you do not know me like Rodán and your father do. They have trusted me. You will learn this also."

"Still—" I started.

"Just know that I have been with you before today, and I am there with you even now. In times of trouble when you will feel most alone, you are not." The glow around her seemed to grow brighter as the day waned.

"Your father and Rodán were successful," she continued. "They knew when to call on me and knew I would provide them enough to prevail if I was able," she continued. "Rodán adhering to that conviction made a difference in your victories."

I tried to process what she was saying. She must have seen the confusion on my face.

"Know that there are powers you can avail yourself of," she said.

I frowned in thought. "What powers? When?"

"You will know when the time comes," she said. "I can't tell you what will happen or how. Only that the evil, the threat is real. The difference can be your belief in the powers available to you."

"I don't understand," I said.

"I will not tell you the outcome. Things look dire now, and hopeless." She was like a patient teacher with a child. "Without faith in what I am saying, following through with the right actions, and using the powers available to you, defeat will follow."

"What about Rodán?" I asked. "He was one of yours, yet an evil has come to him now and he has been turned."

"I have not left Rodán, but sacrifices must be made, Nyx," she said. "Due to the evil of others, sometimes the good of one must be sacrificed for the good of all."

"What can you tell me?" I asked. "What can I do to help my people defeat Volod?"

Her crystal-blue eyes held my gaze. "I will tell you that your victory can come, but only at the cost of your blood. Yet you must trust me and not lose hope, no matter the circumstances."

A chill swept through me. *My blood?* She had to mean me. My blood. My sacrifice. My death.

So be it. What choice did I have? I raised my chin. "I will trust you and do whatever it takes to save paranorms and humans in my adopted Earth Otherworld."

"I know you will." She turned to Colin. "She will need you till the end."

The end. My stomach cramped and my conviction wavered. But I knew what I had to do.

"Thank you." I was grateful to Colin when I felt him take my hand. "I will do anything to defeat Volod. Anything at all."

She gave a slight incline of her head. "I will leave you now."

I opened my mouth to say something then shut it. Instead I bowed my head. When I looked up I saw that Colin had done so as well.

"Farewell, Nyx." She reached up and caressed my cheek. Her touch was soft. I felt an incredible warmth throughout my body again, like a power surge that entered me when she touched me.

"May good fortune be with you." Her last words seemed to be carried on the breeze as they slipped past me.

We watched as the Great Guardian turned away. My skin tingled with the oncoming night, telling me I would be shifting soon. I ignored it and followed her with my gaze.

She walked onto the bridge and paused, then glanced over her shoulder at me. Our gazes met and she gave me a smile again.

Then the Great Guardian turned away and walked the rest of the way across the footbridge before she vanished.

TWENTY-SIX

Wind pulled at Volod's long coat as he stood beside Rodán's grave once again. Clouds obscured the moon, but he did not need its light to see by.

Pleasure swept through him as he waited. It should not be long now.

Monique stood to his right, elegant and lovely in a black evening dress with a matching bolero jacket. Anticipation seemed to thrum around her. She was smiling, her hands clasped before her.

Elizabeth was on his left, wearing a lake-blue dress, her hair swept up and revealing the collar that he hadn't allowed her to take off since Monique put it there. He sensed her anger, but it did not matter to him. What mattered was that she was there to serve him however he chose.

Several Vampire paranorms from Volod's dream team stood by. He wanted them to witness who was now his to command. Who would be their leader as they followed Volod's direction.

The unmarked grave still looked as if it had been in the cemetery for years instead of a mere ten days. But those ten days had seemed very long as he waited for his newly made Vamp to crawl out.

Turning Rodán made him feel triumphant in a way he had not felt before. He, Volod, had captured Rodán of the Light Elves. And now the great Rodán would serve him.

The question of whether or not Rodán would actually rise

from the ground to become a Vampire flickered in Volod's mind. Some paranorms had died in the grave, never to rise.

He immediately dismissed the thought. He truly had no doubt that Rodán would be among the undead soon.

The ground shuddered beneath Volod's feet. He frowned.

Monique bounced up on the toes of her high heels. "He's coming." Her voice quivered with excitement.

Volod wasn't sure exactly what was happening, but it might be a good idea to step back. He grasped Monique's and Elizabeth's arms and drew them back three steps.

A fissure cracked open the earth where Rodán's coffin lay. A low roar came from beneath, the sound of rock and stone churning.

Rocks and dirt burst up into the air, rising in the sky then showering back down. Volod threw up a shield over himself and the two females as he watched and waited.

Rodán rose out of the ground. Not clawing up through the dirt but actually rising as if the earth had decided to give him a ride to the top.

The soil beneath his feet gave way, revealing the simple coffin that Volod had buried him in. The box moved to the side of the grave and settled there.

Rodán stepped onto the ground. Volod tried not to feel any amazement. He'd never seen any being rise like this, nor come out with no dirt clinging to him, and clear-eyed.

The Elf looked from Volod to Elizabeth then settled on Monique. He smiled and revealed his new fangs.

"Rodán." Monique took a step forward, a brilliant smile on her face. She took Rodán's hands in hers. "Welcome to your new world. You have no idea how happy I am that you're here and that we can now share it."

"It is good to see you, love." Rodán embraced Monique, and she gave a happy sigh.

Anger flowed through Volod as he became aware of the members of his dream team looking at Rodán with respect. Each member seemed eager to speak with Rodán, to pay him some sort of homage.

Volod ground his teeth then forced himself to relax. The feelings his Vampire paranorms had for Rodán mattered not. He would maintain ultimate control and use them all for his purposes.

When he was finished with Rodán and the other Vampire paranorm Trackers, he would destroy them all.

Then Volod sucked in his breath as Rodán kissed Monique like a lover, as if Volod, and Elizabeth, and the Vampire paranorms were not there. A slow, deep kiss that had Volod seething. Only knowing that he needed Rodán to draw in Nyx and lead the Vampire paranorms kept him from killing him now.

"Come. Here." Volod spoke the words as a command that could not be ignored by any Vampire he had made.

Rodán broke away from Monique after holding her gaze a fraction longer than Volod would ever allow again. Monique couldn't seem to take her gaze from him.

The Elvin male crossed the few feet it took to stand before Volod. Rodán's eyes were clear, his golden skin only slightly paler than it had been before.

"Bow your head and kneel." Volod kept his features impassive.

Rodán lowered his head and knelt at Volod's feet.

Volod smiled. The great Rodán. His now.

A sliver of moonlight peeked through the cloud cover, and Rodán's long blond hair glittered in its light.

"Who is your master now?" Volod said.

"You are, Volod." Rodán's voice was strong and true.

Satisfaction filled Volod. "And you are mine to direct as I see fit. I made you."

"Yes." Rodán kept his head bowed. "I am yours."

"Then rise." Volod gestured to Rodán's coffin when the Elvin Proctor was on his feet again. "Take your coffin to the hearse parked on the street and we shall leave this place."

Rodán gave a deep nod of acknowledgment. "Of course."

Volod watched as Rodán used his superior Vampire-Elvin strength to pick up the coffin and carry it over his head. Unlike newly made Vamps who had been human before they were turned, Rodán showed no sign of strain or effort. Most Vampire paranorms were much the same. Rodán was exceptional.

With his fingertips at the base of Elizabeth's and Monique's spines, Volod guided them away from the gravesite toward his limo.

When they were seated, he handed Monique a silver leash. Fury flashed in Elizabeth's eyes then faded as she bowed her head. Monique snapped the leash to Elizabeth's collar and held it as they sat on the seat across from Volod.

The sight excited him, made him want to take them both to his bed now. But now was not the time. That would come.

When they arrived at the brownstone that Volod was using as his temporary headquarters, he instructed Rodán to take his coffin down into the basement.

Every Vampire paranorm seemed to be waiting in the huge room on the first floor. Murmurs of excitement went through the crowd as they watched the Elvin Proctor carry his coffin.

Volod studied them. They seemed to be holding their collective breath, waiting for Rodán to return. Rodán would be a popular leader. A powerful leader whom the Vampire paranorms respected. Yet Rodán had bowed and voiced his allegiance. The other paranorms would see this, too.

When Rodán reappeared the Vampire paranorms burst into applause. The Elvin Proctor made a show of humble acceptance, but Volod knew time would tell whether he could truly trust Rodán. He hoped this wasn't a mistake.

No, he was not going to second-guess himself. There was no way for Rodán to break free of Volod's grasp on his undead life. He would serve Volod until his end.

Which would be when Volod had no use for Rodán anymore.

Monique let go of Elizabeth's leash and joined Rodán at the center of the room. Volod frowned inwardly. He had not given her permission to do such a thing. He would deal with her later, when they were alone.

The two Elvin Proctors stood in the midst of all of the Vampire paranorms. Monique took Rodán's hand in hers and smiled at him. Volod had exceptional hearing but Monique spoke so low that he heard nothing when she whispered in Rodán's ear.

Enough. "Monique." Volod kept his tone measured, showing no hint of his anger.

She brought her gaze to his and seemed to come back to herself. She gave a brief nod then slipped her hand from Rodán's and excused herself to return to Volod.

"Take Elizabeth's leash," he ordered Monique.

She obeyed and grasped it in her hand.

Humiliation was in Elizabeth's gaze as she looked away from both of them.

"Stay here." He said the words to both females, then made his way to where Rodán was speaking with several of the Vampire paranorms.

"We have much to discuss," Volod said.

Rodán lowered his head then looked at Volod again. "I am at your service."

Volod snapped his fingers at Monique and Elizabeth and with a gesture instructed them to follow him and Rodán up the stairs.

When they reached the upper level, Volod led the way to his study. Elizabeth closed the door behind them then stood obediently beside Monique.

Volod turned to Rodán. "Take a seat." He pointed toward a pair of chairs in front of the large desk, then settled into the leather desk chair.

Rodán sat. He looked casual, at ease with his surroundings and at being a Vampire paranorm. Humans and paranorms alike accepted, even embraced their fates, easily transitioning into their Vampiric roles.

Somehow he had expected a little resistance from Rodán and was pleased to see none. The Vampire paranorms seemed to readily take to him, as if already looking to him to lead them. That was all well and good, so long as Rodán knew his place.

"I have allowed you to live for two reasons." Volod leaned back in his chair. "One, I need a leader over the Vampire paranorms who will work closely with me. And two, I want you to bring Nyx to me."

A flicker of something passed through Rodán's eyes, a look that made Volod feel as though Rodán was remembering who he'd been.

"Do you plan on killing her?" Rodán asked in a voice that Volod could not read.

"No." Not yet, but Volod was not ready to voice that he intended to eventually rid himself of her permanently. "I can use her as a Vampire paranorm. She is strong and would make a good leader to serve under you."

That wasn't the real reason Volod wanted her. He longed to humiliate her in any way he possibly could, perhaps putting her on a leash, like Elizabeth, and making her follow him on all fours. Certainly she would share his bed. Yes, he would use Nyx until he was through with her. Then she would be killed.

Rodán gave a nod, apparently approving. Yet his eyes gave nothing away. He looked much the same as a Vampire paranorm as he had as a paranorm. Volod had the sense of Rodán putting himself above all others, including Volod.

The thoughts made anger burn in Volod's chest. He would take great pleasure in destroying Rodán when the time came.

For now he would use the Elvin Proctor to lead the Vampire paranorm Night Trackers. They would destroy the paranorm world so that no one would ever have control over Vampires again.

TWENTY-SEVEN

It had been twelve days since Rodán was bitten a second time.

Two days since Rodán should have risen as one of the undead.

Four days since we returned from Otherworld.

I closed my eyes and rubbed the bridge of my nose before looking out my bedroom window again at Central Park, which would soon be dark with the deepening evening. Spring, a time of renewal, had made the park green with life.

But right then what I saw were the branches that were not yet budding, the dead grass not yet taken over by green, the dead leaves still on the ground, and the darkness coming to steal away whatever was good.

All I could think about was Rodán as one of the undead. The beautiful Rodán I'd known didn't exist anymore.

My phone rang. I had turned off the theme to *Rocky* in favor of a traditional ring. Knowing that Rodán should have come out of the grave by now made my heart ache too much for silly ringtones.

The phone number on the caller ID wasn't one I recognized. I glanced out the window as I answered. "This is Nyx."

"Nyx."

I went rigid at the sound of the familiar voice. "Rodán?"

"Are you all right?" Concern was in his tone as I tried to get my bearings. "Is everything okay with you and the other Trackers?"

"What?" I blinked. This was in no way like anything I

had expected. "We're fine." I cleared my throat. "What about you? Are you . . ." I didn't know how to finish.

"I am good." Rodán lowered his voice. "I escaped from nearly being turned and I have been in hiding."

"Really?" Hope bubbled inside of me."You got away?"

"Yes." He said the word with no hesitation. "I need to see you. Tonight."

I paused. Inside I knew he wasn't telling the truth. "Rodán, please don't lie to me and make this worse. You are a Vampire."

A pause. "Why do you say this?"

"Desmond showed us what happened in a hologram. We saw it all, Rodán. The girls with the potion, the fight with Volod and Monique, and Volod biting you. We saw it all. Don't lie."

Another pause. "You are right. I was afraid to tell you because you might not believe me."

My heart sank as I let him go on. "But it is not what you think. I want to meet with you. I need to get to you before Volod does. I will not harm you but I'm afraid Volod will kill you, Nyx. Do you at least believe that I would never hurt you?"

I bit my lower lip before I said, "I want to believe that, but how can I?"

"Nyx, you know that Vampires have controlled themselves without attacks for decades," Rodán said. "I can also."

I remained quiet, not knowing what to say.

"Volod has a bull's-eye on your back," Rodán continued. "I want to meet and protect you."

Confusion made my mind fuzzy. Part of me wanted to say yes, but after all that had happened, I didn't dare jump into anything. Yet what if he was telling the truth?

"Where is it you want to meet?" I asked. "What time?"

"Central Park." As he said it, I looked back out the window. He added, "Cherry Hill Boat Landing. Midnight."

It was a secluded location . . . a perfect hideaway or trap.

"How about the Gapstow Bridge?" I said. Much more open yet secluded enough for a meeting like this.

He paused. "Yes, that would be a good location."

"Rodán?" I needed to be sure it was him. No matter how familiar his voice sounded, there are things in this world not to be trusted. "What did my father say when you told him you wanted to recruit me to be a Night Tracker?"

Rodán laughed. It was so good to hear that sound, it almost made me smile. "He said he would never allow his daughter to leave with the likes of me."

I did smile then. It was him. "Okay," I said. "I'll be there at midnight."

"Nyx." He sounded more serious. "Come alone."

I opened my mouth to answer then stopped. Alone?

"Rodán." I spoke slowly. "Others have been tricked. You know I can't come alone. Why are you asking this of me?"

"It is important that you follow my direction." He sounded like the Proctor who had always been on the lookout for his Trackers. "You will be safe."

I paused before I said, "All right."

"I will see you tonight," Rodán said then disconnected.

The phone felt hard and cool in my hand as I continued holding it to my ear a few seconds longer. My mind whirled.

Rodán would never ask me to put myself in possible danger. He would be the first person to tell me to not go alone, to bring backup with me.

Still, what he'd said was true. Vampires had the ability to suppress their natures and had done so for countless years. Rodán himself was one of the strongest beings I had ever known, and he had never done anything to harm me.

With a frown I turned away from the window. No, I would not go alone. But how I could I bring backup without Rodán sensing it?

I would choose Dopplers with animal forms that you'd find in a park, and Shifters who could choose any animal form they wanted.

What about the gift the Witch had given me? Would I be able to hear Rodán's thoughts? I hadn't been able to over the phone, but maybe it didn't work like that.

I looked at my phone and dialed the first person who came to mind. "Colin," I said. "I need to see you."

Thanks to his Dragon ability to transfer, Colin was knocking at my front door a moment later.

I let him in then hugged him when he closed the door.

"Are you all right?" Colin held me by my shoulders and looked at me. "Something's wrong."

"Yes, I'm fine," I said, wondering if I was telling the truth. "But you're right, something is wrong."

I explained to Colin about the phone call with Rodán—or at least who I thought was Rodán. "He knew what my father said to him when he recruited me as a Tracker," I said, partly to myself, partly to Colin. "So it really is him . . . I just don't know for sure if he was telling the truth."

Colin looked grim. "He might be, but meeting him alone would be foolish. We have to assume he is not being truthful."

"I agree," I said. "Angel can come as a squirrel and Lawan in cat form." I ran through the Trackers. "Ice can be a falcon, and I believe both Gentry and Hades could choose a park animal form."

"Don't forget Nakano. And Kelly is a rabbit—and Phyllis is a Were," Colin said. "And I don't think Joshua can be spotted as shadow."

I nodded. "Yes. That gives us eleven counting you and me." I cocked my head. "Although you're a Dragon. How would Rodán not sense you?"

Colin rubbed my shoulders. "He might sense me as a human, but a lot of humans go through that park. As long as there's only one of me, I think it'll be okay."

He added, "What about Armand and his team?"

I shook my head. "Armand plans to kill Rodán the moment he spots him."

Colin released my shoulders. "I can't help but think we can use all of the help we can get."

I said, "We won't be able to find out if Rodán is really all right if Armand kills him. Rodán might be the key to us getting to Volod."

"That's true," Collin said.

My skin started to tingle as the sun lowered in the sky. I had maybe ten minutes before I shifted. "Let's start making some calls."

My senses were heightened as I walked through the park to Gapstow Bridge at the northeast end of what was named simply "the Pond." I didn't sense Vampires, but that didn't mean they weren't waiting someplace else to come swooping down on me.

We had sent out a recon team. They'd found nothing and had returned to my apartment just minutes ago.

But as I walked through the darkness, and even though I knew I had teammates out there, I still felt alone . . . and like I was headed for a trap.

Maybe this wasn't such a good idea. Maybe I should have said no.

My heart wanted to believe so badly that Rodán really was okay, that he hadn't been turned. This was our chance to find out the truth.

When I reached the foot of the stone bridge, I thought of the small bridge in Otherworld where I'd seen the Great Guardian just days ago. I thought of what she'd told me—that sacrifices must be made. That sometimes one must be sacrificed for the good of all. That this would cost me my blood.

I walked to the center of the bridge, the stone firm beneath my boots. Water sloshed up against the stone below, a quiet sound that moved in time with the brush of wind through the surrounding trees. I scented the air and caught nothing more than leaves, water, and earth.

Even without moonlight, my keen Drow vision allowed me to see my surroundings. My internal clock told me it was now midnight.

Hair at my nape prickled. Someone was behind me.

I drew my Dragon-clawed dagger so quickly that it was in my hand at the same time I whirled to face whatever had come up behind me.

"Rodán?" He stood there looking more beautiful even than I remembered. He wore all black, his long, white-blond hair a bright contrast to his tunic. His eyes looked clear, green, and beautiful.

His hair rose from his shoulders in the light wind. I smelled rain in the air and the coolness of the night on my skin.

And then his thoughts came to me and chills rolled through my body.

I will not hurt her, he told himself. *I will never harm Nyx.*

Confusion made my mind spin as I clenched the hilt of my dagger. What did he mean? Why would he be worried about hurting me?

I am what I am now. His thoughts were as clear as if they were my own. *That will not change.*

Then came a turn in his thoughts I sensed more than heard. His thirst for blood, his desire to take a paranorm, but his will to never take that step. He would fight it. He would survive on synthetic paranorm blood, should a way be found to make it.

I took a step back. I'd been so shocked by his thoughts that I hadn't thought about the real danger I was in.

"They really did get to you." My throat ached from the pain of saying those words. "You're one of them now."

"Yes. But it is unlike anything I have ever known." Rodán's voice was low, urgent. "I never expected this. The beauty of it is almost more than I can believe. The feeling. The power. It is amazing."

I shook my head. "No. I can't believe you'd go to their side and like it."

"It is freeing." Rodán held his hands out to me and I took another step back. "There is nothing even close to being a Vampire paranorm. But I will force no one to join me."

"No." I couldn't stop shaking my head. *"No."* I wouldn't believe it. Couldn't believe it.

"Come with me, Nyx." He stretched out one arm, extending a hand as if to take mine. "Come with me now and join me."

I remembered what Armand said about killing those we

care about when it was too late for them. But I couldn't bring myself to take the dagger I held and use it against Rodán, no matter how much danger I faced at that moment.

His voice turned urgent. "It's safer for you if you come with me now. It is not safe for you out in the world alone. If Volod bites you, you will be drawn to him. You will be his."

"Going off with a Vampire is not what I'd call safe," I said.

I prepared to turn and run.

The place where Volod had bitten me all those months ago started to tingle and burn and I went stiff.

Volod was here.

TWENTY-EIGHT

My heart beat faster and faster. I turned just enough that my back was to the side of the bridge.

Rodán was on my right.

Volod on my left.

Blocking my way down each side of the bridge.

"What are you doing here?" Rodán was looking at Volod. "You told me I could handle this my way, yet you followed me."

As Rodán spoke, I could hear his thoughts as if he were saying them out loud. He was angry at Volod. He hated Volod but he was not going to show his disdain. Rodán felt fear for me. He wanted to protect me from Volod.

This was why I had been given the gift of reading minds. I understood that now. I needed to trust Rodán.

"I told you your way would not work." Volod looked at me. "I have been watching and hearing you. One does not talk a paranorm into becoming a Vampire. One turns a paranorm by attacking. Your method does not work."

Adrenaline rushed through me as the two Vampires closed in on me.

I sucked in my breath.

And backflipped off the side of the bridge.

Before I could hit the water, I grabbed a protruding stone near the underside of the bridge with one hand.

Blood rushed in my head as if water roared under the bridge.

My other hand still gripped my dagger. I held on to the

stone with my upper-body strength as I sheathed my dagger so that I could use both hands on the bridge.

I started to make my way hand over hand to my right but I saw a Vampire waiting there. I looked to my left—another Vampire.

Not just any Vampires, but Vampire paranorms. Shifters.

The only way for me to go was down, into the water.

"Nyx," Rodán called from the bridge. "It will be so much better for you if you come with me."

"Too late for that." Volod's power hummed and as he looked down at me. "We will take her."

My heart beat so hard now that my chest hurt. I had been on the receiving end of Volod's power and I didn't like the idea of being there again.

Tension sparked in the air from my teammates, who waited for my signal.

I dropped into the water. My body cut into its icy chill. I used my water elemental magic to drive me away from the bridge, far enough that it would be safe to get out.

My team members would have come to my aid, but I didn't want to put them in more danger. It was time to cut our losses and get out of there.

Before I had a chance to leave the water, an invisible blast of Volod's power slammed into me.

I cried out as my chest burned and the blast slammed me up against the bank. I tried to get to my feet, but his power had pinned me in the mud and slime.

Vampires were coming at me from the bank above me.

A terrible roar broke through the night as a great Dragon came from the trees and slammed into the Vampires on the bank.

Colin.

And then I heard fighting. The sound of shouts and yells, of sword clanging against sword. The sounds of fierce animals fighting as Shifters fought Shifters.

I tried to move again but Volod's power was too strong. I ground my teeth and raised one arm. I clenched my fist as I called upon my water element again.

A great fist of water rose from the pond. It towered over Volod and Rodán, who were both still on the bridge.

I slammed the water fist down on Volod. It pounded the Master Vampire onto the bridge. With a loud crack and smashing sound, the fist drove Volod through the bridge, down into the water.

His hold on me broke.

I looked up the bank at Colin, in his human form, as he fought against seven Vampires. Where had all these Vamps come from? I had never sensed them. None of us had or we wouldn't be there.

Then I realized what had happened—these were Vampire paranorms, but they didn't smell of Vampire. As Shifters, they would have the same abilities to blend into the forest as our paranorm Trackers had.

One Vampire-Shifter could have been a frog on the edge of the pond, another could have been a swan with its head tucked under its wing, supposedly asleep in a small cove. They could have been anything, anywhere.

Mud and slime coated me as I scrambled up the bank. I didn't have much time. What I'd done to Volod would only piss him off.

Colin used a sword to fight off the Vampire paranorms who were coming at him from all sides.

I drew my dagger, raced up behind one of the Vampires, swung the blade at his neck, and sliced his head clean from his body.

The Vampire next to him whirled. In the same motion he shifted into a Bengal tiger. With a roar it leapt, straight at me.

I called to my air element and shielded myself with it. The tiger slammed into my shield and dropped with catlike grace to the ground, where it watched me.

Hiding behind a shield while my fellow Trackers fought was not an option.

I dropped the shield and called to my water element, then drove it toward the tiger. Before I could use a fist of water to slam into the tiger, it pounced.

While it was still in the air, I dove forward under its great body and came out behind it. The tiger landed and spun. It stared at me, tail twitching.

Behind me was the pond. Directly in front of me was the tiger. Behind it, Colin battled four Vampires.

To my right Lawan fought two Vampires. Beyond her had to be another ten Vampire paranorms who fought several of my teammates. We were unbelievably outnumbered.

Both Volod and Rodán were nowhere to be seen, but the bitch Vampire, Elizabeth, stood off to the side. Beside her was a beautiful Vampire-Elvin female. I'd seen her in the vision—Monique, the San Francisco Proctor.

All of that I absorbed in a flash while still keeping focused on the tiger.

As I leapt toward it, I ordered my earth element to drive the ground beneath the tiger up. The beast was caught off guard.

I jumped on its back, straddling it. The big cat twisted in the air and I had to press my knees in tight to keep from falling off. No human could have managed it, but I'm not wholly human.

The tiger tried to shake me off. I raised my dagger and brought down the blade on its neck.

The tiger shrieked but its neck was so great that my dagger only made it halfway. It was already healing as I brought my dagger down again.

This time the blade sliced the rest of the way through its neck. The tiger collapsed. I jumped and landed on my feet before it hit the ground.

As soon as it did, the great cat's body and head vanished. In its place was the male Shifter's human form and his head.

I didn't look back, just started after another Vampire that was fighting Colin.

Lawan cried out. I pivoted and saw her, pinned up against a Vampire paranorm who had his fangs buried in her neck.

"No!" I shouted as the Vampire dropped her and she slumped to the ground.

I bolted toward the Vampire paranorms who now stood over Lawan's body.

Blood was still on the fangs of the Vampire who had bitten her and rage tore through me. Was she dead?

I grasped the oval buckler at the front of my weapons belt and had it off and flying through the air before I reached the two Vampires. It sliced the head off one of them.

The Vampire paranorm who had bitten Lawan had a wild light in his eyes. I raised my dagger to swing at him.

He morphed into an enormous gray pit bull—at least twice the size of a normal pit bull.

I came up short as the horrendous dog charged. My heart thrummed and I had to keep my focus about me. This was no normal, average, everyday, number-one most vicious dog alive. No, this was probably ten times worse.

Its short neck was so thick, so full of sinew and muscle, that I wondered if my blades could slice through it all.

The pit bull barreled toward me. I dodged to the side—barely. The Vampire-Shifter moved faster than I'd ever have believed.

I was so focused on the dog that I didn't see the Vampire-Shifter who came up from behind me until it was too late.

He knocked my dagger from my hand as he pinned me to him, my arms to my sides, and the pit bull rushed at me again. I struggled to break free as I saw those huge jaws coming straight for my throat—

I called to my earth and water elements at the same time. Water slammed into the pit bull. Jagged rocks thrust up from the earth. My air shield blocked me from the front.

The combination of the water pounding down and the rocks thrusting up impaled the pit bull on the sharpest of them. The dog yelped, its cry long and fierce.

I slammed the back of my head against the face of the Vampire-Shifter who had ahold on me. That gave me just the fraction of a second I needed to break free. I wheeled around at the same time I pulled a wooden stake from my belt then drove it through the heart of the Vampire-Shifter. He dropped.

I turned again, another stake in my hand. The pit bull had shifted back into a male who was impaled on the stone. I took the stake and rammed it into his heart.

The bite mark on my neck burned and I spun. Volod was directly behind me. I turned to run. A Vampire paranorm blocked my way. Then Elizabeth and Monique were on either side of me. I was boxed in.

Real terror tore through me as I twisted around, trying not to let any of them touch me. No matter which way I turned, a Vampire was behind me.

There was no room to jump up. No room to use any of my weapons.

My heart pounded so hard it felt on the verge of exploding. Heat burned in my neck like white-hot flame. I faced Volod. I'd never been so terrified in my life as I was at that moment.

The transference. I'd use it to get away.

I tried to focus on it, but it wouldn't come. It felt like someone was blocking me with their magic. When I saw Monique's expression, I knew it was her.

They were all moving toward me. Closer. Closer yet. So close I could almost feel the press of their bodies to mine. I could smell the ancient dirt and must smells so strong, I could barely breathe.

I didn't know what else to do. I jerked a stake from my weapons belt and dove for Volod.

Strong hands gripped my shoulders from behind, stopping me cold.

Monique and Elizabeth each grasped one of my arms.

I fought against their holds as Volod bared his fangs. Their strength was too much. There were too many.

Volod moved toward me. I could smell his breath. I could feel his excitement. Could see the thrill of victory in his eyes.

"No!" I screamed and tried to kick, but Volod was too close.

I heard Colin shout my name. I heard piercing wails.

I heard the screams of the dying.

Hopelessness and horror closed in on me.

I wouldn't give up without a fight. I wouldn't—

Volod moved so fast. He had been standing before me, then in a blink he had one hand on the back of my head. The other hand on my shoulder.

I screamed and tried to fight.

My neck burned where he'd bitten me before.

I felt the slide of his fangs into my flesh.

No. *No.* This couldn't be happening.

I felt the draw of my blood leaving my body as Volod drank of it.

My body started to go limp.

My vision grew cloudy.

Nothing.

TWENTY-NINE

My thoughts were muddy. I couldn't see. Couldn't think. Couldn't feel.

Something had happened but I couldn't hold on to what it was. A wispy tendril of a thought that kept eluding my grasp every time I reached for it.

Panic made me shiver. I didn't know why I felt panicked, only that something was wrong. Desperately wrong.

I tried to take slow, even breaths. Even that was a struggle.

Then I remembered. A dream.

A nightmare.

My eyes flew open. Darkness. Even though I knew I was awake now, the fogginess of my thoughts wouldn't clear. It was a fight just to think.

The nightmare kept pushing at my mind. I couldn't quite remember it, but I knew it had been a bad one.

A familiar figure entered my thoughts. The face was shadowy. He stepped forward and I saw him clearly.

Volod.

I held back a scream. *Just a nightmare, Nyx. He's not really there.*

I took a deep breath. The air felt close. Confined.

Fear overcame me. I felt as if I had swallowed a mouthful of needles that now stabbed at the inside of my belly.

Pieces of the nightmare started to unfold in agonizingly slow frames. A bridge. Rodán. Volod. Water. Vampires . . . Vampires . . . more Vampires.

Hands grasping me. Me, fighting their holds. Volod's long white fangs coming toward me.

In my mind I heard my own scream as Volod sank his teeth into my neck.

Cold flushed over me from my head to my toes. A nightmare? Or did it really happen?

Of course Volod hadn't bitten me. I'd be dead.

I'd be buried . . .

No.

I put my hands up—

And my palms met a firm, padded surface just inches from my face.

I started to scream but put the back of my hand in my mouth, holding the scream in.

Calm down. Calm . . . down.

The fog of my thoughts wouldn't clear. I moved my hand away from my mouth and hiccuped.

I felt around me, touching the sides and top of the box. Desmond's words came back to me. Drow were immune to a Vampire's bite.

But I was half human, too.

The half-Drow part of me allowed me to see within the total darkness. Above me was the quilted cream-colored satin lining of the inside of a coffin. Each wall around me was padded in satin, and my head was on some kind of small pillow.

It was nighttime and I was in Drow form, my amethyst skin contrasting to the cream lining. I didn't feel the familiar leather fighting suit hugging my body.

I ran my palms down my belly and as far as I could reach in my position. I was wearing some kind of velvet-like gown with bell sleeves, a dress like the ones I'd seen Elizabeth wear. The gown was the same cobalt blue of my hair.

I brought my finger to my mouth and ran it along one of my incisors. The normally tiny fangs that I had as Drow were now long. I pricked my finger on the end of one. Not only long, but sharp, too. The taste of my own blood made my mouth tingle.

An overwhelming urge came over me to get out of the coffin and to the surface. It was almost unnatural in its strength.

My elements. I felt them stir, waiting for me to call on them. My earth magic was strong. I was surrounded by earth, including the six feet of dirt above me.

Grasping something familiar calmed the nerves inside me, and I held on to my earth magic.

Get me out of here, I ordered my element. *Take me to the surface.*

The earth trembled and shook around me. I heard loose dirt slide down the sides of the coffin. And then I felt the coffin begin to rise.

Despite the continued fogginess of my thoughts, I was able to focus on getting out of the grave. Right now nothing else mattered.

The coffin burst free of the ground and I heard rocks and earth pounding on the lid as they rained back down.

Even in the cramped confines I was still able to bring my knee to my chest. I thrust up with my bare feet and hit the lid with all I had.

A thump as the lid swung open and I pushed myself up to stand inside the coffin.

Volod was just feet away, and my neck burned where I had been bitten. I felt a pull toward him. A calling. I felt a desire to go to him and kneel as if he were the Great Guardian.

Five Vampire paranorms stood around the circumference of the grave. Dirt was on their clothing, and vaguely I thought it must have been from the earth that had been blown away from atop of the coffin. Behind them stood Elizabeth and Monique.

My thoughts continued to be twisted, confused as I looked at Volod. I felt as if I was programmed to go to the Master Vampire.

I climbed out of the coffin and my bare feet met loose earth and stones. The long skirts I wore brushed my legs as I walked toward Volod. His dark gaze held mine as he waited without saying anything.

Around me trees bowed in the wind over headstones. The smell of Vampires was strong, blending with the scents of the trees and grass.

When I was standing in front of him my thoughts started to clear a little. That face I hated so much was smiling. A satisfied, triumphant smile.

"Kneel, bitch." Volod's tone was filled with malice.

The loathing I'd felt for him came rushing back and fed the Drow half of me that was fighting Volod's mental hold.

But it wasn't enough to overcome the compelling need to obey him. The human half of me surrendered.

I sank down onto my knees and lowered my head.

Volod laughed. "I control and master the great Rodán . . . and here we have Nyx of the Night Trackers. Now that I have you both, the rest of what I have planned will be easy."

I kept my head bowed as he went on. "You will serve me faithfully until you die." He bent over and murmured, "And you will die, Nyx, if you do not obey me. And perhaps even if I tire of you."

My Drow half continued to war with my human half but I didn't say anything. It became more real with every moment that passed . . . I was a Vampire.

"And in another twenty-four hours you shall have friends join you," he said and I tensed. "Lawan and Gentry will be rising."

Shock tore at my insides. Lawan and Gentry had been turned? Volod must have bitten them a second time twenty-four hours after the first.

He continued, "All of you will join me in my ultimate goal of taking over the paranorm world."

My whole body went still as his words sank in.

The Drow half of me fought harder and harder to take control. But my human half was winning. "Get up." The contempt in Volod's voice was clear. He hated me, but now he had triumphed over both Rodán and me.

I pushed myself to my feet. Dirt trickled down the part of my dress that had been covered in it. When I was standing, Volod gestured toward the coffin I'd been buried in.

"Pick it up and take it to the hearse waiting at the curb." He flicked his fingers in a way that said, *Hurry along.* "By yourself."

It was the first time I'd looked at the coffin itself. It was dark blue, huge. How did he expect me to carry it outside the cemetery?

I knelt beside the coffin—and picked it up. To my shock it felt no heavier than a cardboard box. Without help, I loaded it into a hearse parked on the street outside of the cemetery. Then I closed the hearse's back doors with loud *thunks* that echoed in the night. I glanced down the street and saw a human couple walking along the sidewalk in the opposite direction.

My mouth watered. I thought about how warm their flesh must feel. How salty the taste of their skin. How easily my fangs would slide into their necks. How good their blood would taste.

Horrified, I jerked myself back to reality. My stomach clenched and I thought I might throw up.

Yet at the same time I hungered for blood.

I wanted it. Needed it.

"I'll make sure you are well fed, Nyx." Volod's voice came from beside me, and I cut my attention to him. "But right now I want you hungry." He leaned down and scraped his fangs down the side of my neck. I went rigid. "I want you prepared to do anything I tell you to, just to get your first drop of blood."

He moved away, settled his hand on my shoulder, and began to massage it. "I have other things in store for you as well."

The sudden change from contempt to sensuality had my head spinning. What was happening?

He turned toward a limousine parked in front of the hearse. "Get inside and sit between Monique and Elizabeth."

When the three of us were sitting on the bench seat across from Volod, he said, "You've met Elizabeth."

When I looked at the redheaded Vamp, she showed her fangs and hissed at me. Volod gestured toward the Vampire on the other side of me. I turned my attention to her even though it meant putting my back to Elizabeth, and I didn't feel comfortable with that. But I didn't seem to have a choice.

"And as you may know, this is Monique," Volod said.

Monique gave me a pleasant smile. "Welcome."

I gave a nod. I didn't know what to say.

She touched my shoulder and said the Elvin word for clean. *"Avanna."*

"Thank you," I said as every speck of dirt vanished from my body and clothing. Considering the situation, I really didn't care if I was clean or not, but I felt the ingrained urge to be polite.

Volod had an amused look as he reclined across from us. I could feel hatred rolling from Elizabeth—not just toward me, but I was pretty sure toward Monique, too.

It wasn't long before the limo pulled up in front of a brownstone. Volod had likely been hiding out here all this time.

Volod instructed Elizabeth and Monique to walk in front of us. To my surprise, Monique was leading Elizabeth by a leash. Despite the fact that she must be humiliated, Elizabeth kept her chin raised.

Volod walked beside me, his hand lightly touching my upper arm as if guiding me. I wondered if I still had the Witch's gift. I had read Rodán's mind on the bridge, but I hadn't read Volod's. I couldn't hear his thoughts now, either.

As my mind continued to clear, mixed emotions filled me. I felt a warmth like I had when I was walking up to see my family in the Otherworld after being away for a long time. Another part of me wanted to bolt . . . but I felt a strong contentment here. Like I was home and belonged next to Volod, while somehow I felt disdain for him at the same time.

We walked through the entryway into an enormous room. The downstairs must have been gutted to make the large space.

Fifty or so Vampires were in the room. They went silent when Volod and I entered.

Volod paused at the threshold, and I looked at him. Pure satisfaction radiated from him, enough that my stomach clenched.

"You may remember Nyx of the Night Trackers," Volod said in a loud, clear voice. "She is now one of us."

The room full of Vampire paranorms broke into applause. I wasn't certain if it was because they liked and respected me, or because Volod had conquered me. Probably a little of both.

Volod guided me through the room. My heart leapt when I saw Rodán.

"Nyx." Rodán stepped in front of Volod, and without seeming to care what the Master Vampire thought, he wrapped his arms around me. "I am so happy to see you," he said, but I heard his thoughts: *I am so sorry. So very sorry this has happened against your will. It will work out, though. I will take care of you.*

I hugged Rodán back. "Don't be sorry," I whispered in his ear. "It wasn't your fault."

Rodán raised his head and looked at me. *You can hear my thoughts?* he asked in his mind.

With a nod I whispered, "Yes."

Then know this, he thought, *we will rise above Volod and shall end this.*

Surprise made my eyes widen. Rodán was planning some kind of uprising. As much as I welcomed the thought, I sensed I could not go against Volod. I didn't think I had the strength to break Volod's hold on me.

Volod nearly snarled as he stepped close to us. "You have a team to prepare, Rodán."

"Of course, Volod." He gave me one last long look while he thought, *Be ready. We have much planned. Be ready.* And then Rodán slipped into the crowd.

I followed him with my gaze until I couldn't see him any longer.

Volod startled me when he said, "Is there something going on, my new pet?"

I jerked my attention to him. "Going on?"

He studied me for a moment. "Come."

Obediently I followed him through the room to a set of stairs. The entire way Volod was greeted and congratulated on his victory over Rodán and me.

My mind was less foggy as I followed Volod up the stairs to a study. It was more a library than an office. Bookcases filled with both ancient tomes and modern works.

I still wasn't sure what to think . . . I hated Volod, the passion of that hatred running deep. But I couldn't seem to stop following him, to stop obeying him.

Over and over again, I had been telling myself that I was just going along with this whole thing, but the truth was more like I couldn't stop myself. Volod had a hold on me that I didn't know if I could break.

"Sit." He pushed me to a chair but I recovered and sank into the seat. He scowled as he walked around to the other side of the desk and sat in the leather chair. "I have you. Now what to do with you, you may wonder."

I said nothing.

"You will be trained to lead one of our Vampire paranorm teams." Volod leaned back and steepled his fingers. "I turned you. I bit you twice. Your allegiance to me will be absolute."

"Yes, Volod," I said when he seemed to be waiting for something.

"Tonight I will start releasing greater numbers of Vampires to feed on humans," he said. My stomach churned more. "We have broken the Trackers. There is nothing stopping us in New York. We will begin sending out additional teams of Vampire paranorms to turn or kill more paranorms."

He continued, "We know where they choose to hang out and we know how to take them. Then it is on to the next city—and the next, and the next."

My new allegiance to Volod warred with the need to save those in my prior life. The two worlds were on a collision course inside me, and I wasn't sure I would survive.

"I am bringing in Vampires from all over the United

States and Canada." Volod sounded pleased with himself. "We will have a gathering, a conclave of Vampire leaders from across the continent. Together we shall plan how best to strike paranorms."

"Where are you doing that?" I asked.

Volod waved me off. "I will divulge the location to no one. You will not know where we are going until we arrive."

"When?" I asked.

He studied me for a long moment. I wondered if he was questioning his power over me. "You will learn when the time is right."

"How many Vampires and Vampire paranorms are there?" I held my hands in my lap and laced my fingers together as I struggled to calm myself.

"Truly all of that is none of your concern." He waved off my question. "You need not worry about numbers or who leads the Vampires to turn or kill humans."

He leaned forward and braced his forearms on his desk, his hands folded in front of him. "I will have you work on paranorms."

I listened to what he was saying with mounting fear and confusion. Everything inside me was so twisted. I didn't know how to think or feel because my allegiance to Volod was growing and growing.

"Monique and Rodán are each in charge of a territory. You will serve under Monique." He nodded as if giving himself approval.

"Let us not concern ourselves with talks of our destruction of paranorms," Volod said. "For now our kind must have a night to celebrate victory."

Volod got up from his chair and came around to stand beside me. He held out his hand and I took it, and he drew me up to my feet so that our bodies were touching.

He released me and brought his hands to my neck before he slowly ran the pads of his fingers along my skin. The movement was sexual, his eyes filled with raw lust.

"You will do whatever she or I require of you," he said. "You will even share my bed. Is this clear?"

"Of course." I forced myself to remain still and to agree with him. "I serve you now."

"Of course." Volod echoed my words as he smiled, a slow, evil smile. "I am your Master."

THIRTY

That day I slept like the dead.

Volod had ordered me to sleep in the coffin I'd been buried in, down in the basement. Perhaps forty of his Vampires and Vampire paranorms stayed there.

When I woke, I climbed out of my coffin and almost stumbled. I felt dizzy, light-headed. My stomach growled and my mind went to thoughts of blood and raw meat.

And sex. I wanted sex in the most intense way possible. I'd heard that Vampires associated sex with blood, and now I understood.

That need turned my thoughts to Colin. How could I have not thought of him sooner? It was as if being a Vampire was wiping out my past life.

What about my parents? What about all the people I loved?

"Change into this." Elizabeth came out of nowhere and shoved a dress into my arms. "Volod wants you to wear this, and he wants to see you in his study."

She put her face close to mine. "You'd better watch yourself, bitch. When your end comes, I'll be the one driving a stake through your heart."

"Good morning to you, too," I said beneath my breath as she turned and walked away. "Or rather good night. I guess."

I looked at the royal purple dress she'd handed me. It went well with my amethyst skin tones. I wondered why Volod was having me dress up as if I was in medieval times, like Elizabeth. Monique wore modern and sexy clothes.

The basement was empty save for myself and a whole

bunch of open coffins. In the corner was a screen that I changed behind. I said *"Avanna"* before I put on the clean dress, and the magical cleansing spell of the Elves made me feel as fresh as if I had just taken a shower.

I didn't know what to do with the dress I had been wearing so I folded it and laid it on top of my coffin to worry about later.

No doubt Volod wouldn't be crazy about waiting, so I made my way out of the basement, up the stairs to the second floor.

As I stood at the doorway to Volod's study, he looked up from paperwork on his desk and he frowned. "I do not tolerate those who do not do as they are told when they are told," he said. "I expect no delays whenever I call for you. You simply drop what you are doing and come."

I lowered my gaze. "Yes, Volod."

He got up from his seat behind his desk and came around to where I stood. "You must desire sustenance."

My stomach clenched and growled and I nodded.

"Good." He said the word as if it was meant to be comforting. But I knew what he meant—my hunger gave him control over me.

"Here's one of the paranorms like you requested." A male voice came from the doorway, and I turned to see a middle-aged Doppler female beside a Vampire paranorm.

"Excellent." Volod went to the doorway and took the Doppler by her shoulders. "Wait here," he said to the Vampire paranorm who had brought in the Doppler female.

"Yes, sir." The Vampire paranorm bowed from his shoulders and stood to the side.

"Come here, Nyx," Volod ordered as he turned the Doppler to face me, holding her shoulders from behind. "Vampires understand instinctively how to feed, just as a suckling baby does with its mother. But I will show you the best way. I want to watch you the first time."

My belly twisted as I looked at the Doppler he was holding. I could smell her fear, more intense than I would have smelled even as Drow.

But what called to me more than anything was her blood. My mouth watered. Pain made me wince as my fangs dropped from my gums, where they had retracted.

"Hungry, are you not?" Volod said in a soothing tone that I recognized as him manipulating me.

Yet I couldn't take my attention from the Doppler. I imagined how good her blood would be as it entered my mouth . . .

My stomach twisted harder at the thought of drinking a being's blood. I'd only liked char-burned steaks and super-well-done hamburgers, never anything even slightly pink.

And now I was visualizing myself drinking blood, and even eating bloody hunks of meat.

My stomach growled again. I felt sick at the thought of what I wanted to do. And sick at the thought of doing without.

Volod motioned for me to come closer. I took a step forward.

A look of impatience flashed across his face and I hurried to reach him. He ran a finger down the side of the female's neck. "This is the carotid artery. It is very special. It is what we drink from."

I couldn't take my eyes from that spot. The Doppler's fear excited me while I watched the pulse of her blood in the artery.

Volod traced the vein with his fingertip. "Feed, Nyx."

"No," the Doppler female whispered and began a futile struggle as I lowered my face to her neck. "Please, no."

Every word she said and every struggle she made only made me want what she had to offer even more.

Like the way prey running from an attacker only heightens the instinct to attack. I wanted to attack. Wanted to jerk her to me and ravage her neck.

Instead I moved my head slowly toward the spot and drank in the smell of the sweat of her skin and her lifeblood.

I slid my fangs into the vein Volod had shown me. The taste was incredible. Better than anything I had imagined.

The Doppler female had gone slack but was making soft,

almost erotic whimpers. The power of a Vampire's bite was not only mesmerizing but sexual, too.

"Stop," Volod said after I had taken only a few long draws from her.

The command brought me up short. I didn't want to stop, but I couldn't help myself. I had to do as he ordered—it was built into me somehow.

"I want you hungry for later," Volod said. "This is only a dining lesson."

As I drew away I noticed the two spots leaking blood. Hunger made me lick up the blood. The two holes sealed over, like they had never been there.

"Very good." Volod's tone held a note of approval. He turned to the Vampire paranorm, whom I had forgotten about. "Take her back to the holding cells."

The Vampire paranorm bowed again. "Yes, sir," he said before guiding the now dreamy-looking Doppler away.

"Find Monique," Volod said to me, his tone dismissive. "She is to start your training at once."

"Yes, Volod." I bowed my head in acknowledgment. It was as if I had no control over my thoughts or my words or even my actions. "I'll go to her now."

"Most likely you will find her on the third floor in the bedchambers, the sitting room, or the library." Volod returned to his seat.

"Yes, sir." I got to my feet and left through the door I came in.

I had to pick up my long skirts to make my way up the stairs. As I went I thought about the Doppler female and how good her blood had tasted. Volod had left me hungry, wanting more.

When I reached the landing I heard voices down the hallway and paused at their intimate sound.

With curiosity, I peered around the corner and saw Monique and Rodán standing in the hallway just outside the door. Monique's hair was a little messy—it had been perfect when I'd seen her earlier.

Rodán looked at her with an expression that was so

familiar to me. Sexual and satisfied, in a way that was entirely sensual and always made a woman want to go straight back to bed with him.

The scent of sex met my enhanced senses and I felt myself grow warm. I felt like I was invading a private moment, and I started to turn to go back down the stairs, but stopped and pulled a glamour.

"Monique," Rodán said, "I know I can trust you and I will." She cocked her head, and he continued. "I've planned a coup against Volod." At her surprised look he said, "We must stop him. The destruction he wants is not who we are, Vampire paranorms or not."

"A coup?" Monique sounded stunned, but I couldn't gauge how she felt about his statement. "What do you mean?"

I felt drawn to the conversation. I didn't want to be seen watching, so I pulled a glamour then peeked around the corner again.

Rodán held both of Monique's hands. "All Vampire paranorms are in danger. Volod does not plan to let any of us live once he attains his goal of taking control of the paranorm world."

Monique frowned. "Why do you think this?"

"I have heard what he has said and I've read between the lines. I have watched his disguised disgust for Vampire paranorms. More than that, though, I have seen a vision of it." Rodán reached up and brushed her hair over her ear. "If we do not stop him, it will happen."

"Do you think he is powerful enough to destroy Vampire paranorms?" She was still frowning. "What are you going to do about it?"

"We can talk about all of that later," Rodán said. "There is no time now. We are having the meeting on the first floor in the conference room. I will give you the details after the meeting."

"Should I be at the meeting?" Monique asked.

"From what I have seen, meeting together is not all that unusual here," Rodán said. "From Volod's perspective we could explain in many ways that would be acceptable. It would be unusual for you to be there at this time, however."

Rodán let his fingers trail from her ear to her lips. "I would prefer for you to keep Volod distracted while I meet with the others to avoid any questions at all from him. We won't be long. We're meeting in a few minutes. A brief overview and some planning of our next steps."

Monique's eyes did not leave Rodán's. "Who is attending?"

"Kennedy, Vincent, Stephen, and Frederick will be present. I expect to add Nyx to our ranks, but I need to be convinced Volod doesn't have a hold on her first."

"I assumed Volod had a strong hold on all. How much control do you think he has of her?" Monique asked.

"I don't know yet. I will evaluate her first. I do know that the hold is at its very strongest in the beginning," Rodán said. "I have been observing and listen to many of the Vampire paranorms. The ones I am meeting with I picked out for various reasons. They have all quietly voiced the same concerns to me about Volod that I have had. I trust them."

Monique ran her tongue along her lower lip, a movement that distracted Rodán for a moment. "Do you plan on adding others to your ranks?"

"We will consider who else to add to our group." He continued to stroke her hair almost absently. "For now, the group must be small and restricted to those we know we can trust. Volod has a powerful hold on many who are intoxicated with the power they feel."

Monique said nothing. I wished I knew what she was thinking.

"I can trust you, can't I, Monique?" Rodán said.

Raising an eyebrow and reaching up on tiptoes, Monique kissed him. "Need you ask? Didn't I prove in the bedroom how my feelings have never left you, Rodán?"

"Nor have mine ever fully left you," he said softly.

"And now, just look at you . . . a Vampire." Monique spoke with sensuality and excitement in her tone. "You saw what that does to me, didn't you? Of course you can trust me. Anything for you." Monique reached up and kissed Rodán again. "I'll take care of Volod."

He took her in his arms and gave her a long, lingering kiss. Old feelings for Rodán surfaced and I felt a moment's pang. But that vanished as my thoughts turned for a brief moment to Colin. I pushed them aside. This was not the time.

Monique drew away from Rodán, and he left the opposite way from where I was hiding. I assumed he was heading for a back set of stairs.

Monique walked in my direction and I pressed myself up against the wall so that she wouldn't touch me. She was a powerful paranorm, and I prayed that my new and improved glamour was strong enough. Thank goodness for Desmond's help.

I felt a presence behind me and a shiver ran down my spine. I looked over my shoulder.

Elizabeth.

THIRTY-ONE

"Elizabeth," Monique said as she came around the corner. "Where is Volod?"

"What is going on?" Elizabeth looked at Monique with suspicion in her gaze. She sniffed the air. "You've been with Rodán," she stated. "I saw you disappear with him. Now I can smell sex on you."

"That is none of your business," Monique said, her tone cold.

"Volod will learn of this," Elizabeth said with venom. "You, the great Monique, will feel Volod's wrath." Her lips quivered in anger. "We will see who will be at the end of a leash tomorrow. You will be done. He has no need for Vampire paranorms who don't serve his purpose, and you have betrayed him now. I will see that you are buried wearing a collar and a leash."

Monique and Elizabeth faced each other on the landing as Monique drew her shoulders back and glared. "I did this for a reason. Volod will understand."

Elizabeth eyes showed the humiliation she obviously felt. "We will see about that, you arrow-eared bitch."

Monique narrowed her gaze. "If I was Rodán's, why would I be seeking Volod out right now to tell him of a rebellion against him?" She put her hands on her hips. "A rebellion that Rodán is planning . . . a coup. They're meeting in the conference room in a few minutes.

"So, yes, I was with Rodán. I have nothing to hide," Monique continued with clear confidence in her voice. "Volod will understand. He knows my allegiance is pledged to him alone. Anything that happened in the bedroom served a purpose for Volod."

Shock jolted me. Monique was going to tell Volod? How could Rodán be so wrong in trusting her? Maybe she was suddenly afraid for her life now that Elizabeth knew of her with Rodán. Or maybe she just was in fact Volod's.

It didn't matter. I had to get to Rodán and warn him. Maybe he couldn't trust the others, either.

"An uprising against Volod?" Elizabeth said, surprise on her features.

"Where is he?" Monique asked again. "I need to hurry."

"In his study." Elizabeth gestured downstairs.

Monique turned.

I had started to go to the conference room to warn Rodán when Elizabeth practically flew at Monique.

It happened so fast. The next thing I knew, Elizabeth rammed a stake into Monique's back and drove it through to her heart.

Stunned, I watched as Monique's body slumped to the floor, the stake still protruding through her back. Blood leaked around it. Monique's body was lifeless.

A satisfied smile crept across Elizabeth's face. "Volod will get the news from me."

My surprise shifted to the fact that the odds at this moment were a lot better with Monique dead. She had turned traitor on Rodán and I wasn't going to mourn her.

Now there was only one to worry about. I dropped my glamour.

Elizabeth looked at me with surprise as I called to my elements. Her expression changed to fury. She took a step toward me, and I released my air element.

She gasped as I bound her with air magic. With my element, I gagged her and pinned her arms to her sides. She lost her balance and fell to the carpet with a thump.

I didn't have much time before someone came up the stairs—

A surge of power slammed me up against the wall. I

cried out as my head hit the hard surface. An invisible force held me dazed against the wall. I couldn't move.

The hold I had on Elizabeth failed.

My mind spun. I turned my head just enough to see a figure at the top of the stairs.

Volod.

Fury was on his features as he looked at Monique's body then cut his gaze back to me.

"It was her." Elizabeth pointed to me as she got to her feet. "Monique and Rodán were together and she was jealous. She killed Monique."

"I didn't kill Monique." I tried to shake my head but I couldn't move. It was hard talking the way Volod's power had me pinned against the wall. "Elizabeth did."

"You can't believe that bitch. You know she *lies*." Elizabeth hissed. "Not only did she kill Monique, but she is plotting to overthrow you . . . to kill you."

"Explain what you are talking about." Volod's voice was low, deadly.

"I was standing right behind that wall, near the doorway. I overheard them." Elizabeth lied in an urgent, convincing tone. "Monique and Rodán were planning a coup together." She gestured to me. "This bitch walked up and was in on it all. She knew that they had just screwed each other, and she was angry at them. She confronted them both."

Volod scowled as Elizabeth paused. "Continue. And make it fast."

"Rodán told this one here to focus on what mattered and to meet with the others planning the revolt," Elizabeth said. "They'll be in the conference room within minutes."

Elizabeth glared at me. "When Rodán left, the bitch was furious with jealousy. She stabbed Monique as she walked away."

"She's lying." My stomach twisted. Volod would kill both Rodán and me as soon as he saw that it was true about the revolt. "Elizabeth stabbed Monique in the back, literally. With my powers, I don't need to stab people in the back."

"They are meeting in the conference room now." Elizabeth

went up to Volod. "That will prove to you that I am telling the truth."

Volod released his hold on me. I wasn't expecting it and I dropped to my knees. He walked up to me and yanked me to my feet by my hair.

"Come." Still gripping a fistful of my hair, he jerked me to him. My scalp stung. With his free hand, he brought out a wooden stake and placed it over my heart. The point of the stake dug into my flesh.

Then he started to drag me beside him, going in the same direction Rodán had. "If Elizabeth is being truthful, then you die."

I ran through all the possibilities in my mind and came up feeling helpless and hopeless. Volod would see that what Elizabeth had told him was the truth.

"Elizabeth," he said to her, "I want every one of my Vampire guards at the conference room now."

Elizabeth nodded and flashed a look of pure hatred at me.

"Now," Volod boomed.

She ran off.

He believed her. My throat grew tight. As we moved, the stake he held to my heart bit into my skin through the dress.

The human part of me struggled to break Volod's mental hold. My Drow half was growing stronger and feeding the struggle. It was as if Volod's threat had woken something inside me that had been dulled by his power.

What could I do? How could I warn Rodán?

With Volod still holding the stake over my heart, I didn't see how I could without dying in the process.

Volod kept me close to him as we went down a back staircase. Because I'm Drow, it didn't matter that Volod was dragging me along with him—I simply made no sound as I moved. For the first time I wished I would make noise that would warn Rodán.

On the bottom level, we reached a closed door. I heard voices from inside, one of which was Rodán's. I held my breath as Volod listened at the door.

Volod, like me, had amazing hearing compared with

norms. With his ear pressed up against the door, though, Volod could hear what I could not. His features grew dark with rage.

Volod turned the handle and forced the door open. At the same time he shoved me into the room and knocked me to the floor.

I'd expected a long table with chairs, like a traditional conference room, but it was just a good-size carpeted empty room with barred windows on one side and a door opposite.

Five Vampire paranorms were in the room, including Rodán. Expressions ranged from surprised to fearful.

"Elizabeth was telling the truth." Volod's features grew even darker with his fury. "You plot against me."

Volod raised his hand. I dove for his legs and surprised him by hitting him behind the knees with my shoulder.

He didn't fall, but he stumbled backward.

Rodán emitted the same kind of power I'd seen him use against Demons nearly a year prior. It slammed into Volod, knocking him against the wall.

Rodán bared his fangs as he sent another burst of power at Volod.

Volod threw up a shield, deflecting the magic.

I scrambled to my feet and ran toward Rodán.

Volod's attack on Rodán and me seemed to cut the threads of allegiance that had forced me to obey him. I called to my air element as I reached Rodán.

The Shifter and Doppler Vampires in the room transformed into their animal forms: bear, lion, rottweiler, and coyote.

Behind Rodán the other door of the room opened.

Vampires started pouring in.

I glanced over my shoulder and saw even more Vampires come in behind Volod.

We were outnumbered at least twenty to six in a confined space.

Could Rodán use the transference to get out of here? Could I?

I started to reach for him when I saw a huge blast of power coming straight at me.

It was too close for me to throw up a shield.

Rodán stepped in front of me and took the full blast that had been meant for me.

The power slammed into him so hard it send him flying into me and knocked us both backward, straight into the hands of the Vampires behind us.

Around us the other Vampire paranorms were fighting Vampires. Bodies of Vampires were already dropping, but a couple of the five Vampire paranorms also lay motionless on the floor, stakes through their hearts.

The room smelled of blood and the Vampire stench of old dirt. It was so strong it filled my head.

"Hold him!" Volod shouted as Rodán and I were grabbed.

Rodán glanced at me. "Go," he said in a hoarse voice that wasn't like him at all.

The blast of magic must have injured him far more than I'd realized. I started to shake my head but glimpsed a projectile heading straight for me.

Volod had grabbed a stake gun and raised it at me. Rodán shoved me back behind him.

"No!" I screamed just as the wooden stake buried itself into Rodán's heart.

Rodán slumped against the Vampires who held him. His head fell back. Those crystal-green eyes I'd loved so much stared up at the ceiling, sightless.

Horror, anger, and fear spun through me.

I looked at Volod, who had another stake in the weapon, aimed at me again. I closed my eyes and the first thought that came to me was Colin—

I spun away, into the transference.

THIRTY-TWO

I opened my eyes as I appeared in the darkness on Colin's doorstep.

My stomach heaved and I threw up.

"Nyx?" Colin's shocked voice came from behind me as I wrapped my arms around my belly and heaved again on the ground beside his door.

He hooked his arm around my shoulders, and I wiped my mouth with the back of my hand.

Harsh reality beat at me over and over and over again and I felt a sense of hopelessness. Rodán was murdered. I was a Vampire.

"Talk to me." Colin squeezed my shoulders as I rose.

"Avanna." My throat was tight as I said the Elvin magic word, cleaning away the vomit from the ground and cleaning myself from head to toe. I didn't really care. I did it more for Colin than for myself.

"Hey." Colin brought me around so that I was looking at him. "I can't believe you're alive, that you're here."

I threw myself against him, wrapping my arms around his waist and burying my face against his chest. I just wanted to hold him and not let go.

Pain enveloped me, my whole body shaking with the force of it. I sobbed for Rodán, for all of those lost, and I cried for myself.

And then I realized my face was wet. So was Colin's T-shirt.

I hiccuped as I drew away from Colin. I couldn't speak as I brought my fingers to my face—

And felt wetness.

My eyes were wet.

No coherent thought would come. I put my finger into my mouth. Salty.

Drops leaked from my eyes, and I followed the paths they made with my fingers.

I looked up at Colin. "I'm crying." It didn't make sense. After a lifetime of wishing I had tears, I was now crying.

"You are." Colin caught my chin in his fingers and tilted my head back. "Let's get inside my apartment. I think you have a lot to tell me."

He held my hand and he drew me inside before locking the door shut behind us.

"I'm crying." I felt numb yet confused as I repeated the words.

Colin hugged me close to him and I felt him tense. I squeezed my eyes tight and more tears rolled down my cheeks. He was recognizing now that I was a Vampire.

"Explain everything to me." He didn't sound judgmental. He sounded caring.

I raised my head and looked at him. "You know already. Volod turned me." My Vampire fangs had dropped, and I knew Colin could see them.

Colin dragged his hand down his face then took a deep breath. "All I know is that you're the Nyx I fell in love with." He put his forehead against mine, wrapped his arms around me and held me tight "Even if you do have fangs."

"I love you, too." The words came out in a hoarse whisper.

He drew away and rubbed one of my tears away with his thumb. "Why don't you tell me what happened?"

"I don't know what happened immediately after Volod bit me." I leaned my head against his shoulder. "All I know is that I woke up buried in a coffin and what happened after that."

"And that was?" He prodded gently, as if knowing that right now I needed to talk.

I told him about my initial allegiance to Volod, how Rodán had been planning a coup, Elizabeth killing Monique, and then finished with the fight and how Rodán had died saving my life.

I hiccuped and more tears rolled down my face. "He's really dead now."

The pain I felt was as fresh as when Rodán had been turned. Only this time I had control over my elements. And maybe I handled it better because I'd already been through losing him once.

Colin rocked me as I cried.

When my tears started to dry I straightened in my seat on the couch. "How ironic the tears are now." I wiped the last of them away with my fingers. "I finally learned to cry by becoming the one thing I hate the most."

"So there's a silver lining," he said with a gently teasing expression.

My stomach rumbled and I realized I was hungry. And it wasn't for a hamburger.

I was hungry for blood.

And I could smell Colin's. Sweet, pure paranorm blood. What Volod had given me earlier had only been a taste. A way for him to gain more control over me.

I felt such a mix of emotions bottled up inside me. I could only attribute it to the Drow side fighting the Vampire side. I felt disgust for what I was, yet this intense desire for blood seemed natural and good. I wanted blood. Colin's blood.

"You need to take what I have, Nyx." Colin moved closer to me and I opened my eyes. His scent was raw, masculine, but it was nothing compared with the smell of his blood.

I could picture myself sliding my fangs into his carotid artery like Volod had shown me earlier. I could almost taste Colin's blood. It would be better even than the Doppler female's had been.

It was surreal. How could I be thinking of drinking his blood? Of drinking anyone's? Yet I was and it was powerful.

"You can't hurt me," he said as I opened my eyes. "You

know that Dragons are immune to a Vampire's bite and also to the pain of the bite. You can drink from me."

I felt like I was going to go crazy with the urge to feed while being repulsed by it at the same time. My mouth watered as I looked at him. I shook my head. "I can't—"

"You can." Colin drew his T-shirt away from his neck, exposing the big vein and the life that was pumping through it. "I need you to be fully yourself," he said. "If we're going to fix all this, you can't be hungry and distracted."

It made sense. And the call of his blood was too much for me to resist.

I moved my lips along the soft skin over the vein.

Erotic sensations suddenly filled me, moved through me. At the same time I wanted to drink from him, I wanted him in every other way possible. How could I feel this way after what I'd just experienced?

I straddled his lap and felt his excitement. He groaned as I skimmed his flesh with my fangs before I slid them into the vein.

Colin placed his hands on my hips and pressed me tight against him as I drank of him.

His blood flowed over my tongue, my mouth tingling. It tasted better than the Doppler's had. Colin's was so sweet and pure. Dragon's blood was exquisite.

I felt wild and erotic as I moved against him. He ran his hands up and down my body, exploring my curves. I moaned as I drew what I wanted, what I needed from him.

Then I felt Colin's hand on the back of my head. "I think that's enough, honey," he said. "Why don't you save some for a snack later?"

We both started laughing. How could I laugh now? But maybe I needed it.

If I weren't a Vampire now, my cheeks would have been burning because I'd lost control. I drew my fangs out then licked the spot with my tongue to stop the bleeding, like I'd done instinctively with the Doppler female.

I frowned. "I didn't hurt you when I bit you, did I?"

"I loved it." Colin ran his fingertips down my cheek. He

brought his fingers to my own artery. He kissed me, long and loving.

I rested my head against his chest for a long moment. It felt so good being with him that I didn't want to face reality.

Finally, I took one of his hands in mine. "We have a lot to talk about. Maybe we should have discussed it all sooner—"

"You needed to get your strength," Colin said, interrupting. "It will be better for us to talk about everything now."

I met his gaze and took a deep breath. "What happened after I was taken?" I was almost afraid to ask.

Colin dragged his hand down his face. "We were outnumbered. I tried to get to you before Volod could take you away. Too many Vampires and Vampire paranorms were between me and you." He nearly growled with frustration. "And then you were gone. Those of us who weren't killed or bitten had to retreat."

"Who did we lose?" Fear gripped me as I thought about my fellow Trackers and friends. "Volod told me that Lawan and Gentry have been turned. They were supposed to rise twenty-four hours after me."

"We were afraid of that." Colin looked grim. "Hades and Phyllis are dead."

My face felt drained of all blood. "They're dead?"

He nodded. "Out of the eleven of us, two died and three, counting you, were taken."

I braced my elbows on my knees and put my face in my hands. Their faces spun through my mind. "It's my responsibility," I said as I rose and looked at Colin. "I led the team. I should have brought more of us."

"You did what you had to and the only way that seemed plausible," Colin said. "Don't second-guess yourself on this."

It was hard not to.

"What about my parents and Olivia?" I held my hands to my belly. They would be so devastated right now.

"Olivia is pissed enough to take on Volod herself." Colin gave a grim smile. "I talked with Tristan late last night."

I straightened in my seat. "I need to get word to Olivia, Tristan, and my parents that I'm all right." I pushed my hair out of my face. "Well, as all right as a half-Drow, half-human Vampire can be."

"As you can imagine, your father is furious," Colin said. "I believe he's planning on sending a small contingent of warriors over here with a goal of wiping out Vampires."

I shook my head. "This isn't the way I'd hoped to get his help." I rubbed my palms on the dress that I was still wearing and echoed my earlier thought. "They must be devastated."

"Now that you're back we'll get word to them," Colin said.

"First we call Olivia." I raised my hands as I realized Volod had taken my things. "My phone, weapons . . . everything is gone."

Colin drew his cell phone out of a pocket. "I'm not going to tell her about you over the phone."

I nodded. "That's probably best."

He dialed her number. "Olivia," he said.

I heard her voice from where I was sitting. "What, Smokey?"

Classic Olivia, but I didn't hear the normal sarcastic edge to her voice.

"I need you over at my place as soon as you can get here." Colin cut off what was sure to happen next. "Please don't argue. It's important."

Olivia paused. "Don't get your scales all stuck in a bunch. I'll be right there."

"Thanks." He hung up.

"What else has happened while I've been gone?" I said when I had his attention. "It's been eleven, no, twelve days now."

Colin's expression went dark. "Vampire attacks on norms and paranorms are out of control. We suspect Volod is building his ranks."

"How are we going to stop him?" I rubbed my temples, feeling a headache coming on. "It all seems so hopeless, Colin. After all that we've been through, I never thought it possible."

"Don't give up hope, Nyx." He traced his thumb along my jaw.

"Look at what Volod has done." My voice rose in pitch.

"He has decimated our team. He has turned and controls some of the strongest paranorm Trackers across this continent." I swallowed, my throat feeling raw, almost sore. "It seems impossible to stop him. So hopeless."

"We just need to think it through, Nyx. We are not done for," Colin said. "This isn't the Nyx I know talking."

I paused before I said, "It's obvious, though, that we can't do it on our own. We need help. And more help than Armand and his gang."

"Armand has already been in contact with the Proctor Directorate," Colin said. "Trackers are being recruited all over the United States and Canada, and they'll be arriving within the next day or two."

"What then?" I studied Colin's eyes. "Does Armand have a plan?"

"We're all still working on it." He took my hands in his. "The details of where Volod is, where he's keeping his Vampire ranks—all of that we don't know."

"I know where Volod's place is here in the city." I frowned. "He's probably left by now since I escaped. He won't know whether I came back to you all.

"Maybe we should get a team together now and meet," I added. "Armand should know what I know."

"Nyx." Colin put his hand on mine. "Armand said he'd kill anyone who was turned, and he meant it. He believes he's doing the right thing by eliminating Vampires. He'll kill you, Nyx. He's already said that."

"He told me that before I was bit, but I'm not one of them. I'm not, Colin. I'll control what I am and I'll fight to defeat Volod's evil. I'm not a full Vampire like the others."

"You're right, but I'm afraid Armand won't see it that way," Colin said, shaking his head. "I know he won't.

"Here is what I'll do. We'll call our people . . . our Tracker team, but I won't tell them about you until they're all here. Then we only have to tell everyone once about everything that's happened with you."

My stomach twisted as Colin made the phone calls to all of the Trackers as well as Desmond. Penrod and Tristan were the only beings Colin clued in on my presence. The Sprite and my brother had been in training together.

Thanks to Tristan's inherited ability and Penrod's gift of transference from a Sorceress, they would arrive at the specified time.

I still wore the ridiculous dress, but there hadn't been time to go to my apartment. I wasn't even sure I could in case Armand had it staked out. In order to have *me* staked. After what Colin had said—and what Armand had told me—I figured it was a good bet.

I waited in Colin's bedroom and traced my fingers over the bed's comforter. My mind traveled back to when we had shared his bed. It seemed like another lifetime.

A loud *I am here* knock sounded at the door. It was Olivia's.

I got to my feet and stared at the door. Colin glanced at me before going to it and opening it.

"What's so important that I had to run down—" Olivia's mouth dropped. "Nyx?"

Colin closed the door behind her as she and I walked toward each other.

When we stood face-to-face she put her hands on her hips.

She tried to talk but couldn't.

"I've never seen you speechless," I said with a smile. "Don't worry, I don't bite."

"Better not. Try to suck my blood," she said, "and I'll kick your ass across Manhattan."

"It's all good or I wouldn't have called you," Colin said.

"Yeah, it's all real good, Colin," I added. "I'm glad to see you, too, Olivia." And then I hugged her. I smelled her familiar scent along with the richness of her blood. It was stronger and better than any perfume.

Olivia gave me a fierce hug before she stepped back. "This is growing old—you facing certain death and now dying. I've had it."

I was glad to see she was wearing one of her T-shirts. When I was injected with a lethal serum, she had gone blank-T-shirt on me.

"You're gonna be lucky if someone doesn't stake you the next time they see you." She gestured to my dress. "Hell, I'm ready to stake you for wearing that. You look like a reject from a Renaissance fair."

I raised my hands as I looked down at myself. "And to think I was going to change up my entire wardrobe."

"Start talking," she said. "I want you to tell me every damn thing that happened and how it is that you've gone all Vampire on us but you're standing here."

Another knock at the door. I stilled.

"It's Tristan," Colin said. When he opened the door my brother rushed to me and hugged me tight.

"I cannot lose you, little sister." Tristan rocked me back and forth as he squeezed me. "When Colin told me that you were here and alive, I let Father and your mother know at once. That is what took me so long."

Words were hard to come by, and I choked back more tears. "Thank you for telling them."

When Tristan and I separated, I said, "Let's go into Colin's bedroom." I cocked my head in that direction. "The others will be arriving soon, and I want to wait until they're all here before I come out. I'll tell you everything I can in there."

Olivia smirked. "Always have to make an entrance."

By the time I finished telling Olivia and Tristan my story, nearly everyone had arrived. My nerves had settled—some.

Voices came through the door, and my stomach clenched.

The door to the bedroom opened. Colin peeked his head in and gave me an encouraging smile.

It was now or never.

THIRTY-THREE

I walked toward Colin. Everything seemed to spin in my mind. What if the Trackers wouldn't have anything to do with me now that I was a Vampire?

"Hold on, mush brain." Olivia pushed her way past me, and Tristan joined her. "You're not going out without us to run a little interference in case some dolt has a happy trigger finger."

It was so good to have my partner at my side. Not to mention Colin and Tristan there, too.

At the door to the bedroom I paused. The scent of the warm bodies on the other side of that door was strong, and the scent of their blood, and I was glad I'd fed from Colin or I might not have been able to concentrate.

When I stepped into the living room, conversation came to a complete halt.

"Nyx?" My friend Nadia was the first to speak. *"Nyx?"*

"What the hell?" Ice got to his feet, too, his eyes filled with suspicion. "She's a Vampire. I can smell it."

"She is." Mandisa, who never spoke to anyone, stepped forward. "Nyx is Vampire."

I shivered as they all looked at me.

"Yes, I'm a Vampire." I raised my chin. Colin came up behind me and squeezed my shoulders, giving me strength. "But my Drow half is strong and I can fight it. I am fighting it and I will fight to defeat Volod with you."

Nadia got up from the couch and ran toward me. When she reached me, she enveloped me in a hug and she sobbed close to my ear. Tears leaked from my eyes, surprising me yet again.

When we pulled away, Nadia looked stunned. "You're crying."

I wiped tears away and nodded. "Something about this whole process, this whole transformation, changed me."

Nadia hugged me again. And then Angel and Tracey were right behind her. Before I knew what was happening, I was being passed from one Tracker to another, either being given a hug or one of them shaking my hand.

When Max reached me to take my hand, he looked devastated. I remembered how close he and Lawan had seemed the last time the Trackers got together. He must have been experiencing so much pain to know that Lawan was either dead or turned.

"Did you see her?" Max sounded hesitant, his voice a deep rumble. "Lawan . . ."

"No, she didn't rise when I did." I put my hand on Max's arm. "But she could be like me," I said. "Able to go against Volod's wishes."

Max's face seemed to crumble. I'd just confirmed that Lawan was being turned. He nodded and moved away.

Only a couple stayed back, including Mandisa. I was okay with that. Mandisa and her poison-tipped arrows were on the scary side.

When Penrod shook my hand, he said, "Nyx I will never forget that you accepted me when others didn't. I'm no different from you. When I heard you were in trouble and you needed all the help you could get, I had to come back."

Colin and Olivia stayed close, likely watching to make sure no one staked me.

After everyone greeted me, I stood at the head of the room. So much loss—the Trackers who had died and the ones who had been turned. But along with that pain was determination . . . that those who were responsible would pay.

I shared my story and told them what I'd learned from Volod. It wasn't much, but it was more than what we'd had before.

"We have to do something and soon," I said. "Volod's numbers are strengthening. The more time he has, the harder it's going to be for us."

"Nyx is right." Dave looked thoughtful. "We need to talk with Armand."

I started to protest, to explain why that wasn't a good idea, when the door to Colin's apartment slammed open.

Armand stood in the doorway.

He had a crossbow with a stake aimed at my heart.

"No!" someone shouted.

The stake flew from the gun.

Colin and Olivia slammed me to the floor.

The stake skimmed my head as I went down. I heard the hard *thunk* as it buried itself in the wall.

Desmond whipped out ropes of magic and bound Armand. His stake gun clattered to the floor.

"Release me." Armand didn't look intimidated in the least. His voice was low and deadly. "Do it now and I'll forget about the fact that you're harboring a Vampire."

"Kill him." Ice spoke in a fierce tone. "He won't give up until Nyx is dead. Let's get it over with."

"I agree." Tristan's voice was harsh, his muscles taut and bulging with restrained violence. "We must not let him harm my sister."

Penrod drew his sword. "I would be honored to protect Nyx."

The Sprite raised his sword. I scrambled to my feet, my enhanced Vampire-Drow strength allowing me to push past Colin and Olivia.

"Stop." I put my hand on Penrod's arm. "He's a good man. Don't kill him."

Armand narrowed his eyes. "You will not take me."

I met his gaze. "If I wanted to bite you I would do it now, and you could do nothing about it. But that's not what I'm about. I may be part Vampire, but I am not a true Vampire."

I gestured to the other Trackers. "These people know me. They knew me then and they know me now."

"You are a Vampire," Armand said in a low growl. "I do

not know why you saved me, but it cannot be for any purpose of good."

"Armand," I said. "Listen. Observe. My Drow side is fighting this." I raised my hands. "I went against Volod, and he wants me dead. Rodán was organizing a coup and I was involved. While fighting Volod, I had to watch Rodán, one of the people I love more than anything, die for me."

"You could easily be lying to turn these good Trackers to your side," Armand said.

I wasn't going to let him rattle me. "I will do anything in my power to stop Volod. We are here planning his destruction," I said. "If I wanted to attack paranorms, I would be with Volod right now planning your demise, not here planning his."

Armand didn't say anything. I wondered if I was getting through to him.

"You know that the odds aren't good versus Volod and his growing army of Vampires and Vampire paranorms," I said. "You need every resource available even to have a chance at victory—and you want to want to kill me? The only thing that my death will do is make your enemy, Volod, happy.

"Why?" I continued. "Because he knows I am one of the few threats to him. My people here are willing to fight to the death for me, but you and Volod's team are the ones who want me dead."

The Proctor had started to look like he was considering my words.

"Are you beginning to get a picture that something is wrong here?" I looked at the other Trackers then nodded to Desmond. "Let him up."

Penrod had a pleading note in his voice. "I do not trust him. Let me take his head off. He was trying to kill you, and he will."

I shook my head. "Armand is no fool. He knows he needs me." I looked at Penrod. "I appreciate your loyalty, but please sheathe your sword."

"How did you find out Nyx was here?" Colin asked with a frown.

"I have ways."

"I want to know." Colin's anger was showing through.

Armand paused. "I didn't know," he finally said. "I overheard a few Trackers talking about meeting here. It seemed unusual so I thought I would walk in on it. I didn't know she would be here."

I pointed to Desmond. "Let him up."

Penrod sheathed his sword. The room was taut with tension as Desmond released Armand.

When Armand was on his feet, Desmond turned to us. "I have something to show you."

"Not another hologram." I held my hand to my aching stomach. "I don't know if I can take much more of those."

"Whatever it is, I am meant to show you," Desmond said. "We will see what we are meant to see."

"You don't know?" Olivia put her hands on her hips. "What kind of Sorcerer are you?"

Desmond had almost killed Olivia when she'd been turned into a Zombie. Since then, she hadn't exactly been one of his biggest fans.

"A tired one." Desmond motioned for us to stand so that we were in a circle. Armand was on one side of Desmond, and I was on the other.

The Sorcerer formed a ball of light in his hands and set it free. It floated in the center of our circle, like a toxic green blob. The same color of green as the deadly serum Volod had injected me with not long ago.

An image of Rodán formed where the ball of light had been. This time instead of life-size images, it was small, maybe a foot tall.

Still it was so lifelike that it took my breath away. Rodán. So vibrant. So alive, even in undeath.

Rodán was in the conference room where he had died. He was talking with the four Vampire paranorms who had been in the room with him when Volod learned of his attempt at a coup.

"Nyx will join us in our revolt against Volod," Rodán said.

"I am certain of it. As will Monique, whom I have already spoken with."

That treacherous bitch. Ultimately it was her fault that Rodán was found out. Her fault that he was dead.

"What must we do?" asked one of the Shifters.

"Tell me those whom you believe are dissatisfied with Volod," Rodán said. "I will spend a little time with them to determine who would support our efforts."

Rodán had always had such a good sense for people. The only reason he'd failed to see that Monique was fully in Volod's clutches was that he hadn't wanted to see. They'd had a romantic history.

His love of women once again was his undoing, as it had been with the Nymphs.

The door burst open in the hologram and I had to live everything over again. I watched with horror as the two Dopplers were slaughtered and then Rodán took the blast of power that had been meant for me. I wanted to throw up all over again as I saw the stake bury itself into Rodán's heart.

Then the figure of me vanished a fraction before a stake passed through the place where I'd been only moments before.

Tears rolled down my cheeks as I turned away from the images. Colin rested his arm on my shoulders in a comforting embrace while I wiped tears from my eyes with the backs of my hands.

When I turned back, Desmond looked apologetic and Armand studied me as with a different kind of appreciation than he'd had before.

I think he saw that Trackers who knew me well—Trackers he respected—were prepared to fight for me. It made a difference to him.

"I am sorry," Armand said. "For what you were forced to go through by losing a good friend not once but twice. I cannot apologize for misjudging you because you are a Vampire. But I believe I can trust you from this point on."

"Okay." My voice was shaky. "Thank you."

Armand placed his hand on the hilt of his sword. "Of course if you lean to the Vampire side . . ."

"You'll have to kill me." I tried to smile and failed. "I get that."

"As long as we understand each other," he said.

"Loud and clear." I looked to Desmond. "Was that it?"

"I apologize." Desmond pushed his wild hair out of his eyes. "I guess that's what the Great Guardian wanted us to see. Especially Armand."

In the past I would have been irritated at the Guardian, but not now, not after meeting her. She had been good and pure beyond anything I could have imagined.

I took a deep breath. "I'll fill you in on what happened and what I know that may help us."

Armand listened to me intently as I spoke, interrupting me on occasion to ask a question. I explained that I hadn't been with Volod long enough to find out a lot, but I shared what I did know. It was hard to guess what Armand was thinking as he listened to me.

"We have heard rumors that Volod is amassing a large number of Vampires and Vampire paranorms," Armand said finally. "We believe they intend to attack, and soon."

"I believe that was part of what Rodán was going to talk about," I said.

I went on, "Volod mentioned briefly that he is bringing in Vamps and paranorm Vamps from all over. They're going to meet for some sort of planning conclave. Like I said, he wasn't sharing time, place, or numbers. If there is an attack, that would be the place. We needed to be ready to go on a moment's notice."

I looked around the room at all of the Trackers and Desmond. "We need to find out when and where Vampire paranorms are being taken and if we can get them together."

Armand nodded. "It is a greater problem when they are spread out. It is difficult to take so many out one by one when they are adding to their ranks."

"Yes," I said. "We haven't been on the offensive, and they've taken us by surprise. They know our weaknesses and have hammered our leadership. It's time to change."

When I finished, I asked Armand, "Why don't you take over the meeting now so that you can share with us what is being done and what we need to do next?"

For a moment Armand studied me. I knew he was debating giving me insider information. He still wasn't positive he totally trusted me.

"I am not sure you are aware," Armand said, "that since the Paranorm Council was taken, we have been taking high-profile paranorms into hiding. Part of our focus, too, is protecting Peacekeepers. One of our Soothsayers has also disappeared and we are afraid she has been taken by Volod."

My stomach twisted. "Who?"

"The one named Lulu," Armand said.

Lulu. I shook my head. I'd never liked her, but I would not wish such a fate on anyone.

"We have started bringing in Trackers from across North America," Armand said. "We have just over one hundred amassed."

Over a hundred. That was a sizable number, but I suspected that up against Vampire paranorms, it wasn't enough. I was impressed that so many had gathered already, though.

"Where are you keeping them?" I asked. "It can't be that easy to hide so many."

"We are housing them in a secret location," he said.

I was curious just how much I could get out of Armand. "Where is that?"

He paused as if weighing his decision. "The Vampire pyramid seized in New Jersey last fall."

"You're kidding." Surprise had me shaking my head. "You're housing paranorms in a Vampire sanctuary?"

"Former Vampire sanctuary," Armand said. "It is working quite well for our efforts."

"Yes . . ." I thought about everything that had happened in that pyramid last fall. It certainly had not been easy to take. "I can see how it would."

"A hundred is nowhere near enough paranorms," Colin said.

"We have more Peacekeepers coming in." Armand shifted his stance, his arms crossed over his chest. "The difficulty we face is that most Proctors cannot afford to give up many of their Trackers because they need to protect their own cities."

I glanced at Colin. "You said my father is sending some of his warriors?"

Colin gave a nod. "He said he would be sending twenty of his most elite warriors."

"Twenty Drow warriors is an exceptional asset." Armand looked impressed. "They are skilled fighters and from what we understand are immune to a Vampire's bite."

"That gives us a hundred and twenty." I blew my breath out. "Our odds still aren't that great."

"We can expect probably thirty to forty more . . . maybe. I just don't know when," Armand said. "I'm afraid that is all. I do not believe Volod will have close to those numbers of Vampire paranorms to go up against us. Especially if we are able to have the element of surprise."

Armand looked at all of the Trackers assembled and returned his gaze to me. "I am going to place my trust in those who will follow you and in my gut instinct. You will lead your team. You know the city and the area, and if I'm not mistaken they are willing to follow you."

Again he moved his gaze from one Tracker to the next. "Am I mistaken? If any of you wishes to join my team then speak up. Or if you have anything else that you wish to bring to my attention."

"I will follow Nyx." Ice shocked me by being the first to speak. "She has my trust."

"As she has mine," Joshua said with a calm yet hard edge to his voice. "I have served under Nyx since I joined the Trackers and I can think of no one better to lead us."

"Agreed," Angel said.

"Damn straight," Olivia said.

Murmurs of agreement went around the room. I didn't hear any dissent.

The support of my friends surprised me. For the first time in my life I had to hold back tears.

I addressed them. "We need to strike Volod first, before he can add more Vampires and Vampire paranorms." I pushed my hair out of my face as I tried to work over the problem in my mind. "Now to figure out just where he's hiding all these Vampires."

THIRTY-FOUR

Volod held the Fabergé egg in his palm and stared at it. The jeweled curio was one of the treasures he had amassed over the many years he had lived.

He squeezed his hand and crushed it.

Like he wanted to do to Nyx. What he would do to her. Crush her skull and watch the excruciating pain she would go through as her body healed like a Vampire's. He'd crush her again and again until he finally staked her through the heart.

Volod flung the remnants of the egg across his library hard enough that some of the pieces buried themselves into the wall while the others clattered to the floor.

He moved to the window and looked out into the night from the last major hideaway he had for himself and his people. He had built the twenty-bedroom mansion over a great cavern two centuries ago in case there was ever a need to hide those in his care. It was in a remote area of upper New York State. Every window and door in the house locked down during the day, the metal shutters and doors shielding the occupants from any sunlight.

The huge cavern itself was more than enough to house the Vampires he had brought in from across the United States and Canada. There weren't enough coffins, so most were forced to sleep on the cavern floor during the day. It would not be for long, however.

What he had planned would leave paranorms destroyed or in hiding. Paranorms would then be afraid to come out after dark.

Vampires would soon rule.

Volod turned away from the window. The conclave should be assembled now, the last of them having arrived within the hour.

Pieces of the Fabergé egg crunched beneath his shoe as he strode out of the library toward the drawing room.

Elizabeth waited just outside the library. She looked lovely in her floor-length red gown, her red hair swept up atop her head, her green eyes sparkling.

He came to a stop beside her and took her hands in his. She looked up at him with desire in her gaze, and he brushed his lips over hers.

"I was wrong about Monique. I thought she was loyal," he said as he looked down at Elizabeth's beautiful face. "I wish for you to once again serve at my side."

"Of course, Volod." She looked extraordinarily pleased to be returned to her station.

Monique's duplicity and Rodán's attempt at starting a revolt caused Volod to consider wiping out all Vampire paranorms.

He had expressed to his Vampire paranorms that they would enjoy self-rule as soon as their takeover was complete. His words had been greeted with agreement, He saw no dissension.

He should have seen the signs with Rodán, however. The former Proctor had questioned him and had not liked how Volod had taken Nyx.

Of course he had no intention of allowing so many paranorms to live once he reached his goal. It was far too dangerous. At most he would determine his most loyal individuals. The others he would lay waste to.

Volod schooled his expression as he escorted Elizabeth across the marble floor to the double doors of the drawing room. It would not do for the members of the conclave to harbor any doubt in Volod, his leadership capabilities, or his judgment regarding the Vampire paranorms.

Two Vampires flanked the entrance and two more were stationed inside the drawing room. He acknowledged each with a look that clearly instructed them to maintain their posts.

When he entered the drawing room, the occupants quieted for a moment. And then he was greeted with applause.

Pleasure swept through Volod at the recognition of what he had accomplished thus far. Of course they would applaud him. Truly there should be no question.

The members of the conclave who had made the trip at Volod's request were seated in a semicircle at one end of the drawing room, as if in session.

Excellent. Nine, a simple majority of the seventeen-member North American Conclave, were in attendance. There could be no dissent from those who had chosen not to show up. It had been their choice.

Prolocutor Nicholas smiled at Volod. "You have done well," he said with a deep nod. "You are to be commended."

Volod bowed in return as he played along with the idiotic formalities. "Many thanks to the conclave for the support that has been give since this endeavor began."

"Now tell us of your progress and your plans," Nicholas said.

"The city of New York is almost mine," Volod said. "We will take our forces into the city and overcome all paranorms by eliminating the Trackers and any others who choose to fight us.

"Once New York is captured," Volod continued, "we will focus on Chicago in the Midwest, New Orleans in the South, San Francisco in the West, and Toronto in Canada. These cities will be taken as well, and their Tracker forces wiped out."

Volod looked from one member of the conclave to the next. "We will use those areas as our planning centers to control each region. When we control these cities then we move to places like LA, Seattle, Atlanta, and Montreal. We will control this continent and eventually we move on to Europe."

"Ambitious, are you not?" said Marcus with a scowl.

If Marcus had been prolocutor, Volod would have a more difficult road ahead. Fortunately he wasn't.

"I do only what will benefit our people," Volod said while choking back the reply Marcus deserved.

Marcus had a smug expression as he said, "You put much stock in your Vampire paranorms. Tell us about the uprising led by a newly turned Vampire paranorm named Rodán."

Despite a momentary shock, Volod kept his expression placid and his tone even. "There was no uprising. We had one individual who attempted to stir up trouble. She murdered Rodán and Monique."

"Who was this?" Nicholas said with a frown.

"A paranorm who is half Drow." Volod cleared his throat. "Drow are immune to the Vampire bite. I had hoped her human half could be overcome, but it was not to be."

"That was a significant error in judgment," Marcus said.

"It was determined within twenty-four hours of her arrival that she was not under my control." Volod held back the fury he still felt. "She has been dealt with."

Nicholas did not look like the news bothered him. He seemed to be fully in line with Volod. Marcus on the other hand deserved a stake in the heart.

"What forces have you assembled to date?" Nicholas asked.

"Our forces are sufficient to take out the opposition. They have no idea of our numbers," Volod said. "No one does but me."

Nicholas said, "I have heard figures of close to two hundred fifty Vampires, over seventy Vampire paranorms, and thirty Vampire paranorm Trackers."

"Your sources underestimate what I have accomplished," Volod said.

"Can you take New York with the numbers you have?" Nicholas asked.

"I have no doubt," Volod said.

"What is your plan for finishing off the city?"

Volod paced from one end of the seated conclave members to the other. "With all due respect, I have been successful because I don't boast of my plans. The only one who knows my entire battle plan—or, as I call it, freedom plan—is me.

"I will tell you this," he continued. "I have my resources. Trackers are coming from all over, and I am laying my trap. I will draw them in and crush them. Crush them all."

Volod narrowed his eyes as he thought about the paranorms he would be taking on soon. "In the next few days, New York will be mine, and the other cities will see their ranks crushed there. I will decimate the paranorm teams from all over this continent."

THIRTY-FIVE

Nothing was left at the brownstone but a sense of evil that made me shudder down to my bones.

I rubbed both arms with my hands as my gaze drifted over Volod's cleared-off desk and the empty bookshelves in his study. How had everything been cleaned out so fast? I had searched the study for something that might give us an idea of where they'd gone. Nothing. Not a damn thing.

Colin had used his version of a transference to take us in and out of my apartment, during the day, in case any of Volod's people were staking it out at night. It felt good to have on my leather tracking clothing again.

But my daggers, Kahr 9mm, XPhone—my whole weapons belt was gone. I wondered if I'd find it with Volod. And I would track the bastard down and deal with him.

For now I wore one of my old weapons belts with a sword sheathed at one side instead of my Dragon-clawed daggers.

I had started to grab some of the garlic-and-holy-water defenses but had put them down when I'd started to feel a little sick. Not a lot, but enough that I'd rather stay away from the stuff.

"They're definitely gone." Angel came up beside me. "We've gone through every part of the brownstone." She looked around her. "This place stinks of Vampire." She glanced at me. "Save for present company."

"That's one thing I'd never thought I'd smell like." I shook my head. "Vampire."

"Well, so far so good." Angel patted me on the shoulder. "You still smell like a half-Drow, half-human, uh, individual."

"Thanks," I said. "I think."

Olivia snorted as she walked into the study. "Whoever heard of a purple Vampire?" She cackled in a very Olivia-like manner. "A plum with fangs. At least the points in the fangs match the ears now."

"Ha." I pointed at her. "Well at least I've never been ball-gagged while chained to a bed and abandoned by my boyfriend, likely after being flogged. Your ass did look kinda red."

"You didn't see my ass," Olivia said with a smirk. "It was covered."

"Ball-gagged?" Angel's eyebrows lifted and she looked from me to Olivia. "Flogged?"

"You should try it sometime," Olivia said to me. She nodded to Colin as he walked across the room. "I'm sure Smokey would be glad to oblige."

"Oblige what?" Colin rested his hand on one of my hips.

"Olivia was just talking about how much fun she has being on the receiving end of a whip." I turned to Angel. "Your specialty is the whip. Why don't you let me borrow it?" I narrowed my eyes at Olivia again. "I think I could make good use of it in the office."

Olivia waved me off. "You don't do anything for me, honey." She held out her hand to Angel. "But you can loan me the whip. I'm supposed to meet Scott in an hour."

"This whip isn't touching your ass." Angel grinned and put her hand over the whip looped on her belt. "Find your own. Besides, you never know when I might need it for my fun. It comes in handy."

"Oh great." I rolled my eyes. "It's not just Olivia. We have a room full of kink here."

Olivia cocked her head to the side. "I wish I could do that thing with the vine ropes that some of you paranorms spin out of nothing. Immobilizing someone that way would be useful in sooo many ways."

I managed to hold back a smile. "Guess you'll have to resort to manual labor."

"The Sorcerer would like you to come to the conference room," Dave said as he walked through the door. I flinched at the thought of what had happened in that room. "He said it was really important."

"All right." I took a deep breath and looked at Colin.

He rested one of his hands on my shoulders. "I'm right here."

We went down the stairs toward the room where Rodán had died. Had really and truly died.

My throat ached. I could feel tears waiting at the backs of my eyes as I thought of how my beautiful Rodán had saved my life and lost his own.

When we headed into the conference room, my chest ached. Armand and Desmond were talking near the doorway as we walked in. Olivia, Dave, and Angel followed Colin and me into the room. Max was guarding the front entrance, Nakano the back.

"No more holograms," I said to Desmond. "I can't take another."

"I wasn't going to." Desmond pushed his unruly hair away from his face. "I just need the energy you all carry to enhance my own powers."

"Okay . . . ," I said, but still didn't fully trust what he might do.

At Desmond's direction, those of us in the room held hands. I was between Colin and Desmond, and I felt a wild sort of energy coming from the Sorcerer.

"Close your eyes." Desmond's voice rang stronger than normal as he gave the order. "Concentrate on feeding me your energy."

I closed my eyes and tried to think about currents of energy traveling from my body, through my hand, to Desmond. But my mind was stuck on images of Rodán as he used to be.

"I need more," Desmond said and he squeezed my hand. *"Concentrate."*

I nodded, took a deep breath, and focused harder on my body being a beacon of magic. I used my power over my elements to strengthen me, to give me more of what I needed to help Desmond.

Energy rolled through me from the other Trackers as it traveled through each of us and then was passed on to the Sorcerer through our joined hands.

The room felt alive, brimming with tension and the crackle of magic.

Desmond started humming. A weird sound that reminded me of something electrical vibrating with power.

"I see trees." Desmond spoke slowly, his voice deeper and somehow magnified. "Many. A forest full of them."

I pictured the Vampire pyramid, but I knew that couldn't be it.

"It's dark," he continued. "Cool outside." Desmond paused. "Walking . . . tree after tree."

My heart pounded as Desmond spoke, as if I was on the mental journey with him and discovering what he was seeing for myself.

"A large structure surrounded by a spiked fence," Desmond said. "A fortress." He gripped my fingers tighter. "The structure has many rooms. It is more like a mansion. I see no beings there . . . but I sense them."

Where is it? I asked in my mind.

I felt as if wind was being sucked out of the room—as if we were traveling backward through time.

Desmond was quiet before he said, "It is a long journey to reach this fortress."

He released my hand. The spell he'd cast faded away, breaking up into sparkles in my mind.

I opened my eyes and found my focus wasn't clear. I blinked until my vision returned to normal. I turned to Desmond. "Is that it?"

"Yes." Desmond met my gaze and gave a slow nod. "And I know how to get there."

THIRTY-SIX

Traffic was so bad that evening that I could have run to Jenny Jump State Park in New Jersey faster than we traveled by vehicle. Literally. Two traffic accidents slowed progress. Of course a radar gun could clock me running faster than the speed limit.

I was just thankful that Olivia wasn't at the wheel. No, she was likely scaring Dave to death as she drove the vehicle they were in. Colin was driving our SUV, and there were three others in our little convoy from the city.

It was three days after my return. A recon team had been dispatched to find Volod almost immediately after our visit to the brownstone. They were due back today.

Now it was time for us to reconvene and get ready to go on the offensive against Volod and his forces. We wanted to catch them off guard before they returned to New York City. I only hoped we'd be in time.

When we'd last been in the hardwood forest of the state park it had been late fall, the trees naked. Now it was spring and despite the darkness I could see that everything was alive and green.

Our SUV traveled down the two-lane dirt road into the forest, the headlights cutting through the night.

Shivers ran over my body as we reached the almost invisible mirrored pyramid in an isolated part of the forest, and I ran my fingers along my collar. This was where Volod had injected me with a deadly serum. This was where we'd battled him, where we thought we'd taken down his empire.

When we arrived at the great stone fence that surrounded the property, the huge iron gate creaked open as if someone had been waiting for our arrival.

Mirrored glass covered the imposing pyramid, yet the surface didn't reflect the surroundings. Instead it seemed to absorb the light.

An imposing stone fence around the perimeter was about twelve feet high. Rows of razor wire curled along the top. The sharp barbs gleamed in our headlights.

It didn't look at all like a Vampire lair. It looked more like an Egyptian pyramid—modern style.

As we neared the structure, the ground rumbled and shook, then started to rise in front of us. A great door—about the length of two buses—slowly opened the earth. We drove into the cavernous opening, which slanted down to a concrete parking garage.

The last time I'd been here the garage had been filled with the Vampires' luxury vehicles. Well, those plus an old truck and a Prius. The concept of environmentally conscious Vampires was hard to wrap my mind around.

We entered the pyramid through the garage. Lead seemed to line my belly as we walked to a great foyer that was all too familiar.

The enormous chandelier overhead was still brilliant even though its hundreds of teardrop crystals were dusty. To the right a black marble staircase swept up to where a huge ballroom had held the giant nest of Vampires.

Now voices floated down to us from that direction. I recognized some of the paranorms talking. It was good to hear something familiar coming from what had been one of the worst places I'd ever been to.

Our eight-member team went up the sweeping staircase to a ballroom where about ninety paranorms were gathered.

Armand had told me that he had called ahead and informed the paranorms that they would be working with a Drow-human-Vampire, and he expected no problems.

Some approached and shook my hand while others stared

at me in confusion, wariness, or mistrust. I couldn't blame them. It was certainly a unique situation.

I made my way through the crowd until I reached my brother.

"Tristan." I smiled as he hugged me.

A ringing sound came from a pocket in his leather pants. I raised my eyebrows. "Since when did you start carrying a phone?"

Tristan fumbled with it but managed to get the flip phone open. "Olivia gave it to me while you were gone."

Trust Olivia to give a Drow warrior from Otherworld a phone.

"Yes?" Tristan said when he brought the phone to his ear. He had it upside down so I helped him turn it back. "Hello, hello?"

He listened for a moment, said "Yes, sir," then handed the phone to me. "It is for you."

I blinked in surprise. My brother had a call for me?

"This is Nyx," I said.

"Nyx!" My father's voice boomed over the phone line.

"Father?" My jaw dropped. "How are you calling me?"

"Tristan gave me this damn contraption to reach you when we arrived." He yelled into the phone as if he thought the sound had to carry across the miles.

I winced and pulled the phone away from my ear. "Where are you?"

"I sense we are perhaps five furlongs from you. I transferred my warriors into this—this . . . do you call this a forest?" he said. "It is nothing that compares to Otherworld. I had bad information and didn't make it to our target, so I need someone to come collect us."

"No, the forest doesn't compare." I had to smile at that. When it came to nature, nothing was as pure as Otherworld. "Tristan and I will go out and meet you."

"I shall wait for your arrival," Father said, and then the connection was severed.

"You gave Father a phone?" I handed the device back to Tristan.

He shrugged. "Convenient, is it not?"

I just shook my head at the thought of the warrior king of the Dark Elves having a cell phone.

After making our way out of the pyramid, Tristan and I ran to meet my father.

The evening was cool as we cut through the night. It was impossible to hear or see Elves—Dark or Light—if they didn't want you to. But as Drow, Tristan and I could both sense them.

When we came upon the warriors in the forest, just off the road, they let us by without speaking. Tristan nodded to the warriors we passed. I was aware of their gazes. I wondered what they were thinking now that I was a Vampire.

I was not actually certain they'd all even heard of Vampires before they joined my father's special force.

Father stepped out into the forest, and emotion surged through me. I threw myself into his arms. I didn't care that his warriors were watching. I needed my father.

He embraced me. "Nyx." His voice was thick as he squeezed me tight to him. "You tempt me to take you back to Otherworld and lock you away." He drew away and held my face in his palms. "I have almost lost you too many times."

"I know, Father." I hugged him again and rested my cheek against the cool metal of his breastplate. "I think I need a vacation."

Tristan and I walked with my father and his warriors back to the pyramid. The warriors did not change their bearing, but I could sense the wonder and wariness they all felt at being escorted into this bizarre world.

It made me think of when Rodán had brought me to New York City. The surprise, excitement, and even fear I'd felt in such a strange place. Almost three years later I was a changed person.

We escorted them through the foyer of the pyramid, up the staircase, and to the ballroom. The paranorms had been told to expect a contingent of Dark Elves but there was still a sense of wary interest on both sides.

Colin and my father greeted each other like longtime friends.

There was barely any room to move now. There had to be over a hundred of us packed into the enormous ballroom. When daylight came we would have the Drow warriors sleep inside the pyramid or down in the catacombs.

I left my father and Tristan, and I squeezed through the crowd with Colin to the head of the room where Armand waited. Desmond was there, too.

Armand raised his hands and made a motion for everyone to quiet down and listen.

When the room was silent, he spoke. "Thanks to the Sorcerer Desmond, we have learned where the Vampires are gathered."

A murmur traveled through the crowd of paranorms.

"Based on what Desmond told us, a recon team was sent in. They have just returned," Armand continued, "bringing valuable information."

He gestured for a paranorm to come forward. I recognized a Tracker from upstate New York, a Shifter named John.

Armand clapped a hand on his shoulder. "John, share with everyone what you and your recon team learned."

"By shifting into one of my smaller animal forms, I was able to enter Volod's mansion. I found this." John raised a piece of paper. "This is a list of all Vampires and Vampire paranorms who are or will be at the Vampires' lair shortly. It's a much shorter list than we expected. There are fewer than a hundred names on it."

"How do you know that number is correct?" Dave asked as a murmur traveled through the room.

"It appears very accurate based on the numbers of Vampires I saw." He went on to explain that the compound had human guards on the perimeter while the vampires were asleep, much as when they had controlled the pyramid.

"The guards are replaced by Vampires about ten o'clock. We will need to take care of the guards," John said with a smile. "Which shouldn't be hard being they are human."

He held up the paper again. "This also has an agenda for the next two days. It has times listed down to the quarter hour. From what we observed, they are following that agenda."

We made plans to penetrate the perimeter forest to just outside the main mansion, where there was a huge assembly building. It was just north of the mansion with two huge outdoor fireplaces and chairs set up. A large roll-up door in the rear was unlocked. Not that a lock kept me from getting into anything.

According to John, there was a huge back room that was used for storage, but it had plenty of empty space for our fighters to lie in wait. A drape separated the storage room from the main room. We had to get into place with a large team before the Vampires assembled. Apparently the Vampires generally didn't come out until at least an hour or so after sundown.

"That hour will give our fighters time to set up for the attack," Armand said. "Many of them will be inside. We will plan on having twenty to twenty-five there. The rest will be on the perimeter and will attack the building on signal as well as going after any Vampires who run out of the assembly hall or remain outside or in the mansion."

"Last night," John said, "Volod talked to the Vampires about who they are, what they are entitled to, how they are superior to everyone now. According to their agenda, he's now about to lay out the next step in his plan. He likes to get his troops excited, practically in a frenzy."

"Yeah, I've been to a couple of these meetings," Olivia said. "It was called Amway."

A little laughter was sprinkled around the room. I knew a Shifter who was an Amway distributor and I'd bought soap from him. Still, I doubted that most paranorms had heard of the company.

"We thought we would have to take the Vampires down in tight quarters," Armand said. "This will work out perfectly. We will go through what we know about the Vampire paranorms; we have a dossier on each one, and we know their respective skills. I believe that we have more than enough firepower to take them all out."

It was difficult still to think of destroying these beings, these Vampire paranorms. If they only understood that Volod would ultimately destroy all of them after he was done with them.

Not long ago, we were on the same side fighting Volod. To think we had been so close to destroying him less than a year ago. And now he was on the brink of taking over New York City. I couldn't imagine a more cunning or evil being.

"We have the element of surprise in our favor," Armand said, drawing my attention back to him. "And we have numbers. A numbers advantage was not what we expected. Adding the Drow warriors will help ensure victory."

"Why don't we go in daylight when the Vampires are in coffins or catacombs or wherever the hell they are?" Olivia asked.

Armand turned to her, resting his hand on the hilt of the sword sheathed at his side. "Good question. The mansion is virtually impenetrable when it is locked down. There are also tunnels belowground, so some could escape.

"And there is one we want to look in the eye when he dies." Armand's jaw tightened. "Volod. We don't want him slipping away. Also, a good number of our fighters cannot be out in the daylight."

Armand moved his gaze around the room. "As it is an isolated area with no airport available, we will go by tour bus."

"You're kidding. Tell me you're kidding." Olivia's voice rang out, a hint of laughter in her tone. "A bunch of powerful paranorms have to go to a battle in tour buses?"

Armand managed to look matter-of-fact. "Due to a shield that we believe a Vampire-Sorcerer has put up, we cannot use transference reliably. The shield seems to mess with the transfers. It is just not accurate. We could end up in the middle of the mansion with our entire team, or half of us might land ten miles away. Our recon team had problems with it and had to walk a few miles in. They did not have problems transferring out, however."

There were a few groans mixed with some snickers. I was

one of those who wanted to laugh. I looked up at Colin. "Please tell me you can get us up there without taking a bus."

Colin rested his hand on my shoulder. "Unfortunately, no."

This time I groaned. A tour bus?

"What about the Dark Elves?" I asked. "They can't be out when it's daylight."

"We are specially outfitting one of the buses," Armand said. "We are certain it won't be a problem."

After Armand quieted everyone again, Desmond created a three-dimensional map of the upstate location where Volod's lair was hidden. Armand used the tip of his sword to point out the topography and the layout of the buildings.

Desmond's magic showed us areas we would never have been able to map out otherwise. Still, the recon team had also done a great job gathering information that Desmond could not.

Desmond would be able to use his magic to jam any modern weapons like guns, eliminating that concern.

Armand spent time going over the specifics of our planned attack. He assigned me to lead a team of nine, counting Desmond.

Not all of our Trackers would be able to go, which was one reason why we numbered little over 120, even including the Dark Elves.

"Let me make something very clear." Armand moved his gaze around the room. "You are to kill all Vampires and Vampire paranorms in your paths. Do not allow yourself to feel pity for these beings."

"What about her?" an out-of-town Tracker said. Everyone looked at me.

"Nyx is half Drow, which made her less susceptible to the infection of Vampirism," Armand said. "I have seen for myself her loyalty to our cause and our people. Those of you who know me . . . Do you really believe that if I sensed a threat, she would be here right now? I hope you trust me more than that. She is one of us."

That seemed to stop the questions, but I still sensed lingering distrust.

Armand concluded, "The buses are outside and waiting. Let's clear out of here and ensure that Vampires never harm paranorms again."

The paranorm Trackers in the ballroom cheered and shouted. I could feel the enthusiasm of the crowd sweeping us on to victory.

Armand clenched his jaw as he added, "We know our enemy is formidable, but we have an excellent plan in place. We have great fighters. We outnumber them. We have the element of surprise. This will be the night that Volod will go down. We will not lose."

Cheers erupted in the room from the teams. I felt goose bumps. Yes, this night, Volod would go down.

THIRTY-SEVEN

"If they sing 'one hundred mugs of ale on the bus' one more time I'm going to go bust some skulls." Olivia had her eyes narrowed at the back of the bus, where twenty Drow warriors and a king were being led in a rowdy rendition.

I, on the other hand, was laughing so hard my sides hurt. To see my father and his warriors singing along with other Trackers was almost too much. For Olivia it apparently was.

"Why don't you take a nap?" Nadia turned to Olivia. "You could use one."

"Listen, fish brain," Olivia glared at Nadia, "if I want your opinion I'll . . . come to think of it, I'll never want your opinion."

Nadia gave Olivia a sly look and her sea-green eyes glittered. "From what I hear, whips are your thing. They're not mine."

Olivia glanced at me. I raised my hands in an I-have-no-idea-how-she-found-out gesture.

In the back, they started the next round at forty-nine mugs of ale on the bus.

"I have an idea." Olivia looked immeasurably pleased with herself as she gave Nadia a wicked grin. "Green gills, why don't you sing them to sleep?"

Nadia brightened. "I would love to."

"No." I stood in the aisle and blocked her. "Nooo singing."

"Bummer." Nadia flopped back into her seat. "But it would be soooo much fun."

"Come on," Olivia said. "It'll be great."

"Sirens know one song when it comes to men, and it always means death for the males." I glared at them both. "We need them for this assignment."

Nadia and Olivia looked at each other. "Then we'll do it after," Olivia said and she and Nadia shook on it.

"Forty-eight mugs of ale" floated up from the back and I almost said, *Go for it.*

But no, Nadia would not get to sing. The last time I'd heard her, she'd almost killed two Shifter males at the Pit who'd made some sexist remarks about her.

Sirens hate lewd males. And Sirens from the Bermuda Triangle do not know the meaning of restraint.

She flipped her luscious long red hair over her shoulder. "I think I'll take a nap. Must rest up my voice for the trip back." She covered her mouth in a pretty little yawn and curled up.

Nadia and I had been close friends since I'd arrived in New York City. She'd been one of the first Trackers to ask me out on a girls' night. She adored the opera, and I went with her when I could. The last one we'd gone to was a few weeks ago, *Pelléas et Mélisande* at the Met. She had a lovely singing voice when males weren't around.

Those in the back got even more rowdy at "forty-five mugs of ale on the wall."

Olivia banged her head on the seat in front of her. "I should have gone in the SUV with Armand, even if it meant sitting next to stinky Penrod."

Sprites smell like burned broccoli, so I couldn't blame her. "Desmond cast a spell on everyone," I said. "If you'll notice, you can't smell any odors. It'll keep us from being smelled by Vampires."

"Damn." Olivia banged her head again. "On the way back I am so riding in the SUV."

I glanced over my shoulder at Ice and Cindy, who were seated a couple of rows behind me. I'd never, ever seen Ice act like he did around her—a gentleman instead of a wisecracking jerk. It was amazing. I wanted to ask them if they enjoyed each other more in the form of mice or as they were now.

Megan, the Witch, sat with Bruce, the pit bull, on the cushion beside her. The falcon, Tate, perched on the back of her seat.

I ran my gaze over the other Trackers from Armand's bunch as well as some of the Trackers from states across the continent, in addition to our own from New York City. The fact that we'd all pulled together and were ready to go to war against Volod made me shiver.

Colin made his way from the back of the bus to where I was still standing. With the blacked-out windows and the double-black curtains blocking out the light from the front of the bus, it was dim inside, but I enjoyed the view of the Dragon.

When he reached me, he placed one hand on my hip and kissed me. It was a kiss filled with warmth and restrained passion, one that made me feel all melty and gooey inside.

"Are we there yet?" Kelly flopped back in her seat with a scowl on her usually pretty face. She crossed her arms over her chest. "We've been driving forever and we can't even see out. They're so loud back there. I'm hungry."

Olivia snickered. "I say we stick her under the bus with all of the weapons."

Now, there was a thought with merit.

"Better yet," Olivia said, "since Kelly is a Doppler bunny, she can be our lucky rabbit's foot. We just need to remove one."

I held back a laugh and shook my head instead.

Earlier we'd played a game of twenty questions—Colin did the Otherworld version and Dave did the Earth Otherworld version.

The hardest part for me was being around all those paranorms in a confined space . . . hearing all of those heartbeats . . . smelling all of that rich blood pumping through their veins . . . It was a good thing Colin had insisted I drink from him earlier or I might have gone crazy.

* * *

When we finally reached our destination the Drow warriors and my father stayed on the bus while the rest of us piled out into the afternoon sunlight. My skin reddened immediately. Fortunately I could handle it well enough to be outside without turning into a Drow-human-Vampire blowtorch.

A strong wind bowed the tops of the trees, reminding me of the sound of a rushing river.

"What is this place?" Kelly had her hands on her hips as she looked around. We were surrounded by forest, forest, and oh, more forest. "Where can we go for dinner?"

Megan and Rachel, a Shifter Tracker from Boston, brought up an ice chest and opened it. It was filled with sandwiches. "We have turkey, ham, egg salad, roast beef, and veggie," Rachel announced. "They're wicked good."

Kelly screwed up her face. "There must be a McDonald's nearby. McDonald's are everywhere."

I was surprised she wasn't too good for Mickey D's.

My stomach rumbled and Megan leaned in close to hand me a wrapped package. "Brought a steak sandwich for you. Rare."

"Thanks, Megan." I took it from her and smiled, suddenly wishing I had a pint of blood to wash down the steak.

"How's the 'gift' working for you these days?" she asked as I bit into my sandwich.

I chewed and swallowed. "It helped me a lot and then it stopped." I smiled. "Thank you. It was a special gift."

"I was meant to give it to you." Megan smiled back. "I'm glad it gave you what you needed."

After I finished eating, it was time to get into position.

Volod's mansion sprawled across a huge clearing in the woods. No other homes or buildings were closer than five miles in any direction. According to our recon team, during the day the entire place was locked down with retractable metal shutters and barred entrances.

The buses parked a good two miles away. As various beings got out their bows and arrows and assorted other weapons, Olivia looked at me and shook her head. "How did this happen? A bus full of grunts on the way to fight a Vampire war. This is as bizarre as it gets."

I laughed. "I doubt that. These are paranorms we're talking about. Bizarre is the norm."

Olivia shook her head. "Anyone passes by here now and sees this group will think a Halloween-in-May bus broke down."

With another laugh I walked over to Colin and Armand.

"So you feel pretty comfortable with the recon team's assessment?" I said to Armand.

"Yes." He looked in the distance, in the direction of the mansion. "I sent the best Trackers I have."

I glanced up at Colin. He looked so good to me. His long blond hair lifted away from his face in the wind as his warm burnished-gold eyes focused on me. He was heavily armed with two swords strapped to his back, as well as daggers and stakes on his weapons belt.

For a moment I thought the scaled serpent tattoo on his arm moved, but it was only a trick of the waning light.

We broke into eleven teams with an average of ten paranorms each. My team comprised Colin, Ice, Nadia, Robert, Olivia, Mandisa, Penrod, Desmond, and—I had drawn the short straw—Kelly. We would all be in the assembly hall, waiting for Volod and his Vampires and Vampire paranorms to leave the mansion. The first step was getting to the building without being found out.

Human guards were posted around the perimeter of a great wooden spiked fence. I thought about how nice it would be to see a Vampire impaled on each spike.

When the sun started to set, I slipped into the forest and shifted to Drow. Colin came with me. He didn't like the idea of me being alone, and I didn't mind letting him watch me shift. He said he found it rather sexual, but this was no time to have my thoughts drift there.

Shifting is always difficult when I can't stretch and move into the change, but as a Vampire it seemed to be a little easier. Who'd have thought?

Colin and I moved back to our team. I slipped in the earpiece that Olivia had secured for the leaders. We were in a good location where we could see through the gate to the front of the mansion.

The sun slowly settled over the mountain range. The sky grew completely dark.

It was time.

THIRTY-EIGHT

Metal shutters retracted from the mansion's windows. The bars over the great double front doors did as well.

Lights flickered on in the mansion, yellow beacons that would have appeared warm if it weren't for the fact that the place housed Vampires.

As if a hot coal had been pressed to my skin, my neck burned where Volod had bitten it. I slapped my hand over the location and ground my teeth. It only burned when Volod was close, so he was definitely in there.

I didn't want to count on having a whole hour after sunset before the Vampires came out no matter how much time the recon team said we had. I wanted to get in and get ready.

When I gave the signal, my team moved through the night to the front gate. The wind was stronger, and with it came the threat of a storm. It was oddly reminiscent of the last time we had fought Volod down months ago, to the last moments before I had almost severed his head from his shoulders.

We reached the gate. Ice and Robert took the pair of human guards with no problem, snapping their necks and leaving their bodies behind.

Twenty of us were prepared to go inside the assembly hall and prepare for Volod and his people. That left approximately eighty Trackers to surround the perimeter, along with twenty Drow warriors.

Once we were inside, those of us who could pull glamours could position themselves just about anywhere. The rest would go into the storage room or anyplace else they might find to hide.

Although Volod had been able to sense me in my glamour in our last encounter, I knew it would be different this time.

Ice shifted into his white jaguar form, Robert changed into a cougar, and Kelly became a bunny. They slipped between the bars of the gate.

Nadia, Olivia, Mandisa, Colin, Penrod, and Desmond eased through the night with me. I used my air element to unlock the gates. They swung open, creaking; I hoped the sound of wind helped cover it.

"Stay alert," I said as we slipped into the mansion's driveway. We left the gates open for other teams to follow.

Everything was beyond quiet.

We worked our way to the assembly hall, which had remained dark.

"Teams going into the hall report in." Armand's voice came over the radio, static caused by the wind making it difficult to hear well.

I held my hand to my ear. "Team one, set," I said in a low voice.

"Team three, set," came Angel's voice over the wind.

One by one the rest of the team leaders checked in.

"On my count." Armand's voice was calm and deadly. "Three . . . two . . . one . . . *go*."

Those of us heading into the hall started moving again. We eased from tree or bush to the next as we made our way to the front entrance. I tried the doorknob. It turned easily, and the door slowly opened.

It was a large, mostly empty room, just as John had said. A good place for Volod to hold his rah-rah Vampire rallies.

Windows lined the east, north, and west sides. The south side was attached to the mansion. Across the room was the large roll-up door that John had mentioned. It now rolled up, and Angel's team entered from the back.

We moved into place. Colin nodded to me as he and I took a corner and pulled glamours. I crouched and watched.

One by one Trackers cloaked themselves. Those in the hall slipped into the back room. After closing the roll-up door and the front entrance, the last couple of Trackers vanished behind glamours.

It remained quiet. So quiet.

Light crackled outside, capturing my attention. Through the windows an odd orange lightning spiderwebbed the sky. Prickles ran up and down my spine.

"What the hell?" someone whispered.

My whole body suddenly froze. I couldn't move. I couldn't blink.

I felt my glamour drop away.

No matter how I tried, I couldn't speak. All I could do was hear and see. Even then my vision was limited because I couldn't turn my head. My eyes burned from not being able to blink.

Fear clawed its way up my throat from my chest.

What was happening?

Other Trackers I could see had lost their glamours. No one was moving.

The back door made a rattling sound as it rolled up. Lightning continued to crackle across the sky. The air smelled of ozone.

Vampire paranorms came into the room. My heart pounded so fast my chest hurt.

One of them was headed straight for me.

Instinctively I tried to reach for my weapons, but it was as if my entire body had turned to ice.

When the Vampire paranorm reached me, he leaned down and picked me up under his arm like I was something he'd just purchased. He carried me through the back door and outside.

Between the mansion and the assembly hall, Trackers were being set onto the lawn as if they were great chess pieces on a massive board.

Tracker after Tracker. Each being carried by Vampires and Vampire paranorms.

My heart sank to my belly when I saw my father and his

men being arranged behind the Trackers. All of them faced one direction.

I had the odd thought that the wind might blow one of the frozen paranorms over and trigger a domino effect, with each paranorm Tracker falling against the next.

How had Volod managed to freeze us? It was as if he had a Soothsayer . . .

I mentally shook my head. Impossible. Or was it?

The Vampire paranorm hefted me onto his shoulder once again. And then a silent scream echoed in my head at what I saw.

There had to be over two hundred Vampires and Vampire paranorms. A sea of them.

Our intel had been wrong. Very wrong. How could this be?

The Vampire paranorm carried me through the array of frozen Trackers. I sensed all the tension, the anger, the fear, the fury, of every one of the Trackers and Drow warriors. If thoughts could kill, we'd never see Volod again.

When he reached the front row, he set me down. I was in a crouching position and could only look directly in front of me.

Two Vampires moved within my line of sight. I couldn't look up but I knew instinctively who was staring down at me.

Volod. Elizabeth.

"Unfreeze her." Volod spoke to someone on the other side of me.

"Yes, Volod," came a voice I was more than familiar with.

The orange light streaking the sky sparked. A female wearing a long pink gown that brushed the tops of the grass raised her fingers, and a stream of light traveled from her hand to me. My body went limp and I fell forward. I caught myself with my hands, my arms braced so that I was on my hands and knees.

I tipped my head back and saw Lulu.

Lulu. Volod had taken her, just as we'd feared.

She looked triumphant. In her element. Proud to be a Vampire paranorm.

Pleased to be in control of me.

She stepped aside and I met Volod's eyes. Dark. Burning. Hateful.

"Get her up." Volod glanced to his right.

I followed his gaze and saw two Vampire paranorms I recognized from the brownstone. One of them had brought the Doppler female to me, my first meal. Vaguely I wondered what had happened to that female.

They dragged me to my feet. I felt off balance but my coordination was returning.

My elemental powers. I tried to concentrate on them, to call to the earth to open up a chasm beneath Volod's feet. But I was still too weak.

"Restrain her," Volod said to the two Vampire paranorms.

I tried to shrug off their holds, but together they were incredibly strong. They easily restrained my hands behind my back with Vampire cuffs. As Trackers we were spelled to get out of such handcuffs, but as a part Vampire, I was now unable to.

"Shackle her ankles," Volod said.

The raw edge of panic cut through me. I tried to call to my elements but they wouldn't answer. The cuffs wouldn't allow me to use any of my magic.

I kicked and struggled but they held me tight as a third and fourth Vampire paranorm brought forth a spreader bar with cuffs attached to it. They forced my feet apart and placed the bar between my ankles. If I tried anything with my feet, it would throw me off balance.

"Take off her weapons," Volod said. "She won't be able to use them, anyway, but I want her to feel completely vulnerable."

And then I was stripped of the rest of what could have aided me in fighting Volod. If I'd figured out how to free myself.

"Did you enjoy my surprise?" Volod gestured to Lulu. "Isn't she magnificent? I've been keeping her a secret until she was needed. One never knows who might spoil the element of surprise."

"How does she freeze paranorms?" My throat ached as if

it had been rubbed raw. "And why aren't your people affected?"

"You were the only ones affected because you were the only ones in the area her spell covered. My Vampires poured out of the mansion and all of the hidden cavern exits in the forest after she froze you. And you happened to be in the building she spelled, didn't you?"

I hated to hear his laugh. I hated him relishing victory. I never should have asked.

Lulu looked so smug and beautiful there beside Elizabeth.

"That doesn't explain how she was able to freeze paranorms," I said. "Soothsayers can only freeze humans."

"When she was turned, it enhanced her powers." Volod smiled. "I then took her to our newly turned Sorcerer. He showed her the magic she didn't know she had and helped her strengthen it, until she grew to have the power she now wields.

"He also showed her how to freeze you," he continued, "but keep you fully conscious. Yes, I wanted you to know everything going on.

"As long as she lives, Lulu shall serve me." He lifted his hands and looked to the orange light show in the sky.

Then he put his hands behind himself and turned to the scene before us.

"Not only do I have this precious gem, your Lulu," he said, "but I have your council." He gave a nod to his left. I looked and saw the Paranorm Council standing straight and proud, weapons in their hands. The only one missing was Bethany, and I wondered what had happened to her. Volod gestured to his right. "As well as a pair of your precious Trackers."

My heart ached as I saw Lawan and Gentry.

"We have you far outnumbered," he continued. "I didn't just have the Vampires and Vampire paranorms that you expected. I had another one hundred and fifty below in the caverns."

A cold chill swept over me. "Our forces outnumber yours by what, two or three to one?" He made an offhand gesture.

I felt deflated. Like every good thing had been sucked out of me. Surrounding me were some of the best fighters in the paranorm world. Now every one of them was frozen. At Volod's mercy.

And that was something Volod had none of. Mercy.

Volod motioned for a Vampire paranorm to step forward—Fae, I thought, but not a race I was familiar with. "Meet Christopher." Volod let his gaze drift across the assembled "statues." "Some of you know him. He has the gift of transference."

The Master Vampire patted Christopher on the shoulder. "After my work is finished here, he will take me straight back to my home, the place that will once again be mine. You know it well. The pyramid, I think you call it."

Volod let his gaze drift over the Trackers on either side of me. He stopped at Nadia.

"That one." Volod gave a nod in Nadia's direction. "She is good friends with the Drow bitch. She will be first. Even if I wasn't going to kill all of these Trackers here, she is a Water Fae and cannot be turned. Thus I would never have a use for her anyway."

The thumping of my heart grew faster. "Let her go, Volod." I struggled to keep a pleading note from my words.

Nadia was kneeling in her frozen position. A beautiful ice sculpture. It seemed like her warm and loving nature should be strong enough to melt her ice prison.

"Bring the Siren here." Volod directed his request to a pair of Vampire paranorms to his left.

They hesitated a fraction of a second before following through. Then they picked Nadia up and carried her before Volod.

A great spiked ball lodged in my chest, its metal spines seeming to pierce my organs.

To Lulu he said, "Unfreeze her."

Even Lulu seemed to pause at the request, but she pointed her finger toward Nadia. A small burst of light shot out.

Nadia gasped and sucked in a long breath. Her sea-green eyes were wide. Like me she had heard everything that was happening while she was frozen. And she knew Volod had something planned for her.

She didn't beg, though. It wasn't Nadia's style. Instead she glared at Volod. Her skin took on a light tinge of green as she started to sing her Siren's song. The song that meant certain death to males.

Volod stepped forward. His hand whipped out so fast it was a blur. Metal glinted off a blade.

And he sliced open her throat.

"No!" I screamed and fought against the handcuffs and the two males who held me.

Nadia crumpled to her knees. Blood poured down the front of her, the red spilling over the black leather she wore.

She brought her hands to her throat and collapsed to her side then rolled onto her back. Instead of singing there were only wet, rasping gurgles.

Screams echoed over and over in my head. My heart nearly stopped beating.

Nadia's eyes stared up at the orange sky.

She was dead.

Tears rolled down my cheeks and the pain in my chest was nearly too much to bear. Not my dear friend. Not Nadia. "Please, no."

"Good." Volod's words were chilling. "I will enjoy killing your other friends here while you watch. You will be last."

My head ached, my heart hurt. The pain of Nadia's death began to turn into a hot burning fury.

"Are you not particularly fond of the human?" Volod said with an evil smile.

I tried to keep from revealing anything with my expression but I wasn't successful.

"Yes . . ." A vicious smile curved the corners of his lips. "I can see that you are."

I thought pain was going to rip me in half over Nadia, but now Olivia, too?

No. I couldn't let that happen. I had to stop him somehow.

But as I looked over the sea of Vampires and Vampire

paranorms that surrounded me and the frozen paranorms, I felt utterly helpless.

"Get the human," Volod said to the two Vampire paranorms. "Bring her here."

I wanted to scream. I wanted to shout. But I couldn't. It would only make them more eager to kill Olivia in front of me.

Elizabeth moved to stand beside Volod, her smile as evil as his. The wind teased her hair away from her face. "Why don't you let me have the human?"

It was then that I realized that as the only human, Olivia was probably driving every Vampire in the place crazy with bloodlust.

She was still frozen when they brought her to the front, and Volod ordered Lulu to unfreeze my friend.

Lulu looked nervous and paused. After seeing Nadia murdered, was she having an attack of conscience?

Before Lulu could act, Elizabeth turned her gaze on Volod. "I want her to be one of us. I want to lead this one around on a leash, Volod. Would you permit that?"

"An appealing idea." Volod smiled at Elizabeth. I sucked in my breath. Knowing Olivia, that would be a fate worse than death. "You know me well, Elizabeth. You may take your new pet—after I bite her."

"Wonderful," Elizabeth said with a smile that was pure malice.

"Unfreeze the human." Volod scowled at Lulu. "Now."

"Yes, Volod." Lulu hurried to touch Olivia.

Olivia rushed Volod.

The movement surprised everyone, including Volod.

"I owe you, you fanged piece of slime," Olivia shouted as she tackled him. "For what you've done to my friends." She hit him at the knees with momentum so hard that he should have been bowled over.

Instead, Volod grabbed her by her hair and jerked her up.

"Try to bite me without teeth." Olivia slammed her fist into his jaw, snapping his head to the side. Unfortunately his teeth didn't break.

He grabbed her to him in a rough, harsh movement, bringing her hard against his chest.

"Let go of me, scum." Olivia kicked and fought, but she was no match for the incredible strength of a Master Vampire.

I lunged forward, trying to get to her, trying to help her. But the bar I was shackled to wouldn't let me move.

Volod had Olivia pinned to him. In a blur of movement he lowered his face to her neck and bit.

Olivia shrieked. A moment later she went limp in Volod's arms, just as the Doppler had in mine.

"No." I sagged against my captors. The hopeless feeling inside me grew larger, heavier.

Volod raised his head and licked blood from his lips then ran his tongue over the two puncture wounds on Olivia's neck. He tossed her aside, at Elizabeth's feet.

Olivia landed on her backside. She looked dazed and incapable of speech.

I wanted to scream to cry . . . to rage . . . To kill Volod . . . To truly and finally wipe him out of existence.

Volod turned to me. "You are wondering, of course, how we knew of your coming and of your plans." He glanced at the crowd of Vampires and Vampire paranorms surrounding all of the frozen paranorms. He made a *come here* motion with his fingers.

A Metamorph I recognized as Janet strode forward. I frowned. It had never occurred to me that Volod had turned Metamorphs. But what did Janet have to do with this whole mess?

When Janet reached Volod, she turned and faced us.

And shifted.

Into John. The Tracker from upstate New York who had led the recon team. The one who had come up with this entire plan, including the timing. We had been set up perfectly by Volod.

We'd had a Metamorph in our midst and we hadn't even known it. A Vampire-Metamorph.

The world was crumbling and I didn't know how to stop

it. Rodán was dead. Nadia, dead. Other Trackers, dead. Olivia, bitten. Trackers turned into Vampire paranorms. Me, a Vampire.

And now my people were frozen, surrounded by Vampires and Vampire paranorms.

"Yes, you took the bait, didn't you," Volod said, "and walked right into my trap with your meager force."

I fought to keep from slumping with the weight of the feeling of defeat.

"What are you going to do, Nyx of the Night Trackers?" Volod smiled. "When all that you hold dear is being destroyed before your very eyes."

THIRTY-NINE

I kept my head high, striving for bravado I didn't feel. No matter how I puzzled it out, I couldn't see a way to stop Volod.

"Bring up her family and the friends she holds most dear." The glint in his eye was utterly evil. "I'm not even close to being finished yet."

Chills rolled through me. He was going to kill my family and friends. There had to be something I could do. But what?

The Great Guardian.

What had she told me? That she was with me even in times where it seemed she wasn't.

Nadia had just been killed in front of me. My friends were next. It sure didn't seem like she was now.

Her power was available to me, she'd said. I needed to trust her.

It wasn't just hard. This was impossible.

Maybe what I needed to do was ask.

Great Guardian, I need you now more than ever. I believe you, but help me to believe more.

"Let's start with her friends the Manhattan Trackers." Volod pointed to Desmond, Angel, Joshua, and Ice. "Those four . . . I know for a fact you work intimately with them."

I swallowed hard as those I cared about were brought forward. There were just no words for any of this.

When the Sorcerer Desmond and the three Trackers were arranged in the front, Volod said, "Bring up the one who is her father and the one who is her brother." He looked at me.

"You killed my brother. Now you will watch yours die, along with your father."

My mind churned, my stomach twisted. I thought I was going to throw up.

He must have seen everything written across my face. "Yes, bitch. I know all about you and the ones you care for."

John—Janet—pointed toward the back row. Volod sent several of his Vampire paranorms to get them.

My father looked so regal and proud in his frozen glory. He stood straight and tall, his muscles clearly taut with what I knew to be suppressed violence.

Tristan, a kind soul but a powerful warrior, had his bow and arrow in hand. The diamond arrowhead glinted in the orange lightning that continued overhead.

When their rigid bodies were set next to me, Volod let his gaze slide over the other frozen paranorms.

"There." He nodded in Colin's direction. "The Dragon. I want him next."

I caught my breath.

"Who do you choose to die first?" Volod said. "Your family, your friends, or your Dragon?"

I jerked against the cuffs. I tried to use my elemental powers again, put all my focus into my air magic to unlock the cuffs. I felt nothing. I felt naked without my powers.

And so helpless. I felt so helpless.

Colin was brought to the front and the sickness in my belly increased.

"Your Dragon will be next," said Volod. "And I will keep them all frozen. Each will be completely aware of what is happening."

Volod put his hands behind his back and swept his gaze again over the frozen paranorms. "I have no reason to have any of these unfrozen."

I wanted to beg but I knew it would do no good. He'd enjoy hurting them even more.

He moved his gaze back to me. "I will kill them. All of your Trackers and your visitors from afar will die today. I already have all the Vampire paranorms and powers that I need.

"And I have no need of you except to watch you suffer through your last moments."

One of the Vampire paranorms who had carried my father to the front said, "You told us we would feast tonight and turn many."

"Shut up." Volod narrowed his gaze at the one who had spoken. "You Vampire paranorms were created to serve me. There will be others. I want every one of these Trackers wiped out."

"Don't you understand?" I raised my voice to be heard over the wind as I spoke to the Vampire paranorms. "Volod will kill you all when he has finished using you. I have been turned, too, but I will not fight for his gain."

"Shut up or I will have you frozen again," Volod growled.

"Volod killed Rodán and Monique," I shouted. "I was there when both were murdered."

A rumble rose from the crowd.

"Freeze her!" Volod screamed to Lulu.

Lulu was wide-eyed, looking from Volod to me to the crowd.

The Vampire paranorm who had spoken up shouted, "I, too, saw Volod murder Rodán."

Volod grabbed a sword from the Vampire Shifter next to him. He raised it and swung it at the outspoken Vampire paranorm. The being's head flew out in front of the crowd and rolled to a stop.

Silence.

Then someone shouted, "You killed Mark."

Another—then another—started yelling.

"You killed him!"

"You went back on your word!"

"Nyx is right."

"Volod said they would be turned, not killed," said another.

"Volod has tried to fool us," a Vampire paranorm growled. "We won't stand for this."

"What Volod is doing is wrong." It was Leticia, the chief of the Paranorm Council. "Volod is going to slaughter all of these paranorms. We are seeing his true intentions here. Being a part of the murder of all of these helpless paranorms—this is not what we are or who we are. They are our brothers and sisters."

"None of that is the truth," Volod shouted, but beings in the crowd only yelled louder.

"Freeze them," Volod ordered Lulu. "All of the rebellious ones."

"Don't do it," someone yelled. "Unfreeze our brother paranorms instead."

"Do what I instructed you to do, Lulu." It was clear Volod was using his mental control over Lulu. I could see her shake and tremble and try to fight him off, but she mentally wasn't strong enough. She wasn't meant to be a fighter. Soothsayers in general were fragile compared to Trackers.

"Yes, Master," she whispered.

Lulu stepped forward and raised her hands.

"Do it, Lulu," Volod shouted. "Now!"

A wooden missile flew out from the crowd.

The stake buried itself in Lulu's heart.

Volod took a step back in shock.

The guards holding me let go.

Shouts and gasps filled the air as all of my people were set free from the spell.

Immediately Colin was at my side, using Dragon fire to melt and disintegrate my cuffs and the spreader bar and cuffs at my ankles without touching my flesh.

"Get them!" Volod was shouting to his Vampires and Vampire paranorms. "Kill them all!"

Colin jerked me back by my arm with the others. We were trapped. A hundred and twenty of us surrounded by over 250 of Volod's Vampires and Vampire paranorms.

Through a lifetime of training and from instinct, the Trackers and Dark Elves moved in sync. We put our backs to the center, now facing all Volod's forces so that we were in huge circles within circles.

Someone shouted, "The paranorms and the paranorm

Vampires are brothers. Death to the true Vampires!" Other voices joined in.

Cries and the sound of battle reigned as Vampires and Vampire paranorms started fighting each other. I saw Lawan, Gentry, and members of the former Paranorm Council attacking Vampires.

Armand's magically enhanced voice shouted, "Kill all Vampires. Do not kill the Vampire paranorms."

Our people didn't hesitate. Heads were flying, bodies falling.

My attention had never fully left Volod and Elizabeth. "Christopher!" Volod was shouting. "Take me out of here. I'll give you anything you have ever wanted. I'll make you a leader."

Christopher, an obviously traitorous Vampire paranorm, hurried to Volod's side and grabbed his arm. Volod reached for Elizabeth's hand.

"No way, you fanged bitch." Olivia's shout came from just feet away. In the next instant, Olivia was flying at Elizabeth, driving her to the ground before Volod could grasp her hand.

Elizabeth screamed and clawed at Olivia. But my friend and partner had the element of surprise.

Olivia raised her hand, a stake in her fist.

Elizabeth tried to shove her away, but Olivia had momentum and fearless determination on her side.

She drove the stake into Elizabeth's heart.

"Take that, Vampire bitch," Olivia growled. "Red looks good on you," she added as small trails of blood leaked from around the stake.

"Get me out of here!" Volod screamed again.

I dove for my weapons belt and jerked a stake out. Just as the images of Volod and Christopher started to waver, I flung the stake.

It pierced Christopher in the heart.

They vanished.

"No!" I shouted.

"He can't be far," Colin said. "Christopher died. Volod would have fallen out of the transference."

My neck burned where Volod had bitten me. "Yes. He's near." I picked up my weapons belt and slung it around my hips. "We have to find him."

A battle raged around us. Paranorms worked side by side with Vampire paranorms to eliminate the Vampires.

"Where do we start?" A crawling sensation ran up and down my arms as a sense of urgency nearly overwhelmed me. "We have to get to Volod before he escapes."

"Look." Desmond came up beside me. He was studying the forest to the east of us. I followed his gaze and in the moonlight I saw a thin, silvery trail. "That's it," he said.

"A trail of bread crumbs?" I stared at the wispy rope of silver. "You're sure?"

"Must be." Desmond looked from the trail to me. "It's the magical signature of a Fae being. Christopher was Fae."

Colin took my hand and Desmond's upper arm. In a blink we were standing in the forest, silver light floating like fog around our feet.

"It's Christopher." Desmond was kneeling beside a body. "Just as we thought, he's dead."

"Footprints." Colin was studying the ground. He nodded to the east. "That way."

Colin went ahead of me, then paused and came back. "Lost the trail. He's got to be here somewhere, though."

Desmond joined us. "Likely falling out of a transference wasn't an easy thing to go through. He could be hurt."

"If only we're so lucky." I would truly be surprised if Volod was actually injured. "We need to split up." I said. Colin looked like he was going to argue, but I didn't give him time. "If you come across him, just shout."

The bite on my neck was burning even more. Volod couldn't be far.

I called to my air and earth elements as I jogged through the trees. I sent out tentacles of magic, searching the forest ahead of me for Volod.

My magic wrapped around something so evil my stomach cramped. I stopped short. The evil vanished. Volod had raised a shield to hide himself from my magic.

I ducked around bushes and trees, searching. Ahead I heard footsteps. Without pause, I jumped up, grabbed a branch, and swung myself up into a tree. I silently ran along large branches and jumped from tree to tree while Volod's shoes slapped against leaves.

I couldn't call out to Colin and Desmond without alerting Volod. I'd let them know when the time was right.

In moments I was above him. He looked over his shoulder as if knowing someone or something was after him. I kept him in sight as I continued following him through the treetops.

My heart pounded. Blood thrummed in my veins. The Drow half of me thrived on the chase. The thrill of the hunt was on.

When I was directly over Volod he came to a stop. I paused, judging the distance from the tree to his head.

I crouched to jump.

Volod shot his gaze and his arm up.

And shot a bolt of power at me.

"Bitch!" His power slammed into me with so much force I flew from the branch, back against the tree trunk.

I cried out from shock and pain. My chest burned from his magic.

Volod shot another burst of power from his hand.

I pulled a glamour and moved just in time to avoid getting hit.

Splinters flew from the tree trunk. Several buried themselves in my biceps, and one in my neck. I winced but held back a cry of pain.

Volod looked for me but my glamour was too strong.

He sniffed the air. "I can smell you. I can smell your blood." His voice was low and dangerous. "I can feel you. You're still mine to command, Nyx."

I got to my feet and pulled out the splinters, gritting my teeth from the pain.

"Come out and play," he said then shot a burst of his power in my direction.

I barely dodged it and barely maintained my glamour. I drew my sword. I'd have to come out of glamour to fight him, but I'd kill him. This time I'd do it right.

Sword in hand, I charged him. I let my glamour drop just as I raised my sword.

Volod threw up a shield. I hit the shield hard and bounced off it, landing on my backside.

I vanished again behind a glamour. I'd play cat-and-mouse with him a little more. He'd have to drop that shield to try to harm me with his power.

Slowly I walked in a circle around him. He sniffed the night air and turned in the same direction I was moving.

"Avanna," I murmured to cleanse myself of the blood. He was tracking me just by the smell.

I continued moving, but he paused. When I was behind him, I raised my sword and dropped my glamour.

"You're dead," I growled.

Volod whirled, his hand ready to send power at me as he dropped his shield.

I stepped into his space, swinging my sword.

His power hit my sword so hard that I lost my grip on it. It flew from my hands and clanged against a stone on the forest floor.

I grabbed a stake from my weapons belt and charged him, my arm raised with the stake in my fist.

Volod blocked me with one arm and sent his other fist into my gut.

Air whooshed out of my lungs. I stumbled back.

He dove for my sword and grabbed it before I could reach him.

Volod swung the sword at me. I ducked and somersaulted backward out of reach.

My breathing was coming harder now as adrenaline pumped through my body.

I clenched the stake in my left fist. With my right I drew a dagger. I missed my Dragon-clawed daggers, but this would do.

Volod lunged for me with the sword. Instead of backing up, I tucked myself in a ball and somersaulted forward.

I felt the dangerous flash in my eyes as I came to a stop and shouted over the wind, "This is for Rodán!" I jabbed the dagger into his belly and opened it up.

Volod cried out, clearly in pain as he instinctively grabbed his belly. I surged up and slit his throat. "And that's for Nadia." Blood gushed from his wound and sprayed me.

"This is courtesy of me to you." I rammed the dagger into his chest and impaled his heart, twisting the blade. "For everything you've done."

Volod went instantly stiff. Then in what felt like slow motion, he rocked on his heels and fell to the forest floor, landing on his back.

I stood over him, staring down at the eyes that could no longer see the trees they were staring at. The cruel mouth that would no longer give orders that would destroy lives.

My whole body trembled as my mind tried to process the facts.

Volod was dead.

Volod was dead.

He would never harm another paranorm or human again.

I dropped to my knees and tears flooded my face. I sobbed for the people I loved, their lives forever lost.

And I cried for myself.

FORTY

"Let's go, honey." Colin wrapped his strong arm around my shoulders and helped me to my feet. "It's all over."

I didn't know if my legs would hold me as I rose and looked down.

All the evil, all the pain associated with Volod, over.

It didn't seem real, but there he was at my feet. That cold lifeless face with a permanent look of surprise. I didn't think it had ever occurred to him that he could lose. That I could kill him.

"We should take him back to the others." Desmond walked up to the opposite side of me. "They need to see that he's dead."

I nodded slowly. "Yes. They do."

"Grab my arms." Colin glanced from me to Desmond before he crouched and gripped Volod's ankle with his hand.

The moment Desmond and I each had a hold on Colin, we flew through the transference. In a breath we were back at the spot where Volod had slit Nadia's throat and lined up my family and friends.

Devastation.

A bloody battlefield. Beheaded and staked Vampires were lying everywhere. But not just Vampires—a couple of Trackers and Vampire paranorms were also dead . . .

Desmond having jammed their guns obviously stifled what little firepower the Vampires had possessed over paranorms. The Vampires were no match for us without their weapons.

But there were no Vampires still living. They were all dead. Volod had no chance when the Vamp paranorms turned on him.

No mercy to the Vampires. They had deserved none.

I saw my father and brother with the Drow warriors. I was never so grateful as I was at that moment to see them okay.

It occurred to me then. The Great Guardian had said my blood would be sacrificed. It was. I was now a Vampire. My people are my blood, and their blood was sacrificed also. Rodán's blood. Nadia's.

With my heart in my throat, I turned to Colin, buried my face in his chest, and cried. I cried real tears.

Other Trackers started coming up. Angel touched my shoulder and I turned and hugged her. "Volod is dead, Nyx," she said.

Then Angel turned to the Trackers walking among the bodies and repeated loud enough that her voice carried across the battlefield. "Volod is dead!"

A shocked silence was followed by cheers. Applause and shouts so loud that goose bumps broke out along my arms.

Through the sadness I felt, there was an overwhelming relief. We had won. We stopped the great evil, and miraculously there were few of our own who had fallen in the last battle. I had to focus on the victory. We won. *We won.*

I hugged Colin again. He knew it was best just to hold me. He needed to say nothing. The strength of his touch said it all.

With the back of my hand I wiped the tears from my eyes then turned to Desmond, Ice, Joshua, and Penrod. And hugged each of them.

Colin, Desmond, and I stepped away from Volod's body so that anyone who wanted to could come up and see.

"Yes." I released my hold on Colin and raised my hands for quiet. "Volod is finished. He'll never terrorize humans or paranorms again."

More cheering. I rubbed my arms as chills continued to roll over me.

Everyone who still lived started hugging. At first paranorms and Vampire paranorms stood separately, but eventually they joined and embraced, too.

A lump rose in my throat when I saw Max take Lawan into his arms and hold her close.

Olivia came up in front of me and I hugged her. "Never thought I'd be even partially related to a Vampire." Olivia rubbed her neck where Volod had bitten her. She patted me on the shoulder. "I'm ready for steak, bloody rare."

I appreciated her attempt at a little levity in the midst of so much tragedy.

The crowd grew quiet and I turned to see that Leticia had joined us. She had been regal as a paranorm. As a Vampire paranorm, she was even more so. She had her hands raised and motioned for quiet like I had.

"Thank you for your trust in the Vampire paranorms," she said. "We wish only to coexist with our brethren."

Murmurs traveled through the crowd, mostly of approval.

"Vampires have been able to survive on synthetic blood all of these years," she continued. "Vampire paranorms will do the same. We do not wish to drink the blood of our brothers and sisters. We wish only to be accepted for what we were made to be, which was not of our choice.

"We of the former Paranorm Council will surrender our positions to paranorms who will vote in new leaders. We ask, however, that you allow Vampire paranorms one seat on the council, to represent those who wish to live in peace with our brethren."

Leticia stepped back and Armand took her place.

"Vampire paranorms have proven they have a place among paranorms." Armand swept his gaze from one fighter to the next. "We will work closely with our brothers and sisters."

The paranorms and Vampire paranorms across the battlefield applauded.

Armand looked to me and said loudly enough for everyone to hear, "You may fight on my team anytime, Nyx Ciar."

I inclined my head. "It will always be my pleasure to serve with those like you who keep our world safe from evil."

"As for Volod," Armand said to the crowd. "We shall burn what is left of him."

Armand began giving orders on disposing of the dead. Not only would we set fire to Volod's body, but we would burn all of the other Vampires as well.

As everyone set off on their tasks, I hurried to my father's side.

"Father." I flung my arms around him and he wrapped his own around me.

"I am so proud of you, my princess."

"Thank you for coming." I kissed him on the cheek. "Thank you."

"I could not see you hurt anymore." Father looked around at the paranorms working side by side with Vampire paranorms. "Your people fought well."

"They did," I said. "As did you and your warriors."

"Of course," Father said in Drow. "For I brought only the finest."

I kissed Father then hugged my brother. "Thank you, Tristan."

"I did no more than anyone else," he said. "You are the one to be commended for all that you have done."

"No." I shook my head. "These people are the reason why we survived and ultimately why I was able to kill Volod. It is they who deserve praise."

Tristan kissed my cheek and hugged me again.

For a long time I walked through the battlefield, talking with Trackers, paranorm and Vampire paranorm alike. A heaviness weighted me down as I thought about all that I had loved and lost because of Volod.

I tried to think of Nadia how I'd known her. Radiant and beautiful, full of life and love. And not to think of her as Volod had left her.

When my thoughts turned to Rodán, I remembered all of the good times we'd enjoyed since he had recruited me. My former lover, friend, confidant, mentor, and Proctor. He had been so many things to me. The emptiness he left behind would never be filled.

The two of them had left an indelible stamp upon my life and I would think of them always.

Later, when it was getting close to daylight and time to burn Volod's body, Colin and I met up again and he put his arm around my shoulders. We didn't talk at all for a long time as we watched Volod's body burn to ash.

"He almost had victory but he got too greedy," Colin said.

"And evil." I shook my head. So much evil I didn't even want to think about it.

After a while I sighed and looked up at him. "I need a vacation."

He touched the tip of my nose with his finger. "You deserve one."

"Where do Vampires and Dragons go on vacation?" Olivia said as she walked up to face Colin and me.

I lightly punched her arm. "Anyplace that doesn't involve other Vampires of any kind."

Colin tilted his head to the side. "I think I might know just the spot."

Rain pattered on the windowpanes of our New Hampshire cabin. It was dark outside, branches scraping across the panes as a late-spring storm whirled its way through the country.

Colin and I snuggled up under a blanket in front of the fireplace. I rested my head on his shoulder.

"Demons, Werewolves, Vampires, Zombies, and more Vampires." I sighed. "I've had enough excitement in the last year than most people face in a lifetime."

"Just Zombies and Vampires were enough for me." Colin stroked my hair, the feel of his fingers sending delightful shivers through me.

"Nice of Armand to give us a two-month paid leave of absence along with a nice fat bonus." I tilted my head up to meet Colin's beautiful gaze. "And I want to spend all of it with you."

"I wouldn't have it any other way." He continued to run his fingers through my hair, soft and wonderful. "I wasn't about to let you go off without me."

"Olivia should be having fun with her boyfriend in the Bahamas," I said. "Wonder if they brought the whips and chains with them."

Colin snorted with laughter. "Knowing Olivia, I am sure."

I snuggled deeper in our blanket, enjoying the warmth of Colin's body. Loving his scent, loving everything about him.

"Do that little bite thing you do," Colin murmured, his words rumbling in his chest. "I love it."

"I thought you would never ask." My fangs dropped at the mere mention of biting him and I licked his neck then scraped my fangs along his neck.

He hugged me tight. "I love you, Nyx."

"Mmmmm . . ." I moved my lips to his ear. "I love you, Colin," I whispered. "I love you."

FOR CHEYENNE'S READERS

Be sure to go to CheyenneMcCray.com to sign up for her PRIVATE book announcement list. Please feel free to e-mail her at chey@cheyennemccray.com. She would love to hear from you.